M. H. BONHAM

Save a Tree Program

At Dragon Moon Press, our carbon footprint is significantly higher than average and we plan to do something about it. For every tree Dragon Moon uses in printing our books, we are helping to plant new trees to reduce our carbon footprint so that the next generation can breathe clean air, keeping our planet and it's inhabitants healthy.

LACHLEI

M. H. BONHAM

Dragon Moon

www.dragonmoonpress.com

Lachlei

ISBN 10 1-896944-69-8 Print Edition
ISBN 13 978-1-896944-69-2

ISBN 10 1-896944-71-X Electronic Edition
ISBN 13 978-1-896944-71-5
CIP Data on file with the National Library of Canada

Dragon Moon Press is an Imprint of Hades Publications Inc.
P.O. Box 1714, Calgary, Alberta, T2P 2L7, Canada

Dragon Moon Press and Hades Publications, Inc. acknowledges the ongoing support of the Canada Council for the Arts and the Alberta Foundation for the Arts for our publishing programme.

Alberta Foundation for the Arts   Canada Council for the Arts   Conseil des Arts du Canada

Printed and bound in Canada
www.dragonmoonpress.com

DEDICATION

To Larry, as always.

ACKNOWLEDGEMENTS

I want to thank to following people for their help on *Lachlei* (in no particular order):

• My husband, Larry, and my good friend, Deb Eldredge, for being first readers. My husband, Larry, for being my editor as well.

• The good folks at Yard Dog Press (www.yarddogpress.com) who introduced fans to this world. If you're interested in other stories, check out my other books, *Prophecy of Swords* and *Runestone of Teiwas,* which are in the same universe. A huge thanks to Selina Rosen and Lynn Stranathan. Thanks to Lynn for edits.

• My thanks to Gwen Gades, publisher at Dragon Moon Press, for taking this book on, and Brian Hades of Edge Science Fiction and Fantasy.

• Thanks to the guys at Podiobooks.com, the coolest bunch of people around. Especially to Evo Terra for giving me another way to promote. Listen to their books. Thanks to Tee Morris, who actually inspired me to submit to Dragon Moon Press.

• A huge thanks to Laura Diehl, for the awesome cover.

CHAPTER ONE

The world was gone.

Rhyn'athel, the god of warriors stood on the charred mound that was once a towering peak within the Shadow Mountains. Nothing but burnt and smoldering ruins and corpses filled the land to the glowing red horizon and beyond. The acrid smell of burning flesh and death reached his nostrils. To a mortal, the stench would have been overwhelming.

But there were no mortals. There was nothing living now. All the races were gone along with the green fields, the majestic forests of pine, oak, and elm, the streams, the rivers, the mountains and the valleys. All laid waste in one single battle.

Rhyn'athel doubted anything could have survived the torrent of flames and the massive destruction that followed. He sheathed his sword, *Teiwaz*, in anger and pulled off his helm and mail coif, revealing the red mane streaked with gold.

Such waste! The gods of light would have to begin again.

Rhyn'athel was a tall god, but he could see no further than perhaps a mile. The thick clouds of smoke were too dense and piles of burning corpses too tall to see beyond. His silver eyes scanned the battlefield.

He caught movement and drew *Teiwaz* once again. Had the demon god returned? What could Areyn Sehduk, the god of death, want with this world now? Areyn had razed the world with the *Fyr*, the Eternal Fire, and nothing could stand in its way.

Teiwaz, the Sword of Power, glowed a menacing blue-white against the blood-red sky. Rhyn'athel relaxed when he saw the movement was a silver wolf padding through the piles of ashes and charred remains.

"Ni'yah," Rhyn'athel said.

The wolf transformed into a god wearing mail. He was shorter than Rhyn'athel, with a wolf-gray mane and brass-colored eyes. Still, the familial resemblance remained. "Brother," he greeted the warrior god. "Where is Areyn Sehduk?"

"Back in the world of the dead, I hope," Rhyn'athel replied. "What of the other worlds?"

"Much the same as this," Ni'yah said. "Except our own world, *Athelren*. The other gods and goddesses were able to hold off the Eternal Fire to protect the Hall of the Gods."

"Nothing more?"

"Nothing more."

Rhyn'athel shook his head. "Then the *Eleion*..."

Ni'yah grinned wryly.

Rhyn'athel stared. "Why do you smile? Areyn destroyed everything! Everything!"

"Not completely, my brother."

Rhyn'athel blinked. "What?"

"You don't think I would let the *Eleion* perish, do you?" Ni'yah asked. "They were, after all, my idea."

A grin spread across Rhyn'athel's face. "Who's alive?"

Ni'yah shook his head. "I couldn't save all. But it's enough to return the *Eleion* and the *Ansgar* races to this world. There's enough of each of the Nine Kindreds. But yes, your son, Lochvaur, is alive."

"You brought them to *Athelren*—to the Hall of the Gods?"

"It was the safest place—considering there were no safe places," Ni'yah said. "So, what did you get out of Areyn?"

"A truce," Rhyn'athel said. "We've divided the Nine."

"Equally?"

Rhyn'athel nodded.

Ni'yah frowned. "Next time, have me negotiate. We won, my brother—we should've gotten the majority."

"I tried—but even with *Teiwaz* run through him and pinned to the World Tree, Areyn wouldn't concede his four," Rhyn'athel said. "And this world, the fifth world, can't be touched by either side until the end of time. It's neutral ground."

"What of the *Eleion* and *Ansgar*?"

"This will be their world now."

"No bargain," Ni'yah said. "The *Jotunn* and demons can still walk these worlds—they'll decimate our people."

"Neither the *Jotunn* nor the demons can enter this world– not while under the truce," Rhyn'athel said. "But neither I nor Areyn can enter this world as long as the truce is in effect."

"I didn't agree to this," Ni'yah said, crossing his arms.

"You will abide by it."

"No."

Rhyn'athel glared at his brother. "You dare defy me?"

"Yes," Ni'yah said. "This is foolish—you brokered no peace, brother, you simply delayed the inevitable."

"And what would you do?" Rhyn'athel demanded. "Areyn can't be destroyed anymore than you or I. Without a reasonable offer, Areyn has no motivation to keep the truce and then, we are back to this." He waved a gauntleted hand at the desolation.

Ni'yah shook his head and said nothing. His brass eyes hardened as he gazed at the destroyed world. "What Areyn did is unforgivable."

"What would you have done?"

A silence ensued. At last, Ni'yah nodded. "I would've brokered peace the best I could," he admitted.

"Which I have done," Rhyn'athel replied. He gripped his brother's arm affectionately. "I know it's a delay, but what else can I do?"

"Let's hope it's enough," the wolf-god replied.

CHAPTER TWO

TWO THOUSAND YEARS LATER

The air smelled of death.

Areyn Sehduk watched the small band of warriors ride towards him. The death god smiled as their horses skittered nervously to an uneasy stop. He had chosen to wait here for them—here along the King's Highway—amid the fir trees and dark pines under a moonless night. Few traveled this stretch of road that wound from the North Marches to the city fortress Caer Lochvaren. They weren't far from the *Silren's* border—no doubt the *Silren* would take the blame for what Areyn Sehduk was about to do. That suited the death god just fine.

There were five in all. They were none other than *Chi'lan* warriors—men sworn to serve Areyn Sehduk's enemy, Rhyn'athel,. They wore red and gold, the colors of Rhyn'athel. The colors of the *Lochvaur* kindred.

The colors of the enemy.

One warrior rode forward. He was handsome with a lean, muscular build and a flowing red mane streaked with gold, typical for the *Lochvaur*. He wore a gold circlet on his brow, denoting his rank. His piercing silver eyes met the death god's gaze.

This one is Fialan, the god thought.

"Who are you?" Fialan demanded. "Why do you seek to waylay us?" He drew his sword.

Areyn Sehduk laughed. Even in his mortal guise, the laugh grated on Areyn's ears. The body he took was of a tall, lanky *Silren* with a long, white mane and ice-blue eyes. It fit him well, although he preferred the dark hair and eyes of the *Eltar*. His mail was dark, but he wore the traditional colors of the *Silren*: a silver eight-rayed star adorned his blue surcoat. "I will waylay whomever I please."

"I am king..."

"I know who you are, Fialan," Areyn replied coldly. "Your precious titles mean nothing to me."

At that, the other four *Chi'lan* drew their swords. *Not that it mattered,* Areyn thought. With a single glance, all four horses and riders fell over dead. The horses screamed and thrashed, bloody foam spewing from their nostrils as they collapsed. The men screamed once before collapsing with their horses. Their swords clattered uselessly to the ground.

Now, Fialan was alone.

Fialan stared at the dead men and then back at Areyn Sehduk. Fear crept into Fialan's eyes for a brief instant, but the *Lochvaur* king steeled his gaze, much to his credit. "By Rhyn'athel's sword, who are you? What manner of wizardry is this?"

Areyn Sehduk grinned. *This would be great sport.* "Why don't you come down from your horse and find out, *King*?" he taunted, drawing his dark blade.

There was no hesitation now. Fialan dismounted, drawing his adamantine blade. Areyn had seen the look in the king's eyes before many times. Fialan showed no fear, but it mattered not. It was still the look of a dead man.

Fialan circled warily, keeping his guard up. Areyn lunged, swinging his sword. Fialan parried and riposted. Areyn parried.

They broke off and circled.

"Who are you?" Fialan demanded. "Silvain and my father signed a treaty nearly a hundred years ago. The *Silren* and the *Lochvaur* are at peace..."

Areyn chuckled. "No longer, it would appear..."

Fialan attacked now, swinging the long sword. Areyn slid to the side and parried, but too late — Fialan's blade sliced through Areyn's armor into flesh. Pain shot through Areyn, but he ignored it. Instead, the death god laughed.

Fialan stared. Blood poured from the *Silren's* chest as Fialan pulled his long sword away. The blow would be a mortal wound to any *Eleion*—even to a first-blood, those born with gods' blood in them.

"What are you?" Fialan demanded. "Demon?" Sweat dripped from his brow, and Areyn knew Fialan was afraid.

Areyn grinned. "I am your death," he replied. "I grow weary of this game."

With that, an invisible force ripped Fialan's sword from his hands. Areyn Sehduk approached, and Fialan found he could not move; some infernal power rooted him to the ground. Fialan could do nothing but watch helplessly as the death god, almost lazily, plunged the sword into his chest.

Fialan collapsed, writhing in pain for a moment before lying still. His silver eyes stared unblinking into the dark sky. Areyn chuckled. "I suppose it is some consolation to know that you would've won," he remarked. He pulled the dark blade from the dead king and gazed at the blood as it rolled down its edge. "But no mere mortal will defeat me."

Areyn Sehduk turned and for a moment saw movement in the dark forest. Ice-blue eyes scanned the silent pines and caught a glimpse of a wolf padding away. He turned back to the dead king and grinned. "And now, the fun begins."

◆◆◆◆

The wolf waited until the death god had passed. It watched as Areyn Sehduk turned and walked northward along the King's Highway. Then, it slowly crept from its hiding place to survey the damage.

It was a large beast—nearly twice the size of a normal wolf — with black-tipped agouti fur. It padded around the bodies of the dead *Chi'lan* and then halted as it stood before Fialan, gazing with his brass-colored eyes at the dead king.

"A terrible loss," the wolf said to no one in particular. He turned and disappeared into the forest.

CHAPTER THREE

Lachlei awoke shivering.

She huddled in the thick blankets, her silver eyes staring into the blackness of the room. She ran her hand through her red-gold mane and tried to remember the dream. Lachlei had dreamt of a battle—a slaughter. Five *Chi'lan* cut down in cold blood.

It was just a dream, Lachlei told herself. *A terrible nightmare.* But Lachlei's dreams had a habit of becoming reality. It was the price of being first-blood, and the price of having the Sight.

Lachlei slid out of bed and wrapped herself with a robe. With a single word, the candles in the room jumped to life, filling the darkness with a soft glow. She strode to the cradle where her son, Haellsil, still lay sleeping. Lachlei looked down on the infant and smiled. Haellsil looked much like Fialan. So much so that nearly every *Chi'lan* warrior had proclaimed Haellsil would become a great warrior in his own right. *How could he not, being Fialan's son?*

How could he not being Lachlei's son? Lachlei added silently. Lachlei glanced at her old sword, hanging on the wall. She too had been *Chi'lan.* Lachlei had been a good warrior, serving the old king, Lochalan, before he died in battle. Fialan, Lochalan's son, had proven himself in battle and the *Lochvaur* Council had made Fialan king after Lochalan's death.

Lachlei had fallen in love with Fialan. She had accepted his proposal, giving up her sword to become the *Lochvaur* queen. She hadn't regretted the choice in the three years she had been Fialan's consort. But occasionally, Lachlei missed being *Chi'lan.*

Yet now, something was amiss. Lachlei dressed and slid from her private chambers to the mead hall where the *Chi'lan* warriors slept. The room was dark save for the ruddy glow from the firepit's dying embers and the stars that glowed above through the hole in the roof where the smoke could escape. The mead hall was hewn from thick oaken logs, with exposed beams and rafters. On one end were hers and Fialan's private quarters, behind the small dais where massive oaken thrones sat. The firepit lay in the middle. The mead benches and tables that usually stood around it were pushed to the side to make room for those *Chi'lan* who were the king's personal guard to sleep. Lachlei stepped carefully over sleeping warriors and past the great battle hounds. One dog looked up at her curiously, and she ran her fingers through its coarse, curly fur as she passed by.

Lachlei pulled on one of the oaken double doors that led from the mead hall to outside. At the door stood a *Chi'lan* sentry. It was Cahal—a tall, young *Lochvaur* who had recently made *Chi'lan.*

"Lachlei, my queen," Cahal stammered.

Lachlei raised a finger to her lips and he fell silent, his silver eyes almost smoke-gray in the darkness. "When is Fialan expected to return?" she whispered.

"The day after next," said Cahal and then hesitated. "Certainly, you know that…"

But Lachlei's eyes widened. "Fialan!" she gasped. "No!" Pain shot through her as she felt the mind-link sever between herself and Fialan. Lachlei collapsed, but Cahal caught her before she hit the ground.

"What is it?" Cahal said, holding Lachlei as she wept.

The torches within the mead hall sprang to life. *Chi'lan* warriors poured from the hall, some with swords drawn. They stood in bewilderment to see Cahal holding Lachlei.

"What happened? What is it?" Voices babbled around her.

"What is it, Lachlei?" Cahal asked, this time gently.

Lachlei shook her head. "Fialan," she whispered. "Fialan is dead."

◆◆◆◆

"It was Areyn Sehduk," the wolf said. He glared at the god, his brass eyes glinting menacingly.

Rhyn'athel, the warrior god, sat on his throne in the Hall of the Gods, his silver eyes revealing his doubts. God of the *Lochvaur*, the kindred bore his silver eyes and red-gold mane. He wore mail and sat on his throne beside the other thrones of the nine gods and goddesses of light. All were empty now, save his. "How can you be so certain it is our old enemy, Ni'yah? After all, you say you saw a *Silren* kill Fialan."

"It was Areyn," Ni'yah repeated stubbornly. "No *Silren*, not even Silvain, could use that magic. When will you learn, my brother, that Areyn uses the Truce to keep you out of his way?"

Rhyn'athel frowned. "And when will you quit meddling in the affairs of the *Eleion*? You will bring the war back to the Fifth World if Areyn recognizes you in your current form."

"Then, let him!" Ni'yah snapped. "This charade has gone on long enough, my brother. Areyn is in *Elren*, and you are a coward for not standing up to him."

Rhyn'athel's face darkened. He stood up, his hand straying to the sword hilt at his side. "Who are you calling a coward, Ni'yah?" he growled. "I don't slink around like some common cur, meddling in affairs I have no business in."

Ni'yah transformed to his god form. He was shorter than Rhyn'athel nearly half a foot, but the other god's impressive stature did nothing to intimidate him. "Are you threatening me?" Ni'yah demanded. "If you are, then you choose your battles poorly, my brother. You can't defeat Areyn Sehduk without me."

Anger glinted in Rhyn'athel's steel eyes, and for a moment the two brothers stood, gazes locked. Then, Rhyn'athel began to chuckle. "Damn you, Ni'yah!" he said, shaking his head. "You're incorrigible! If you were anyone else…"

Ni'yah smiled wryly. "You'd teach me a terrible lesson—but you won't."

Rhyn'athel gazed at his brother. "Someday, you may get yourself into trouble that not even I can get you out of."

"Perhaps," the wolf-god shrugged. "But that time is not now. Fialan is dead. Areyn killed him..."

"You don't know that."

"I know the mark of an immortal's work. Who else would desire to destroy the peace we've achieved?"

Rhyn'athel shook his head. "It could be followers of Areyn ..."

"As long as the Fifth World remains under both your and Areyn's control, there will be no peace. Areyn will not settle for the Nine Worlds being equally divided." Ni'yah sighed. "With Fialan dead, the power will shift—you know that."

"Fialan was my champion," Rhyn'athel agreed. "There will have to be another."

Ni'yah frowned. "You said that when Lochvaur died—and there has been no equal to him. That was another time when you gave into Areyn's demands..."

Rhyn'athel's gaze hardened and Ni'yah knew the barb had hit its mark. "Don't you think I rue that decision, Ni'yah? Lochvaur and I agreed that for the sake of the Truce, he should remain in Areyn's realm. You, I remember, talked me into it."

"You've given too much for peace, brother."

Rhyn'athel's face was expressionless, but Ni'yah knew he had pushed the warrior god past his limit. "Don't you think I regret every day that Lochvaur stays under Areyn's power? Don't you think I regret that my *Chi'lan* feed that demon god's power? Ni'yah, if it were not for the living..."

"And now, without a champion, we risk that, too. There's no other living right now who could rival Fialan," said Ni'yah. He paused and a glint entered his eyes. "Save one."

"Who?"

"Lachlei." Ni'yah's eyes gleamed now. "She could do it."

Rhyn'athel scowled. "Fialan's consort?" He searched his memory for the *Lochvaur* woman's image. None came readily to mind.

"Lachlei is *Chi'lan*," said Ni'yah. "She trained under Lochalan; she's a distant cousin. And she's half *Laddel* as well. Her mother Ladara was Laddel's granddaughter..."

"Then, she's first-blood," Rhyn'athel mused.

"Oh yes, she is," Ni'yah grinned. "She's *twice* first-blood, from both the *Lochvaur* and *Laddel* lines. Very powerful—if she'd use her magic. She was an exceptional warrior before she became Fialan's queen." He paused and glanced sideways at his brother. "She's beautiful, too."

Rhyn'athel stared at Ni'yah. "You've been among the mortals for far too long."

Ni'yah chuckled. "I have—I won't deny it. I've learned to appreciate what the Fifth World has to offer." He paused. "But Lachlei can't handle Areyn Sehduk alone, my brother. She'll need your help."

Rhyn'athel shook his head. "I'm sworn by the Truce to not become involved."

"Then, at least come to *Elren* and see what Areyn has done," Ni'yah said. "Observe what has happened first hand, and then tell me this is not the work of the death god."

Rhyn'athel hesitated. He knew Ni'yah had a good reason for being persistent, even if his brother was a rogue. Rhyn'athel stood for a moment, arms crossed, vexed at the choice he had to make.

Ni'yah smiled slyly as he watched his brother weigh the options, his brass eyes glittering with mischief. "Observe—that's all," Ni'yah said. "You don't need to act…"

"Observe," repeated Rhyn'athel. It sounded harmless, but it was Ni'yah and Rhyn'athel knew it wasn't. Ni'yah had one final trick to play. He sighed. "Very well," Rhyn'athel said, at last. "I will observe—that is all."

"That's all," said Ni'yah, triumph ringing in his voice.

Rhyn'athel fixed him with a stare. "That *is* all," he said with finality.

CHAPTER FOUR

Lachlei watched the wagons enter Caer Lochvaren. The iron gates swung wide to admit the slow and somber procession. All along the wall, walks, and towers of the fortress city, *Chi'lan* warriors turned in respect towards the wagons bearing the bodies of the king and his guard.

By *Eleion* standards, Caer Lochvaren was a small fortress city. It had a single keep and bailey, with no other towers and no buildings larger than two stories. The whole fortress was little more than the fortified settlement it replaced. Only the keep and curtain walls were made from stone. All other buildings were wooden, built from timber taken from the surrounding forests. Another cluster of homes and shops lay just beyond the walls, protected by a palisade and moat as a secondary defense.

Not much more than a grody, Fialan had said. Lachlei smiled sadly at her husband's words. Fialan would never get the chance to see the *Lochvaur* to the greatness he envisioned. Of all the *Chi'lan*, Lachlei believed Fialan could have done it. Fialan had the strength, determination, and the power to make the *Lochvaur* into the greatest kindred.

Now, Fialan was dead.

The *Lochvaur* had never been the largest kindred of the Nine. Even so, the *Chi'lan* warriors had become legendary as they defended themselves against larger, more aggressive kindreds like the *Silren*, *Eltar*, and *Redel*. Warriors who preferred peace to war, the *Chi'lan* had always sought to settle their differences with treaty, but were never afraid to fight or die.

Now, the *Chi'lan* and the *Lochvaur* were leaderless.

Lachlei walked slowly from the mead hall. Gone were the tears, replaced by cold anger. Gone too was the finery of the office. Lachlei now wore her old mail and badges of a *Chi'lan* warrior. Her surcoat and cloak still shone bright red-gold, and her old broadsword hung at her side.

"My queen," Cahal said, standing by her side.

"*Chi'lan* Lachlei," she corrected him. "I am no longer your queen, Cahal. I ceased being your queen when Fialan died—it is up to the Council to decide who will be the next king."

Cahal stared for a moment and then shook his head. "It's hard to believe that Fialan is really dead," he said.

Lachlei smiled sadly. The ever-present mind-link that connected her with Fialan was gone. "It isn't to me." Her silver eyes followed the slow procession. Each wagon, draped with red and gold cloth, bore a warrior. Two horses drew each wagon. The last one, Lachlei knew, was Fialan's.

A tall *Chi'lan* approached Lachlei. Kellachan, her cousin, stood beside her. "Lachlei, the Council will meet…" he began.

Lachlei held up her hand. "Not now, cousin," she said.

"I will ask that they choose you as…"

"No."

Kellachan blinked. "But you are the queen."

"I *was* your queen," Lachlei said bitterly. "I have neither right nor title to the throne, save perhaps being first-blood. The Council has not chosen me, nor would I accept it. I don't deserve it."

"Lachlei," said Cahal. "Reconsider this. Of all the *Chi'lan*, you alone can see our kindred to greatness."

Lachlei shook her head as she walked towards the wagons. The lead *Chi'lan*, astride a battle horse, raised his hand to halt as he saw her walk forward. As Lachlei approached, the stench of death filled her nostrils. She fought the gorge that threatened to rise in her throat.

Instead, Lachlei turned to the commander of the accompanying *Chi'lan*. "Kian, how did they die?"

Kian turned to her, his face ashen. "Fialan took a blade to the chest," he replied. "The others…" He shuddered.

Lachlei turned to the first wagon. She stepped up on the running boards and peered at the corpse. A wave of dark magic assailed her, and she shuddered involuntarily. Despite her nausea, she pulled the cloth back from the corpse. Bright red blood stained its mouth as though the man had just died.

Lachlei frowned. She didn't want to touch the thing—it reeked of foul magic—but she had to know. She reached out and touched the corpse on the forehead.

Hot pain shot through her. "By Rhyn'athel's sword!" she yelped, pulling her hand back. She looked at her fingers and saw blisters form on them.

Cahal stood beside her. "What is it?"

Lachlei showed him her fingers. "I would wager all the bodies are like that," she said.

"Magic?"

"Dark magic—a heinous kind."

"Did you feel anything when you touched the corpses?" Cahal asked, turning to Kian.

Kian shook his head. "No, but we didn't touch the bodies directly."

Lachlei focused on her fingers. The blisters absorbed into the skin and healed. Part of the powers of a first-blood was the ability to heal oneself and others—even from terrible wounds. She gazed at the corpse. "He didn't die through normal means," she said at last.

Kian and Cahal glanced at each other. "What happened?" Cahal ventured.

"His heart and lungs burst," she said. "Were all the others like this?"

"All save Fialan." Kian suppressed a shudder. "The horses, too."

Cahal met Lachlei's gaze. "Do you know what caused it?"

Lachlei stepped from the wagon's footboards. "Dark magic," she said. She walked towards the last wagon, dreading what she knew she would find.

Cahal caught up to her and gripped her arm. Lachlei turned towards him, her eyes haunted. "You don't have to do this," he said.

Lachlei shook her head. "But I do, Cahal. I do." She glanced at his hand. "Let me go."

Cahal released her and Lachlei climbed onto the running boards of the last wagon. Fialan's corpse was covered with a red shroud. Lachlei hesitated for a moment and then grasped the shroud, pulling it back. She caught her breath as she gazed into her husband's dead face.

A wave of emotion flooded her as she looked in his unseeing eyes, glazed with death. Pain and sorrow threatened to overwhelm her again, but this time she fought it. She focused on the anger as it welled inside. Some *thing* had done this to Fialan. Lachlei was going to find out what.

Fialan's pale face betrayed nothing of the horror he had felt in the last seconds of his life. Like the others, his body stank of foul magic. Lachlei didn't dare repeat touching his body for fear of the same result.

Lachlei forced herself to look away from the face and look at the blood-soaked armor. She saw only one wound to his chest—a single sword cut. She frowned. Fialan was too great a warrior and too powerful a first-blood to let someone surprise him. If thieves or soldiers had caught him, Fialan would have fought and suffered many more wounds than this. Seldom did *Chi'lan* die with only one sword wound.

Her gaze drifted to the long sword, *Fyren*, which lay beside him. Lachlei reached out and touched the adamantine blade's hilt lightly, half expecting to be burned. Instead, the blade felt cold and hard to her touch.

"What is it?" Cahal asked as she picked up the sword and held the blade to the sun's rays.

"I don't know," she murmured, gazing at the discolored blade. She stretched out with her powers, hoping to gain a sense of what had killed Fialan.

Death.

Lachlei recoiled in horror, almost dropping the sword. Her mind reeled.

"Lachlei?" Cahal grasped her shoulders.

She shuddered and then gazed at Cahal. "By Rhyn'athel's sword! It's the blood of the thing that killed Fialan."

CHAPTER FIVE

"Fialan is dead."

Areyn Sehduk stood in the throne room of the *Silren*, a smile played across his lips. In his current form, the death god was the warrior, Akwel, one of the *Silren* nobles. He had ambushed Akwel, taking the *Silren's* body as the warrior rode alone in the forest. He consumed the hapless *Silren's* soul, using Akwel's energy to feed his power while he stayed in this world. Areyn would soon have to feed again.

The sun shone brightly through the stained glass windows, casting a rainbow of color across the granite floors. The dark blue colors of the *Silren* standard hung overhead, emblazoned with a silver, eight-rayed star, contrasting against the light gray stone.

In the bright sunlight, none, not even Silvain, suspected that the man who stood before them was the death god. Silvain, the king of the *Silren*, sat on the intricately carved throne, listening to Areyn's words. The son of the goddess, Elisila, was old, even though his body had remained young. None here knew his age, save Areyn. The godling was over three thousand years old and had seen many battles—including the first battle against Areyn Sehduk.

Areyn remembered the king of the *Silren* and despised him. During that battle, the kindreds had reunited under godlings such as Silvain and Lochvaur. They had fought with Rhyn'athel to overthrow Areyn. None here save Silvain remembered that battle. None here save Areyn, himself.

Areyn had been hesitant at first to approach Silvain in his new body. Silvain had powers beyond even a normal first-blood, but Areyn soon discovered that the godling could not see beyond his disguise. No one could, save perhaps another god, and even then, Areyn doubted one of the lesser gods could recognize him. Areyn guessed that only Rhyn'athel could, but Rhyn'athel wasn't here.

Rhyn'athel wouldn't get involved. That was the beauty of the Truce. Only when it was too late would the warrior god enter the fray. By that time, *Elren* would be Areyn's and the power would shift. With the power of five worlds under his command, Areyn knew the other four would eventually fall.

It was a good plan. It would work. Even the meddling Ni'yah couldn't do much about it. Areyn had seen a wolf after he had killed Fialan, and that had troubled him at first. Could it have been the meddling god? But the wolf had fled, not confronted him, and Areyn had sensed nothing special about that wolf.

Behind Areyn sat the *Silren* nobles, many who gazed at him in admiration. He knew the *Silren's* minds and now was the time to put into words their desires.

"With the *Lochvaur* champion gone, the *Lochvaur* are leaderless," Areyn said. "Their confusion is our gain. Now is the time for the *Silren* to take back the lands that are rightfully ours."

A murmur of assent rippled through the *Silren* nobles. There was no love between the *Lochvaur* and *Silren*.

Silvain raised his hand for silence and the room stilled. He met Areyn's gaze. "We are at peace with the *Lochvaur*. We agreed to the treaty Lochalan and I signed nearly a hundred years ago."

Areyn laughed. "Have the *Silren* gone soft? Were not the lands the *Lochvaur* now occupied once ours?"

"The North Marches have been in dispute for many centuries," Silvain said evenly. "I remember when Lochvaur, himself, claimed those lands."

"Yes, but so did you," Areyn replied. "They were our lands first."

The nobles looked to Silvain.

The king of the *Silren* smiled, his ice-blue eyes met the gods. "Indeed, they were our lands," he admitted. "Akwel, you know our history very well. Very well indeed."

Better than you think, Areyn Sehduk thought darkly.

"But what of the *Chi'lan*?" one voice objected. The *Silren* warriors parted and a tall woman clad in mail approached the throne. Her ice blue eyes considered Areyn with contempt.

"Rhyn'athel's dogs," Areyn scoffed. "With the *Elesil*, we can defeat the *Chi'lan* and take back our lands."

"*Rhyn'athel's dogs,* as you call them, are the best warriors in the Nine Worlds," she said. "We spilt much blood to obtain that treaty, and you would throw it away on a worthless scrap of land?"

"North Marches is hardly worthless, Cara, my daughter," Silvain said. "It has been traditionally our lands before Lochalan."

Cara met her father's gaze. "The *Elesil* will not enter the fight with us."

A sardonic smile played on Areyn lips. "Conlan has assured me his support. The *Elesil* want their lands to the east almost as much as we desire ours. Now is the time to act, while the *Lochvaur* are leaderless."

"You're insane—the *Laddel* and *Haell* will assuredly come to the *Lochvaur* aid," Cara objected.

"I hear the prattle of women," Areyn spoke. Many of the nobles chuckled in response.

Cara drew her sword and started forward.

"Commander, no!" A *Silren* captain named Haukel caught her arm.

Cara wheeled around. "Not here," Haukel said, giving her a knowing look. "Not now."

"Yes," said Areyn grinning as he watched Cara seethe. "Those of you who care to listen to women prattle are as much cowards as they are. The *Lochvaur* have our lands—it is time we took them back!"

The *Silren* warriors cheered, drowning out the dissenters. Areyn gave Cara a sly smile. She turned and left, flanked by a few warriors.

"Then, it is decided," Silvain said. "We take back the North Marches."

The stars shone brightly in the sky as Lachlei thrust the torch into the pyre on which laid the five dead *Chi'lan*. The other *Chi'lan* followed, tossing their burning torches into the wood. The dry kindling caught and the flames leapt up, ensconcing the body of Fialan and the men who died to protect him.

It had taken most of the day to build the pyre on the mountain overlooking Caer Lochvaren. Lachlei had helped the *Chi'lan* construct the pyre, carrying the logs and branches necessary to feed the flames. The air had a hint of frost in it, and the trees were already changing color.

A change was in the air.

Lachlei watched as the flames obscured the bodies. She had tried what she could to remove the foul magic from them, but the stench remained.

It will not leave Fialan alone, even in death, she thought. *What powerful magic could do this?*

Beside Lachlei stood her kinsman, Kellachan, and her personal guard, even though *Lochvaur* law didn't require their service to her anymore. Cahal stood loyally by—a reminder of the ardent loyalty Fialan commanded among the *Chi'lan*. Lachlei thought now about her infant son, Haellsil. He would become a great warrior like his father—if he lived long enough.

The *Lochvaur* were vulnerable; there was no great champion now. The other kindreds would sense the vulnerability and gather like wolves awaiting the death of a wounded moose. The pack would draw closer and eventually tear them apart. Unless…

Unless there was a champion to take Fialan's place.

But Lachlei knew there was no *Chi'lan* warrior alive who could. She knew the *Chi'lan* and their capabilities, but first-bloods from the line of Lochvaur were rare. Fialan was one; she was another. Lachlei and Fialan had been related only distantly with six generations between a common ancestor. Kellachan was even more distantly related, without the powers a first-blood should possess. No wonder that the *Chi'lan* turned to her.

Lachlei strode away from the fire, wanting to be alone. Her sorrow now turned to anger—whatever had killed Fialan was evil, that much she was certain of. She looked into the sky to see the moons rise slowly above the horizon. Tomah and Iamar rose, followed by a third moon, Mani. She stared at the golden moon in amazement. Mani often was the portent of great and terrible things.

Her hand strayed to her side and brushed against the sword hilt. She had sheathed *Fyren*, her husband's blade earlier, not thinking. Lachlei now drew the blade and held it upward towards the moon. The smoke from the pyre drifted overhead, turning the moon blood red.

Rhyn'athel, she spoke silently. *Great god of warriors, hear me! By the blood that burns in the Lochvaur veins, by the blood that burns in my veins, grant me the power to find the evil that killed Fialan, your champion. By my blood, I will avenge you, Fialan, even at the cost of my own life.* Lachlei brandished the sword and for a moment, the great sword glowed.

Lachlei turned around, resolve in her face. She gazed at the pyre. "You will be avenged, my Fialan. And may the gods have no pity on the one who did this to you."

CHAPTER SIX

Rhyn'athel stared at the *Chi'lan* woman who stood in the moonlight, her face filled with anger and resolve. Even angry, she was beautiful—she rivaled the beauty of the eight goddesses.

"This—is Lachlei?" he asked. Rhyn'athel turned towards Ni'yah, but found he could not tear his gaze from her. Lachlei was a true *Chi'lan*, athletic and powerful, and yet her beauty…

"She is rather pretty, isn't she?" Ni'yah said wryly, his brass eyes gleaming. "I thought you might like her."

Rhyn'athel continued to stare at Lachlei, entranced. Suddenly, the Truce meant nothing to him. Rhyn'athel had forgotten how long it had been since he had been in *Elren*. How much he loved the world and the *Eleion*. And how much he had fought to stay away from it.

Lachlei brought back those old emotions. Emotions Rhyn'athel had long buried inside him for the sake of the Truce. Emotions he could not afford to have, and yet still did. The god continued to stare at her. Lachlei was a creature of light. He could sense the power within her—the power that belied her mortality.

He wanted her.

"How long has it been since you were with a woman?" the wolf-god asked. "Two thousand years, I'd wager—maybe longer. Not since the Truce, certainly…"

The remarks snapped Rhyn'athel out of his reverie and he wheeled on his brother. "You knew this would happen."

"Not, *exactly*…"

"You've just complicated matters."

"I always do," Ni'yah agreed. He paused and became serious. "Listen, I would wager half my powers that Areyn Sehduk killed Fialan. I saw your champion die, my brother, and nothing should have been able to hold Fialan's powers back, save a god. Fialan was the strongest champion you've had since Lochvaur, and his powers equaled most godlings."

Rhyn'athel reluctantly turned his gaze from Lachlei to his brother. He nodded. "That is true—Fialan was powerful."

"The bodies stink of Areyn's magic," Ni'yah replied. "Even Lachlei can feel it, but she doesn't recognize it because she's never been up against Areyn. I have."

"What would you have me do? Destroy the Truce? It will start another war bloodier than the last. And to what purpose, Ni'yah? I can't kill Areyn anymore than he can destroy me."

"The problems with being immortal," Ni'yah remarked dryly.

"We would raze the Nine Worlds," Rhyn'athel said. "Everything you see here and now would be gone…"

"Lachlei has sworn blood vengeance," Ni'yah said.

Silence ensued.

"I know. I heard her," Rhyn'athel replied.

Another silence followed.

"Lachlei will not rest until she avenges Fialan's death or is dead."

"What would you have me do?" Rhyn'athel snapped. He turned around and crossed his arms.

"She'll be lost to Areyn Sehduk if you do nothing," Ni'yah replied.

"We don't know Areyn killed Fialan."

"Yes, we do, but you won't admit it," Ni'yah replied. "The sword Lachlei carries is Fialan's. Fialan blooded it on Areyn before Areyn killed him."

Rhyn'athel turned around with a fierce gleam in his eyes. "He did? I'm glad to see Fialan gave Areyn something to think about."

"Indeed and no doubt Fialan is paying for that boldness in Areyn's realm," Ni'yah said. "But, the proof you seek is on the blade."

"Indeed," Rhyn'athel said. His gaze lingered on Lachlei. She had sheathed the sword and now sat cross-legged on the grass, looking into the night's sky. He could hear her thoughts and feel her underlying power as she stared at the stars. *How had he overlooked her?* he wondered. *Perhaps he had been afraid.*

The thought amused the god, but there was some validity. Had Rhyn'athel paid more attention to Lachlei, he might have been tempted to enter the Fifth World—as he was doing so now. If Areyn Sehduk learned of the transgression—however minor, Areyn would use that as an excuse to raze this world. He would destroy the *Eleion* as he had destroyed the others that had occupied the worlds he took—in favor of his own twisted creations. The *Eleion* would be no more, nor would their descendants, the *Ansgar,* hope to survive under Areyn's reign. Areyn ruled the dead as well—taking away Rhyn'athel's warriors as he had done with Fialan.

Rhyn'athel's gaze lingered on Lachlei. To allow her to die—to be taken from him until the end of time—was unbearable. Rhyn'athel turned his gaze inward, using the Sight to look into the future…

"Brother?"

Rhyn'athel's silver eyes had glazed over. They now snapped back to attention, and he stared at Ni'yah. Resolution within them told Ni'yah that Rhyn'athel had seen something the wolf-god could not. "You meddler!" he growled and with that, Rhyn'athel vanished, leaving Ni'yah bemused.

◆◆◆◆

"By Rhyn'athel's sword!" Cara swore. "What is happening to our people?" The daughter of Silvain stood under the stars with the few warriors who were loyal to her. Twenty *Silren* warriors had agreed to meet in the rolling plains, far from the silver fortress to debate the turn of events. They had ridden their horses under the night's sky until they reached a small hillock called *Silwar.*

Silwar had been an old temple or shrine to Elisila, one of the goddesses of light and the goddess of the *Silren* and *Elesil.* The ruins had been there longer than Cara remembered—indeed, it had been there before the Truce. The *Fyr* had destroyed life throughout the Nine Worlds, but it did not destroy everything from the earlier times. The warriors dismounted and sat amid the broken stones and Cara stood before them.

"I wouldn't say that too loudly, Commander," Haukel remarked. "Silvain would have our heads if he knew there were followers of the warrior god amidst his kindred."

"I am his daughter," Cara replied brusquely. "His only heir."

"I don't even think that will save us, if Silvain finds out," a woman warrior named Tora spoke. "Gods protect us, but there is something wrong with Akwel."

"You noticed that too?" Cara remarked and glanced at the others for confirmation. There was a murmur of consensus. "Akwel and I have never been friends, but I sense something is terribly wrong. To go against the *Chi'lan* warriors is folly."

"But what can we do?" Haukel said, his hands outstretched in a helpless gesture. "Rhyn'athel knows Silvain won't listen to reason."

Cara met his gaze. "He may listen to me," she said. "I am his only heir."

"Too risky," Haukel replied. "There are too many warriors against us. As Akwel grows in power, he will have your father's ear."

"Then, we'd better act now," Cara remarked. "Before it's too late."

"No, we can't risk you," Haukel said. The *Silren* broke into arguing.

"Enough!" spoke Cara, causing the warriors to fall silent. "I alone will speak to Silvain, though I may risk exile because of it. I am his only heir, and that may stop him from having me put to death as a traitor."

"If he exiles you, what then?" Haukel asked.

Cara shook her head, her pale blue eyes filled with worry. "I don't know, Haukel. I don't know."

CHAPTER SEVEN

Lachlei walked from the quietness of the hill. She didn't want to leave—for the first time, she had felt close to the warrior god. Fialan had often told her that Rhyn'athel held the *Lochvaur* and especially the *Chi'lan* in the highest regard, but she had never felt the closeness to Rhyn'athel that Fialan felt. Fialan's power, he had said, came from Rhyn'athel, himself.

As Lachlei turned to gaze at the dying flames of the pyre, she couldn't help but wonder what went wrong. Why had the warrior god failed Fialan at this last moment? What creature was powerful enough to destroy a *Chi'lan* champion? She drew the sword, *Fyren*, again and gazed on the darkened blade, but did not use her powers for fear of the same reaction. *Something vile had killed Fialan. Something vile that bled,* she thought darkly.

If it could bleed, it could die.

She sheathed the sword again. Lachlei had heard of vile creatures from Areyn's realm. Demons capable of destroying lives. The *Lochvaur* had fought against such creatures in the times before the Truce between Areyn Sehduk and Rhyn'athel. Maybe there was one left in this world.

But the wars between the gods happened over two thousand years before. Would a demon be lurking within the Shadow Mountains all these many years without the *Lochvaur* knowing of it? Somehow, she thought it unlikely.

"Lachlei!"

Lachlei turned to see Cahal and Kellachan striding towards her.

Cahal's face shown with worry. "We've been looking for you," he said.

She smiled. "I'm sorry, Cahal, but I needed some time alone," she said.

He nodded. "I understand—but you shouldn't be without your guard."

She sighed. "Cahal, I don't need a guard any longer. I am not in power..."

The two men exchanged glances. "You will be," said Kellachan quietly. "The Council has voted unanimously that you remain queen until they decide on challengers."

Lachlei stared. "How? Who nominated me? Didn't you tell them..." Her voice trailed off. "Gods! Kellachan!" she swore, her eyes glowing with anger. "You didn't tell them!"

"No, I didn't," Kellachan said quietly. "But I didn't nominate you. Laewynd did. No one else contested, and no one else was nominated."

"I wasn't consulted!"

"Lachlei," Kellachan said. "Who else is there?"

"There's you," Lachlei said, but the words sounded false, even to her ears. "You're first-blood..."

"I have no power," Kellachan replied. "You know this—you and your son are the last of Lochvaur's true heirs." He paused. "Before you married Fialan, you were the greatest *Chi'lan* warrior we'd seen in many centuries..."

"Fialan was," she stated.

"You were equals," Kellachan said. "You simply deferred to Fialan because you loved him…"

Lachlei stared at her cousin, shocked at his words. "How dare you!" she snarled when she found her voice. "Fialan is barely dead and you mock his memory!" She turned and stormed off.

"Lachlei!" Kellachan began, but Cahal gripped the *Chi'lan's* shoulder.

"Wait. Let me talk to her," Cahal said.

Kellachan nodded. "Make sure she's ok—we don't need anything to happen to her."

Cahal nodded and followed her. "Lachlei!"

"Leave me alone, Cahal," she said, turning around.

"Wait—hear me out," Cahal said. "Lachlei—the *Chi'lan* are leaderless. Without a strong first-blood, the *Lochvaur* will be vulnerable to the other kindreds."

"I don't want the throne."

"Then, all the more reason you should be our queen in the interim," Cahal said. "You won't abuse the power."

Lachlei shook her head. "Cahal, I can't…"

"Why?"

"I'm not the warrior Fialan was—there's never been a woman champion," Lachlei said.

"Perhaps it's time there was one," Cahal replied. "We have always had women *Chi'lan*—why not a champion? Until the Council chooses a champion, or until one wins in trial by combat, you're the only one who can keep the *Lochvaur* together."

"Trial by combat? A champion hasn't been chosen like that in centuries."

"Maybe they should—that's how Rhyn'athel chose his champions in earlier times."

Lachlei smiled wryly, wiping her eyes. "Don't tell me you believe in those old stories?"

"Why not?" Cahal said with a shrug. "I do believe that I am looking at his next champion."

"I'm sure others have something to say about that."

"Perhaps," he said. "Let's go. Your warriors await you."

Chapter Eight

The weeks that followed were difficult for Lachlei. With her appointment to queen in the interim, she had to rule the *Lochvaur* and perform her duties as *Chi'lan* as well. Laewynd, the head of the High Council, seemed content to take over her administrative duties, and for that Lachlei was thankful. Yet, as each day passed, something began to gnaw on her.

Perhaps it had been the method of Fialan's death that left her uneasy. Perhaps it was the Sight. Rumors abounded of a massing of armies in the North. The *Silren*, it was said, were on the move. But, the *Elesil* and *Redel* were also gathering, and Lachlei suspected that the *Lochvaur* might have to defend their lands. Lachlei found herself riding outside of the Caer Lochvaren's gates more often to clear her mind. She began to detest the confining walls now, seeking the solace of the mountains or the windswept plains.

"Scouts have returned from North Marches," Cahal said as Lachlei rode beside him outside of Caer Lochvaren. Despite her protestations, Cahal refused to allow her to travel alone. "The news is not good."

"The *Silren*?" Lachlei asked.

"There are signs that the *Silren* are massing. For what, we can't be certain."

Lachlei said nothing. Instead, she looked ahead. They were riding in the foothills of the Lochvaren Mountains, not far from the hill where Fialan's pyre had been. The aspen and birch were beginning to change color now—brilliant gold and fire red against the conifers. The path was well-traveled; it made its way through a cleft and wound its way deep into the mountains.

It had been a month since Fialan's pyre had lit the sky above Caer Lochvaren, and still nothing had been decided. The High Council had not appointed a king, and there were rumors of an impending war.

"Lachlei?" Cahal asked. He had become used to her moodiness, knowing well that she thought constantly about Fialan in her sojourns.

"Laewynd assures me that we have naught to fear," Lachlei replied heavily. "The army isn't mine to command..."

"What of the *Chi'lan*?" demanded Cahal. "They are your guard."

"Two thousand," Lachlei replied heavily. "Two thousand against the *Silren* and *Elesil* armies? Even though we are *Chi'lan*, it will be a slaughter. Laewynd assures me that something will be done if the *Lochvaur* are attacked."

"Laewynd," Cahal spat. "A disgrace to the *Chi'lan* if there was one."

"He is our oldest and most experienced warrior," Lachlei said.

"Laewynd is a coward," Cahal replied. "He became *Chi'lan* to become a member of the High Council—nothing more. He is no warrior."

Lachlei smiled slightly at his outburst. "Fialan thought he was useful."

"Fialan knew how to use the Council," Cahal said. "He didn't let Laewynd get his way. How old is he? Five hundred years, if a day."

Lachlei chuckled. "He did avoid the *Chi'lan's* early death," she admitted. "But you can hardly blame him. I have no desire to meet the death god, either."

Cahal shrugged. "None of us do, Lachlei, but we are still *Chi'lan* and bound to serve the warrior god. I see none of that loyalty to Rhyn'athel. I only see ambition."

"As do I," Lachlei admitted. "But Laewynd is happy to work behind the scenes—not take power. That is his way, Cahal. Laewynd is the High Council, and the High Council is Laewynd. I must work with him if I am to have the army."

Cahal shook his head. The late afternoon sun was already behind the mountains and the shadows were long. "We should be heading back, my queen," he said. "It will soon be nightfall."

Lachlei nodded, feeling tired. "Indeed," she said. "I'm sorry I'm a disappointment to the *Chi'lan*," she said softly as they rode side-by-side.

"Disappointment?" Cahal asked sharply. "Why do you say that?"

"I can see it in my warriors' eyes," she said. "I let the Council make me queen for the interim because there was no one else, and yet, I feel powerless. I'm not the champion Fialan was."

Cahal smiled. "Maybe you should not try to be like Fialan," he said. "Fialan was a great warrior, but you are not Fialan. Maybe Rhyn'athel has different plans for you."

Lachlei halted her horse and stared up at the hill overlooking Caer Lochvaren. They were at the base of the hill now. "Perhaps he does," she said. She dismounted and handed him the reins. "I want to be alone for a while."

"I'll wait," he said knowingly. Lachlei nodded and walked up the hill.

◆◆◆◆

Rhyn'athel stared into the twin suns of *Athelren*; their golden glow bathed the world in warmth. It was springtime now in the high mountains where the warrior god's shimmering white-walled fortress stood. Even on the fortress parapets, the drowsy smell of pine reached Rhyn'athel's nostrils as he looked over his world.

The mountains, covered with spruce, pine, and other coniferous trees stretched for miles in all directions. To the west, the rivers poured into the great sea. To the east and south, vast tracts of fields and fertile ground stretched endlessly. Rhyn'athel knew he had created the perfect world when he had created *Athelren*.

And yet, his mind strayed to *Elren*—the fifth world—and to the *Chi'lan* woman who inhabited it. For weeks, Rhyn'athel tried to put Lachlei's vision from his mind, but each time his thoughts returned to her. She was beautiful and strong—a warrior among warriors—and he felt himself drawn to her, despite logic or reason.

Now, a month later, Rhyn'athel decided to return to *Elren*. *Athelren* held no pleasure for him, and he longed to see Lachlei again. It violated the Truce, but he reminded himself that if he did not show himself to Lachlei, Areyn Sehduk was unlikely to know he had entered the Middle World.

Rhyn'athel appeared within the forest on the hilltop overlooking Caer Lochvaren where he last saw Lachlei. It was dusk in *Elren*, and he glanced at the sky as the first stars became visible. He was going to look for Lachlei when he saw her walk along the stone path to the hill's summit where he had seen her make her blood oath.

Lachlei was as beautiful as he remembered her, and he caught his breath as she turned and looked his direction. She was smaller than he remembered—her height due to her *Laddel* inheritance—but she was as beautiful. She wore her mail as she had the night he had seen her.

She looked at him. Rhyn'athel knew she could not see him, despite her first-blood powers, but felt a shiver as their gazes met. Seeing her beneath the stars, he was entranced. "Rhyn'athel," she whispered. "Rhyn'athel—do you even hear your *Chi'lan's* prayer? Something terrible killed Fialan; the Council sits and does nothing. The *Chi'lan* are leaderless. Help us."

Rhyn'athel stood close to her—so close that he could have touched her and taken her in his arms. But he would then give himself away and violate the Truce. But hadn't his presence already violated the Truce? To hold her this once...

"I was wondering where you were."

Rhyn'athel turned and saw Ni'yah leaning against a tree. "Ni'yah..." Rhyn'athel growled and the wolf-god smiled wryly. "You troublemaker!"

Ni'yah grinned. "This isn't keeping with the Truce, is it?"

"You knew I'd fall in love with her!"

Ni'yah retreated, his hands open in a helpless gesture. "I didn't exactly *know*," he said. "More like *suspected* you might." He grinned at Rhyn'athel's scowl.

"You would have a war started for the sake of a woman!"

"For the sake of the Nine Worlds," Ni'yah replied. "Lachlei was just the bait. You know this was due for some time."

"Indeed," Rhyn'athel admitted reluctantly, his gaze drifting back to Lachlei. "Are you certain that Areyn is here?"

"What do you think?"

Rhyn'athel nodded. "Very well," he said at last.

Much to Rhyn'athel's annoyance, triumph gleamed in Ni'yah's eyes. "I knew you wouldn't let the *Eleion* down."

"But I can't remain here—not without Areyn detecting me," Rhyn'athel said. "What can I do?"

"We can beat Areyn at his own game," Ni'yah said. "We know he is in mortal form now, but he wouldn't expect you to take mortal form."

"I'll become an *Eleion*—a *Chi'lan*." He grinned. "Brilliant, my brother."

"They don't call me a trickster god for naught."

"But, won't Areyn recognize me?"

"He shouldn't—not if you keep your power and your defenses up," Ni'yah said. "You should garner no more attention than a powerful first-blood. Unless he presses your defenses, Areyn will never know."

Rhyn'athel nodded. "Let's do it."

Ni'yah stared at his brother. "Now?"

Rhyn'athel turned to gaze on Lachlei. She had sat cross-legged on the ground, looking up into the sky. Now, she stood up slowly, rubbing the stiffness from her limbs. She turned for a moment to look towards the two gods. Even though Rhyn'athel knew she couldn't see or hear them, he nearly held his breath as she looked at the place where he stood. Again, he desired her. Perhaps he could have her if he were *Eleion*...

"Rhyn'athel?" Ni'yah's voice brought him back. "Are you sure you wish to do this?"

Rhyn'athel grinned. "Never more certain," he said.

CHAPTER NINE

Cara stood in the hall of the *Silren* king. The sun had set and the torches and firepits were lit. Already the mead benches and trestle tables were out; servants brought prepared cooked meats and wine. Silvain, her father, sat at the head of the noble's table as he and Akwel spoke.

Cara studied the expression on her father's face. Silvain looked tired, but was still the great warrior and first-blood. Pale blue eyes, pale skin with a slight silver sheen, and white mane flecked with silver, Silvain was the embodiment of the *Silren*.

As cold as the evening star, Cara thought. *And as forgiving...*

This would be a difficult conversation—the *Silren* and *Lochvaur* were traditionally enemies. A son of the goddess Elisila, Silvain resented the power Rhyn'athel and his kindred wielded. Silvain would disown her if he knew she was one of the few warriors of Rhyn'athel within the *Silren*.

Akwel turned and met her gaze and she shivered involuntarily. Something terrible within his gaze that told her Akwel was not quite *Eleion*. Cara took a deep breath and stepped forward.

"Father," she said, interrupting the two men. Silvain looked up. "I wish a word with you in private."

"Certainly, my daughter," said Silvain.

Akwel considered her thoughtfully. *And what do you plan to tell him, Chi'lan?*

Cara started and stared at Akwel. "Did you say something?"

"What is it, my daughter?" Silvain asked. He glanced at Akwel, who held Cara's gaze.

Akwel leaned back. *It would be a pity if Silvain learned of the little meeting you and your pathetic traitors called at Silwar.*

Cara swallowed once. Akwel knew—somehow, he knew of Cara's allegiance to Rhyn'athel. Cara forced a smile. "Nothing, my father. Nothing." She turned and left.

◆◆◆◆

Lachlei left the glade. Cahal was waiting for her below, and she knew she had tarried longer than she should have. As she walked towards the rough-hewn stairs, she saw Cahal and Kellachan walking towards her. "Lachlei!" Kellachan waved. "Where have you been?"

"Riding," she said, looking at Cahal, who nodded. "What brings you here?"

"The Council has finally decided on the next champion," Kellachan said.

"Good," she said. "We can stop this nonsense once and for all. Who'd they choose—you? Kieran?"

Kellachan and Cahal exchanged glances. Lachlei stared at Kellachan, a lump growing in her throat. "Kel? Who is it?"

"You," Kellachan said.

Lachlei opened her mouth to speak, but found she could not. She exhaled in frustration and shook her head.

"Listen—Laewynd, Moira, and the others in the Council felt you were most qualified. None of us have the powers you…"

Lachlei did not hear his explanation. She turned around and ran up the hill as fast as she could.

"Lachlei!" Cahal shouted, sprinting after her.

◆◆◆◆

Rhyn'athel watched as Lachlei left the quiet glade. She had been oblivious of the two gods who spoke. He turned and met Ni'yah's gaze appraisingly. "If it is true that Areyn is here, then I have no choice but to act." He shook his head. "It has been too long since I have been in this world."

With those words, Rhyn'athel turned his power inward. All at once, he felt smaller and vulnerable. At the same time, he became more aware of everything physical around him, while simultaneously, his other senses dimmed. The cold wind blew against him. The acrid smell of fires from Caer Lochvaren reached his nostrils as he breathed in the air. He shivered in the cold, wrapping himself with his cloak.

Rhyn'athel turned to see that he was still not completely alone. Ni'yah still stood there, though his form was nearly invisible to him.

You're using your mortal senses, Ni'yah remarked in mindspeak. *It takes a bit of getting used to.*

Rhyn'athel concentrated and found that Ni'yah's form sharpened. "That's better," Rhyn'athel remarked and then stopped. His voice sounded strange to his ears.

Ni'yah was chuckling. *Not quite the resonance, is there?*

"No," Rhyn'athel admitted. He looked at his hand in amazement as he flexed his fingers, relishing in the sensation. "Are their senses always so inundated?"

I'm afraid so—it's one of many distractions they suffer.

"Really?" Rhyn'athel grinned. "How do you deal with it when you're in their forms?"

In time, you get used to it, Ni'yah said, grinning back. *Wait until you're hungry—or worse yet, have to relieve yourself…*

Rhyn'athel chuckled. "Part of being mortal."

Ni'yah's gaze drifted behind him. *So is she…*

Rhyn'athel turned and this time, did catch his breath. Lachlei entered into view again, now, with another *Chi'lan* warrior. Rhyn'athel searched his memory. *Cahal,* he recalled. A young warrior recently appointed to her guard.

Lachlei strode right towards Rhyn'athel as he stood in the darkness and at the same time glanced behind at the *Chi'lan* following her. "Leave me alone, Cahal! I won't accept the throne!" She ran right into the warrior god.

Rhyn'athel caught her and held her for a moment in surprise. The power he had sensed in Lachlei in his immortal form ran through him now like a shock. Amusement played across his face as she gasped and pulled back. "You should watch where you're going," he said.

Her sword was out and so was Cahal's. Lachlei backed up. "Who are you? What are you doing here?"

"I am Rhyn…" and Rhyn'athel's voice trailed off. He heard Ni'yah chuckling in his ear and shot an angry glance towards his brother. In the heady excitement of becoming mortal, Rhyn'athel hadn't thought this through.

"Rhyn?" Lachlei repeated.

Rhyn'athel smiled in amusement. "I am *Chi'lan* Rhyn from the North Marches," he said. "We heard of Fialan's death." He was pleased to have thought of this so quickly.

"News travels fast," said Cahal, eyeing Rhyn'athel suspiciously. "It takes nearly a fortnight to travel from the North Marches to Caer Lochvaren. Assuming we sent messengers…"

Ni'yah's chuckle turned to a roar of laughter in his ears. Rhyn'athel reminded himself to make the wolf-god pay for his mirth when Rhyn'athel returned to his god form. *Of course, travel was slow here,* he reminded himself ruefully. "I was on the King's Highway—a week's travel north of here. When I heard the news, I came quickly." He paused, hoping perhaps that would make sense. "I'm looking for Queen Lachlei—the *Lochvaur* guards in the city said she would be here."

Nice touch, Ni'yah remarked.

Rhyn'athel made no reply.

Lachlei glared at Cahal. "Does everyone know other than me?" she demanded.

Cahal gave Rhyn'athel a helpless look. "I—I'm not sure…"

"Know what?" the god asked and was rewarded with a relieved look from Cahal.

"That I was voted queen by the Council."

"I had not heard," he said truthfully. "But it would make sense. Your reputation is well-known throughout the *Lochvaur* lands." He smiled, meeting her angry gaze. "Even in the North Marches."

Lachlei met his gaze. The anger within her disappeared, and she found herself grinning foolishly back. Cahal relaxed in relief and they both sheathed their swords. "I'm sorry," she said. "This has been a very trying time."

"Indeed."

Lachlei paused, gazing at the god. "I didn't expect someone to be here," she said awkwardly. She paused. "Where's your horse?"

Ni'yah's laughter echoed once more in Rhyn'athel's ears, but the warrior god shook his head. "He's in one of the stables—after such a long ride, I didn't want to risk an injury on this mountain."

Lachlei nodded, obviously mollified with his explanation. "You must be tired and hungry from your journey."

Say 'yes,' Ni'yah's voice echoed in his head.

"Indeed, I am," Rhyn'athel said.

Lachlei glanced at the *Chi'lan* beside her. "Come on, Cahal, let's find Kellachan. After I apologize, we'll show our guest our hospitality."

CHAPTER TEN

After a brief introduction, Lachlei led Rhyn'athel, Cahal, and Kellachan down the mountain towards Caer Lochvaren. It was dark now and the stars shone overhead. The cold wind bit through them as they walked along the rough-hewn steps leading down to the fortress-city. They retrieved the horses Cahal had tied to a tree, choosing to walk back since Rhyn and Kellachan had no horses with them.

As Lachlei walked beside the new *Chi'lan*, she had a chance to study him. Rhyn was tall even for a *Lochvaur*, being nearly six and a half feet, with a muscular frame that spoke of power. He was handsome too, with a strong, chiseled jaw and silver eyes. His red-gold mane was long for a warrior, and he had no visible scars.

Odd, she thought. She had never known a seasoned *Chi'lan* to not bear a scar or two. Even a first-blood had scars he or she couldn't completely heal. Lachlei guessed by his demeanor and build, he might be a few hundred years old—young for an *Eleion*, but a veteran for a *Chi'lan*. Most *Chi'lan* met their deaths within their first hundred years.

The name, Rhyn, was odd too. It meant "warrior" in the *Eleion* tongue, but the word was often paired with another to form a name: Rhyn'el, *warrior Eleion*, Rhyn'ar, *warrior spear*, Rhyn'athel, *warrior god-king*. Perhaps it was normal for those *Lochvaur* of the North Marches to use shortened names. Or perhaps Rhyn was not really his name.

Lachlei carefully probed his mind and met such a strong mental defense, it sent her mind reeling backwards. *First-blood,* she thought immediately. *A powerful one.* The only one who she had known this powerful was Fialan. The sidelong glance from Rhyn told Lachlei that her clumsy attempts at reading his mind did not go unnoticed. The slight smile that parted his lips told her he was not offended.

Lachlei decided on a new tact. "So, Rhyn, what bloodlines do you come from?"

Rhyn'athel had been expecting such a question. "From Lochvaur's line, his youngest son, Rhyn'ar, who came to the Northern Marches."

Lachlei nodded. She remembered hearing of Lochvaur's son, Rhyn'ar. "I had no idea, Rhyn'ar had any descendants."

"Do you want me to repeat all ten generations?" he asked wryly.

Lachlei smiled in spite of herself. She found she liked Rhyn. He had a manner about him that put her at ease, even though he seemed a bit mysterious. "Not necessary," she said. "You're a first-blood then. We thought that Fialan, Kellachan, and I were the only first-bloods left…" Lachlei hesitated as she realized she had used Fialan's name as though he were still alive. She stopped and turned away, blinking back the hot tears.

Rhyn'athel stood beside her, feeling helpless. He could sense the emotions that boiling up inside her—her anger at both the warrior god and fate for her husband's death. Lachlei felt as though Rhyn'athel had deserted Fialan when his champion had needed him most.

The god part of Rhyn'athel reminded him that he had been blamed for far worse; but the mortal part of Rhyn'athel stung with the rebuke. He should have been there, protecting his champion, Rhyn'athel thought darkly. If it were Areyn Sehduk as Ni'yah had surmised, Rhyn'athel should have stepped in.

But at what cost?

"Lachlei," he whispered, gripping her shoulder. Again, he felt the shock run through him, but this time did not release her.

Lachlei turned around, her eyes red from fighting the tears. She took a deep breath and met his gaze. "I'm sorry," she said.

"Don't be," he said. "Fialan was a great champion."

Lachlei wiped her eyes. "That he was, Rhyn," she said. "Gods, I miss Fialan! I don't know why Rhyn'athel let this happen."

The warrior god shook his head. "I don't know why either."

◆◆◆◆

Areyn gazed at the small, fortified village of North Marches. The village was not much more than a small grody with a stockade, built on earthenwork fortifications. A few thousand inhabitants—*Lochvaur* mostly, but there were other kindreds mixed in. *Redel*, *Lochel*, and even some *Silren* made their homes among the *Lochvaur* of North Marches.

It was dark, and the moon, Mani, rose overhead. Twice, Areyn had felt something stir within his god senses, making him uneasy. He scanned the area, searching for the wolf that he had seen earlier, but found nothing. Doubt played in his mind now—obviously from being mortal, he decided, but Areyn could not shake the feeling. Something had changed now—something he could not quite sense. That bothered him.

Instead, Areyn turned his attention to what lay before him. He gazed at the village with a hunger that could not be suppressed. Although he had taken an *Eleion* body, Areyn was still the god of destruction. Killing Fialan and his guard had only temporarily sated the bloodlust. He needed to feed again.

Areyn's mount shifted uneasily. He patted the warhorse's neck. *Easy, Slayer,* he mindspoke to his mount. *We will be feasting on blood soon.*

Slayer's red eyes considered the death god thoughtfully. No living thing would bear Areyn Sehduk even in mortal form, so the god was forced to summon one of his own demons to be a mount. It had taken quite a bit of magic to hide the demon's true nature from a godling like Silvain, but Areyn had done it. Even so, the *Silren* sensed Slayer's evil and wisely avoided the horse. Areyn was not certain how long between feedings the demon would go before it started taking *Silren* to sate its bloodlust. Only its fear of Areyn Sehduk kept the demon in check.

"This looks like an easy fight," remarked Galen, a *Silren* noble who sat beside Areyn Sehduk.

Areyn nodded in acknowledgment, but chuckled inside. *Easy fight, indeed. It will be a slaughter.* There were only a few hundred *Chi'lan* to guard the village along with other soldiers. While each *Chi'lan* was worth five *Silren* in battle, Areyn had ten thousand troops. He had already planned for the logistics of moving the army, having prepared for it months before.

Moving ten thousand troops a hundred miles across the border without being seen had been simple. Areyn used his magic to conceal the troops and speed up their movement. They moved now at demon speeds.

Areyn gazed into the dark night. Something still did not feel right. He turned to Galen and fixed the *Silren* with a cold smile.

"Patience, my friend," the death god said at last. "We'll attack an hour before dawn."

CHAPTER ELEVEN

Fialan awoke to darkness. He lay against hard ground and groaned. *How long had he been out?* he wondered. *Not long,* he thought, as he gazed into the dark sky. It had been night when they had been attacked on the King's Highway. Perhaps it had only been a few hours.

And yet, Fialan's mind whirled with the inconsistencies. Something was different now. Despite his dizziness and confusion, Fialan felt no pain. The night had been a rare moonless night, but now as Fialan opened his eyes again, he realized that there were no stars. It was truly dark here.

Fialan sat up. The memories flooded back. He had been in a forest when the *Silren* had attacked. No, not a *Silren*, Fialan corrected himself. It had been a demon of some sort. It had killed his entire personal *Chi'lan* guard and their horses with a glance. He had wounded the demon and it had…

No!

Fialan looked around frantically for some familiarity, but saw none. He was no longer in a forest, but instead sat on a cold, windswept plain covered with dry grasses that looked sharp to the touch. The sky was beginning to turn blood red in what he could only guess as being east.

He shut his eyes again as he remembered the demon looming over him. The intense pain as he felt his very life force sucked away to feed it…

"So, you've finally come around," came a voice. A feminine voice.

Fialan turned and saw a female *Chi'lan* standing next to him. She was tall, wearing old-style scale mail sewn into a jack, and a conical helm with a noseguard. She leaned against a polearm as she offered him her hand.

Fialan took her hand and stood up. He could barely make out her features in the dim light, but he could tell she was beautiful. "Who are you?" he asked. "Where am I?"

She looked as if she had answered the questions many times before. "I am Eshe, *Chi'lan* warrior. I died in the Battle of the Nine Worlds, killed by a *Jotunn*. You're in Areyn's Realm, called *Tarentor*. You're dead."

◆◆◆◆

The walk from the mountain to Caer Lochvaren had tired Rhyn'athel. While his body was in peak condition, the god hadn't expected the limits a mortal body imposed. Rhyn'athel had eaten no food, and he suspected part of the weariness was due to lack of it. He could augment his strength using his own powers, but Rhyn'athel thought it might attract unwanted attention from Areyn. If he couldn't handle the basics of being mortal without using his powers, what chance did he have convincing Areyn Sehduk he *was* simply a mortal?

Lachlei led the three into Caer Lochvaren, past the guards and the torchlight at the stockade fence, and through the cobblestone streets of the lower grody.

Caer Lochvaren had been built on the side of a mountain in the Lochvaren Mountains, ringed by valleys and hills. Outside the city, vast fields of wheat and barley lay cut, already harvested and laying fallow until the spring.

Merchant shops and taverns lined the streets of the grody. The buildings were wooden or wattle and daub, suggesting a certain amount of recentness or impermanence to the structures. Rhyn'athel noted that while most of the dwellers were *Lochvaur*, there were many other kindreds here and even a few *Ansgar*. Despite the time of night, the buildings were lit and there were people walking about.

"Caer Lochvaren has grown considerably within the past few centuries. Since our truce with the *Silren*, we've been able to focus on our lives, not war," Lachlei said, seeing Rhyn's interest in his surroundings.

"Indeed," Rhyn said. The sensations of this world were almost overwhelming, and he realized he was grinning foolishly.

"It's not much," she ventured. "But we've had so very little time to put up better defenses."

Rhyn nodded. "It's larger than North Marches," he said, trying to sound casual. "How many live here?"

Lachlei smiled. "The city, itself, has only forty thousand or so—but not all are *Lochvaur*, as you can see." She paused. "The outlying areas, maybe a hundred thousand more. Fifty thousand soldiers; maybe of those, two thousand *Chi'lan*."

"How many *Chi'lan* are there in North Marches?" Cahal asked.

Rhyn thought of North Marches, his supposed home. *How many were there in that village?* His mind reached out to survey the village and felt the equivalent of a hard slap. He hesitated, trying again to focus on the village...

"Rhyn?" Lachlei asked, breaking the god's concentration. His eyes had become glassy. They now returned to meet her gaze. "Are you all right?"

Rhyn smiled weakly. "Sorry, I get distracted when I'm tired."

Lachlei shook her head. "Of course, you've had a long ride." She turned to Cahal. "Can you bring him to the Great Hall and see to his needs, Cahal? I must meet the Council and discuss this vote with them. Kellachan?"

Rhyn was going to object, but nodded instead. He didn't want to leave her — now that he was mortal. But he didn't want her to suspect he was anything other than a *Chi'lan*. Not yet. Not now. "I will see you later?"

"I'm sure you will," she said. Lachlei turned to her cousin and motioned him to follow her.

Rhyn watched Lachlei as she disappeared from sight and felt a tap on his shoulder. He turned to see Cahal grinning at him.

"She is beautiful, isn't she?" the *Chi'lan* remarked.

"That she is," Rhyn agreed.

"Come on, let's get you some food," Cahal said and led Rhyn in the opposite direction.

Rhyn'athel followed silently, lost in his thoughts. He felt rather foolish at his reaction to her and everything around him. He felt so transparent—it would be simple for Areyn Sehduk to find him if he continued to act as if everything was new. He was a god—he created most of the things in this world. He knew the very secrets of the Nine Worlds—where the Runestones lay, where the Web of Wyrd touched the fabric of this world, where the *Fyr* lay chained—but he gawked at simple things like a village or a woman. Rhyn'athel had thought that knowing was the same as experiencing. He was quickly getting a lesson in the experience area.

"I'd be a little more subtle, if I were you," Cahal remarked, breaking the god out of his reverie. They halted at the main gates to Caer Lochvaren. *Chi'lan* and soldiers guarded the massive iron gates that protected the fortress inside. They nodded to Cahal as both he and Rhyn'athel passed through.

Rhyn'athel hesitated, but he could see Cahal smiling. "Don't worry—I won't say anything," the *Chi'lan* assured him. "That's the first time Lachlei has smiled since Fialan's death. And Rhyn'athel only knows why she decided to accept the throne. Lachlei wouldn't even consider it before you appeared."

CHAPTER TWELVE

Fialan stared at Eshe. "What? I can't be dead!"

Eshe smirked as she leaned against the polearm. "Really?" she said. "What was the last thing you remember before you woke up here?"

"I was in a battle with a demon that looked like a *Silren...*" he began. He paused as the voices came unbidden to his mind.

"What are you? Demon?"

"Your death. I grow weary of this game."

"I can't be dead. What about Lachlei? My son, Haellsil? My kingdom?" He tried desperately to access the mind-link he shared with Lachlei, but it was gone. Fialan stared at Eshe in disbelief. "The mind-link—what happened to it?"

Eshe sighed, looking bored. "They all say this—or something like it." She eyed him in amusement. "So, you were a king?"

"Heir of Lochvaur," he said. "First-blood."

"You'll find Lochvaur here too," she said. "I fought for him. Your titles and bloodlines have little meaning here. Your first-blood powers will not work anymore."

Fialan drew a sharp inward breath and then shook his head. "I can't be dead—I breathe."

"You have a body in this world," said Eshe. "Courtesy of Areyn." She turned and began to walk away.

"Where are you going?" Fialan called after her, running to catch up.

"Back to the others," Eshe said. "My job with you is done until Areyn calls me again."

"Areyn calls you again?" Fialan repeated. "What is that supposed to mean?"

Eshe turned to him and for a moment, she looked as though she might strike him. Instead, something flickered in her eyes—*pity?* Her silver eyes then hardened. "You'll learn soon enough, Fialan."

◆◆◆◆

Lachlei strode into the High Council of the *Lochvaur*. The Council room was a large hall, hewn from oak, with exposed rafters and tall clerestories that brought in light. It was dark and smoky inside. A firepit with a crackling fire sat in the middle with rows of benches arranged before it for the nobles. The ruddy light cast shadows on the nobles' faces, but she could see that many were still here. A small dais with two thrones sat along the back wall. Red and gold tapestries lined the walls and the *Lochvaur* banners hung overhead. The tapestries depicted heroic battles in *Lochvaur* history.

One tapestry, which Lachlei had always loved, was of Lochvaur fighting side-by-side with Rhyn'athel, the god of warriors. All first-bloods could trace their lineage back over two thousand years to Lochvaur, the son of Rhyn'athel. She gazed at the creatures they were fighting—dark, shadow-like things with teeth and claws. They were demons—creatures of Areyn Sehduk's creation. Like so many things touched by the god of death, these creatures lived only to destroy.

Lachlei suppressed a shudder. She had sensed the vile magic that had tainted the bodies and wondered about the demons yet again. Lachlei had considered herself a powerful first-blood, and though she was loathed to admit Kellachan was right, she had been Fialan's equal in many ways.

Her mind strayed to Rhyn for a moment. The handsome *Chi'lan* was a bit of an enigma for her. She had never felt someone with that much defense, nor had her mental probes ever been detected. Could he be the next *Lochvaur* champion?

Lachlei turned and glanced at Kellachan, who nodded to her. She strode in and met the chief of the High Council, Laewynd. Laewynd was possibly the oldest *Lochvaur* alive, being nearly five hundred years. Most *Eleion* were not much older than Lachlei, herself, because of the frequent warring between the kindreds. Despite his age, Laewynd looked only slightly older than Lachlei, but no longer had the hardness of the warrior build.

Lachlei was surprised to see most of the council members present. Six men and one woman made up the *Lochvaur* High Council. Tarchon, Moira, and Kieran sat alongside Laewynd, but Lachlei noted Talar and Elrys were absent. Her cousin Kellachan was the youngest council member, chosen because of his first-blood. All had been *Chi'lan* at one time—each bearing the scars of battle. Of all the council members, the only two Lachlei had known well were Laewynd and Kellachan. Lachlei had known Moira as a *Chi'lan* since Lochalan's rule. Moira had been a *Chi'lan* when Lachlei had earned her badge, but had left the *Chi'lan* to become a council member soon after. Kieran and Kellachan were the only active *Chi'lan* warriors on the High Council who had served Fialan and now served her.

Lachlei grasped Laewynd's arms in the traditional *Chi'lan* greeting and noted the softness of his hands as her own fingers brushed the backs of them. *Not the hands of a warrior,* she thought. She wondered if the *Lochvaur* had been imprudent to have someone who wasn't *Chi'lan* anymore in charge of the High Council.

"My queen, Lachlei," Laewynd spoke.

"You've presumed much, Laewynd," Lachlei said crossly. "I am *Chi'lan...*"

"I know, I've heard," Laewynd said. "And I want you to stop this foolishness..."

Lachlei stared at him speechlessly.

"We all know that you are the last first-blood with power—save perhaps your son, Haellsil, but he is an infant," the chief councilmember said. "There is no other choice, Lachlei, you must be queen."

Lachlei shook her head. "There must be others..." she hesitated as she saw the nobles shake their heads. "There is first-blood in North Marches..." she began.

"And we know nothing of them," Kellachan said. "Lachlei," he said, turning to her. "You, alone, know what killed Fialan—I can see it in your eyes. You know what we may be up against. The High Council agrees—those with the Sight have seen darkness ahead. We believe you alone might see us through."

Lachlei looked around at the familiar faces. They had served her husband well. Now, they were putting their trust in her. As the commander of the *Chi'lan*. As queen. Her gaze strayed back to the tapestry of Lochvaur and Rhyn'athel. Did she really know what killed Fialan? Did they really suspect something as sinister as she did?

Her thoughts turned to her son, Haellsil. If there were a demon out there, as she suspected, the creature might not be satisfied with Fialan's life. If it targeted Fialan, what was the chance that it might search for Haellsil?

Cold fear gripped her. Haellsil would not have a chance to grow up, much less make *Chi'lan* or become king. She tried to remember the old stories about demons. They didn't simply go away after they killed—they drank the life force of those who held power. The demon may have killed Fialan because he was a powerful *Lochvaur*. Would she simple sit idly by and let the demon grow more powerful until it came for her and her son?

Lachlei knew the answer. For a moment, she thought of Rhyn and his power. Perhaps he too sensed the demon. Perhaps he knew something she didn't.

Lachlei sighed and shook her head. "Very well," she said, meeting Laewynd's gaze. "I don't want the throne, but I will take it. At least until my son is old enough to become *Chi'lan* and prove himself."

CHAPTER THIRTEEN

Cahal led Rhyn into the mead hall where the warriors had gathered. The enticing aroma of cooked meats reminded Rhyn how hungry he was. In the smoky light, he could see warriors drinking, talking, and playing various games with dice or daggers around the lit firepit. Rhyn hadn't expected the chatter to be so loud, but he felt at ease here. These were his *Chi'lan*—the soldiers sworn to the warrior god—and he knew each of them by name.

Cahal nudged him forward, and together they walked in. Heads turned to see the new *Chi'lan* as he strode by. Cahal led him to a bench just beside the fire, not far from the gamers. Servants brought them plates of food and mugs with amber liquid in them.

Rhyn'athel took a swallow of the amber liquid and grinned. It tasted honey-sweet with spices. Picking up one of the pieces of venison, he bit into it. The hot meat tasted salty with herbs. This was something he could get used to, he decided.

"I'd be careful with the metheglyn," a familiar voice said. Rhyn'athel looked up to see his brother standing beside him, arms crossed. Suddenly, the room became still as the god halted time.

Rhyn'athel glared at him. "This will draw Areyn's attention."

"Not likely—I've done it before," Ni'yah remarked. "We need to talk."

"About what?"

"Metheglyn," he said pointing to the mead. "You're not used to it and it affects gods more than it does mortals."

"How would you know?" Rhyn'athel replied, taking another gulp of the mead.

"Experience," Ni'yah said. "I once fell unconscious after downing a flagon."

"First time you ever stopped talking?"

"Not funny," Ni'yah replied. "The first-bloods avoid it because they have no resistance, thanks to our blood. It affects demons too, so they don't drink it either."

"I'll remember to offer Areyn a drink the next time I see him," the warrior god remarked.

"Do you want my help or not?"

"I seemed to be doing all right," Rhyn'athel said smugly.

"Well, you haven't gotten yourself killed, I'll give you that," Ni'yah said. "But this is a tough crowd."

Rhyn'athel chuckled. "They're *Chi'lan*."

"They may be your *Chi'lan* but you're not one of them," Ni'yah warned. "You're their commander. Even if you look like a *Chi'lan*, they'll challenge you until you fit in or flee like a whipped cur."

"I can handle myself," Rhyn'athel said, taking another bite of the meat, but pushing the mead flagon away. Despite his desire to not admit that his brother was right, the god began to feel the metheglyn affect him.

Ni'yah grinned. "We'll see."

Ni'yah vanished and simultaneously the entire hall became alive again. Rhyn'athel chuckled. He knew Ni'yah meant well and was touched by his brother's concern. But, Rhyn'athel was still a god—the most powerful god of all the gods of light, and arguably, more powerful than any other god. He chose this form, but if necessary, he could shed it.

"You must have been hungry," Cahal remarked, looking at Rhyn's empty plate.

"I was," Rhyn admitted. He leaned back and watched two *Chi'lan* near the fire try to hit a mark someone had cut in an upturned table. One *Chi'lan* was a heavily scarred warrior with a broken nose. His frame was large for a *Lochvaur*—indeed, for any *Eleion*—making Rhyn look small in comparison.

"That's Tamar," said Cahal.

The big man looked up on hearing his name. He saw Rhyn and scowled. "So, this is the *Chi'lan* from North Marches," he said, sizing Rhyn up.

"I am," said Rhyn.

"Who made you *Chi'lan*? You don't look like much to me." His speech was slurred, suggesting he had drunk more than even his frame could handle.

Rhyn shrugged. "*Chi'lan* Ronan of the Marches..."

"Then, you're no *Chi'lan*," Tamar said. "I don't know any *Chi'lan* Ronan. Only Fialan made *Chi'lan*."

"Easy, Tamar, he's first-blood," Cahal said.

"First-blood!" Tamar spat. "First-blood? Does he think he's better than us?"

Rhyn stood up. "I don't want a quarrel..."

"Then, get out," Tamar growled.

Rhyn glanced around. The other *Chi'lan* seemed mildly interested in the argument, but no one was eager to aid him, save Cahal. But Cahal was young and inexperienced.

"Tamar..." began Cahal.

"Cahal, stay out of this," Rhyn said. "I can defend myself."

"Can you?" Tamar said, drawing closer. Rhyn noted that he still held the dagger. "You don't look like much of a *Chi'lan*. No scars."

Rhyn shrugged. "Maybe I know how to get out of the way."

Cahal chuckled.

Tamar glared. "You don't drink mead either."

"I didn't know that was a prerequisite for a *Chi'lan*." Rhyn smiled. "It's quite good—you can have mine, if you'd like."

Tamar glared. "I wouldn't want anything that a *Shara'kai*, half-breed from the North Marches touched."

Cahal glanced at Rhyn. The new *Chi'lan* seemed relaxed and unoffended. "Rhyn, he just called you a half-breed."

The god looked bored. "I've seen better *Ansgar* warriors than him."

Tamar lunged, slashing with his dagger. Rhyn stepped to the right and used the big man's momentum to toss Tamar aside. A moment later, Rhyn stood over the *Chi'lan*, his sword drawn. Tamar scrambled to stand, but was met with the tip of Rhyn's blade inches from his face. The sword glowed blue-white in the dim light.

A murmur rippled through the *Chi'lan* and the entire mead hall became silent. Everyone stared at the Sword of Power and at the man who wielded it.

"I would be very careful whom you choose as your enemy," Rhyn said, an edge to his voice. "Especially one who would be your friend."

Tamar blinked. Beads of sweat trickled down his brow as he met the god's gaze. Rhyn smiled and lowered his blade. He offered Tamar his hand.

Tamar hesitated and then took the god's hand. Rhyn pulled the big man up and they stared at each other for a moment. Tamar smiled and Rhyn sheathed his sword. Laughter erupted throughout the *Chi'lan*. Several clapped Rhyn on the back before going back to their mead. Many went back to their business.

Tamar chuckled but he gave Rhyn an appraising look. "Where did you learn to fight like that?" he asked. "I've never had anyone move so quickly that they could take me down."

"*Chi'lan* training," Rhyn replied grinning.

Cahal stood beside them and chuckled. "Perhaps, but I've never seen anyone move so fast." He nodded at the sword that hung at Rhyn's side. "Nor have I seen a Sword of Power. I thought they were all destroyed before the Truce—where did you get that?"

Rhyn shrugged. "From my father."

A lie? Ni'yah's voice echoed in his head. *My, are we taking this mortal thing a little too seriously?*

A necessity, Rhyn'athel replied. He met Tamar's gaze and saw that the *Chi'lan* was studying him curiously.

"You're more than first-blood," Tamar said at last. He turned and took another flagon of mead before returning to the knife game.

Chapter Fourteen

Lachlei left the council's chambers. The cold air bit into her face as she strode back to the great hall. Laewynd was a fool, she decided. His faith and trust in her were misplaced. She couldn't lead the *Lochvaur* against their enemies, let alone to the greatness Fialan envisioned. And yet, there was no one else. There was no other first-blood capable of doing what she could.

But, even as she thought this, Lachlei knew she was wrong. There was Rhyn. Lachlei could sense that Rhyn was as powerful as Fialan had been. Maybe even more so. But Rhyn was a stranger and was not of Caer Lochvaren. Indeed, he was not of any *Lochvaur* line known to exist. How could the *Lochvaur* of Caer Lochvaren have missed such a bloodline? Lachlei couldn't imagine it. Even the North Marches were not so remote when it came to blood kin.

"I told you Laewynd would make you queen," said Kellachan as he strode beside her.

Lachlei glared at him. "Damn it, Kel, I'm not fit to lead the army."

Kellachan grinned. "Yes, you are—only you won't admit it."

Lachlei shook her head. "Kel, my husband is dead and I must find his murderers. They have used dark magic against him."

Kellachan nodded. "I know," he said. He met her gaze earnestly. "Lachlei—have you thought that those who killed Fialan were not looking merely to slay him?"

Lachlei stared. She thought of the demon. "You think it was an attack against the *Lochvaur*?"

"What do you think?"

Lachlei gazed into the starry sky. She had thought the demon killed Fialan because he was a powerful *Lochvaur*. She had not thought about the consequences of his death. Of course, now that Fialan was gone, there was no one to protect the kindred. She shook her head, lost in her own muddled thoughts. "I think I am very tired," she said at last. She reached the door to the great hall and pulled it open.

The noise of the hall poured into the darkness. Lachlei smiled as she saw that the warriors were still drinking. Of course, they would still be drinking. Lachlei would have crept to her private chambers unnoticed if she had a choice. But Cahal spied her as she slid through the door with Kellachan beside her. Cahal stood at attention and other *Chi'lan* followed, including Rhyn. His silver eyes seemed to cut right through her. The hall fell silent.

Lachlei frowned. She knew they were expecting her to say something. The weariness of the month filled her. She simply wanted to sleep.

"It appears that both Laewynd and the High Council have overridden my personal desires," she said without preamble. She glanced at Kellachan who smiled at her. "The High Council has chosen me as your queen."

A deafening roar drowned out her words. The *Chi'lan* cheered and pulled their daggers from their belts. "Lachlei! Lachlei!" they chanted and pounded their pommels against the tables to their words.

Lachlei raised her hands for silence, but they only shouted louder. Mead flowed from the barrels into flagons and someone handed her a cup. Lachlei grinned and took a gulp of the spiced honey-wine as the chanting grew louder. Almost immediately, she felt the heady rush from the drink.

"Lachlei!" Cahal said.

Lachlei turned and smiled at the younger *Chi'lan*. "What is it, Cahal?"

Cahal paused, noting her eyes were bright from the mead. "Perhaps we should talk later."

"Perhaps we should talk now," she said with a smile. "What is it?"

"The new *Chi'lan*, Rhyn…" he began.

"What about him?"

"He bested Tamar."

Lachlei turned to see Rhyn gazing at her from across the room. He had been talking to Tamar and looked up, somehow sensing that she was looking at him. He was handsome, she decided, and a sly smile crept across her face. "Is that so? He bested Tamar?"

"He has a Sword of Power," Cahal added.

Lachlei stared. "Really? Are you sure?" Even in her inebriated state, Lachlei knew the implications.

"Quite," Cahal said. "The sword glowed."

Lachlei considered Rhyn thoughtfully. "A Sword of Power. This is very interesting, Cahal. Who knows about this?"

Cahal shrugged. "Everyone. Rhyn took Tamar on right here in the hall."

"There are no Swords of Power left."

"Rhyn said he inherited the blade from his father."

Lachlei shook her head. "No, Cahal. Swords of Power disintegrate when the forger dies. Only godlings have strong enough magic to forge a Sword of Power. Are you sure what you saw?"

"Ask anyone here if you don't believe me."

"I believe you," she said, glancing at Rhyn. "I just find it extraordinary."

Cahal glanced at Rhyn and then back at Lachlei. "Do you think he's lying?"

Lachlei shrugged. "Not necessarily, but I think Rhyn isn't telling us everything." She glanced at Rhyn, and his steady silver eyes met hers. For a moment, she felt as though he had knocked down her mental defenses with ease. She shivered and broke eye contact, glancing into the empty mead cup. She turned to Cahal. "See that I'm not disturbed," she said. She strode to the door to her private chambers and left the hall.

◆◆◆◆

Lachlei found that she couldn't sleep at first, despite the mead. She had checked on her sleeping son and Wynne, his nanny, before collapsing in exhaustion. She had wept for weeks since Fialan's death. Now, she could weep no more—instead, she began to think about the demon that killed Fialan.

She felt edgy—as though something was about to happen. The Sight did that to her frequently, but gave her only hints and clues as to the future. A random image here or there or a fleeting thought would come to her. It didn't come when bidden, but sometimes Lachlei could summon the visions without controlling what she was summoning. The Wyrd—the fabric of the past, present, and future—was like that. Only the gods had the ability to see the entire Wyrd, but even they could not control it. Very few first-bloods had been able to summon visions and those had been primarily godlings.

Lachlei let herself drift, allowing the Sight to permeate her senses. Fialan had better control over the Sight than she had, but he too found it difficult to interpret. The Sight certainly didn't save Fialan's life—if Fialan had seen the demon, he would have avoided it.

Lachlei saw nothing save darkness. It would be dawn in a few hours and she knew she would need her rest for the work ahead. Exhausted, she fell into an uneasy sleep.

CHAPTER FIFTEEN

Fialan followed Eshe across the plains as the "sun" rose into the dark sky. Unlike Sowelu, the sun of *Elren*, this sun was swollen and red, but cast little heat and almost no light. It provided little warmth in this barren place. Fialan wrapped his cloak around himself, but the cold wind cut through it.

Fialan marveled that he was still dressed much the same as he had when he died—assuming he had died. He didn't quite believe the *Chi'lan* named Eshe. She didn't talk or look back as she walked across the barren landscape towards what appeared to be cliffs in the distance.

And yet, the world was as alien as anything Fialan had ever dreamed of. It was bleak and red, obviously due to a play of the sun's light on the land. As his eyes began to adjust to the dimness, he could see other *Eleion* wandering the vast plains. Some huddled in groups; some alone. Occasionally, a few considered him with interest, but most ignored his presence and none spoke to him.

Fialan caught up with Eshe and grasped her arm. She had drawn her cowl over her head and wrapped the cloak tightly around herself against the cold. "Will you talk to me?"

Eshe paused. "Why?"

"You spoke to me earlier."

"That's because I had to," she said, pulling her arm from his grasp.

"Why?" Fialan asked.

"Because I had to," she said and turned to leave. He caught her arm again. "Leave me alone, Fialan."

"No," Fialan said. "How long have you been here?"

"Time doesn't mean anything here."

"It must," Fialan mused. "You said you served Lochvaur in the Battle of the Nine Worlds?"

Eshe glared at him. Fialan held her arm. "Yes," she said at last. "Let me go."

"No. I won't unless you answer my questions."

"I could use my polearm."

"And I could use my sword," Fialan said. "But if what you say is true, and I am dead, then you can't kill me again."

"You'll feel pain," Eshe replied.

A smile played across Fialan's lips. "Really?"

"What's so amusing?" She stared at him.

"You and I could fight each other and not die," he said.

"You'll regenerate your body."

"Courtesy of Areyn Sehduk?"

Her eyes hardened—steel points within the darkness of the cowl. "Yes."

"But I am Rhyn'athel's champion," he said.

"*Were* Rhyn'athel's champion," she said. "Rhyn'athel has no power here."

"Why do you say that?" he said. "You're *Chi'lan*—you're Rhyn'athel's warrior."

Eshe shook her head. "I *was* Rhyn'athel's warrior," she said. "Rhyn'athel abandoned us to Areyn after the war. Areyn took the dead, Fialan. We are beholden to the death god."

"I don't believe that," Fialan said.

"You've just died, you don't know..."

"Don't know what?"

Again, the hatred glowed in her eyes. "You'll learn..."

"Learn what?"

Eshe took a breath. "You have no will save Areyn's. You will do as he commands." She looked on him in pity. "Fialan, Rhyn'athel has abandoned us to our fate with the death god. Rhyn'athel has abandoned his own son, Lochvaur, to Areyn for the sake of the Nine Worlds. No one, save perhaps Lochvaur and a few of his followers believe that Rhyn'athel will return for us. It has been so long, Fialan."

"So, you believe you should just give up?" Fialan asked.

Eshe shook her head. "Fialan, I used to believe as you do. But Areyn uses us; he drains us of our life force like a leech until we can barely survive. But, we are creations of Rhyn'athel and we grow strong again—only to feed Areyn." She shuddered and pulled herself away. "It's awful—and we don't speak of it ever. You'll learn."

Fialan let her go and she shuffled away from him. The thought of having his life force drained filled him with horror, but he pushed it from his mind.

"Lochvaur hasn't given up—why?" Fialan asked.

Eshe stopped and shook her head. "I don't know."

"Eshe—wait!" Fialan called to her. At first, he thought she would continue forward, but she stopped and turned around. "I'll leave you alone after this—I promise."

Eshe's eyes glinted under her dark cowl. "What is it?"

"I have been the strongest *Chi'lan* champion since Lochvaur. No mortal creature slew me, Eshe."

"It doesn't matter."

"It *does* matter. It matters not just to me, but to the Nine Worlds. I was Rhyn'athel's champion and the creature that killed me should have died when I thrust my blade into it."

Eshe lowered her hood. "You killed it?"

"It was supposedly a *Silren*, Eshe, but it killed my *Chi'lan* warriors with a glance. I struck it in the chest. It would've killed a first-blood, Eshe. My sword was a magical weapon."

Eshe paused. "Your sword was adamantine?"

"From *Athelren*. Nothing could've survived *Fyren's* blow."

"*Fyren*?" she whispered. "*Fyren*?"

"You know the blade, then?"

"*Fyren* is a legendary demon slayer," Eshe said. "It was Lochvaur's blade before he forged his own Sword of Power. No demon could withstand that sword."

"Whatever killed me did," Fialan said. "I buried *Fyren* into its chest. It prevented me from using my powers."

A glint of hope shone in Eshe's eyes. "There are very few that could withstand that blade. That who could withstand *Fyren*, would violate the Truce…"

Fialan grinned. "My thoughts exactly."

"What do you want of me?"

"Take me to Lochvaur," he said.

CHAPTER SIXTEEN

Something wasn't right.

Ronan walked along the stockade fencing of North Marches, his senses at peak awareness. As commanding *Chi'lan*, Ronan was in charge of North Marches defenses, such as they were. Although he was not first-blood, Ronan came from ancient lines, and his instincts were sharply aware of both magical and non-magical dangers. His instincts told him something was about to happen.

Ronan nodded to one of the sentries he passed along the earthen ramparts. It was quiet tonight, and the soldiers were making their rounds as they always had. It was routine, and yet…

Ronan gazed into the darkness. The forest that surrounded the village of North Marches crested a hill to the north—the beginnings of the Lochvaren Mountains lay to the north and west. To the east lay the *Silren* lands. Ronan had never been fond of the *Silren*—what he had seen of them. Most avoided the village of North Marches, but a few did make their way here. Despite the *Lochvaur* attempt in friendship, most *Silren* preferred to avoid the *Lochvaur*.

"*Silren*," he muttered as he walked towards one of the other *Chi'lan* stationed along the ramparts. "Alasila, do you see anything tonight?"

"Ronan," the woman nodded. Alasila was one of the many women *Chi'lan* in North Marches. "Nothing save the cursed moon."

Ronan chuckled, looking up at the pale moon. "Tomah and Iamar don't even show themselves with that evil thing. I was wondering if you had seen anything to worry about."

Alasila shook her head. "Nothing." She gave Ronan an appraising look. "Do you sense something?"

"Maybe," Ronan said. He gazed out at the forest and saw a shadow creep along the ground. "What do you make of that?"

Alasila looked out at the shadow as it crept towards the village. "Fog, maybe?"

Ronan frowned. "The fog comes from the valleys, not the hills." He stared at it for a minute. "Signal the watch," he said. "It's an army."

"An army?" Alasila glanced at the shadow. She could see nothing unusual about it.

"Do what I say!" Ronan snarled. "We need all available warriors here now!"

◆◆◆◆

The bells of North Marches pealed across the land. Deep within the mist, the *Silren* army rode with Areyn at the lead. Areyn swore and reined the demon horse as the watch fires along the North Marches' ramparts sprang to life.

"They've seen us," said Galen.

Areyn almost killed the commander, but held his temper. The fool would die soon enough, but now Areyn needed him. "Give the command to charge," Areyn said.

"But the ramparts…"

"I'll take care of the ramparts," Areyn said. "Lead them!"

Galen nodded and turned to his warriors. "The order has been given! Charge!"

All at once, the mist blew away, revealing thousands of *Silren* riders. Galen brandished his sword and with a cry, spurred his horse forward. The entire cavalry charged with him.

Areyn gazed at the ramparts. With a single thought, the entire wall blew apart, throwing soldiers and *Chi'lan* everywhere. Areyn Sehduk felt the surge of power as he sensed the soldiers deaths. He grinned, almost giddy. It would be a good night.

◆◆◆◆

Ronan lay half covered with rubble. The explosion had thrown him and the other soldiers from the rampart. Even now, he could see the *Silren* cavalry ride through the breech. He realized they had made a tactical error by stationing so many guards along the ramparts. Still, he hadn't expected the *Silren* to destroy the wall so easily.

The chaos of battle surrounded him, but Ronan could do nothing. He couldn't feel his legs. Blood was everywhere, and Ronan could see that his lower body was twisted at an odd angle. His sword was gone. Alasila lay nearby, her eyes half open and glazed over.

Chi'lan fought against the mounted warriors, but there were too many *Silren*. One man, cleaved from shoulder to chest, collapsed on top of Ronan, but the dying *Chi'lan* could do nothing. He heard those who were still alive sound the retreat and flee, leaving him alone to die.

Then he felt it. Cold seemed to grip his very soul, and Ronan turned to see the dark rider as he rode through the breech. The rider approached slowly, carefully, as though studying the dead. He halted at Alasila and his mount lowered its head as though to inspect its grisly work.

"Leave her alone!" Ronan said, without thinking.

The dark warrior turned towards Ronan, a sardonic smile on his face. "Well, Slayer, one still lives."

The beast turned its gaze towards Ronan, and Ronan stared at the demon. Gone were the trappings of a horse. Instead, red eyes glowed above a maw of sharp teeth. Its legs weren't horse-like at all—instead it was muscular with sharp claws. Why had Ronan thought it was a horse?

"By Rhyn'athel's sword," Ronan whispered.

The rider was grinning broadly now. "Rhyn'athel has no power here," he said. "But I do."

The beast rose up and turned on Ronan, silencing the *Chi'lan* even before he could scream.

◆◆◆◆

Lachlei awoke in a sweat. She sat up straight, shivering violently. The last thing she could remember was some *thing* leaning over her, drinking the life from her body. She shuddered, pulling the bedclothes around her. She tried desperately to recall what she dreamt, but only violent images remained. A battle? It seemed more like a slaughter.

The mead hall was silent now, leaving her in the darkness and alone. Lachlei slid from the bed and leaned over Haellsil's cradle to check on him. The rhythmic rise and fall of his chest assured Lachlei he was all right. She hastily dressed in a tunic and breeches, fastened on her swordbelt, and opened the locked doors to the hall.

Outside, the guard was standing there. A quick shake of her head told him that he was to say nothing. Lachlei peered out and saw that the fire in the firepit was dying and cast the entire hall in shadows. The warriors lay stretched out around the fire, sleeping the mead off in their bedrolls. A few quietly played dice in the corner, but overall, the room was still.

A hand on her shoulder brought her around abruptly. It was Rhyn, and his expression was grave.

"North Marches has just been attacked," he said.

CHAPTER SEVENTEEN

"Are you sure?" Lachlei whispered as Rhyn led her past the sleeping warriors.

"Quite sure—you dreamt it too, didn't you?" Rhyn said, anger and helplessness glinting in his silver eyes. "I should've listened to my brother—he warned me..." he said more to himself than to her.

"How could your brother know?"

Rhyn paused and realized what he had said. "He couldn't," he said quickly. "Listen, what you saw tonight was the Wyrd. You saw the attack of North Marches."

"It was a slaughter," she whispered. "You saw it?"

"I did," he said grimly. "It woke me too. Tell me what you saw."

"A creature bending over me—wanting to suck out my life."

Areyn, Rhyn'athel thought darkly. *Or a demon.*

"It's the same creature that killed Fialan, isn't it?" Lachlei asked.

Rhyn'athel stared. "What do you know about the creature that killed Fialan?" he asked sharply.

"It was a demon, wasn't it?" she asked.

Rhyn'athel gazed at her dumbfounded. How did Lachlei recognize Areyn Sehduk or his demon mount? Rhyn'athel began to wonder if perhaps he had underestimated the *Eleion*, and especially, the *Lochvaur*. "A type of demon, yes," said Rhyn'athel at last.

Lachlei met his gaze. "What are you, Rhyn?" she asked.

"What do you mean?"

"You're more powerful than any first-blood I've ever seen. You've appeared with Fialan's death. You've bested Tamar—our strongest warrior. And you have a Sword of Power. You're not an ordinary warrior or just a *Chi'lan* for that matter..."

Rhyn'athel frowned and turned away. Was it that obvious? He looked in askance for Ni'yah, but his brother wasn't there. Rhyn'athel guessed that the wolf-god was at North Marches, having sensed Areyn's work.

"No, I'm not," he said at last. "I'm a demon slayer of sorts."

"A demon slayer? Like Lochvaur?" Lachlei stared at him dumbfounded.

Rhyn'athel nodded. It was a partial truth. "Fialan's death brought me here."

Lachlei shook her head. "I thought a demon killed Fialan. I could sense the foul magic on the corpses." She buried her face in her hands and began to weep softly.

Rhyn'athel hesitated and then gently put his arms around her. Again, he felt the pleasant shock of her touch; again, he was reminded why he had been so eager to take a mortal form. She did not resist. "I can't rest until the demon is gone from this world," he said.

Lachlei looked up, her eyes bright with tears. "You will avenge Fialan's death?"

"Fialan was blood kin, albeit distantly," Rhyn said. "I have slain demons before."

Lachlei paused. "How can this be? The duty falls on me, since I was his consort."

"But you don't have ..." Rhyn paused.

"What?"

"Nothing," Rhyn replied.

"You were going to say that I don't have the power to kill a demon," Lachlei said.

Rhyn'athel stared at her again. *Were his defenses down? Could she read his mind?* A quick check told him they were in place. "Yes," he admitted. "You don't. Fialan didn't."

"Teach me."

Rhyn paused. "You want me to teach you how to fight a demon?"

"We will have to go to North Marches," she said. "We must avenge their murders and take back our lands."

Rhyn'athel nodded, considering her thoughtfully. Could he possibly teach the *Eleion* to kill demons? His son, Lochvaur, had fought demons fifteen hundred years before—but Lochvaur had been a godling, not just a first-blood. Still, the prospect intrigued Rhyn'athel. "Yes, we do."

"I have a score to settle with this demon," she said.

So do I, Rhyn'athel thought.

◆◆◆◆

Dawn came cold and blood-red over North Marches. Ravens and other scavengers slunk around the bodies of the slain. The acrid smell of smoke wafted through the battlefield. All that was left of North Marches was a smoldering ruin. The *Silren* had torched the village, setting many occupied buildings alight and shooting those who dared try to escape the merciless flames.

Areyn stood among the bodies, reveling in the death while the *Silren* searched for survivors. There would be none—Areyn had made certain of it. Thousands of *Lochvaur* had perished in a few short hours, either at the hand of the *Silren* or through Areyn Sehduk, himself.

Areyn's demon mount was nowhere to be found. Areyn suspected the demon was looking for more dying souls. It had been a good feeding, and the demon was seeking the remnants of the slaughter. It would return once it was sated.

Galen strode towards Areyn. "There are no survivors."

"Good," Areyn replied. "This will help clean the *Lochvaur* plague from *Silren* lands."

"Indeed," the general said. "But we could've used the women and children for the slave trade."

"Maybe next time," Areyn replied, but he doubted it. Areyn Sehduk enjoyed the slave trade immensely, but he needed deaths now. It took power to hold this guise. Unlike the gods of light, Areyn needed the life force of the dying. Their lives made him Rhyn'athel's equal. Without their deaths, Areyn would be little more than a demon, himself.

Out of the corner of his eye, Areyn saw a silver wolf slink away. He turned towards it and grinned. *Spying for your brother again, Ni'yah?*

The wolf made no reply, but paused and glared at Areyn balefully with his brass eyes. The wolf turned and fled into the dark forest with Areyn's mocking laughter ringing in his ears.

Chapter Eighteen

Imdyr lay naked against the cold, stone altar of Fala and closed her eyes. For nearly a month, Imdyr had lain against the winged goddess's altar, searching for some sign. Imdyr had been the goddess's high priestess for five years; Fala had chosen her when she was twelve after the old priestess had died.

Long raven-black hair framed an angular face. Her eyes were obsidian black, contrasting sharply with sallow skin. Her thin body showed her ribs below her small, firm breasts, and her hip bones protruded. She was like all those born of the *Eltar* kindred, tall, lithe, and fair skinned. She had been beautiful at one time, but the darkness in the temple had made her pale and emaciated. Even so, the power still remained.

Imdyr was first-blood. She came from the line of Fala when the goddess had walked among mortals before the wars between the gods. The *Eltar* and the *Falarel* had been her kindreds, and yet, they could not gain any greatness over the others.

Where was the promise of Fala? Imdyr demanded. To her demands came no reply.

Imdyr had waited—in vain. Fala no longer held power in the Fifth World. She was a dark goddess who hated both the gods of light and gods of darkness, favoring her own magic. For this, Fala was an outcast—eschewed by both sides. Her kindreds weak and forgotten.

A surge of power ran through her, and Imdyr sat up. Reaching out with her Sight, she saw a dark figure on a horse—but it was no horse. Within her mind's eye, Imdyr saw the slaughter unfold. Entranced, she felt horrified at first, but she could not tear herself away from the vision. The dark rider came forward, wielding his blade.

She saw a village in her vision and watched as it burst into flames. Pale warriors—*Silren*, by their looks—attacked with a blood-frenzy. Some of their victims ran, but a few stood and fought. The warriors had red-gold manes—*Lochvaur*. But, there were too many *Silren* and the *Lochvaur* were soon overwhelmed.

Imdyr found herself standing on the battlefield, the cold wind whipping across her body. She shivered, but not because she was cold. The carnage excited her—she could taste the blood in her mouth. Then the dark warrior rode towards her. Imdyr could see his face clearly as he turned his demon-mount aside. He was a *Silren* with ice-blue eyes. *Silren*, and yet, not *Silren*.

Imdyr smiled. She looked into his pale eyes. "I know who you are," she whispered. "Areyn Sehduk."

◆◆◆◆

"It was Areyn," Ni'yah said, his brass eyes hard. "He mocks me and he mocks you." He stood on the parapets of Caer Lochvaren next to Rhyn'athel as the warrior god gazed over the forests in the dawn's light. The warming sun's rays brought little comfort to either of them. To the casual observer, they looked like two *Eleion* soldiers conversing—not two of the most powerful gods in the Nine Worlds.

"I know," Rhyn'athel said, his voice heavy. "I should've seen it—in fact, I felt Areyn's shield earlier before the attack, only I was too preoccupied. I won't make that mistake again."

"What are you going to do about it?"

"What indeed? The Truce is in shambles."

"No thanks to Areyn."

"And no thanks to you—or me," Rhyn'athel said. "We've all violated it, despite our intentions."

"Areyn has slaughtered an entire village, and you're worried about *your* violation?"

Rhyn'athel shook his head grimly. "I had hoped to avoid this war, and yet, it seems inevitable. Total, utter destruction—as it was in the last war."

"But we won."

Rhyn'athel chuckled ruefully. "Did we? Yes, I suppose in a way, you could call it a victory. But what did we accomplish?"

"The *Jotunn* and demons no longer walk this world or any of our worlds," Ni'yah replied. "The *Eleion* live here instead of Areyn's spawn."

"But as long as Areyn Sehduk exists, there will be no peace," Rhyn'athel replied. "And he is an *Athel'cen*, a god from the Wyrd—as you and I are. We can't be destroyed. You know as well as I do that the Truce was the only way to preserve what little we've created. And now, that's gone." Silence ensued.

"He has a demon with him," Ni'yah ventured.

Rhyn'athel smiled grimly. "That news does not surprise me." He crossed his arms and leaned against the parapet. "Areyn is a coward—he will not confront me directly because he knows he will lose. So, he takes the guise of a warrior to destroy my kindred and my power in this world, hoping to catch me unawares."

"But now he's gotten bold," Ni'yah remarked. "Bold enough to taunt me."

"Arrogance," Rhyn'athel replied. "The blood-feeding does that to him. Areyn will regret it in a few days when his power levels out."

"What do we do?"

Rhyn'athel made no response. Instead, he gazed below into the bailey. Ni'yah followed his gaze until it rested on Lachlei who had entered the inner courtyards. Ni'yah grinned. "She is very beautiful, isn't she?"

"Damn you for bringing me here," Rhyn'athel said. "You knew all the time she would be my weakness."

Ni'yah shrugged. "I knew you wouldn't let her die—especially now that the Wyrd is weaving a different pattern."

Rhyn'athel took a deep breath, his eyes becoming glassy as he concentrated his powers on the Sight. It was harder to do, now that he had a mortal body, but not impossible. The silver threads of the future shimmered in his vision, and he stared as he saw the path they would take. His eyes snapped back into focus. "I've changed the Wyrd with my presence."

"Can't be helped," Ni'yah said dismissively. "Whenever any of the gods of the Wyrd enter this world, it forever changes the Wyrd's pattern."

"You knew this and yet you continue to meddle," Rhyn'athel accused.

Ni'yah shrugged. "I hate knowing everything that happens—it makes for a very boring life as a god. Besides, it's not just me, now—it's you and Areyn. You have the strongest link to the Wyrd, which is why it is so interesting to see it change around Lachlei…"

"Lachlei," Rhyn'athel repeated distractedly. There were two paths now—both would shift the balance of power. Both hinged on Lachlei.

"You know that not everything is set and the Wyrd doesn't reveal the full future. But Lachlei will…"

Rhyn'athel's face became stern. "Speak of this to no one."

"Areyn may learn of this," Ni'yah said. "Areyn will seek Lachlei out, himself."

Rhyn'athel could feel his face flush with rage, but he held it back. "Not while I am still the warrior god."

Ni'yah nodded. "So, what will you do?"

"Lachlei wants me to teach her how to kill a demon."

"She knows?" Ni'yah gazed at his brother. "Did you…?"

The warrior god shook his head. "Lachlei sensed Areyn, herself. The slaughter woke her."

"I only thought godlings like Lochvaur and Laddel could recognize demons."

"Lachlei can." Rhyn'athel's gaze drifted back to her. "The *Silren* are under Areyn's power. If the *Lochvaur* fall, so will the other kindreds."

"What are you going to do?"

"Stop Areyn here and now," Rhyn'athel said. "Lachlei will be my champion."

Ni'yah grinned. "I knew you wouldn't stand by idly."

Rhyn'athel nodded. "As much as I hate to admit it, you were right." He paused. "We will need more than the *Lochvaur*, though. Your son, Laddel is still alive?"

"He is," Ni'yah said. "And the *Laddel* are a strong kindred—one of the few who use longbows. I will speak with Laddel, if you wish."

Rhyn'athel nodded. "Do that. And speak to Elisila about her *Silren*…"

Ni'yah smirked. "You wouldn't wish to talk with her yourself?"

The warrior god glared.

Ni'yah chuckled. "I thought not," he said and vanished.

CHAPTER NINETEEN

Eshe led Fialan towards the cliffs. She had agreed to take him to Lochvaur and for the first time, seemed actually cheered by his presence. "Lochvaur has a fortification within the cliffs, themselves," she said as they walked.

"Fortification? Is there are need for a fortress here?" Fialan asked, looking around at the bleak landscape.

Eshe laughed; her voice almost musical in that dismal place. Fialan smiled. "By the gods, no!" she said. "If the demons want you, no tiny fortress would keep them at bay."

"Are there any animals here?"

Eshe shook her head. "No—no need to feed us. These shells Areyn has given us don't require food or water."

"Or sleep?"

Eshe shook her head. "Except when Areyn..." She shuddered.

"Why would Lochvaur build a fortress?" Fialan asked, changing the subject back to avoid the topic.

"Most of the dead thought it was foolish," said Eshe. "But, perhaps it's a way to show defiance against Areyn. Or maybe it was simply something to take up time. Regardless, it has had an effect of sorts. Areyn won't come near Lochvaur."

Fialan laughed. "He won't? I wonder why?"

"Lochvaur is part Rhyn'athel," she said. "Areyn won't touch Lochvaur's power or he'll poison himself."

"I thought you said that first-bloods no longer have their powers."

"They don't," she said. "But a godling is different, and even though Lochvaur has no power here, Areyn fears him."

The swollen red sun made its way slowly across the sky. Despite the shock of discovering he was dead, Fialan was glad he didn't need food or rest. He guessed by the sun's movement that *Tarentor's* day was much longer than the *Elren's* day. The barren plains became rolling hills and still, they walked. He could see the mountains loom ahead like sharp, jagged teeth.

"There isn't much to build with around here," Fialan remarked.

Eshe chuckled. "Just twisted ironwood and rock—and the damn saw grass. I hate the stuff! It'll cut through everything except armor."

Fialan laughed with her. "Are all Areyn's worlds this dismal?"

Eshe grinned. "They say he made this world especially for Rhyn'athel's warriors," she said. "He's not fond of the *Chi'lan*."

"But he has other worlds."

"Oh yes—that's no lie," she said. "I hear *Jotnar* is similar enough to our *Elren*, but it is colder. And of course, it's the land of the *Jotunn*, the frost giants."

"You were killed by a *Jotunn*," he said.

"Yes," she said. "Nasty creatures—I supposed you've never seen one."

Fialan shook his head.

"Well, that's one good thing that came from the Truce, I suppose. They used to inhabit our world."

"I hear they were tough to kill," Fialan said.

Eshe chuckled. "You're talkative for a dead man," she said. "This has probably been the most I've said since I've been here."

"Why?"

"Well, you're different. Most when they realize they're dead are resigned to it. They want to see their parents or dead loved ones or whatever..."

"I've made my peace with the dead long ago," he said. "And if what you say is true, I have a long time to see my dead loved ones. My concern, Eshe, is with the living."

Eshe paused and considered him thoughtfully. "You are different, Fialan. Perhaps I was hasty to think otherwise."

◆◆◆◆

The swollen red sun was slipping below the horizon when Eshe led Fialan into a red canyon. The canyon led along the ruddy desert cliffs where a fortress cut from stone sat hewn from the sandstone walls. Fialan stared at the structure in awe. A keep, fortified by a large curtain wall, complete with defensible towers, sat in the high cliffs. It was as large as Caer Lochvaren.

"How long did it take to build that?" he asked.

Eshe shrugged. "When you have all the time in the Nine Worlds, what does it matter?"

"But how did they get the tools?"

Eshe shook her head. "I don't know, but the sandstone is soft. It wouldn't survive a siege."

"Still, wouldn't it give people hope?"

"I suppose it gives hope to some," Eshe said slowly. "But most feel it is folly."

Fialan laughed. "A fool's fight, eh? Then, no doubt you consider me a fool."

Eshe shook her head. "I think your quest may be in vain, Fialan, but I don't consider you a fool."

As they walked towards the cliff, they saw that stairs had been painstakingly hewn in the red cliff face to provide a way up towards the fortress. The trail crisscrossed the face of the rock, with many switchbacks that allowed a steep but traversable climb. Fialan hesitated as Eshe grasped the handholds that led to the stairs.

"What's wrong?" Eshe asked, glancing behind.

"There are no guards."

"Who would you guard against?" Eshe asked. "The demons can come and go as they please, but they don't enter this place. Those who seek refuge—if you want to call it that—are welcome since they are fellow *Eleion*. Most who come here are *Chi'lan*, but there are a few *Lochvaur* soldiers and some from other kindreds. Mostly first-bloods, like yourself, but there are many of common birth."

"Were you first-blood?"

"Do I look first-blood?"

"I don't know—I didn't know first-bloods had a *look* about them," Fialan said.

"They do," Eshe said. "When you see Lochvaur, you'll see what I mean." She started climbing.

"Then you've stayed in the fortress for some time," Fialan said as he climbed behind her.

Eshe stepped onto the stairs and frowned. "Yes, I did." She climbed the stairs until it leveled out onto a shelf. "Aren't you ever silent?"

"No," Fialan said with a grin. "Why did you leave?"

"Why did you die?"

"Who says I'm dead?" Fialan said. "Now, why did you leave?" He stepped onto the stairs and glanced down. The drop was thirty feet. "I guess it's a good thing I can't die now." He looked at Eshe. "Why'd you leave?"

Eshe shook her head. "I don't know. I guess I lost hope." She started to walk away as he stepped onto the ledge.

"Wait!" he said.

Eshe glanced behind, her face no longer a mask. "Leave me alone."

"Why?" He gripped her arm.

He stared as he saw tears streaming down her face. "It's been so long, Fialan," she said. Eshe closed her eyes and wept, burying her face in his shoulder.

Fialan held her. "Eshe, Eshe!" he said. "I'm sorry."

"How long has it been since the Battle of the Nine Worlds?" she asked.

Fialan looked down at her. "Is time the same here as *Elren*?"

"I don't know—some say it is, but Lochvaur is not certain about that. How long has it been in the world of the living?"

Fialan sighed. "It's been two thousand years, Eshe."

"I have been dead for over two thousand years," Eshe said, letting the words sink in. "Fialan, how can one hope after so long?"

Fialan looked into Eshe's eyes. "I don't know, Eshe, but if Lochvaur still has hope, then I will have hope."

"If Lochvaur does not?" she asked.

Fialan grinned. "Then, I will still have hope."

CHAPTER TWENTY

"The *Silren* have attacked North Marches," Lachlei said, flinging open the doors to the High Council. It was morning when she strode in, dressed as a *Chi'lan*, her mail ringing with each step. Lachlei noted, much to her anger, that not one of the Council had risen in her presence. Laewynd gazed at her, his silver eyes unperturbed.

"We know, Lachlei," he said. "Some of us on the Council *do* have the Sight."

Lachlei flushed at the rebuke. "Then you know that they put every man, woman, and child to the sword?"

The council members glanced at each other, but said nothing.

"We were discussing what action we should take."

"Discussing? Discussing!" Lachlei stared at Laewynd. "Are you joking? We've been attacked."

"North Marches has been attacked," Laewynd said. "Not Caer Lochvaren."

"*Lochvaren* has been attacked," Lachlei corrected him. "And North Marches is as much a part of Lochvaren as Caer Lochvaren."

"The land has been under dispute for some time," said Moira. "Fialan's father, Lochalan, negotiated these lands from Silvain."

Lachlei stared at Moira and then at the others. "The demon who killed Fialan leads their army. We are not safe—he will march to Caer Lochvaren..."

Laewynd raised his hand. "We don't know that, Lachlei—we can only speculate."

She stared. "You would stand by idly and do nothing?"

Laewynd shook his head. "I wouldn't act in such haste."

"But haste is what we need!" She paused and met his gaze. "I'll take the army to North Marches."

The council members glanced at each other. "That may not be wise," said Laewynd at last.

"Why?"

"Our intelligence indicates that the *Elesil* may be massing an army to attack us."

Of course. Lachlei frowned. The *Elesil* were related to the *Silren* and held treaties with them. "But the *Silren* and the *Elesil* may join together to siege Caer Lochvaren—certainly we should stop the *Silren* before they get too far south."

"Not necessarily."

"I will lead an army to North Marches..."

"No."

"No?" She stared at them aghast.

"You're not queen yet, Lachlei," Laewynd said. "Despite our vote, you won't be queen until the coronation tonight—assuming there is no challenger."

"A technicality."

"A reality," said Laewynd. "Don't give us cause to reconsider."

"You wouldn't dare. You can't change your vote once the Council has decided."

"Can't I?" Laewynd smiled. "Perhaps I can't change the vote according to *Chi'lan* law, but there are other ways to stop you from taking the throne."

Lachlei met his gaze. She knew those ways. "You wouldn't dare."

"Wouldn't I?" Laewynd leaned back and smiled. "A word to one of the more ambitious *Chi'lan* might result in a challenger. And the last time I checked, *Chi'lan* Lachlei, you haven't seen a battle in three years."

"You'd challenge after you voted me as queen?"

"Not I," Laewynd said. "I have no taste for the throne. But there are some who do. Now, forget about North Marches, Lachlei. The *Lochvaur* have other pressing issues."

"You would've never denied Fialan the army."

"Fialan would've weighed the decision more carefully," Laewynd replied. "You are new at this."

Lachlei now understood. The platitudes they had spoken before had been to appease her. They had chosen her precisely because she hadn't wanted the position, and yet, none would argue with it. The High Council had hoped to take advantage of her. They would've never dared with Fialan in power.

"Very well," Lachlei said. She turned and left before any could reply.

◆◆◆◆

Lachlei entered the bailey and looked around. Rhyn hadn't been in the great hall when she had woken, nor had he been to the High Council.

Fools! she thought. They didn't sense what she and Rhyn sensed. Perhaps if Rhyn would speak to the High Council, they would understand the urgency. She looked up and saw Rhyn looking down on her. She climbed the tower stairs that led to the wall walk. As she approached Rhyn, she saw that he was lost in thought.

"Rhyn!" she called.

The North Marches *Chi'lan* turned to her, a concerned look on his face. "You've been to the High Council."

Lachlei nodded. "They won't give me the troops to meet the *Silren* at North Marches."

"What does that leave you with?"

"My own *Chi'lan*—two thousand total," Lachlei said. "It's not enough."

Rhyn frowned. "No, it's not," he agreed. He knew that the *Laddel* were Ni'yah's to command, but how many would remain to be seen. Laddel, Ni'yah's son, would be obliged to his father, but even Laddel would have his limits. Without the full force of the *Lochvaur*, the *Laddel* would not be willing to give their entire army to stop Areyn. It would be too late by the time the *Lochvaur* entered the fight. "What if the *Silren* obtain the *Elesil's* aid?"

Lachlei shook her head. "The *Elesil* are traditionally allied with the *Silren*. If they enter the fray, we'll be overwhelmed without aid from our allies. But the *Laddel* are some distance away and the *Haell* allegiance is tenuous at best."

Then, let us hope Ni'yah does his work, Rhyn'athel thought darkly. *If I have to intervene, this could escalate...*

Lachlei studied Rhyn's face curiously. "What of the *Lochvaur* surrounding North Marches?"

Rhyn hesitated. "There are maybe a few thousand. Of those, a few hundred warriors."

"That's a few hundred we don't have now." She fell silent, her face pensive.

"Something is wrong."

Lachlei shook her head. "It's nothing."

"No, it's something," Rhyn paused. He brushed her thoughts and frowned. "Laewynd threatened your crown?"

"It's nothing," Lachlei said.

"No," he replied, feeling his anger rise. "Laewynd threatened you with a challenger, didn't he?"

She took a deep breath. "Yes."

Rhyn frowned. His link with the Web of Wyrd was tenuous in his new form. Even so, he could see that it was changing because of his very presence. "I don't know what's exactly ahead," he said. "But I can promise you none of your *Chi'lan* will challenge you. Nor will I."

"That is some comfort, I suppose." Lachlei's smile was forced. "What will you do now that you have no home to return to?"

"The land is burnt, the people dead, and there is nothing for me. I must seek the demon that killed them."

"Then, our paths still cross," she murmured. "I was hoping that perhaps you would consider joining my *Chi'lan*," she said. "We need warriors, Rhyn." She met his gaze. "*I* need warriors. You're first-blood, and that's a rare commodity nowadays."

Rhyn stared for a long moment, amazed at his luck. "I would be honored," he said.

"Then, stand beside me tonight at coronation," she said. "If I fail, I would have you challenge the victor. I don't know who Laewynd may put up to challenge me, but he will be nothing more than a puppet."

Rhyn shook his head. "No, Lachlei, you won't fail."

"Laewynd reminded me that I haven't seen battle in years—against a battle-hardened warrior, I may fall. You are the only *Chi'lan* I've seen who is worthy enough for the throne."

"I can't accept."

She took his hands and once again, Rhyn felt the charge run through him. "Please, Rhyn, I know you're a first-blood and I know you have a Sword of Power. Cahal told me how you've defeated Tamar."

Rhyn looked into her eyes and felt his resolve slip away. *How could a woman weaken the determination of the most powerful god in the Nine Worlds?* "I accept, Lachlei," he heard himself say. "But you will not fail."

◆◆◆◆

Imdyr rode her black horse towards the *Silren* encampment. It was late afternoon and the sun was already sinking behind the Lochvaren Mountains. Before her lay the tents and watch fires of the *Silren* army, nestled deep within the forest surrounding the King's Highway.

Her horse's hooves made no noise, and Imdyr traveled like a shadow in the oncoming darkness. Imdyr's dark hair and black cloak flowed behind her. She was now dressed in dark adamantine mail and a short sword hung at her side.

The *Silren* guards did not see Imdyr as she rode by, cloaked in her own powers of invisibility. Even with Areyn's shields, Imdyr could sense the death god nearby; his power seemed to draw her in. Imdyr dismounted and entered Areyn's tent.

Incense greeted her as she entered the dark tent. Another odor that she couldn't place—a sweet musky smell—seemed to permeate her senses. As her eyes became used to the dark, Imdyr saw that the tent was empty. Empty, and yet, not. Imdyr could feel Areyn's power everywhere—it was as tangible as the incense that wafted through the tent. She took a step forward.

Suddenly, she felt a strong hand grasp her neck from behind and pull her backwards. Another hand clamped around her mouth so she could not scream. Imdyr turned to see ice-blue eyes glitter with a red light in the darkness.

Who are you?

Imdyr smiled inwardly, despite her fear. *I have come for you, Areyn Sehduk.*

A hesitation. *I am Akwel.*

Is that what the god of destruction calls himself?

Areyn released her, his eyes glowing menacingly. "What are you?" he growled.

"I am Imdyr, High Priestess of Fala," she said.

"An *Eltar*," Areyn said. He gazed at her, trying to read her mind and found it was shut to him. "A daughter of the winged goddess. Why do you seek a *Silren*? We consider you a little more than animals."

"Which is why it surprises me that you took a *Silren* body," Imdyr remarked, appraisingly. She approached him and put her arms around his neck. "It is said that Fala was once your lover…" Imdyr kissed him passionately.

Areyn pulled away. "Who sent you?" he demanded. It bothered him that he couldn't read her mind. "How did you get past the guards?"

"All in due time," she said, kissing him again. "If you please me, I might grant you what you most desire."

"There is nothing that you would have that I would want."

"Really?" Imdyr said, pulling away and feigning surprise. "Then, I suppose I could offer Rhyn'athel the same. Maybe a god of light would be more appreciative of my gifts…"

Areyn curbed his temper as his curiosity took hold. "What gifts?"

"The Nine Worlds, of course."

Areyn licked his lips; hunger glittering in his eyes. "Perhaps I was being hasty," he said. "I will listen."

"Later," she said, sliding out of her clothes. "You must please me first."

CHAPTER TWENTY-ONE

Lachlei stood on the hill overlooking Caer Lochvaren. The stars shone brightly overhead as the three moons, Tomah, Iamar, and Mani, crested the horizon. As it had been in ancient times, the *Chi'lan* now met to choose their ruler and champion. Her personal guard, *Chi'lan* warriors all, stood beside her. Over five hundred warriors, torches blazing, stood around Lachlei as she faced Laewynd. She was ready for combat.

"Does anyone challenge the *Lochvaur* champion?" Laewynd spoke. He held a small circlet in both hands, awaiting a response.

Silence ensued. Lachlei glanced at her *Chi'lan*. Rhyn stood beside her, as promised. One by one, she met the gazes of the warriors she thought capable of challenging her. Rhyn, Cahal, Tamar, Kellachan... One by one, the warriors shook their heads. Lachlei smiled. If none challenged her right, she would be Rhyn'athel's champion and queen of the *Lochvaur*. She recalled how Fialan had taken the throne without a single challenge. None dared challenge what was Fialan's right...

"I challenge."

A voice broke her from her reverie, and she focused on the speaker. Murmurs ran through the *Chi'lan*—there had not been a challenger in over five hundred years. Lachlei turned to see Kieran from the High Council step forward.

"I challenge her blood-right," he said, his silver eyes narrowing.

Lachlei met the man's gaze. "You challenge me?" she asked. Despite Laewynd's threats and her earlier fears, she had not expected a challenge—especially from one of the Council members. But Laewynd had not said the Council vote was unanimous. Indeed, it did not have to be—Fialan had won the crown through a simple majority.

The thought of fighting another *Chi'lan* dismayed Lachlei. She now considered her opponent.

Kieran was an older warrior, loyal to Fialan, but Lachlei knew little about him, save that he had been in Fialan's guard. He wore an older-style scale hauberk and his broadsword was made from darkened steel. One eye was glass-blue—cloudy—from an injury sustained long ago. Kieran steeled his jaw as he spoke. "It is my right as *Chi'lan*," he said. "Regardless of whether I am first-blood."

Lachlei glanced at Cahal, who nodded grimly. That was technically true—any *Chi'lan* had the right to challenge for kingship. She saw Rhyn's eyes harden.

"That is your right, Kieran," she agreed. "But, I would ask you to reconsider."

"Does Fialan's consort fear a fight?" the warrior replied. "Or has the trappings of royalty dulled your skills?"

Murmurs ran through the *Chi'lan*. Lachlei smiled slightly. "No, but evidently my appointment has sharpened your tongue," she replied. "I suspect it is sharper than your sword."

Laewynd stood between them. "Is this an official challenge?"

Kieran drew his sword. "It is."

Laewynd looked at Lachlei. "Do you accept?"

Lachlei drew *Fyren*. Cahal pulled her aside, concern in his eyes. "Lachlei," he whispered. "Are you sure you want to do this?"

Lachlei took a deep breath. It would be a fight to the death or unless a contender yielded. "Why is he challenging me?" she whispered back. "I thought the *Chi'lan* were all of one mind."

"Kieran challenges because of Laewynd," Rhyn replied as he stood beside her. "He was the dissenting vote in the Council. There are those who believe you would be a pawn for the Council."

Lachlei frowned. "A pawn?" She met his gaze. "Do others believe that?"

"Some," admitted Cahal. "But I am not one of them."

Lachlei turned to Rhyn. "Do you believe that?"

"I believe you will be Rhyn'athel's champion," the god replied. "I believe you are *Chi'lan*."

She met his steady gaze and smiled. "Yes," she shouted so all could hear. "I accept the challenge!"

Cheers ran through the crowd. She turned away, and felt Rhyn grip her arm.

Kieran is blind in his left eye, Rhyn informed her in mindspeak. *He's very strong, but not as fast—use that to your advantage.*

Lachlei nodded. She crouched into a defensive position, holding *Fyren* ready. The warriors began to bang their weapons against their shields in time. Kieran dropped into a defensive position and they circled slowly, gauging each other. Lachlei kept her breathing measured. Time seemed to slow as she studied her adversary. Kieran was not only a seasoned warrior, but also much heavier and stronger. He had at least fifty pounds on her, and his height left her at a disadvantage. She would have to either hang back and wait for an opening or press her attack and risk taking a hit.

She could see in Kieran's good eye that he too was weighing potential strategies. He had her at a disadvantage, but he knew she was *Chi'lan* trained. He circled and feinted, trying to draw her in. Lachlei backed away slightly. She took another breath and focused now—the roar from the *Chi'lan*, the beating of the weapons, everything was gone, save she and Kieran.

Without warning Kieran attacked. Lachlei parried and riposted, swinging *Fyren* around. Kieran parried again; the force of his blow jarred her arm. She slipped to his left side and swung *Fyren*. Kieran barely managed to parry the blow. Lachlei skittered out of range as he brought his own sword crashing down.

She smiled inwardly. Rhyn was right. She nearly got a blow in on Kieran's left. It meant he was vulnerable there. Kieran would also be more protective of that side, knowing his limitations.

Before she could react, Kieran lunged at her, swinging his broadsword. Lachlei parried and attacked. Kieran countered. Lachlei took the full brunt of the blow on *Fyren*. The blow jarred her arm, threatening to numb it. She slipped inside, and *Fyren* twisted upward, cutting into Kieran's arm.

The *Chi'lan* warrior yelled and backed off as *Fyren's* adamantine blade drew first blood just above the elbow. Lachlei followed, *Chi'lan* bloodlust in her eyes, as she swung the battle blade. Another cut, this time across the chest, but the scale armor held. Lachlei realized too late that Kieran had her where he wanted her.

Kieran swung his own blade. Lachlei backed off as the blade hit her helm hard and bounced into her left shoulder, biting through mail. She felt the snap as the heavy sword broke her collarbone, and she screamed as the sword continued to bite in. The pain blinded and sickened her and she dropped to her knees.

"Do you yield?" she heard a voice somewhere beyond the pain.

Lachlei opened her eyes. She had dropped *Fyren* and was now on her hands and knees, leaning into her right hand to keep from collapsing to the ground.

"Do you yield?" The voice came again.

Lachlei closed her eyes again. Her mouth was dry and she could not speak. The pain was intense.

You are first-blood. Is this how Rhyn'athel's champion would die?

Lachlei hesitated. She concentrated on the pain and found it lessening. Like all first-bloods, she could heal—but could she heal herself? She now focused on the wound.

"Do you yield?"

Silence ensued. The drumming stopped, and the warriors were silent.

Lachlei continued to concentrate, and her shoulder became warm. The pain disappeared and she could feel the bone begin to knit.

You are first-blood.

Lachlei raised her head and met Kieran's gaze defiantly. "I am first-blood," she said, her voice strong. "I do not yield!"

Kieran raised his sword for the final blow. Lachlei leapt to her feet, slamming her foot into his knee and taking him down, sweeping his legs out from under him. Kieran fell, dropping the sword and grasping Lachlei as he went down. Lachlei struck his jaw with a solid palm heel strike and rolled from his grasp. She rolled onto *Fyren* and leapt to her feet, sword in hand. Kieran was armed and on his feet as well, but not as steady. Lachlei had not broken his knee, but she had done damage to his right leg.

Lachlei knew by the look in Kieran's eyes that the *Chi'lan* would show no mercy now. He swung his sword, pressing her backwards. Lachlei tried to slip under his attacks, but each time she was driven back.

Hold your ground.

Lachlei heard the voice in her head, but made no reply. She was drenched in sweat and blood, and was tiring now. She could not see how she could hold her ground without losing her head to Kieran's blade. Kieran slammed his blade down as Lachlei brought *Fyren* up. This time, as the blades chattered against each other, she twisted *Fyren* and caught both blades, redirecting them down, point first into the ground. Using the momentum, she leapt up and threw a round kick to Kieran's blind side, hitting him in the head.

The kick sent Kieran sprawling, and Lachlei pulled both swords from the ground. She stood over the fallen *Chi'lan* with both blades pointed at Kieran's throat.

"Yield!" she demanded. Silence ensued.

Kieran looked up, his face bloody from the broken nose and smashed jaw. He shook his head. "I will not."

Lachlei let the sword blade linger for a moment as it touched his neck. "Kieran, I need good warriors like you. Yield—you are no good to me serving Areyn Sehduk."

"I won't serve a pawn."

"Then, serve a *Chi'lan*," she said. "For I am *Chi'lan*, though perhaps in the past three years I may have forsaken the path. I swear by Rhyn'athel's blood I serve the warrior god first." She looked up and met Rhyn's piercing gaze. *I know what I am now,* she thought. "Kieran, I am Rhyn'athel's champion." With that, she thrust his blade into the ground.

A thunderclap shook the hill as white fire flew from the blade. For a moment, the white-hot fire surrounded her. The *Chi'lan* drew back in surprise and then the flames vanished. Burning pain shot through Lachlei's forearm, and she almost dropped *Fyren*. Carefully, she sheathed her sword, pulled the gauntlet off, and pulled back the mail and sleeve of her arming shirt. She stared at her right arm.

"What is it?" Cahal asked as Kieran's eyes widened.

Lachlei met Kieran's gaze, and the defeated *Chi'lan* nodded. "It's true, then," he said.

Lachlei looked up and met Rhyn's gaze. "I've been chosen," she whispered. She brandished her forearm to show the new mark of a black dragon still forming on her skin.

CHAPTER TWENTY-TWO

"Quite showy, wasn't it?" Ni'yah remarked as Rhyn'athel followed the warriors down the hill to the mead hall. After Lachlei had won the fight, Laewynd had placed the circlet on Lachlei's head and pronounced her queen of the *Lochvaur*. Lachlei accepted the title and led the warriors back to Caer Lochvaren.

The two gods walked together at the back of the crowd; their conversation concealed from anyone who might listen in. If anyone had paid attention, they would have seen Rhyn speaking with another *Lochvaur*.

"They needed a sign—I gave them one," Rhyn'athel replied dismissively. "Lachlei is my champion. She's proven herself—Kieran was a tough opponent."

"With a little help from you," Ni'yah remarked.

Rhyn'athel caught his gaze and held it. "Lachlei defeated Kieran on her own. I merely encouraged her."

Ni'yah grinned. "She's good, isn't she?"

"She's a better fighter than I expected," Rhyn'athel admitted. "But she's inexperienced."

"Her first-blood capabilities are equal to Fialan's," Ni'yah said. "I was disappointed when Lachlei chose to marry him—of all *Laddel's* progeny, she's shown the most promise."

Rhyn'athel looked at him, arching his eyebrow. "I believe you're disappointed she's *Lochvaur*."

"She's half *Laddel* and has more of my blood in her than yours. How many generations removed from Lochvaur is she?"

"Ten."

"At least ten. She should've had silver hair and golden eyes, if it hadn't been for those damn dominant traits of yours..."

Rhyn'athel chuckled. "She's shorter than a *Lochvaur* ought to be. Can she transmute?"

Ni'yah shrugged. "I don't know—she's never tried. I don't think she knows her full capabilities."

The two gods walked down the hill to the open gate. Ni'yah stopped and gave his brother a measuring look. "Once in a while, the Wyrd weaves a strange pattern that none of us can fathom. Have you looked at the Wyrd lately?"

Rhyn'athel shook his head. "Not in its entirety since becoming mortal, why?"

Ni'yah looked above them and nodded. The warrior god followed his brother's gaze, seeing the slender filaments of the Wyrd as they made up the fabric of the world. "I've seen only a few times when the Wyrd behaved like this. One was with Lochvaur; the other was with our own creation within the Wyrd."

"Are you saying that Lachlei affects the Wyrd?"

"I'm saying that with three *Athel'cen*, our appearance has changed the very fabric of the Wyrd. Lachlei is more than simply a pawn; she may be a player..."

Rhyn'athel frowned. "Then, she may control our fate."

"And the fate of the Nine Worlds," Ni'yah said. "You were wise to make her your champion."

Rhyn'athel stared ahead at the guards at the gate, but his mind was on Lachlei. "It is more than that," he admitted.

Ni'yah nodded. "Indeed, my brother."

Rhyn'athel looked at Ni'yah in mild annoyance. "Don't you have work to do with the *Laddel*?"

Ni'yah chuckled. "I suppose I do." He vanished, leaving the warrior god to continue though the gates of Caer Lochvaren.

◆◆◆◆

The mead hall was dark with only a faint glow from the firepit when Rhyn'athel entered. Most of the warriors had fallen asleep beside the fire with only a few still awake. Lachlei sat at a table near the fire beside Cahal. She looked up as the god entered and smiled.

She had not seen Rhyn since her fight with Kieran. Lachlei had removed her armor and was now wearing a simple tunic and breeches. Her forearms were bare, and she gazed at the dragon marking on her arm: the mark of Rhyn'athel. She smiled as she saw him enter.

"Where have you been?" she asked.

Rhyn's silver eyes glittered in the dark. "I had some unfinished business." He sat down beside her, and his gaze fell on the dragon mark. "Does it still hurt?"

"A little," she admitted and then looked at him curiously. "How do you know it hurt?"

Rhyn smiled wryly. "It looked like it hurt."

Lachlei gazed at him in puzzlement. "You know, Fialan never had the mark of Rhyn'athel," she said. "But Fialan wasn't challenged, either."

Rhyn slid his fingers along the mark. Lachlei suppressed a shiver as he touched the darkened skin. His touch was feather-light and gentle as he traced the mark. The pain subsided and he withdrew his hand. "You did very well against Kieran," he said.

She met his gaze. "I must thank you for the information," she said. "I don't think I would've had an advantage otherwise."

"Do you believe that?"

Lachlei shook her head. "I don't know what I believe anymore," she admitted. "I thought I didn't want the crown."

"It's not what you expected."

"No. I thought most of what Fialan did was placate Laewynd and the Council. I had no desire for politics." She stared at the firepit. "I always assumed I was a warrior, Rhyn, even when I chose to become Fialan's consort and drift into the background. I felt more comfortable with the *Chi'lan* than I did at the affairs of state."

"It is one thing to win the crown; it is quite another to hold it."

"Fialan used to say that." She smiled sadly.

"Did he? So, if you didn't want the crown, why insist on it?"

Lachlei shook her head. "I don't know," she admitted. "But I know that Kieran, for all his strength as a warrior, doesn't have first-blood powers. The demon that killed Fialan is still out there. The *Lochvaur* don't need a politician, Rhyn. They need a champion—a first-blood— one who could take on a demon. Maybe someone like you." She considered him thoughtfully. *Rhyn would make a great king,* she decided. He was a powerful first-blood, if enigmatic. "Why didn't you try for the throne?"

Rhyn shrugged. "Rhyn'athel chose you."

"Indeed, and maybe I am that champion, but I don't know. A few weeks ago, I wouldn't have believed it, but now, I'm not sure."

"What changed your mind?"

"I think Rhyn'athel spoke to me."

"The warrior god?"

She grinned foolishly. "Sounds idiotic, doesn't it?"

"No," Rhyn said quickly. "What did he say?"

"He reminded me I was first-blood," she said. She fell silent and stared for a while at the mark. "I don't know why Rhyn'athel chose me," she said. "I never thought I would've made a champion. There are other warriors with far more experience—who are better fighters than I."

"But none with first-blood powers," Rhyn reminded her.

"No, none. Save you," she said. "Rhyn, my inexperience nearly killed me, but my first-blood powers saved my life." She shook her head.

"Lachlei, there have been greater *Eleion* born of godling blood, who have shown less strength and determination than you," he said, taking her hands in his own. "And there are heroes within *Eleion* history who had not a drop of gods' blood in their veins. The Wyrd hands us the fate we must deal with. It is our choices and our resolve that decide whether or not we are great." He pulled her hands to his lips and kissed them before releasing her. He met her gaze. "Go to sleep, my queen. You are Rhyn'athel's champion."

Lachlei stood up slowly, touching the hand where Rhyn had kissed her. "Thank you," she murmured as she slipped quietly towards the door that led to her chambers. She paused, still feeling his gaze before leaving the room.

The glow from the fireplace was the only light in her chambers. Lachlei had thought the quarters were too small when Fialan was there; now it seemed extraordinarily huge. In the dim light, Fialan's weapons and extra armor cast shadows across the room. Sparsely furnished, there was not much more than a table and chairs sitting on a thick carpet of rushes. Beside the fire, Wynne sat, holding Lachlei's son wrapped in a warm blanket.

Wynne's brass eyes reflected the flames as she looked up at the queen. Wynne was from the *Laddel* kindred, the clan of Lachlei's mother. Wynne had come with Ladara many years before when the *Laddel* princess agreed to become the consort of a *Lochvaur* prince. Even after Ladara's death in battle, Wynne had chosen to stay with Lachlei. Now, she cared for Lachlei's son and she had cared for Lachlei.

"Wynne..." Lachlei began.

Wynne put a finger to her lips. "He just fell asleep," she said, beaming at the infant. She stood up slowly and walked over to Lachlei, who beamed at her son. The baby held a braided tress from Wynne's wolf-gray hair. Lachlei gently removed the lock and gazed into the child's face.

"He looks like his father," Lachlei remarked, taking Haellsil from Wynne's arms. The baby yawned and nestled deeper into the warmth of the blanket.

"That he does," Wynne replied.

Lachlei closed her eyes and turned away. "He'll never know his father."

Wynne shook her head. "You knew the risk, being *Chi'lan*," she replied. "Ladara did when she chose your father."

"A lecture, Wynne?"

"A reality, Lachlei. Those born to the warrior god's kindred are short lived because of the life they choose."

"The *Laddel* are no better."

"No, we're not, and that makes you doubly cursed, perhaps," she said. "I worry that Haellsil may not know his mother, either."

"That is a risk," Lachlei replied. She walked over to the baby's crib and gently laid him down. She was greeted with a soft whine and a tail thump from Strang, Fialan's warhound. She knelt down and ran her hands through the warhound's coarse red fur. "Strang," she whispered as the big war dog licked her. "Do you miss your master?" The dog looked up at her with soulful eyes. "I do, too," she admitted.

"I heard about the fight between you and Kieran." Wynne leaned in the doorway.

Lachlei shrugged. "He challenged my right."

"I thought you didn't want the throne."

Lachlei shook her head but said nothing.

"It's that new *Chi'lan*, isn't it?"

"What makes you say that?" Lachlei said a little too sharply.

"I know you better than you think," Wynne said. "He's a handsome one."

Lachlei stared at Wynne. "I can't believe you," she whispered. "Fialan is barely dead..."

"And you are alone," Wynne remarked.

"I can take care of myself."

"No one is denying that, *Chi'lan* Lachlei," Wynne replied. "But you are taking on more than anyone expects you to. What is his name? Rhyn, is it?"

"Wynne..."

The *Laddel* woman met Lachlei's gaze. "What happened?"

Lachlei bared her right arm. "Wynne—I've been chosen."

Wynne stared at the dragon mark. "By the wolf's fur," she whispered. "Rhyn'athel has chosen you?"

Lachlei nodded. "I'm now his champion."

Wynne hugged her gently. "May the warrior god protect you," she said with a smile. "Then, I believe that Rhyn was sent."

"Sent?" Lachlei asked, looking at the nurse in puzzlement.

"A Guardian, perhaps, or a spirit guide," Wynne said.

Lachlei laughed. "He seems *Eleion* enough to me."

"Perhaps." She smiled. "If you won't be needing me?"

Lachlei nodded. "Good night, Wynne."

Wynne nodded and left Lachlei's private chambers. Lachlei walked to the door and for a moment thought about opening the door to see if Rhyn was still awake. Instead, she locked the door and walked to her bedroom; Strang following her faithfully. She lay down, letting the warhound lay beside her and ran her fingers through its coarse hair. As she fell asleep, her last thoughts were of Rhyn.

CHAPTER TWENTY-THREE

Lachlei strode towards the hall of the *Lochvaur* High Council. As queen and Rhyn'athel's champion, none could dispute she had the right to demand the army. The night before burned in her mind just as the mark of the warrior god burned in her skin. All who saw her now met her gaze in deference. She was Rhyn'athel's champion.

Movement beside her stirred her from her thoughts. Lachlei turned to see Rhyn walking silently next to her. She smiled, despite herself. The North Marches *Chi'lan* shadowed her almost as much as Cahal did now. She welcomed his presence.

"Rhyn," she chided lightly. "I was unaware I was in need of a bodyguard."

"The queen shouldn't go anywhere without one of the *Chi'lan*," Rhyn replied.

Lachlei scowled. "Cahal sent you."

"And if he did, would you send me away?"

She smiled coyly. "Perhaps I should."

"I don't think Cahal would like that."

Now, Lachlei scowled. "Go back to Cahal and tell him that I don't need protection." She turned and walked away. Rhyn followed, much to her irritation. She turned and glowered at him, seeing a slight smile on his lips. "Are you going to ignore a direct order?"

"Yes," he said.

"I should…" She fell silent, trying to think of something.

Rhyn's smile grew wider. "You'll what? Fight me?"

Lachlei laughed. "Yes, that's what I'll do. Fight you."

"You'd lose."

Lachlei sobered and eyed him. "I would, would I?"

She considered him for the first time as a potential opponent. He was tall and muscular, but not so tall that his height would be a handicap in a fight. She had seen no apparent weakness in his stride or either side. Cahal told her that he handled a sword in both hands with ease. At another time, before Fialan, Lachlei would have found him desirable. "How did you best Tamar?"

Rhyn shrugged. "Tamar was drunk and sloppy—I was not."

She paused as her gaze fell on the Sword of Power that hung at his side. "I never properly thanked you for your help through this," she said, drawing closer to him. "You have been invaluable to me, Rhyn. If there is anything…"

A flicker of emotion glinted in the *Chi'lan's* eyes, but it flitted so quickly that she was unable to read it. He smiled. "It is my privilege to serve Rhyn'athel's champion," he said.

Lachlei could feel her pulse quicken as they stood facing each other. She glanced down at the Sword of Power. The rune of *Teiwas* — the rune of

Rhyn'athel—carved into the hilt, caught her attention. "So, tell me how you came by a Sword of Power."

Rhyn stiffened slightly as if snapped from reverie. "My father gave it to me."

Lachlei smiled at his discomfort. She drew closer so that they were barely inches apart. "Is that so? Swords of Power disintegrate when the forger dies."

"Not all," Rhyn assured her. "Although their preservation requires special circumstances..."

"Such as?" Their gazes locked.

Rhyn leaned forward; his lips drew closer to hers. "Such as changes in the Web of Wyrd as those by *Athel'cen*..."

"Lachlei?"

Lachlei broke from him and turned to Kellachan. "What is it, Kel?"

Kellachan glanced at Rhyn and then looked at her. "Was I interrupting?"

Lachlei glanced at Rhyn who met her gaze steadily. "No," she said. "I was going to speak to the Council."

"Good," Kellachan said. "Laewynd is here. He's expecting you." Kellachan led her up the stairs to the Council's hall.

Laewynd will not listen to your demands, Rhyn said to her in mindspeak. *Take the army, Lachlei, no one will dispute you're Rhyn'athel's champion.*

Lachlei made no acknowledgment. Instead, she walked in, flanked by both *Chi'lan*.

The Council room was dark, despite it being daylight. The tallow candles within cast a smoky light on the Council members; the air was acrid and stale as Lachlei took a breath. Dark and musty, she wanted to throw open the doors and the windows and expose the room to the bright sunshine outside. She glanced from face-to-face: Moira, Kieran, Elrys, Tarchon, Talar. All stood as they met her gaze. Only Laewynd sat in his Council seat.

"You will rise," Lachlei said evenly. She did not have to glance behind her to know that Rhyn and Kellachan had their hands on their hilts. "And give me the respect due."

Laewynd stood, his face pale as he met her gaze. "Respect is earned, Lachlei."

"Still at odds with me, Laewynd?" She smiled at Kieran. "Thought I would play the Council's fool?" Kieran smiled back.

"No," said Laewynd, "but I would've expected more sense from you."

"I need the army, and I need it now," Lachlei said. "The *Silren* will cross the Lochvaren Mountains and will march on Caer Lochvaren if we do not stop them. I demand the *Lochvaur* army."

"Such as it is?" Moira said.

Lachlei turned to the Council member. "What do you mean?"

"It will take a month to bring all forty thousand to Caer Lochvaren," she said.

"Even ten thousand..." Lachlei began.

"We can't spare," Tarchon said. "Haven't you heard? The *Redel* kindred to the west are showing signs of restlessness. We can't risk leaving Caer Lochvaren exposed."

Lachlei glanced at Kellachan and Rhyn, who stood beside her. *What has happened, Kel?*

The Council has already taken a vote, her cousin replied. *Despite your popularity, only Kieran and I voted in your favor.*

"You see, Lachlei, you can't force your agenda on the Council," Laewynd smiled smugly. "Even if we *would* give you the army, we couldn't."

Lachlei glanced at Rhyn. *Your recommendations?*

Gather who you can, Rhyn replied. *Go around the Council.*

"Very well," Lachlei said. She met Laewynd's gaze. "I know where your loyalties lie. I will take my own *Chi'lan* to meet the *Silren.*" She turned and left, followed by Rhyn and Kellachan. "Damn them!" she snarled after the doors shut.

"You could take the army, yourself," Rhyn said. "You have that right."

Kellachan shook his head. "If she does, she'll alienate the nobles. For whatever we think of the Council, the people chose them to lead."

"No one, save the Council members, chose Laewynd as Council leader," Lachlei said.

"Kieran and I don't make a majority, even without Laewynd," her cousin said. "As much as you are Rhyn'athel's champion, and as much as you're popular among the people, you won't be able to take the army."

Lachlei turned to Rhyn. "What do you think?"

"I think that you're Rhyn'athel's champion," he said. "One *Chi'lan* is worth ten soldiers."

Lachlei met his gaze and smiled. His faith in her strengthened her resolve. She nodded. "Find Cahal and prepare the *Chi'lan.* We leave tomorrow for North Marches."

CHAPTER TWENTY-FOUR

The autumn air of the Lochvaren Mountains held a bite, Lachlei decided. She sat on her warhorse, looking back at the *Chi'lan* warriors who rode behind her. She pulled her cloak more closely around her. Two thousand of her personal guard followed her to fight against the demon who sought to destroy her people. Two thousand *Chi'lan* out of forty-five thousand total warriors. She wished the Council had granted her part of the army.

It had been a fortnight since they left Caer Lochvaren and headed northward along the King's Highway. Snow was already falling in the higher passes, and the trees were flocked with the last night's snow. Lachlei stared ahead. More forest lay before them with a steep climb as they headed towards one of the smaller passes. It was rocky, and the snow blanketed the ground. She patted her warhorse's neck as steam issued from its nostrils. She glanced behind again. Despite the cold, the army was in good spirits and the warriors were well equipped.

"I think we should make camp once we cross the pass," Rhyn said. "We'll have to camp in the lower forest—it'll provide some protection against the wind at night." Rhyn rode beside her and Cahal. It seemed natural for the North Marches *Chi'lan* to ride next to her. He proved to be invaluable as they rode northward, demonstrating his knowledge of the land and obstacles ahead.

Lachlei gazed at the road as it wound its way through the trees. She could just see the pass beyond a small break ahead. "What about avalanches?"

Rhyn shook his head. "Too early in the season just yet, but we're going to have to be careful. In a few weeks, the snow may block our route back along the King's Highway."

"Alternatives?"

Rhyn frowned. "We could go around onto the northern edge of Darkling Plain, but that will lead us through *Elesil* and *Eltar* territory. It'll probably be our only option once the snow becomes deep."

"Damn inconvenient time to start a war," Lachlei remarked. "Who fights with winter coming on?"

"The *Silren*, evidently," Cahal remarked dryly.

They rode forward, leading the *Chi'lan* across the first pass. The snow was a little more than a half foot deep, easy enough for their horses to plow through. Once on top of the pass, Lachlei gazed eastward across the mountains and could barely see the brown and gold plains beyond. How many miles would it be out of their way if they had to take that route? A hundred or more, certainly.

They continued farther down the mountain until they found a relatively flat area where the army could camp. Weary from exertion, the *Chi'lan* made camp and prepared for the night.

Lachlei entered her own tent and found a small woodstove with a flue had been set up. The air was warm inside, making her drowsy and she stripped off her cloak, layers of furs, and mail down to her tunic and breeches. A small kettle of water was already boiling on the hot stove and she poured herself a cup.

"May I enter?" she heard Rhyn's voice from outside the door.

"Please, come in," Lachlei said. She poured him a cup of hot water and offered it to him. "I'm sorry it's not spiced wine."

"I'm not," Rhyn replied, gratefully accepting the cup and drinking. "We need our wits about us. Our scouts just came back—the *Silren* are camped in the next valley."

"Are you sure?" Lachlei said, lowering her cup and staring. "My Sight has shown nothing."

"Something is blocking our ability to see exactly where they are," Rhyn replied. "But, the shield goes both ways; we've been able to keep our own army's precise location hidden from them."

"Until now," Lachlei remarked. She shook her head. "They're bound to have scouts."

"No doubt," the *Chi'lan* said. "They'll wait for us, though. The *Silren* will prefer to fight rested."

"Can we wait for them?"

Rhyn shook his head. "Inadvisable. We're heavily outnumbered, and we'll give up our advantage if we fail to take the higher ground."

"Your recommendations?" Lachlei asked.

"Rest tonight," Rhyn said. "We have a day's march between us, so it is unlikely that the *Silren* will try anything tonight, but we'll post a watch just in case. We can awaken before dawn and bring our army to the ridgeline along the pass. At that point, we'll prepare and bivouac there. Then, we'll attack at dusk."

Lachlei nodded. "Are there really ten thousand of them?"

He gulped the rest of the water. "That's what the scouts are reporting." He paused. "The lay of the land will dictate the battle." He smiled at her. "We both need rest. Don't worry just yet, Lachlei. Something will present itself."

Lachlei watched as he left. "I hope you're right, Rhyn."

◆◆◆◆

Laddel stood along the parapets of Caer Ladren and gazed into the crimson sunset. He was a shorter *Eleion* with an agouti mane and brass eyes like his father, Ni'yah, the wolf-god. He was ancient by *Eleion* standards, having lived through the war between the gods nearly two thousand years before. The last war was still vividly etched in his mind.

The *Laddel* fortress-city towered over the forest that stretched for miles in all directions. Hewn from the native red sandstone, the city was a beacon of the *Laddel* might. The towers curved upward, carved with symbols of the forest and the wolf. The main keep sat in the center of the towers, the green and silver banners hung from the walls. Along the parapets, silver-haired *Laddel* warriors kept watch, their green and silver cloaks flashed in the sunlight. They had grown from a small kindred to a powerful nation within the two thousand years. None dared challenge the *Laddel.*

And yet, Laddel stood alone with his dark thoughts. Twice he had felt the tremor that ran through the world's core. The first time, that tremor bought terrible destruction on the *Eleion.* Laddel had been young then—not much more than boy—when the war of the gods began. Those were the days when the gods of light walked among the *Eleion.* Before the Eternal Fire and before the Truce.

Before Areyn Sehduk's vengeance.

"Of all the living first-bloods, you alone recognize Areyn's stench in this world," came a voice from behind him.

"It isn't hard," Laddel replied and turned to Ni'yah. "I've had plenty of past experience." He paused and smiled. "I was wondering when you might return to Caer Ladren, Father."

Ni'yah nodded. The wolf-god leaned against a merlon. "I wish I came with happier news."

"Areyn Sehduk has returned?"

"Indeed."

"What of the Truce?"

"Areyn has taken the form of a *Silren,*" Ni'yah replied. "He thought to dupe Rhyn'athel and me by his disguise. Even now, he is marching on the *Lochvaur.*"

"The *Lochvaur.*" Laddel gazed into the setting sun. "We had heard of Fialan's demise. It was no accident."

"Indeed," Ni'yah said. "Lachlei, Fialan's consort, is leading the *Chi'lan* against the *Silren.*"

"Lachlei—Ladara's daughter?"

"The same," said Ni'yah, a glint in his eyes. "Lachlei is your great-granddaughter."

Laddel chuckled. "A *Laddel* blood on the throne of the *Lochvaur.*"

"Indeed—and a twice first-blood—Lachlei is quite powerful. Areyn doesn't know this yet."

Laddel shrugged. "So, why are you here? The *Chi'lan* are legendary—they will turn the *Silren* army."

"Lachlei only has the *Chi'lan.* The Council wouldn't grant her the army."

Laddel shook his head and turned away. "The Truce has been broken, father, and now you are asking me to lead my warriors against the *Silren* when Rhyn'athel's own kindred won't fight for themselves? You ask that the *Laddel* give up our lives in defense of another kindred?"

"If you do not fight Areyn Sehduk now with the *Lochvaur,* you will find yourself fighting Areyn alone," said the wolf-god, his tone low and menacing. "And even I may not be able to help you."

"The *Lochvaur* are Rhyn'athel's kindred. The Truce has been broken. If the *Lochvaur* are so important, then let Rhyn'athel save them."

"You would defy me?"

"I would defy folly," Laddel replied, turning and walking away. "My father, you are a meddler. If it were so serious, Rhyn'athel would join the fray." He sighed and shook his head as he continued down the wall walk towards the tower.

"He has."

Laddel halted and turned around once more. "What did you say?"

Ni'yah's face was grim. "Rhyn'athel has already joined in the fight," he said. "I didn't want to tell you this, but you've left me with no choice."

Laddel stared. "Rhyn'athel is *here*?"

"Yes. He's leading the *Chi'lan* against Areyn Sehduk."

Silence followed as Laddel met the wolf-god's gaze. "Who knows?"

"No one, save you and I," Ni'yah replied. "Not even Rhyn'athel's own *Chi'lan* know that he is among them. If Areyn were to learn this, it would take the war to the next stage." He paused. "I know you're powerful enough to keep that secret from Areyn, but no one else must know."

"Rhyn'athel has joined the fight," Laddel mused. "Even with my silence, Areyn will learn soon enough."

Ni'yah nodded. "Yes, he will."

"The *Laddel* will be dragged into this regardless of our wishes."

"You can meet Areyn on his terms or on yours." The god shrugged. "The choice is yours." With that, the god vanished.

Laddel sighed and shook his head. He leaned against the merlon, catching the last rays of the setting sun and gazing into the dark sky.

"Father, was that the wolf-god?"

Laddel turned his gaze to his son, Ladsil. Ladsil was a much younger version of himself with the same wolf eyes and agouti hair. Laddel consider his son thoughtfully. He had been about Ladsil's age when the war between the gods began. "Yes, it was," he said.

"What did he say?"

"The *Lochvaur* need our help. Prepare the army—we'll be marching from Caer Ladren within the week."

CHAPTER TWENTY-FIVE

Lachlei looked down into the valley where the *Silren* army waited. Ten thousand warriors stood ready to fight her and her *Chi'lan*. Overhead, the sky was dark with approaching storm clouds and a cold wind blew from the east. They broke camp early and marched to the top of the next ridgeline above the valley where the *Silren* army sat.

Beside her rode Rhyn, his steel gaze studying the *Silren* lines, his face grim. She tried to discern what Rhyn was sensing, but she could sense nothing save the massive shield that seemed impervious to her power.

"Is the demon there?" she asked tentatively.

Rhyn nodded once and continued to gaze into the valley. "He's planning on trapping us within the valley and crushing our army with his numbers."

"That would make sense," Lachlei said and fell silent, seeing Rhyn lost in thought.

Rhyn gazed at the *Silren* army. Without the full *Lochvaur* army, the *Lochvaur* had no chance against an army five times their size. A ride into that valley would be suicide.

"Is there any way for us to lure him from the valley?"

"Lure?" Rhyn glanced at her and then back to the valley. A slow smile crept across his face. "Lure—that's it..."

Lachlei gazed at him. "Do you have an idea?"

"Of course. It's simple, but he's arrogant enough to fall for it."

Lachlei gazed at Rhyn curiously. "Who's arrogant? Do you have an idea?"

"Yes," he said, grinning. "You gave me the idea—I need five hundred of your troops."

"Five hundred?" she stared. "That isn't enough against ten thousand."

"No, it's not—but it will be enough to draw him out."

Lachlei's eyes glinted as realization dawned in them. "Of course," she said. "We'll be ready for them."

"Then we'll charge at dusk."

◆◆◆◆

Areyn gazed at the southern ridges. The *Lochvaur* were there, waiting. Areyn could wait, too. At some point, the *Lochvaur* would have to ride down through the pass and engage the army. With the *Silren's* overwhelming numbers, it would be a slaughter.

The *Lochvaur* had other possible choices. One would be to retreat. The other would be to try to circle around, but their way would be blocked. No, the *Lochvaur* would come to him in good time.

Imdyr sat beside him, clad in her black mail. The *Lochvaur* were there as she had told him. In fact, everything Imdyr had told him had come to pass.

Areyn considered the priestess with some puzzlement. She seemed able to get around the barriers he could not. It was as though she had a goddess's powers. And yet, Areyn Sehduk could sense that she was mortal and nothing more. He reached out with his senses to see how many of the *Lochvaur* army was marching against them and abruptly was shoved back.

"How many?" Areyn asked.

Imdyr looked sideways at the death god as if he had taunted her. "There are only two thousand," she said. "They will attack—there!" She pointed to the cleft in the ravine.

Areyn gazed at the ravine. "That takes no sorcery to figure out," he said. "Unless the *Lochvaur* are suicidal, there is no other way."

Imdyr's gaze narrowed, but said naught for some time. "There is a god among the *Lochvaur*," she said at length.

Areyn started. "A god—are you sure?"

Imdyr closed her eyes as her battle horse stomped impatiently. She opened her eyes and met the death god's gaze. "I am certain of it."

Areyn paused. "It must be Ni'yah—I've seen the cur skulking around. Little matter—he hasn't the power to defeat me."

"What of Rhyn'athel?" Imdyr asked.

"Rhyn'athel?" Areyn spoke sharply. Imdyr smiled mockingly at the fear in his voice. "Rhyn'athel wouldn't dare; his precious Truce means more to him than a minor encroachment. Ni'yah, however, would become involved."

"The god I sense is powerful," Imdyr remarked. "I hope that it is the wolf-god as you think."

Areyn looked at the mountains, trying to sense the god. How Imdyr was able to break through barriers he could not was indeed puzzling. "It is Ni'yah," he replied. "Only the wolf-god would be so bold."

◆◆◆◆

The sun was beginning to sink low in the horizon when Rhyn began to select the warriors for the assault. He rode among the *Chi'lan*, choosing the best riders he could find. When he had picked his five hundred, Rhyn returned to the front lines where Lachlei and Cahal waited.

"I've chosen my warriors," Rhyn said. "I'll be taking Cahal, if you can spare him."

"I can't," Lachlei said. "He'll be with the remainder of the army."

"You're coming with us?"

"Yes," Lachlei said with a sly smile. "Any objections?"

"Yes," Rhyn said. "Who will lead the army?"

"Cahal will."

"Cahal?" he said. "And if you fall?"

"I'm Rhyn'athel's champion, am I not?" she asked. "I'm your queen. I should lead the attack." She crossed her arms. "If Fialan were alive, you'd expect no less from him."

"We wouldn't put Fialan under undue risk," Cahal replied. "They'll be plenty of fighting here with the rest of the army."

"I know," she said. "But I'll be risking my life regardless of where I am, save perhaps, behind the walls of Caer Lochvaren. I am your champion and your queen. I will lead the charge." With that, Lachlei rode off.

Rhyn glanced at Cahal, who gave the *Chi'lan* a helpless shrug. Rhyn followed her.

Lachlei glanced back, irritated. "Rhyn, you don't need to follow me—I've made up my mind."

"You don't trust me leading the attack."

Lachlei met Rhyn's gaze. His silver eyes betrayed no emotion. "Of course, I do," she said, a slight hesitation in her voice. "That's not what's at issue here."

"What *is* at issue?"

Lachlei paused and silence ensued. She turned her horse away, unwilling to have Rhyn see her expression. She knew her face was red from anger and shame. "You wouldn't understand."

"Wouldn't I?"

Lachlei turned her horse around. Rhyn was still gazing at her with those steady silver eyes, his expression thoughtful, neither disapproving or condescending. "The High Council…" she began and her voice trailed off. Her horse nickered softly and pawed the ground. She shook her head. "Never mind."

"I am not the High Council," Rhyn said. "I care little what the High Council thinks of you. Nor do the *Chi'lan* serve the High Council. The *Chi'lan* serve the king—or queen of the *Lochvaur*—and Rhyn'athel."

"The High Council chose me because they believed they could bend me to their will."

"Can they?"

Rhyn's words stung, even if the question was a simple one. Had she given into the High Council's demands by not challenging Laewynd? What would Fialan have done in this situation? Lachlei felt her fist tighten on her horse's reins and the stallion tossed its head in displeasure. "They wouldn't give me warriors."

"The *Chi'lan* are your warriors."

"But the soldiers…"

"A *Chi'lan* is worth ten soldiers."

"There are ten thousand *Silren* and a demon waiting to attack us," Lachlei said, her face flushing.

"I would say our odds are about even," Rhyn'athel said wryly.

For a moment, their gazes locked. Rhyn'athel smiled, and Lachlei chuckled. "Rhyn," she said, shaking her head. "If I only had such faith as you."

"Lachlei," he said. "Let me lead the attack. The rest of the army will stand ready with you. There is little chance of me being ransomed; however, you will sorely test Laewynd's loyalty if you are captured."

Lachlei laughed. "I can imagine Laewynd's expression if I were ransomed. He would probably appoint Kellachan or another warrior in my stead." She paused. "Maybe even you."

Rhyn chuckled. "I wouldn't take it."

"Why not?" *Rhyn would be a perfect champion,* she thought. He was a powerful first-blood and a natural leader. The *Chi'lan* respected him too—a respect not easily won.

He paused and became serious. "Because the *Lochvaur* already have a queen and Rhyn'athel already has a champion."

Lachlei met his gaze. "Very well, Rhyn, take the charge. I will be waiting for your return."

Rhyn'athel grinned. "Don't worry—I'll be chased by plenty of *Silren*."

CHAPTER TWENTY-SIX

Eshe pulled her helm off and dried her eyes. She wore no mail coif, leaving her neck somewhat exposed. Her wavy red-gold hair was braided in tresses and for the first time, Fialan saw her face fully. She was pretty in a rough sort of way and typically *Chi'lan*. Her nose had been broken at one time and was set slightly askew, and a scar ran from her right lower ear lobe down her neck where a lucky cut slipped between her helm and gorget. Her silver eyes were almost smoke-gray in the waning light. She was tall and athletically built as many *Lochvaur*, and Fialan found her attractive, despite his loyalty to Lachlei. He wondered if she had been married in her previous life.

"I'm sorry," she said. "I've been so alone for so long."

Fialan shrugged. "That was two thousand years worth of emotion."

She shivered. "We should continue," she said, looking into the twilight-deepening sky. "It'll be dark soon, and we won't be able to see." She slipped her helm on.

"Well, if we fall, we won't die," Fialan said lightly.

Eshe grimaced. "It'll still hurt—I once took a tumble off of a ledge farther up." She stood up slowly and turned to him. "Grasp hold of my cloak," she said. "And watch your footing." She began walking upward towards the fortress.

Fialan followed Eshe, watching where she walked. The path was ingeniously cut for those who knew the way. As he had surmised, Eshe knew the trail even in the dark and led him without a misstep.

"Careful. Fialan," Eshe said, at last. "We're almost to the top. Only twenty feet to go."

They had negotiated a path of switchbacks and stairs. Fialan had followed Eshe silently until now. The last twenty feet were straight up the rock face. It was completely dark now, and Fialan could see nothing save Eshe's form and the cliff before her.

"How do we get up that?" he asked.

"There are handholds and footholds," she replied. "You'll have to do everything by feel."

Fialan stared at the rock face. When he was alive, he would use his mental powers to augment his sense of touch. But now, he had nothing. Nothing except faith in a *Chi'lan* woman who had died two thousand years before. "All right," he said, taking a deep breath. The fall from this height would hurt; thankfully, he could only see blackness below.

"I'll go first," she said. "Watch me as I climb. The handholds and footholds are evenly spaced, so you shouldn't have any problems. Wait for me to call to you—that means I've made it. Don't start climbing until then—I could fall and take us both out." She paused. "If I do fall, go on ahead. I'll catch up as soon as I'm able to."

"Very well," he said. He watched as her fingers ran along the rock face and slid into a handhold. Stepping carefully, Eshe slid her feet into each foothold and slowly searched for the next handhold. Fialan watched her climb, slowly, deliberately, until she vanished into the darkness above her. His sharp ears could still hear the scraping of her boots on the footholds and her labored breath.

He heard her grunt and some scraping above.

"Eshe?" came a voice from somewhere above Fialan. The voice sounded pleased.

"Yes, Kiril, it's me," Eshe said.

"What are you doing here?" Kiril asked. "You left us."

"There's a new first-blood who insists on speaking with Lochvaur," said Eshe.

"Demon fodder," Kiril spat. "They like the first-bloods."

"His name's Fialan. He has some news that might change things."

Fialan frowned. *Demon fodder?* He searched until he found the handholds and then slipped his feet carefully in the footholds.

"So, he's a first-blood?" Kiril asked. "From Lochvaur?"

"Yes." Eshe sighed. "Listen, Kiril. He's different. He's like Lochvaur—he thinks the Truce is broken…"

"Eshe," Kiril laughed. "No one believes Lochvaur any longer—you know that. We stay here because the demons won't come here."

"Have you ever thought why they don't come?" Fialan said as he pulled himself over the final ledge. He could barely see the two speaking. "Don't you have torches or doesn't fire work in this world?"

Kiril was a heavy-boned *Chi'lan*—unusual since most *Eleion* were medium to light framed. His thicker face and jaw line suggested *Laddel* blood, but his skin that gave away his true lineage. It was deep bronze—a sure sign Kiril was *Shara'kai*—a half-breed of *Ansgar* and *Eleion*. Even so, in the dim light, he reminded Fialan of *Chi'lan* Tamar. "Wood and pitch are a premium here. We don't waste it."

"I didn't know there were any *Shara'kai Lochvaur*," he remarked. "Let alone, *Chi'lan*. Where did you come from?"

Kiril flinched imperceptibly at the word '*Shara'kai*.' "From the North, near the Tundra Steppes."

Fialan nodded. "Be careful, *Shara'kai*, how you sling insults. Or this 'demon fodder' will show you what a first-blood can do, even without his powers."

Kiril lunged and Fialan drew his sword. "Stop it! Both of you!" Eshe snapped, stepping between both men. "You serve only Areyn Sehduk with your quarrel."

Kiril eyed Fialan mistrustfully. "Indeed," he said.

"I would have no quarrel with you, Kiril," Fialan said and turned his gaze on the blade he held in his hand. He hadn't drawn it since he died, but now he gazed at it in amazement. It *looked* like *Fyren*.

"What's wrong?" Eshe asked as she noticed Fialan's interest.

"This is *Fyren*, but it's not," Fialan said, studying the blade.

"It's a ghost weapon," Eshe said. "Same as your armor and body. Like what you had in life, but not." Eshe grinned at Kiril. "Thankfully."

"Why is that?"

"A *Jotunn* axe separated Eshe's head from her shoulders," Kiril said with a grin. "You came here in one piece didn't you?"

"A ghost weapon—then, it's not real?" Fialan asked.

"It's real, all right, but it's a doppelganger of the real thing. Right down to the metal, but it doesn't hold the essence of the other blade," said Kiril.

"The only exception to that are the Swords of Power," Eshe added. "Those are real."

"Is that really *Fyren*?" Kiril asked, looking at the blade inquisitively.

"Look, you can even see the blood where I cut the demon..." Fialan began and stopped, staring at the blood. It glowed blue-black in the dark and dripped down the blade as if he had just used it. "By Rhyn'athel's sword!" he exclaimed, nearly dropping the blade.

Kiril and Eshe glanced at each other. "Kiril—you fought demons before—have you ever seen anything like that?" Eshe asked. Her eyes were wide with fear.

Kiril shook his head. "Never—and I'd bet no one else has seen such magic—save perhaps Lochvaur." He looked at Fialan in respect. "What did you strike?"

"Something that should've died by my sword but did not. Something that robbed me of my first-blood magic."

A cold wind blew through them. A lone cry echoed across that desolate land. Eshe shivered. "We'd better get inside, Kiril."

Kiril nodded. "Sheathe your sword, first-blood. I think Lochvaur will want to hear what you have to say."

CHAPTER TWENTY-SEVEN

Fog began to seep down the hills and into the valley where Rhyn'athel knew his enemy lay in wait. The warrior god rode forward, flanked by Cahal and Tamar. The King's Highway was barely a road here, just wide enough for horses to scramble through. The road was marked with occasional cairn stones, carved with ancient runes. Rhyn'athel glanced at them—they spoke of the builders of the roads—*Eleion* who were no more. At one time, they had been Rhyn'athel's warriors; now they belonged to Areyn Sehduk.

Rhyn led the warriors down the narrow ravine, through the talus and scree and into the deep pines, silent in his musings. He had lost many warriors to Areyn—too many. Areyn's power came from the energy of those who died.

"Strange," said Cahal, interrupting the god's thoughts. He glanced apprehensively at Rhyn'athel.

"What?" the god asked. He glanced around in the growing dusk. The fog made the pine trees look ethereal, but he could sense nothing worrisome.

"The fog," the *Chi'lan* said. "It moves with us. Fog normally comes from the valleys, not the hills."

Rhyn smiled slyly. "Then, we are indeed fortunate—it will hide our actual numbers," he remarked.

Tamar glanced at Cahal. "Sorcery of some sort or I'm not *Chi'lan*," he growled.

"Perhaps," Rhyn shrugged. "Perhaps not. As long as it remains in our favor, I am not concerned." He halted his stallion and held up his hand, scanning the area where he knew Areyn's troops lay in wait. While Rhyn'athel couldn't quite sense Areyn Sehduk, himself, Rhyn'athel could feel the death god's power. There was no disguising Areyn's stench and the warrior god bristled in anger at the thought of Areyn being within this world.

Areyn is bold if he thinks I will stand idly by and let him tilt the balance, he thought darkly. For a moment, he felt a dark power that seemed to reach out and brush his mind, but he turned it aside. *Areyn is getting bolder,* he thought.

"The *Silren* will expect us to attack through that cleft," said Cahal. "It'll be suicide for us to attack them there—they'll cut us down."

"But there is no other way through," Tamar said. "The cliffs are too steep for our horses."

Rhyn'athel grinned. "Don't worry—just be prepared to attack when I give the signal."

◆◆◆◆

Imdyr frowned. "Something isn't right," she said as the mist crept forward into their lines. She shivered and pulled her cloak around her tightly as though to ward off a spell. A silence had fallen over the *Silren* army as they waited amid the trees. Hours passed and still the *Lochvaur* army failed to charge through the gorge. The last rays of the sun went behind the mountains, throwing everything into shadow.

Imdyr tried to sense the *Lochvaur* and was abruptly swatted aside like a gnat. She tried again, only to find greater resistance.

"What is wrong?" Areyn said, seeing her vexed.

"I've never seen such power," she murmured.

Galen rode beside Areyn. "Akwel, there's something amiss with this fog—it comes from the wrong direction." He stared at Imdyr. "What is *that* doing here?"

Areyn glanced at Imdyr. "She is a sorceress…"

"Demoness!" Galen spat. He drew his sword and pointed it at Imdyr as she huddled in her cloak. "The *Eltar* are Fala's minions!"

Areyn gazed at the *Silren* warrior in boredom. Pity he would have to kill Galen now…

Screams rang through the army, and the *Silren* broke ranks. Flames shot from behind the lines as an army on horseback attacked from behind. Thousands of *Lochvaur* warriors seemingly appeared out of nowhere, charging directly into the *Silren* flank.

Areyn reined Slayer, cursing. "Damn it, bitch!" he snapped at Imdyr. "I thought you said they were attacking from the cleft!" Before Imdyr could reply, Areyn rode towards the warriors, brandishing his sword. "Attack! Attack!"

The *Silren* turned and attacked. Suddenly, the army vanished before their eyes. Bewildered, the *Silren* soldiers halted.

Areyn stared wide-eyed, realizing the trick too late. "What kind of treachery is this?" he snarled, turning the demon mount. A battle cry rang out as the *Lochvaur* attacked. Rhyn led the *Lochvaur* through the cleft and attacked the *Silren* on what was now their flank. The *Silren* were thrown into complete confusion, many breaking ranks and fleeing.

"To me! To me!" Areyn shouted, hoping to rally the *Silren*. He spurred the demon horse and rode towards the *Lochvaur*.

◆◆◆◆

Rhyn'athel swung the great Sword of Power, cleaving through mail, sinew, and bone. The *Silren* warrior he had fought shuddered and collapsed as the warrior god withdrew the Sword, felt the man's final death rattle and saw the light fade from his eyes.

The waste, Rhyn'athel thought. He hated killing mortals—especially *Eleion*—but it really couldn't be helped. Not while Areyn had the *Silren* under his sway. Demons, undead, and *Jotunn* were more to Rhyn'athel's liking—they already belonged to Areyn.

He hadn't expected the illusion to work as well as it did—especially against Areyn Sehduk. *Areyn is out of practice,* Rhyn'athel thought wryly. In the wars before the Truce, such deceptions were commonplace and most gods saw through them. But Areyn did not know he was fighting a god now—certainly not Rhyn'athel, himself.

The screams of battle and blood-rage pounded in Rhyn'athel's veins, and he grinned as he saw the *Chi'lan* force the *Silren* warriors into a hasty retreat. He was still very much the god of warriors, despite the mortal body. He spurred the warhorse forward, brandishing his sword, screaming a battle cry that hadn't been heard in over a thousand years. He led the charge into the fleeing *Silren* lines.

Then, Rhyn'athel saw the dark warlord on his demon steed. Cold hatred filled the warrior god as he gazed on the warrior called Akwel. The man was *Silren*, with ice-blue eyes and a long white mane, but Rhyn'athel immediately saw through the guise. Areyn rode one of his demons as a mount. The creature snarled and slavered as blood and foam dripped from its fangs. Instead of hooves, it had thick, rippling muscles and massive clawed feet. It turned its red eyes on Rhyn'athel.

The warrior god screamed in rage, ready to leap from his own horse and kill the vile thing. *How dare Areyn bring this creature into this world!*

"Rhyn! Rhyn!"

Cahal's voice brought the god back. Cahal was shouting. "We've got to go! Now!" Fear was in the *Chi'lan's* voice, and Rhyn'athel surveyed the situation. Thousands of *Silren* had turned to fight, and the *Lochvaur* were now fighting for their lives.

For a second, the warrior god hesitated. Areyn was still too far away for Rhyn'athel to reach him. He reined his horse hard. "Let's get out of here!" he ordered. There would be another time.

◆◆◆◆

Flames exploded between the *Silren* and the *Lochvaur*. The *Silren* jerked back, fearful, but Areyn laughed. "After them!" he shouted.

CHAPTER TWENTY-EIGHT

Lachlei sat on her mount, anger building within her. She shouldn't have let Rhyn convince her to wait with the rest of the army. She should be with him, leading the attack. The *Silren* and the demon had killed Fialan—she wanted her revenge. The sheer arrogance of the *Silren* galled Lachlei and she wanted blood.

All around her, the *Chi'lan* stood ready. She had lined up five hundred longbow men behind the main cavalry. Even the archers had their mounts ready if they needed to flee. Still, Lachlei knew the longbows were the *Lochvaur's* greatest defense. She wished she had more *Chi'lan* to use as bowmen, but she didn't dare spread her warriors too thin.

Not that the enemy would know, she thought. It was almost dark and in the dim light and the fog, she couldn't see the end of her battle lines. She had forbidden the use of fire—it would betray their position and their numbers.

Lachlei reached out with her powers, trying to sense the battle ahead. Her Sight was limited, but she did see flashes of the battle. Rhyn's image came to mind, and she saw him charge against the *Silren*, wielding his great Sword of Power. She watched unable to turn away from the vision, but fearful that the North Marches *Chi'lan* might die. Cahal flashed into her vision, pulling Rhyn away and the image faded. Lachlei concentrated, trying desperately to bring the vision back…

"Lachlei!" Kellachan's voice brought her back to the present.

She turned to Kellachan as he rode towards her. "What is it, Kel?"

"Our scouts have returned—Rhyn is leading the retreat. They'll be here any moment."

Suddenly, the sounds of battle rang through the hills.

Steady! she mindspoke to her warriors. *Don't attack our own.*

Horses and *Chi'lan* burst through the fog towards the army, some hundred yards out. The *Chi'lan* army held fast.

Rhyn led the retreat, his great gray horse moving like a shadow through the mist. *Get ready!* he shouted mentally with such power that Lachlei was certain the hills were ringing with his voice.

Archers! she called mentally. *Steady!*

The longbow men had already nocked their arrows. They pulled back, waiting for the command.

The *Silren* warriors burst through the fog, their torches lit. They rode bearing their blue and silver colors as they chased the *Chi'lan*. Some saw the army, and their horses skidded to a halt as they reined them hard, but others, intent on their quarry, continued to charge headlong towards the *Lochvaur* army.

Fire! Lachlei shouted in mindspeak. A storm of arrows flew overhead as the longbow men released their bowstrings. Volley after volley of arrows flew towards the *Silren*, cutting down the soldiers.

Rhyn reined his horse and looked questioningly at Lachlei. She sat sternly on her mount, watching the arrows provide an invincible wall against the *Silren*. The *Silren* turned and fled, chased into the fog by the lethal rain from the *Lochvaur* archers.

But Lachlei knew it couldn't last. She glanced at Kellachan, who rode among the archers. He nodded and gave her a knowing look.

We'll be out of arrows within a few minutes, Kellachan said in mindspeak.

◆◆◆◆

Areyn cursed as he watched the *Silren* retreat. He had expected heavy casualties, but not this great. Few *Lochvaur* had fallen in the initial attack and retreat, but now the wall of arrows seemed impenetrable.

The explosions and subsequent illusions had been impressive. So impressive that Areyn Sehduk had wondered if the wolf-god were nearby. Still, a powerful first-blood could pull it off—if there were one. Areyn searched his memory for Rhyn'athel's first-bloods—who could possibly have such power? Fialan, certainly, but he was dead. The only other first-bloods were Fialan's consort, Lachlei, and a cousin, Kellachan; neither had seemed very powerful. But there had been another face among the warriors that charged. A familiar face…

Slayer champed in vexation, and Areyn looked up. Already, the *Silren* line was retreating towards him. Sighing with boredom and annoyance, Areyn rode forward. The *Eltar* witch was nowhere to be seen. Typical. Imdyr had fled at the sight of the *Lochvaur* attack. He would deal with her later.

Galen rode towards him. The commander was covered in blood and grime. Some of it was his own blood—Areyn was certain Galen would die from a painful infection. The thought cheered him greatly.

"Their arrows are keeping us back," Galen said. "They have longbow men."

Areyn shook his head. "They're almost out, you fool! Gather your men and prepare for another attack. This time, we'll break right through their lines."

◆◆◆◆

The flicker of torches through the fog told Lachlei that the *Silren* army was massing for another attack. *How many were there?* she wondered, trying to gain a sense for the numbers of dead on both sides. The fog was still thick, and now smoke choked the air.

Night had fallen, and Lachlei could see the reddish glow of the moons overhead through the thick smoke and fog. She could hardly tell the difference between the smoke and the mist anymore, but both had helped their cause. Lachlei could sense the magic that pervaded the woods around them—the fog and the smoke were supernatural as though a first-blood had used his power to ward off the approaching army.

Rhyn, she thought. The first-blood *Chi'lan* had to be the reason. If it were he, then Rhyn was more powerful than Fialan had been. Indeed, she doubted the world had seen a first-blood like him since Lochvaur.

As much as Lachlei hated to admit it, Rhyn intrigued her. He was remarkably open and vulnerable— and yet, beneath the apparent openness was extraordinary power. Rhyn had admitted he was a demon killer—something certainly not seen since the wars between the gods—and he carried a Sword of Power. That alone was a relic from those ancient times.

But there was more to Rhyn than his apparent power. Lachlei felt comfortable around him in the same way she had felt around Fialan. She didn't know why or how the *Chi'lan* had made her feel at ease, but she felt she could trust him with her life. Perhaps it was the blood. First-bloods instinctively knew each other; they shared a link with the warrior god himself.

Rhyn rode up beside her. He was covered with blood and dirt; his cloak was gone, and his armor had some rents. Although he looked unscathed, those silver eyes were no longer steady and didn't hold her gaze long.

Rhyn is weary, she realized. "Are you all right?" she asked tentatively.

Rhyn nodded. "We lost Trayhan and Haelle," he said, taking a gulp of water from a canteen and then splashing the water on his face. "But we surprised them." He paused. "How long can the archers hold the line?"

"We're almost out of arrows," she said grimly. "How many do you think we've slain?"

"Maybe three thousand," Rhyn said. "The arrows have been keeping the *Silren* from advancing on us, but we've been unable to kill many more after the first assault."

Lachlei shook her head. "That still leaves the majority of their army." She paused. "Is there any way for us to lure them back in?"

"I'm surprised we killed this many with the demon there."

"Did you see the demon?"

Rhyn nodded. "Yes, but he was too far back in the lines for anyone to reach him."

"What did it look like?"

"*Silren,*" Rhyn replied. "He's tall and wears black armor, unlike the other *Silren,* so there's no mistaking him. He rides a black charger I think is from Areyn's realm."

"How do you kill it?" she asked.

Rhyn shook his head. "You don't. There's a trick to fighting him."

"I'll kill it," she said, biting her lower lip. The pain of losing Fialan returned as she recalled gazing on his corpse. "*Fyren* took a bite out of it—that means the demon can be killed."

Rhyn looked at her curiously. "And Fialan paid for that lucky hit with his life."

Lachlei stared at him. "What?" she said as she felt herself flush in anger.

Rhyn ran his hand across his face. "I didn't mean it quite that way," he said. "Forgive me—I'm tired."

"It's all right," Lachlei found herself saying to her surprise. "You caught me off guard—that's all."

"No," he said. "I shouldn't have said it. Fialan was a great warrior..." His voice trailed off, unwilling to say anything more.

"But he wasn't a demon killer," she said, finishing Rhyn's thought. She paused and considered him carefully. "It must take quite a bit of power to maintain this fog."

Rhyn looked uncomfortable but said nothing.

"Cahal told me of the illusions," she ventured. "Fialan could do illusions, but not like this."

Rhyn shrugged. "The demon no doubt is aware of these little tricks—the *Silren* won't be fooled so easily now."

"Can you still maintain the fog?"

Rhyn nodded. "I should be able to. But that won't help our current situation much. What should we do? We can't wait until we run out of arrows."

Lachlei shook her head. "I don't know. We're still outnumbered by over three to one."

CHAPTER TWENTY-NINE

Areyn closed his eyes, summoning the power deep within him. Areyn now called upon the hatred and desire to destroy this world. He had kept that power in check while mortal, but now, he relied on it. The rage within him fed the power. He felt the magic fill him; its power raced along his skin. Slayer began to slaver again, feeling the need to feast. Areyn Sehduk too felt the need for death. The *Silren* deaths were good, but he desired the blood of *Lochvaur*.

The fog had been troublesome. Areyn had tried to cause it to dissipate more than once, but without much success. He could cause it to dissipate in one place, only to have more roll in when he focused on another section. The enchantment was stronger than anything he had yet encountered in this world. Perhaps it was the price of assuming a mortal's body. Akwel hadn't been a particularly powerful first-blood *Silren*, but had been powerful enough. The mesh between the mortal's body and Areyn's mind hadn't been perfect.

Reining his mount around, Areyn's eyes flashed. "Charge! Damn you! Charge!"

The *Silren* nearby cowered. Galen shook his head. "Charge? Are you mad? The *Lochvaur* longbows will cut us down before we even reach them."

"Are you a coward?" Areyn snarled.

Galen hesitated, meeting the death god's gaze. "I am no coward, Akwel, but I know when we are outmatched. North Marches was one thing; fighting the entire *Chi'lan* army…"

He never finished his sentence. With a sudden shudder, Galen collapsed dead. His horse spooked and took off. Areyn turned to the others. "We fight or we die."

◆◆◆◆

Lachlei drew her sword and urged her horse forward. She stared into the mist, trying to discern the power she felt all around. It was dark and sinister—she could feel it as she could feel it on the blade, *Fyren*. And yet, the power was different. More diffused and less tangible.

Was the demon leaving or was something else happening?

She turned to Rhyn queriously. "What am I sensing?" she asked.

Rhyn made no reply, his eyes glazed over as though in a trance.

"Rhyn?" she said.

Rhyn's eyes snapped back into focus. "They're charging," he said.

"Charging?" Lachlei repeated. "Then, the demon knows we're almost out of arrows."

Rhyn nodded.

Lachlei turned to Cahal and Kellachan, who had ridden towards her for orders. "I want both of you to take fifteen hundred of our warriors, retreat uphill and wait for the rest of us."

"The rest of you?" Kellachan asked.

"Rhyn and I will lead five hundred *Chi'lan* into the fray and then fall back to our next position. If we can spread out the *Silren* troops, maybe we have a better chance of killing them." She paused and scanned the lights within the mist. "If the fog holds up, it will be our advantage."

"But the fog is not likely to cover the higher ground," Cahal objected.

"I think it will," Lachlei replied. She glanced at Rhyn knowingly. Rhyn nodded in acknowledgment. *How long will Rhyn be able to keep the fog going?* she wondered. *Certainly, the demon is trying to counteract his magic.*

A cry echoed through the hills—a scream both otherworldly and terrifying. Black fire shot through the *Chi'lan* ranks, causing even the warhorses to panic. Lachlei reined her mount. "Go! Go! Go!" she shouted to Cahal and Kellachan. "We'll hold the lines so you can regroup!"

The two *Chi'lan* commanders turned their steeds and began shouting orders. Rhyn was already gathering the front lines, and Lachlei spurred her horse towards him. The *Silren* exploded through the fog, and a line of dark flame rolled over the *Chi'lan*. Lachlei instinctively threw up her hands, feeling the hot flames lick around her. Yet, as soon as she thought they would be burned alive, the fire dissipated. She glanced at Rhyn, whose attention was fixed ahead.

Heartened by the small victory, the *Chi'lan* archers were notching and firing what few arrows they had left. Those who emptied their quivers mounted their horses and drew their swords, preparing for the onslaught.

The *Silren* charged, and the *Lochvaur Chi'lan* met them head on. Two *Silren* charged Lachlei on horseback, swinging their broadswords. She parried one, but was unable to block both, and the *Silren's* sword slashed deep into her horse's neck. The horse screamed and collapsed. Lachlei leapt off as more *Silren* charged, wielding their blades. She dodged one as he passed. She turned and cut into the second horsemen's legs as he bore down on her. *Fyren* bit deep through bone and flesh and into the horse, itself. Both horse and rider went down and she quickly dispatched them.

Lachlei turned as another *Silren* warrior tried to run her down, armed now with a mace. Unprepared, she barely brought *Fyren* up to parry. The force of the blow sent *Fyren* flying from her grasp and threw her backwards. The *Silren* turned the battle horse and spurred it towards her, intending to trample her under the hooves. Lachlei leapt to her feet in time to see the warrior swing the mace. She dodged and with first-blood speed grasped the man's arm as he swung.

She wasn't heavy enough to pull him from the horse, but she unbalanced him and used his arm to leap behind the warrior. The horse bolted downhill into the *Silren* lines as they struggled. The *Silren* warrior flailed, trying to knock her from behind, but Lachlei grasped his head and with a quick snap, broke the man's neck. She pushed the dead soldier from the horse and reined it to a stop. At that moment, she spied the demon.

He was as Rhyn had described him: a tall *Silren* wearing black armor astride a black charger with glowing red eyes. Lachlei hesitated. She had lost *Fyren* in the fight. A hand and a half bastard sword forged of fine adamantine hung from a scabbard on the horse's saddle, but she doubted it could kill a demon. Still, this might be her only chance to avenge Fialan's death. Lachlei drew the sword and with a yell, spurred the horse towards Areyn Sehduk.

CHAPTER THIRTY

Kiril led them through a stone archway leading into the fortress. It was dark, save for the occasional torch and firepit. Like the fortress itself, the interior was red sandstone, and the sconces cast eerie shadows across the narrow corridors. The acrid smoke from the ironwood and coal wafted through the corridors, stinging their eyes and throats.

Fialan had expected the fortress to be empty, but it was far from it. They passed many *Chi'lan* warriors, hooded and cloaked as if to hide their identities. Most were huddled in groups beside firepits. Their furtive glances as he passed suggested that they had no desire to reveal themselves, although they were curious over the new warrior who strode through their halls, unafraid to show his face.

Here are the kings and the warriors of Rhyn'athel, Fialan thought angrily. *Brought down to huddling around tiny fires. Look what the Truce has brought us.*

Kiril led them deeper into the fortress until they came to a wrought-iron door. It was crudely forged, but impressive given the lack of raw materials. The two *Chi'lan* who stood at the door gazed at Fialan curiously, but said nothing and let the three pass. Fialan could see their eyes gleam in the darkness.

Fialan blinked as he entered the room. The room was well lit compared to the rest of the fortress, with a large firepit in the center that burned red hot with coal and ironwood. The walls, doors, pillars, floors and ceiling were all carved with runes. Fialan recognized them as being from the ancient tongue—the tongue of the gods. Some were used as wards against demons; others were prayers to the gods of light. Rhyn'athel's rune, the rune of *Teiwas*, figured prominently throughout. The room was thick with smoke, and the ruddy light cast ethereal shadows throughout it.

Chi'lan warriors stood or sat on either side, many with their cowls drawn, but some were bareheaded like Fialan. They turned to see the newcomers and to stare at Fialan as he strode into the room. But, Fialan's eyes were fixed on the warrior who sat on the throne at the back.

"Welcome, Fialan," the warrior said. "I've been waiting for you."

◆◆◆◆

Fialan stared at Lochvaur as the son of Rhyn'athel stood to greet him. *Here is the warrior's god's own son,* he thought. For Lochvaur was every bit a godling. He stood proud and tall; his frame muscular and battle-hardened. Fialan saw the resemblance between himself and the godling immediately—their features were similar enough to suggest a blood-tie. And yet Fialan knew the blood of Rhyn'athel ran thin in his veins compared to Lochvaur. Lochvaur's eyes held power that Fialan couldn't begin to guess. This was a man who slew demons and *Jotunn* fearlessly.

In his life, Fialan had heard himself compared to Lochvaur. But, standing before Rhyn'athel's son, Fialan knew there was no comparison. Lochvaur was power incarnate.

Fialan glanced at Eshe. "I thought you said that Lochvaur has none of his former powers."

Eshe shook her head. "He doesn't."

Fialan steeled his jaw and stepped forward. "My lord," he said as he strode towards Lochvaur.

"Fialan," Lochvaur smiled warmly and gripped Fialan's arms in the traditional *Chi'lan* greeting. "We don't stand much on ceremony here with so many warriors and kings around."

"I would imagine not," Fialan said wryly. "But how do you know me?"

Lochvaur grinned. "Areyn can't quite take all my power from me. I can't foresee everything, but I can gain glimpses into the Wyrd."

"You're still linked with the Wyrd?" Fialan breathed, not daring to believe his ears.

"Oh yes—despite what the naysayers would claim," said Lochvaur. "I have more power than even Areyn suspects, but he knows I'm dangerous, so he leaves me alone."

"Why haven't you challenged him?"

"Because Areyn is a god—and I am not quite. Even Ni'yah can't defeat Areyn—and he is the most powerful of the gods of light next to Rhyn'athel. Rhyn'athel is the only god who can defeat Areyn." He paused. "You've brought me something. Something I should see?"

"I and my personal guard were attacked along the King's Highway," Fialan said. "A single warrior attacked us. I was able to thrust *Fyren* into his chest, and yet he lived." He drew the ghost blade. The black blood glowed as he held it up for Lochvaur to see.

Murmurs ran through the hall as Lochvaur gazed silently at the ghost blade. "May I take it?" he asked at last. Fialan nodded and offered the blade. Lochvaur took the sword and a slight smile crept across his face. "*Fyren*, my old blade," he murmured. He turned to Fialan with a smile. "Not quite *Fyren*, but close. It was my first sword as a *Chi'lan*."

Fialan nodded. "What of the blood?'

Lochvaur's grin widened. "I'm sure Areyn didn't appreciate being bested."

"Areyn? Areyn Sehduk?" Fialan asked incredulously.

"Oh yes," Lochvaur laughed. "He would've killed you for your impudence, if naught else."

Eshe and Kiril stared at Fialan. "Are you saying Fialan fought the death god himself?" Eshe asked. A look of wonder filled her face.

"Not just fought," Lochvaur replied. "He bested Areyn." He grinned wryly at Fialan. "Not bad for one of my heirs."

"Then, the Truce…" Fialan began.

"Is over," Lochvaur replied. "Your death, Fialan, as unfortunate as it is, has brought us freedom."

"What freedom?" Kiril said. "We are still here in *Tarentor*, Lochvaur. We are still under Areyn's control. We still hear the demon screams outside the fortress at night, and they still come for us."

"Patience, Kiril," Lochvaur growled.

"Patience! Patience?" Kiril shouted. "We have been patient, Lochvaur. When will you accept Rhyn'athel has abandoned us?"

Lochvaur's eyes glinted menacingly and held Kiril's gaze. "Do you believe that, Kiril?"

Kiril said nothing.

"If so, then you are free to leave—to join the rest if you wish. Serve Areyn, if you choose. I will not stop you."

"How can you be patient after so many years? After so many of us have lost hope?" Eshe spoke.

"Because I have seen more than you," Lochvaur replied. "And I know what will be." He smiled. "Don't worry, my friends, Rhyn'athel already knows that Areyn has violated the Truce." He handed the ghost blade back to Fialan.

This will be a trying time for you, Fialan heard Lochvaur's voice in his head. *As it will for us all, but especially for you. Remember, you are Chi'lan first and always.*

CHAPTER THIRTY-ONE

Rhyn'athel rode, the glowing Sword of Power, *Teiwaz*, in his hands. Once the *Silren* charged, Rhyn'athel could only think of the battle and naught else. The mortal body had limits, and he quickly became fatigued. In his god form, he could fight all day without feeling pain or exhaustion. Now, he experienced both.

The first *Silren* he fought slipped a lucky blow past his guard, and the sword glanced off the warrior god's adamantine armor on his left arm. Pain shot through Rhyn'athel's arm as he felt the crushing blow and the snap of a bone. The god bellowed in rage and pain. The Sword of Power flashed as Rhyn'athel brought the blade down on the *Silren* warrior. The *Silren* parried, but the warrior's sword could not withstand the god's blade. *Teiwaz* shattered the sword and cleaved deep into the man's chest. The light faded from the man's ice-blue eyes, and Rhyn'athel withdrew the Sword of Power.

Rhyn'athel looked around and saw that the battle had moved farther down the hill. The *Lochvaur Chi'lan*, as few as they were, had stopped the first attack. A first-blood like Lachlei and Fialan could heal themselves as well as others, but it took time and a large amount of power. The warrior god didn't have the time to keep appearances up. Rhyn'athel paused and let the bones knit and the break heal in his arm.

He looked around for Lachlei, but saw nothing. Bewildered, he scanned the battlefield and a glint caught his eye. He urged the stallion forward until he saw *Fyren* as it lay in the mud. Glancing around, he quickly dismounted and picked up the sword. Lachlei would not have left Fialan's sword lying around. Rhyn'athel used the Sight and, to his horror, saw Lachlei behind the *Silren* lines attacking Areyn.

"Lachlei!" he gasped. He leapt on his horse and spurred it into the battle.

◆◆◆◆

Areyn Sehduk rode forward amid the *Silren* as they began their advance. The *Lochvaur* were out of arrows and despite their brave charge, there was not enough of them to hold back the *Silren* tide. The *Silren* would destroy the *Chi'lan* and then march on to Caer Lochvaren.

Yet, even in his gloating, something nagged Areyn. Something had turned aside his magic. Something very powerful—more powerful than an ordinary first-blood. His magic should have incinerated the *Chi'lan* along the front lines. Instead, the fire had washed over them like a harmless breeze. Could it have been Ni'yah? He searched the area with his senses, but there was no sign of the wolf-god. Still, there was something familiar…

"Demon!" he heard shouting. Areyn Sehduk looked up to see a *Lochvaur* woman astride a horse, wielding a hand and a half. She spurred the horse towards him, swinging the sword overhead.

Areyn barely had time to parry as Lachlei brought the sword down. He was amazed at her fierceness and strength. Slayer leapt up and ripped into her horse, but the *Chi'lan* woman was too quick. She leapt off the horse and slashed the adamantine blade into the demon.

Slayer howled in pain and rage. The adamantine blade cut deep into the demon—not enough to fatally wound it, but enough to anger it. It slavered and snapped at Lachlei.

"Demon!" she roared at Areyn. "You killed Fialan!"

Areyn smiled. "So, you're Fialan's mate, Lachlei?" He searched his memory, but had none of her. *Odd...*

"I am Lachlei, daughter of Lochynvaur and Ladara. *Chi'lan* warrior and Queen of the *Lochvaur*," she said, keeping her silver eyes fixed on the demon horse. She could see now that it was not a horse, but a demon with sharp teeth and claws. Black blood oozed from its wound. Before her eyes, the wound closed and the demon was unscathed.

Areyn chuckled. "Well, Queen Lachlei, we shall see how well you can fight demons."

Suddenly, dark flames exploded around them. A wall of black fire formed a fifty-foot ring around them. Lachlei stared at the flames and then turned back to Areyn. "What is your game, demon?"

The death god laughed. "To watch you die, of course. If you can take care of my little pet, perhaps I'll consider fighting you."

Slayer hissed in anger and lunged at her. Lachlei leapt aside, barely escaping the demon's massive teeth. She wielded the sword only to have it glance off on the creature's scaly hide. Slayer snarled and lunged at her again. Lachlei parried, only to have the demon catch the sword in its teeth and rip it from her hands. Weaponless, save for a small killing dagger, Lachlei backed up. She pulled the small dagger from her belt and tried to focus on her power.

As the demon approached, Lachlei tried to conjure something—anything—to help her with her fight, but to no avail. Something seemed to prevent her from using her powers. She could hear Areyn's laughter as she retreated from the demon steed.

This was how Fialan died, she thought as she held her dagger up in defense.

◆◆◆◆

Rhyn'athel watched as a wall of flame shot into the sky. "Areyn," he whispered as he saw the flames course overhead. What was the death god doing? Rhyn'athel dared not use his full powers, but he had to know...

Tamar paused beside Rhyn and stared. "What does it mean?"

Rhyn'athel touched something familiar. "Lachlei!" he said. "Lachlei is facing the demon."

◆◆◆◆

A thunderclap followed by a brilliant flash of light shook the ground. Rhyn appeared from the smoke and light, riding through the wall of flame and wielding his Sword of Power. He slammed the Sword into the demon horse, severing its neck.

Areyn stared aghast—the warrior had broken through all his defenses. He called up his powers and hurled flames at the *Chi'lan* warrior. Rhyn brushed them aside and rode towards Lachlei on his gray stallion.

"Are you all right?" he asked, reaching down to offer his hand.

She grinned. "What took you so long?" She grasped his hand and leapt behind him.

Rhyn'athel turned to Areyn. The death god drew his dark blade and strode towards him. Areyn focused his power to destroy the newcomer, only to have his power dissipate on an invisible shield. Areyn Sehduk gazed into those steady silver eyes and saw no fear, only hatred.

"Let's finish this now," Rhyn'athel said. His voice held an edge that Areyn recognized. For a moment, the death god felt fear.

Was this Rhyn'athel?

Like many *Lochvaur* first-bloods, the newcomer bore a resemblance to the warrior god. But, did that mean he *was* the warrior god? Areyn tried to sense what lay beyond the man who sat on the gray charger. He was abruptly slapped back.

"I grow weary of your games," the *Chi'lan* spoke.

Areyn hesitated. It might be Ni'yah. If so, Areyn knew that although he could defeat the wolf-god, it would take much of his energy. He would lose his form and expose himself to Rhyn'athel.

Suddenly, the wall of flames disappeared. They stood now facing each other as the *Silren* army charged towards them. Rhyn'athel paused for a moment.

Another time, Areyn... Rhyn's voice rang clearly in the death god's mind. He turned his horse and urged it back towards the *Lochvaur* lines.

CHAPTER THIRTY-TWO

Lachlei held onto Rhyn'athel from behind as the god urged the horse back to the *Chi'lan* lines. The smoke and fog were dissipating. Much to Lachlei's surprise, the *Silren* did not pursue them much further, nor were there any living *Silren* ahead as they rode through the battlefield. Dead *Silren* warriors lay everywhere, only occasionally did Lachlei see a flash of red from a *Lochvaur*.

The archers did their work, Rhyn remarked in mindspeak. *We lost far fewer because of that.*

They fell silent as they rode towards the *Lochvaur* lines.

Thank you for getting me out of there, Lachlei said at last. She knew if it had not been for Rhyn, she would have been dead. Lachlei doubted she could have killed the demon horse, let alone its rider.

You shouldn't have confronted him, Rhyn replied tersely. *You could've been killed.*

I didn't mean to go so far behind the enemy's lines, she replied. *The demon was there.*

Rhyn hesitated. *What did you see?*

What do you mean? She paused. *Do you mean the demon steed?*

You saw that.

Yes.

And the Silren warrior?

Lachlei paused. What had she seen exactly? Now that Rhyn mentioned it, there had been something peculiar about the *Silren* who led the charge. But, what it was, she couldn't be certain. It was as though she had looked at two different creatures. One, a *Silren*; the other, a dark and sinister being. *I saw something,* she said hesitantly. *It was Silren, but it was not.*

The watch fires along the hillside glowed red. Lachlei stared at the encampment as they rode towards it.

Where are we? What happened? she asked.

After the demon brought up the wall of fire, he was so focused on destroying you that he neglected the army, Rhyn said. *We were able to drive the Silren into a retreat.*

Lachlei shook her head. *How can that be? Only an hour has passed.*

Look at the sky, Rhyn said.

Lachlei looked up and saw that the sky was lightening in the east. She gripped Rhyn harder. *What happened?*

The demon thought you were using your power against his army. While you were in the wall of flames, time slowed down. Or sped up, depending on your perspective. We were able to charge while he was focused on you.

Then, the fight was a delay—and he was toying with me, Lachlei said. *He would've killed me. But I thought only a god could affect time.*

Rhyn made no reply. They rode in silence for some time as they drew closer to the watch fires.

As they approached, Rhyn mindspoke to the guards. *It's Rhyn and Lachlei—don't shoot!*

The sun just crested the hill as they rode into the *Lochvaur* encampment. Cahal greeted them. "Lachlei!" he said. "We thought you were lost."

"No," she said as Rhyn reined the stallion and she slid off. "Just a little misplaced." She glanced at Rhyn, who had a thoughtful look on his face. "I just wish we had the ability to take on the demon."

"You saw the demon?" Cahal asked. "The one that killed Fialan?"

"Yes," said Rhyn, abruptly cutting them off. "We gave the *Silren* a good swat, too—something they're not likely to forget for some time."

"Our casualties?" Lachlei asked.

"A score dead," Cahal said. "About twice that many wounded, but few seriously."

Lachlei stared. "Is that possible? How many slain on the *Silren* side?"

"My estimates may be conservative," Cahal said. He glanced at Rhyn. "How many would you say? Five thousand?"

Rhyn nodded. "I would say that. Maybe more. The archers did most of the work."

Five thousand! Lachlei shook her head, trying to grasp the enormity of that number.

"We pushed them back to the other side of the valley—scouts say they're still in retreat."

"We should pursue them," Lachlei said.

"We will," said Rhyn. "But not now. Our army is exhausted, and we can't go much farther."

"But the *Silren*..."

"The *Silren* will not get much farther today." Rhyn smiled as he dismounted his horse. "Trust me."

Lachlei hadn't realized how exhausted she was. Now that the battle was over fatigue set in, and Lachlei found she could barely stand. She felt Rhyn's strong arms catch her as she teetered. For a moment, she turned and gazed into his steady silver eyes, her arms around his neck. Then, realizing her position, she pulled away and shook her head. "I'm sorry," she muttered. "I didn't realize how tired I was."

Rhyn nodded. "You need rest." He led her to a tent.

Lachlei noted that the *Lochvaur* had raised a wall tent for her in her absence. Rhyn nodded to the guard at the doorway as he led her inside. Oil lamps burned smoky and hung from the tent's supports. There wasn't much in the tent save a cot, a table, and some low canvas chairs. A small stove sat in the back with a small flue that extended out of the back of the tent. The warm air made her feel drowsy.

"It's not much," Rhyn said as he slipped a small kettle of hot water on top of the stove and tossed some herbs into it.

"All the comforts of home," Lachlei replied wryly, noting that the cot had thick moose and elk hides as blankets. They looked warm and inviting. She nearly collapsed as she sat in one of the chairs. "Are you sure that the enemy is still fleeing?"

"Quite," he said. "They won't stop until they reach North Marches."

"We should pursue them."

Rhyn shook his head. "No—we need to wait for reinforcements." He handed her a mug of steaming tea that he poured from the kettle.

"Reinforcements?" Lachlei sniffed the water. "Tea?"

Rhyn nodded. "It'll help you rest."

She scrubbed her face with her hands. "I don't think I need help with that," she said. "I can barely stand as it is."

Rhyn chuckled. "I know—I'm tired, too," he admitted.

"What reinforcements, Rhyn?" she asked. "Laewynd isn't sending me more soldiers."

"No, the warriors are coming from the *Laddel*."

"The *Laddel*? My mother's kindred?" She took a sip of the tea, which tasted faintly of cinnamon and cardamom. "Why would they come to the *Lochvaur's* aid?"

"I'm calling in some old debts the *Laddel* owe me," Rhyn replied.

"Debts? What could you have done to make an entire kindred in your debt?" Lachlei looked at him, intrigued. "Are you a Free-lancer?"

"A mercenary?" Rhyn said, amused. "Let us say I am older than I look, and I fight those battles I deem necessary."

"But you're unscathed for a warrior," she noted.

Rhyn shrugged. "Luck, I suppose."

"Not luck," she said, studying him carefully as if for the first time. She had thought him maybe a few hundred years old, but now, she began to wonder. "A warrior like you survives because you're a good fighter. I saw you fight, Rhyn. You're better than any warrior I've seen. Where'd you learn to fight like that? And don't tell me the North Marches."

Rhyn chuckled. "No, not the North Marches. No one taught me how to fight."

"A natural fighter?" Lachlei eyed him. She drained her cup and felt the herbs take effect. "There is more to you than meets the eye."

"Perhaps—but we should discuss this some other time," Rhyn remarked. "Unless you find the mail comfortable to sleep in, I suggest you remove it."

Lachlei didn't argue when he helped her pull off her boots, armor, or padded arming shirt. Beneath her armor, she wore a tunic and breeches. While they were stiff from sweat and grime, they were comfortable enough. She was so tired that she hardly noticed him leading her to the cot or covering her with the thick blankets. Rhyn sat beside her for a moment as she dropped off to sleep before kissing her. He ran his fingers through her red-gold hair and gazed longingly at the form beneath the fur blankets.

Rhyn'athel stood up. *Patience,* he reminded himself. The Web of Wyrd showed a future that in time would unfold.

If the warrior god was patient enough.

CHAPTER THIRTY-THREE

Morning dawned bright and cold when the *Silren* halted their retreat. They had come to the edge of the valley leading up to the northern end of the Shadow Mountains where the peaks jutted eastward towards the *Silren* lands. A great rolling plain stretched for miles as the *Silren* army followed the King's Highway northward towards the ransacked village of North Marches.

Five thousand troops dead and half again wounded. Fatigued and battle-weary, the *Silren* halted their forced march as the sun rose in the sky. Too weary to set up proper tents, they chose to bivouac in the frosty air.

Areyn Sehduk strode through camp. His demon steed dead, no living creature would bear him. The *Silren* glanced up at him, terror mixed with exhaustion in their eyes. Without Galen and the other nobles to lead, there was no defiance. Most of the injured would not live beyond the day, much less a week; their wounds were either too serious or had already begun to fester.

At any other time, Areyn would have delighted in the *Silren's* misfortune, but now he found it a terrible inconvenience. Their lives were his already, but without the destruction of the *Lochvaur* kindred; they had not served his purpose.

The *Chi'lan* warrior who had rescued Lachlei troubled Areyn. Was it Rhyn'athel? The *Lochvaur* had called Areyn Sehduk by name and destroyed Slayer. Moreover, he wielded a Sword of Power, the likes of which Areyn had not seen since the War between the Gods. And yet, Areyn could not sense if the *Lochvaur* was Rhyn'athel in disguise or whether he was only a first-blood. Had Rhyn'athel grown so powerful in the two millennia since their fight?

The old fear began to gnaw at Areyn. As much as he hated Rhyn'athel, Areyn knew he could not hope to defeat the warrior god. In their last fight, Rhyn'athel had threatened to chain Areyn for eternity. Areyn didn't relish the thought. Perhaps that kept the death god from becoming too bold. But, Areyn knew Rhyn'athel couldn't keep truly him chained for that long. There would be mistakes—errors that would be costly. All it took was one of Areyn's minions to slip by a Guardian, and Areyn would once again be free. And both gods knew that if Rhyn'athel dared to chain Areyn, there would be nothing left of the Nine Worlds if he were ever to get free.

Stalemate—as it had always been. But the game was far more complex than a board game. Areyn could never gain the upper hand, and Rhyn'athel could never destroy him fully. The gods of light against the gods of darkness.

And yet, there was something else that hung in the balance…

"So, the warrior god is here," came a voice.

Areyn turned and saw the *Eltar* sorceress standing beside him. *How did she do that?* he thought. "I was wondering when you would show up," he said irritably.

"I am not your slave, Areyn," Imdyr replied.

"All are my slaves," the god remarked. "And all serve me in the end."

"Then, why do you fear a single warrior?"

Areyn glowered at her. "I didn't see you anywhere nearby when the battle started." He started walking away.

"The warrior is a god," she said.

Areyn halted, the old fear starting to rise in his gorge. "Is it Rhyn'athel?" he asked, still not looking at her. "Do you know for sure?"

"It might be," she said.

"You don't know."

"No," said Imdyr. "Not that it matters..."

Areyn turned on her, snarling. "It matters!"

Imdyr fell silent and Areyn wanted to kill her desperately. He wondered now if she was withhold something from him—something he would gladly kill her for. But if she were dead, he could do little to coax that information from her. As hungry as he was for mortal blood, he needed to know more.

"If the warrior is Rhyn'athel, then why hasn't he challenged me directly?" the god asked.

Imdyr shrugged. "He did challenge you, but the *Silren* attacked," she reminded him. "And there is a little matter of the bitch he keeps."

"Lachlei?"

"Yes—or are you Wyrd-blind now that you've taken mortal form?"

Despite her goad, Areyn turned his gaze to the delicate strands of the Wyrd. In them, he found the answer.

"Lachlei..." he murmured. He turned to the *Eltar* sorceress. "She is why Rhyn'athel is here."

"Indeed, and Lachlei is why Rhyn'athel will not force another war," Imdyr said. "For as long as she is alive, she and her sons will tip the balance of power."

Areyn gazed into the Wyrd again. It showed two paths clearly—one with the sons of Rhyn'athel; the other, with the sons of Areyn Sehduk. "Lachlei," he repeated.

"Seldom does the Wyrd bring the opportunity for victory with one defining moment."

Lachlei...

The fate of the Nine Worlds lay directly with the *Lochvaur* champion.

CHAPTER THIRTY-FOUR

Night passed into day and Fialan gazed at the swollen red sun appearing on the horizon. He stood on the battlements that had been hewn from stone long ago. The shelf above him made a natural shelter, overhanging the battlements and protecting the warriors as they kept watch.

Fialan stared out at that bleak land and thought of Lachlei and his son, Haellsil.

He had accepted that he was dead. Not because of anything Eshe said, or because of his meeting with Lochvaur, but because there simply was no mind-link. It was as though the mind-link had never existed. Gone, too, was his ability to sense things with his mind. Everything was flat and emotionless around him. He felt blind without his powers.

Fialan wondered if Lachlei and his son were all right without him. Lachlei was a survivor, he decided, and she would do everything she could to make certain both she and their son lived. He missed them terribly, but he certainly didn't wish to see them if that meant they would join him here in Areyn's realm.

Who would become the next Lochvaur king and Chi'lan champion? he wondered. Laewynd was the most likely candidate with his political maneuverings, but he was not a first-blood, and he had never aspired to take the crown when he could deal behind the scenes. Being king meant shouldering the responsibility for failures as well as successes. Laewynd preferred manipulation to outright confrontation—something unusual for a *Chi'lan*. Laewynd had supported Fialan only to discover that Fialan wouldn't be manipulated.

Kellachan was certainly the next first-blood in line, if he had had the first-blood powers. But a twist of fate had made him bereft of all first-blood power; just as fate had made Fialan powerful. Fialan's son, Haellsil, would prove a powerful warrior in due time, but he was yet too young. The only other first-blood was Lachlei.

Fialan smiled at the thought of her being the next champion and queen. Lachlei could do it, if she wanted it. But she had always been satisfied to stay in his shadow. Yet he knew she could have challenged him—and maybe won. She was almost as powerful as Fialan, and she had been a *Chi'lan*. Fialan had never discouraged her, yet Lachlei had seemed content to stay away from politics.

Eshe stood beside him and gazed at him. "Was she beautiful?"

Fialan blinked, startled from his reverie. "Lachlei? Why do you ask?"

"You have that faraway look of a man who longs for his home," Eshe said. She stared out into the barren land. "Lachlei—that was the name of your wife, wasn't it?"

"Yes," he said. "She is very beautiful and a great warrior."

"Do you miss her?"

"If I told you otherwise, I would be lying," he said.

"She can never be with you as long as she is alive," Eshe said.

A shrill, chilling scream echoed across the battlements. Eshe shivered and pulled her cloak around her body.

"What is that?" he asked. "Demons?"

Eshe nodded and lowered her gaze. "There are no animals here—the call you hear is one of the demons seeking victims for Areyn." She paused. "You are not afraid."

Fialan lifted her chin with his finger. "Of course I'm not," he said. "It can't kill me."

"It can do much worse—when it takes your essence."

"Then, perhaps, I will be afraid," Fialan said with a smile. "But not now."

"How can you be so brave?" she asked. "Have you never feared?"

Fialan met her gaze. "Oh, I have," he admitted. "Before Areyn killed me, I knew fear such that I had never known."

"Really? Then, why don't you fear the demons?"

"Because they can't destroy me, Eshe," Fialan said. "They've already taken my life, but they can't destroy what I am anymore than they can destroy you. Don't you see, Eshe? Lochvaur is right."

Eshe turned to look over the desert land. "I wish I could accept that. But you've never been Areyn's victim."

"I haven't?" Fialan asked wryly.

Silence ensued. "If Areyn slew you, he would've feasted," she said at last.

"As I thought," Fialan said. He stared into the red sun as it rose. "Eshe, can you see that this is just part of the battle between Rhyn'athel and Areyn? How many *Eleion* were alive after Areyn destroyed the Nine Worlds?"

"Only those who Ni'yah managed to bring behind the walls of *Athelren*," she said. "Or so they tell me. I was already dead by then."

"The Truce was to bring us back—to give us a chance at life again," Fialan replied.

"That is what they told us," she said. "But you have never been to *Athelren*."

Fialan paused. "Have you?"

Eshe nodded. "Yes, many of the old *Lochvaur* have. *Athelren* was our home, Fialan."

He stared out at the dead world. "That is why the bitterness," he said at last.

She smiled ruefully. "You didn't know?"

"Much of what came before the Battle of the Nine Worlds is lost to us," he said. "I always thought *Elren* was our home."

A loud, piercing cry exploded around them. Eshe trembled and collapsed. Fialan knelt beside her huddled form and wrapped his arms around her. "Eshe! Eshe!" he called.

Another scream made him look up. He was looking into the dark eyes of a demon.

The demon was huge, nearly filling the covered battlement. It was black with shiny scales and had a large head like that of a dragon. Snake-like eyes gleamed beneath horned ridges, denoting supernatural intelligence. Its torso was that of a large man, but its lower body was clawed. It had a long, barbed tail like a scorpion and bat-like wings. An impossible fusion of dragon, scorpion, and man.

Fialan drew the ghost blade, but felt Eshe tug at his arm. "You can't kill it," she whispered. "Sheathe your sword."

Fialan glared at the creature. "No. I won't," he said. "I won't lie down like a coward."

"Spoken like a true first-blood," the demon said sardonically. Its voice grated in the cold air. "More strength than sense. But I don't come for you, this time, Fialan. I come for Lochvaur."

CHAPTER THIRTY-FIVE

"How do you kill a demon?"

Rhyn turned around and stared at Lachlei. She stood in full mail, arms crossed. It was late afternoon, and the army was breaking camp. Rhyn had supervised most of the preparations for the march ahead. They would follow the *Silren* until they caught up with Areyn.

Rhyn grinned. "Demons?"

"You promised me you would show me how you kill demons," Lachlei said.

"That I did," he admitted. "But there are no demons here."

"Not yet," said Lachlei. "But that will change."

"Indeed it will," Rhyn agreed. "But we have some time."

"Not enough time," she said crossly. "Now, are you going to show me?"

Rhyn chuckled. "Yes." He glanced at the sword, *Fyren*, that hung at her side. "May I see your sword?"

Lachlei hesitated. "This was Fialan's sword," she said, drawing it and holding it up to the sunlight. The adamantine shone bright, except where a large black stain discolored the blade. "No matter what I try, I can't remove the discoloration."

Areyn's blood. Rhyn'athel smiled inwardly as he gazed at it. Fialan had cut into the death god, as Ni'yah had said. "May I hold it?" he asked.

Lachlei nodded and watched as Rhyn took the blade. At his touch, *Fyren* flashed with a blinding light and glowed. "Sweet gods," she whispered. "How did you do that?"

Rhyn smiled slyly. "It's a good blade. The metal is from *Athelren*. It was forged before the Truce."

Lachlei nodded in amazement and watched as Rhyn made a few experimental cuts in the air. "I thought the stain was the blood of the demon."

Rhyn nodded. "It is, but this demon is very powerful for it to have stained the metal in this fashion. Although *Fyren* is a good blade, it isn't a Sword of Power. Lochvaur's Sword of Power disintegrated when he died. This was Lochvaur's first blade, before he forged his Sword of Power."

"How did you know this was *Fyren*?" Lachlei asked.

Rhyn pointed to the runes along the blade. "It says so."

Lachlei knew the blade was marked, but she was certain Rhyn hadn't looked to see the blade's name. *How does he know the blade?* she wondered. Instead, she decided to try a different tact.

"But what of Lochvaur's Sword of Power?" she began. "How do you…?"

Rhyn'athel chuckled. "Swords of Power were common among the strongest godlings such as Lochvaur. The gods encouraged these Swords because they channeled their power more effectively. The gods actually created similar devices when they weren't as strong. You may have heard of Runestones or other talismans."

"The Runestones of Teiwas?" she said. "I thought they were a myth."

"No myth," Rhyn said. "But Rhyn'athel created those long before the gods learned to forge Swords of Power. The Swords of Power were the culmination of Rhyn'athel's earlier works."

"Must I forge one of these blades?" she asked.

Rhyn shook his head. "You're not a godling—you haven't the power to forge one. Anyway, there is no fire hot enough in this world anymore to forge one. *Fyren* should work, even though it isn't a true Sword of Power," Rhyn replied. "Actually any adamantine blade will work, but the bearer must have enough power to use it." He handed her the blade. "Hold *Fyren* and concentrate on it."

Lachlei held *Fyren* in both hands. She stared at the blade, trying to imagine it sparking to life. It felt heavy and cold in her hands. She turned to Rhyn'athel with a puzzled expression. "I feel nothing."

"Relax," he said. "Focus on your power."

Lachlei closed her eyes and took a deep breath. She exhaled slowly and tried to clear her mind. Lachlei became more aware of Rhyn's presence beside her—each breath he took, his nearness…

"Don't focus on me," Rhyn said. "On the sword."

Lachlei smiled slyly. She turned her mind towards the sword, focusing on her power. *Fyren* began to warm in her hands. She opened her eyes and saw it glowing silver-white. She caught her breath.

"Keep focusing," Rhyn said, his voice stern.

"It takes a lot of power," she whispered.

"It will."

Lachlei reached deep within herself. This was the sword she would kill the demon who murdered Fialan. She would take her revenge…

The sword flared with her anger and burned her fingers. She cried out and nearly dropped it in pain and surprise. Rhyn's hands wrapped around hers as she dropped to her knees. *Fyren* clattered to the ground.

"Lachlei!" he said. "Lachlei!"

Lachlei gripped his hands. They felt remarkably soothing. She did not pull away and looked into his eyes and saw worry. "Rhyn, it burned me…" She turned her hands over and saw no blisters or scars. "What happened?" she whispered.

"You must have tapped your rage," Rhyn said. "It is a powerful weapon, but one that cuts both ways."

"You mean my anger can destroy a demon?"

"It could," he admitted. "But it might destroy you as well."

"If need be," Lachlei said.

Rhyn shook his head. "I would not like that," he said, gently running his fingers through her hair.

It was then Lachlei realized that she was in Rhyn's arms. He leaned over and kissed her, and for a moment, she responded. In the month that followed Fialan's death, Rhyn had been beside her, and yet, she had never thought…

"No!" Lachlei pulled herself away.

A mixture of bewilderment and anger flashed across Rhyn's face, and Lachlei became afraid. The hint of power that she sensed in Rhyn blazed through him like a door that had been cracked open and then shut. Then, he became Rhyn once more. "I'm sorry," he said. "I shouldn't have done that." He released her and she scrambled to her feet. He followed slowly, meeting her gaze.

Lachlei stared. *Did he love her?* She had not given any thought about all the time they had spent with each other. She had thought of Rhyn as a warrior and a friend…

"It's all right," she found herself saying, but it sounded false to her ears. She picked up *Fyren* and sheathed the sword. "I'm just very tired and …"

Rhyn's face was a mask. "It's all right—I understand."

Lachlei barely heard his words as she turned and fled to her tent.

CHAPTER THIRTY-SIX

"Lochvaur?" Fialan repeated. He raised the ghost blade above his head in a defensive posture. Perhaps it did not have *Fyren's* power, but maybe the blade would hold its own.

He felt a steady hand on his shoulder. He turned to see Lochvaur standing beside him. "Easy, Fialan," the godling said. "I've been expecting this."

Fialan lowered his sword. "What?"

"Flayer, it's been a long time," Lochvaur said, facing the demon. "What does your lord want with me?"

Flayer's teeth shone. "My lord wants to speak to you now. There has been a *change*."

Lochvaur glanced at Fialan. "I was aware of this change," he said. "What does that have to do with me?"

"I suggest you ask Areyn Sehduk, yourself."

"Very well, take me to him," Lochvaur sighed.

"Wait!" said Fialan. "You're not going without at least one guard."

The demon and Lochvaur gazed at him curiously. "A guard?" Lochvaur repeated.

"You can't go without a *Chi'lan* guard," Fialan said.

"And who would be my guard?" Lochvaur said. "I can't promise their safety, nor can they ensure mine."

Fialan's gaze steeled. "I'll go."

"What are you saying?" Eshe gasped. "Are you insane?"

"Perhaps," said Fialan. "Perhaps not. But I think I deserve to look on the face of the god who killed me." He sheathed his sword.

Lochvaur grinned. "Perhaps insane, Eshe, but very brave. I couldn't ask for a more loyal guard, Fialan." He turned to Flayer. "Take us both to Areyn now."

The demon's jaw opened as though in mocking laughter, but no sound came from it. Instead, it beat its vast wings, and in a sudden rush of darkness both Lochvaur and Fialan were pulled away.

◆◆◆◆

Rhyn'athel had left the encampment and stood within a meadow surrounded by trees. Ancient cairns and rune stones dotted the field. At one time, this had been sacred ground—a small temple to the warrior god had stood here. Even now, the place felt clean and unspoiled.

He sat on a smooth stone and gazed up at Sowelu, the sun, feeling its cold rays on his face. *There was much to learn about being mortal,* he decided. Far more than he had thought necessary. Had he been so out of touch with this world in two thousand years?

Never had Rhyn'athel experienced such a confusing mix of emotions: his desire for Lachlei and his determination to not hurt her. It was a frustrating merging of passion and restraint. In an earlier time, there would have been no restraint, and as a god, Rhyn'athel would have appeared to Lachlei and loved her. But the Truce had changed everything. He found himself cursing the very Truce he had sought to uphold.

"Welcome to mortality, brother." The wolf-god leaned against a large cairn. "You were doing well until you kissed her..."

Rhyn'athel glared. "If Lachlei knew who I was..."

"If Lachlei knew who you were, so would Areyn Sehduk," Ni'yah reminded him.

"I'm a god—the most powerful god in the Nine Worlds—and yet, I can't even woo a woman. It shouldn't be this difficult."

"Need some pointers?" Ni'yah asked wryly.

"Lachlei loves me," Rhyn'athel replied stubbornly. "I could feel it when I kissed her. I know her heart, but she turns from me."

"Fialan's ashes are barely scattered," Ni'yah said. "Even if she knew who you were, I wonder if Lachlei could love you. She loved Fialan deeply."

"I can't bring Fialan back," the warrior god said. "I'm a god of the living, not the dead. The dead are Areyn's. Even my own son belongs to him."

"Which makes Areyn Sehduk powerful." Ni'yah agreed. "Hence, your dilemma."

"And then, there is the Wyrd," Rhyn'athel said. "Damn it, Ni'yah! She must be mine, and yet, I can't have her."

"You could trick her—become Fialan..."

"No." Rhyn'athel said it so emphatically that Ni'yah fell silent. "I will not stoop to Areyn's tactics." He paused. "And besides, Lachlei would know."

"And there is a chance Areyn would learn of it," Ni'yah mused. He paused and a wicked gleam entered his eyes. "I'll talk to her."

"No!"

Ni'yah grinned evilly. "Yes—I'll talk to her."

"Don't you dare..."

"Or what?" the wolf-god laughed.

Rhyn'athel drew his sword.

Ni'yah vanished.

CHAPTER THIRTY-SEVEN

Bright light blinded Fialan for a moment, and he held his hands up to shelter his gaze. He could hear quiet, mocking laughter as his eyes adjusted to the blinding glare.

"Some protector, Lochvaur," came a voice. A familiar voice. "He can't even see."

"Give him a moment, Areyn," Lochvaur's voice rang clear. "I'd love to see the scar he left you with on your last encounter."

A silence ensued, and the world came into sharp focus. It was daylight, bright and warm. The world they were in was brighter than *Tarentor*. Fialan could now tell that they were in a tent, but where, Fialan couldn't fathom. It felt familiar somehow...

Areyn Sehduk stood in the form of a *Silren*—the *Silren* that Fialan remembered before his death. But now the guise looked incomplete, as though the *Eleion* shell would not hold. His eyes were a mix of black and ice-blue; his hair was not quite white. Yet his mannerisms still shone with unspeakable power.

Lochvaur held the death god's gaze boldly. Indeed, Lochvaur looked more enraged than afraid of Areyn Sehduk, and there was a glint of something within Areyn's eyes. Fear?

Fialan had seen enough fear in other's eyes to recognize the fear in the death god's gaze. *Why does Areyn Sehduk fear Lochvaur, when the god holds our very souls?*

Because it is not what I have done, but what I can do. I bide my time, Areyn, you know this...

Areyn laughed, breaking eye contact first. "Your threats are unfounded, Lochvaur..."

"Are they?" Lochvaur asked. "Then, why do you bring me here? Rhyn'athel knows you've broken the Truce."

"So, it *was* Rhyn'athel I fought," Areyn mused. "He seemed very interested in preserving the *Lochvaur* bitch..." His eyes glinted as they fell on Fialan. "Lachlei."

Fialan nearly jumped at the mention of her name. "Lachlei?" he said. "What does she have to do with any of this?"

Areyn grinned. "Why, she's Rhyn'athel's new champion—and little wonder—since she holds the key to the Nine Worlds..."

Fialan stared. "What do you mean?"

"Enough, Areyn—you wanted me, remember?" Lochvaur snarled.

"It would be difficult to watch a loved one fought over like a scrap of meat between two dogs. Or should I say gods? The Wyrd has woven some very interesting possibilities..."

"Enough!" snapped Lochvaur, drawing his Sword of Power. The Sword glowed brightly in the tent.

Fialan stared speechlessly. How was Lachlei involved, and why would both Rhyn'athel and Areyn Sehduk want her? How could she hold the fate of the Nine Worlds? He looked questioningly at Lochvaur, but the godling's gaze was fixed on Areyn.

"Why did you bring us to *Elren*?" Lochvaur demanded. "Certainly, not to torment us."

"We're in *Elren*?" Fialan asked.

"Indeed," Lochvaur said. "Why, Areyn?"

"Select your best men, Lochvaur. I need them."

"I won't give them for you to drain—choose your own!"

"Not to drain—to fight for me," Areyn replied. "I need warriors to fight the *Chi'lan*."

"Have your own demons fight for you—or choose some other Undead," Lochvaur replied. "I won't lead a charge against my own people."

"You'll do as I say—you have no will," Areyn replied. "Or I can make *Tarentor* very unpleasant."

"Burning rivers of flame? Frozen wastelands?" Lochvaur asked, his voice now mocking. "Come now, Areyn, you can think up far worse tortures."

"I have—and have done so," Areyn smiled coldly. "I have taken your will. You have no choice but to obey me. Yes, yes, I've allowed your foolish attempts at defying me, but in the end, Lochvaur, you are still mine. Go, select you best men. If you do not, I will choose them myself and any that fails me, will serve me in other ways."

Lochvaur stood rigid, his steel eyes cold and filled with hate. "You would make me go against my father and my blood?"

"Indeed," said Areyn. "Pity, that you have no choice." He paused. "Are you going to use that weapon, Lochvaur, or merely threaten me with it?"

Fialan watched as he saw a great struggle of wills ensue. Lochvaur raised his sword as though to strike Areyn, but something caught him as though invisible hands gripped his arms. Lochvaur shook under the power, fighting it desperately. Areyn smiled coldly as the godling's knees buckled and he collapsed to the ground. The Sword fell from his hands and clattered against the floor. Fialan wanted to rush forward to help Lochvaur, but found himself unable to move.

Areyn casually stood before Lochvaur. The godling's face was filled with hate and rage. "Remember, son of Rhyn'athel, who owns you."

"There will be a day, Areyn, when I will exact my revenge."

"Really? Or will you let your brother do that?" Areyn sneered. "Pick up your sword, Lochvaur, and choose your men. I'll send Flayer for them within a *Tarentor* day."

Lochvaur glared as he stood and retrieved the Sword of Power. "There will come a day, Areyn…"

Areyn laughed, and the world spun around them. Suddenly, both Lochvaur and Fialan stood on the battlement as though they had never left.

"Lochvaur!" Kiril gasped as the two appeared. The other *Lochvaur* stood around them, staring at the two men.

"Fialan!" said Eshe. "What happened?"

Lochvaur looked grim and said naught. He nodded to Fialan and strode away without a word.

CHAPTER THIRTY-EIGHT

Lachlei entered her tent and found that almost everything had been packed. She unfolded one of the chairs and sat down. Her face was red and when she rubbed it, she found that she had been crying. Why?

It was one kiss—just one. But that kiss held unspoken passion behind it and she had responded. Had her love for Fialan been so cheap that she would throw it away for desire? Desire that she never knew she had?

Lachlei looked at Rhyn differently now. Had she encouraged this? She had been comfortable around him and willing to give him command of the army—because he was capable? Or because she wished him to be around. Certainly, Cahal and the other *Chi'lan* were just as capable, weren't they?

Lachlei knew the answer. No one was quite like Rhyn. He was as though a legend had suddenly come to life—a first-blood from a time before the War between the Gods. He was a demon killer and wielded a Sword of Power—something that hadn't been known to exist. How could someone not love a legend?

And yet, there was her love for Fialan…

Lachlei cursed silently. Her reaction had been all wrong. First, she had responded to him, and then she had pulled away in fear. Was this the reaction of a *Chi'lan*? Of Rhyn'athel's champion?

It was *her* reaction. She hadn't wanted to be queen, but she was. Her warriors had faith in her, but her success was due to Rhyn…

"Have you seen Rhyn?" came a voice.

Lachlei turned to see Cahal standing in the doorway.

"What?" she began, feeling her face flush.

"Rhyn isn't in camp," Cahal said. He gazed at her for a moment. "Are you all right?"

"Yes," she stammered. "No. I mean, I haven't seen Rhyn."

Cahal studied her briefly. "I thought you were going to ask him how he killed demons."

"I did," Lachlei said. "Perhaps he's overseeing the archers."

"I checked—he's not there." He paused. "Are you all right?"

Her eyes steeled. "I'm fine," she said. "I'm sure you'll find Rhyn someplace."

Cahal nodded. "The army will be ready by nightfall."

"Good, see to it."

Cahal left and Lachlei shook her head. Exhaustion crept over her and she closed her eyes.

It wasn't long before Lachlei sensed another presence in the room. She kept her eyes closed but allowed her hand to drop to her hilt.

"Not a bad trick, but it needs more subtlety," remarked Rhyn.

Lachlei opened her eyes. "What are you doing here?" she demanded.

A glint of puzzlement shone in Rhyn's eyes. "Lachlei, I came to apologize," he said. "I didn't mean to hurt you..."

Lachlei's gaze narrowed. "You didn't hurt me," she said. Even to her ears, her tone was clipped.

Rhyn straightened slightly. "Perhaps I didn't," he said, his voice neutral. He turned to leave.

"Wait..." Lachlei hesitated. Rhyn turned around and gave her an appraising look. "Listen, Rhyn," she whispered. "I'm sorry—it's just too soon."

Resignation filled his eyes. "Of course, Lachlei, I understand."

She shook her head. "That's good, because I don't," she admitted. "You're still my commander, Rhyn."

He smiled wryly. "I didn't think you'd demote me just yet." He paused. "Let's go—the army is almost ready to leave."

◆◆◆◆

Fialan stared into the swollen red sun of *Tarentor*. What had Areyn meant that Lachlei was to be fought over by two gods? The two gods were obvious—Rhyn'athel and Areyn Sehduk—but why? Why did she hold the fate of the Nine Worlds?

Returning to *Elren* had awakened a burning desire to return to the world of the living. Areyn could not have been crueler by offering a drowning man a gulp of air. Fialan knew he could not return as one of the living, but would he return to fight against his own people? Part of him loathed the prospect; but another part desired to return to *Elren*. Even if it meant killing his own kindred.

He had seen nothing of Lochvaur since they had returned. No doubt Lochvaur was fuming over his failure to break Areyn's power. But it was not much of a failure, Fialan thought. No god, save Rhyn'athel—not even the only other *Athel'cen*, Ni'yah—could defeat Areyn Sehduk. Lochvaur was *Eleion*—he couldn't expect to defeat a Wyrd-born god.

Eshe stood beside Fialan silently. She hadn't pressed him for answers when he chose to remain silent. Now he simply stood on the battlement, leaning against a merlon, while she kept him company. It was nearly midday when Fialan decided to enter into the great hall.

Fialan strode through the labyrinth of corridors to the great hall, Eshe following him like a shadow. Lochvaur sat on the throne, his eyes dark and angry at what he had to do. Fialan strode to the throne; those around him parted at his presence. Lochvaur's gaze fell on Fialan and a rueful smile crossed the godling's lips. "It wasn't what either of us expected, was it, Fialan?"

Fialan took a deep breath. "What did Areyn mean when he spoke of Lachlei?"

Pity entered Lochvaur's eyes. "I had hoped you'd be spared the knowledge," he admitted. "I told you, Fialan, that this would be a trying time for you..."

"What?"

"The Wyrd, Fialan, has changed." He shook his head. "There is no easy way to tell you. Lachlei will bear sons who will end this conflict."

Fialan paused. "My son, Haellsil?"

Lochvaur shook his head. "Twin sons—the sons of a god. The sons of one of the *Athel'cen*."

Silence ensued. "Lachlei is my wife…"

"*Was* your wife," Lochvaur corrected. "Death has a nasty habit of changing things. The vows you took to each other are no more."

"And so either Rhyn'athel or Areyn is going to bed her like some common whore?" Fialan snarled.

"Fialan!"

"And I'm supposed to accept this—be the good *Chi'lan* warrior that I am and accept that my own god is…" Fialan fell silent in disbelief.

"Fialan," whispered Eshe.

"Leave me alone, Eshe!" he snapped.

Lochvaur drew himself up to full height. "You were never intended for Lachlei, Fialan. The Wyrd has a habit of correcting itself when there is a dead-end. No one discerned Lachlei's pattern until Rhyn'athel saw her for the first time and the Wyrd rewove itself."

"You're in league with this," Fialan snarled. He turned to leave. "Keep me out of it and leave me alone."

"If I could," Lochvaur replied. "I certainly would. But I have no will in this, Fialan. You are in the thick of this battle, whether you choose to accept it or not." He paused. "And you will fight beside me in *Elren*."

"No, I won't," Fialan replied. He shot Lochvaur a withering look before storming out of the hall.

CHAPTER THIRTY-NINE

"Fialan?" Eshe said tentatively. Fialan sat on a windswept hill, dotted with saw grass. He stared into the cloudless, dark sky. He had left the fortress and climbed the hill as far away from people and the fortress as he could. She had followed him silently and waited as he sat there overlooking the plains.

"Leave me alone, Eshe," he said. The anger was hot inside him. How could Rhyn'athel betray him? The warrior god had allowed Areyn to kill him and now Rhyn'athel would bed Lachlei.

"No, Fialan," she said, crouching beside him. "I know you're in a lot of pain right now…"

"Eshe, you have no idea…"

"I think I do," she said. "Fialan, I thought you were stronger than that."

He stared at her. "What do you know of strength?"

"I have suffered here every day since I died. I saw my two sons die in battle before me. I saw my husband and fellow *Chi'lan* die…"

"Then you at least have them," he said, turning away.

"No, I don't," Eshe said. "Oh yes, they exist in this world, but they are gone. Gone for good."

Fialan stared at her. "What do you mean? You say we can't die here."

"We can't die, but there's something like death here," Eshe said. "We're all going through it, even now. Each day, this world robs us of ourselves, Fialan. Each day, we die a little more. Haven't you noticed the warriors here, Fialan? How flat and emotionless they've become? They've lost hope, until now. Until you told us the Truce has ended."

Tears ran down her face and he reached out and touched her cheek. "I don't understand, Eshe."

"My family is out there, somewhere. They neither recognize me nor acknowledge my presence. They've each become one of the soulless, Fialan. They remain mindless, emotionless…" Her voice wavered. "They are truly Undead."

"Eshe, I…"

"I was becoming one of those, Fialan, until you arrived…"

Fialan fell silent. "But, Eshe, I have lost my beloved wife…"

"Lachlei is lost to you," she said. "You can never see or touch her again until she dies. Even then, your love will not be the same."

"But the gods…"

"Be glad Lachlei is part of this conflict," she said. "And be glad Rhyn'athel may love her—he will save her from this cursed existence."

Fialan said nothing, but did not push her away as she rested her hand on his shoulder. Instead, Fialan held it gently as they both watched the sun disappear below the horizon.

◆◆◆◆

Imdyr lay naked across the cot within Areyn Sehduk's tent. She laid on several thick layers of bear skins, her gleaming form contrasting against the russet fur. Her gaunt body looked almost too fragile for the power within it.

Two days had passed since the retreat. As daylight approached, Areyn risked setting up camp. His instinct was to keep pressing forward until he could bring reinforcements, but the *Silren* were exhausted and at the edge of rebellion. Using the Sight, he realized that the *Lochvaur* stayed their pursuit, choosing to rest. He ordered the army to make camp and posted a watch.

As Areyn walked into the tent, his gaze swept over her once before glancing at the oil lamps and setting them ablaze. "Get dressed," he said. "We have work to do."

"*You* have work," Imdyr said. "I will be no part of it."

Areyn hesitated and met her dark eyes. Her tone suggested she was angry. At what, Areyn did not know, nor cared. "You will serve me."

"I serve whom I please," she replied. "Or who pleases me. Don't forget that I am the one who can hand you victory against the god of warriors. No one else."

Areyn laughed at her boldness. "And what is this about?"

"Lachlei," Imdyr said.

Areyn considered her thoughtfully. He searched the memories of the dead *Silren*. He smiled slowly. "Jealousy, Imdyr?"

She flushed, unable to hide the anger. "I am not jealous."

"You lie poorly," Areyn said amused. Her face became redder now and he sat beside her. "Need I remind you that you were the one who showed me Lachlei?"

"Kill her—you'll maintain the balance."

"The balance isn't what I want," Areyn replied. "Neither I nor Rhyn'athel will be satisfied with anything less than complete victory."

"And why should I accept this fate?" she asked. "You will use me and toss me aside when I'm no longer any use. As long as I can see past the enemy's defenses, you find me intriguing, but once I can't..."

"Do you think I would feel anything towards Lachlei?" Areyn asked.

"I don't know what you feel," Imdyr replied. "Save perhaps the lust for the power that the dead give you." Imdyr rose slowly and slid her arms around his neck. "I could give you sons as powerful as those Lachlei would bear." Her heady musk fragrance filled his nostrils as she lightly ran her teeth along his jaw. "How many lovers have you had, Areyn? How many have satisfied you the way I have?"

Areyn allowed the instincts of the body he had stolen to take over, kissing her passionately in response. He had many lovers before the Truce, some goddesses like Fala; others, mortals like the *Eleion*. The woman who lay in his bed was not much more than a child, really. Pliable and easily duped. He smiled as she unfastened his armor. "None," he said.

"You lie," she replied.

He gazed at her with his ice-cold eyes. "It is what you want to hear," he said, grasping her by the shoulders and pushing her back on the cot. "Isn't it?" he asked as he slid on top of her. "This is what you want."

"Perhaps," she said.

CHAPTER FORTY

"An army approaches from the south," Cahal announced as he rode to the front lines. Lachlei reined her horse and considered his words. They had followed the *Silren* army for two days without any sign of Areyn's army being willing to fight. It looked as though they could drive the *Silren* back through North Marches and into their own lands.

The sun had already set and twilight had shrouded the land. Lachlei raised her hand to halt the weary *Chi'lan*. The pursuit was wearing on her troops and still they had not caught up with Areyn.

"Army?" she asked. "Whose army?"

"*Laddel*," said Cahal. "They have fifteen thousand warriors total."

"Where's Rhyn?" Lachlei said. "He said the *Laddel* were coming to reinforce us."

Cahal stared at her. "Reinforcements? How?" He shook his head. "The *Laddel* have always been our allies, but why would they come to aid us now at a mere *Chi'lan's* word?"

"I don't know," Lachlei confessed. "There is more to Rhyn than he has told us." She paused. "Where is he?" She scanned her ranks of officers, but did not see him among them.

"He's with the archers," Cahal said. "I'll get him."

Lachlei nodded and watched as Cahal rode towards the back of the army. She had only seen Rhyn twice since he left her tent. Those two times he had seemed subdued, no doubt due to her overreaction.

The pursuit had given her time to think. It was natural that she would be drawn to him as much as he was attracted to her. They had worked closely together—closer than even she and Fialan had worked when they were *Chi'lan*. Yet Lachlei was surprised at the intensity of her reaction; she had never felt so driven by desire. It frightened her.

Cahal rode back with Rhyn riding beside him. Rhyn met her gaze steadily, forcing her to look away. "Cahal tells me your *Laddel* are here."

"I know," he said.

"Commander, I want you to come with me when I meet with them, since you have a better understanding of this alliance than I do," Lachlei said, finally meeting his gaze. "I'd reprimand you for not telling me about your *Laddel* contacts, Rhyn, but we may need them. I want you to tell me about those connections."

"Blood," Rhyn said without hesitation.

Lachlei stared. "You're part *Laddel*?" She gazed at him in wonder, but could not see any *Laddel* features.

Rhyn shook his head. "Not exactly. I have some close relatives who are, though."

"Really?" she said. "If they were in North Marches…" Her voice trailed off. "I'm sorry."

"North Marches is *Laddel* concern, if not *Laddel* territory," Rhyn replied. "I had sent a messenger to Caer Ladren the night we left Caer Lochvaren. I couldn't guarantee troops."

Lachlei smiled wryly. "You're not as good a liar as you think," she replied. "But I will accept that explanation — for the time being." She turned to Cahal. "Can we outrun them, if necessary?"

"Outrun them?" Cahal asked, puzzled.

"Despite Rhyn's assurances, I can't consider any army that large to be anything but a threat until I meet with their commander," Lachlei said, glancing at Rhyn. "The *Laddel* have no love for the *Silren*, and I trust Rhyn's judgment, but my instinct tells me to be wary."

"Wise in any encounter," said Rhyn. "But I think you'll find me right in this."

"Let us hope so," she said. "Our warriors are weary from the chase and need rest. They do not need a battle."

◆◆◆◆

Mani, the third moon, had risen and brought its baleful glow on the two armies when the messengers returned from the *Laddel* army. Lachlei had lined her chase-weary *Chi'lan* ready for battle, if necessary. Over a rise, the *Laddel* army stood ready as their messengers rode forward. They bore the standards of the wolf and the silver and green colors of Ni'yah's kindred.

Lachlei rode out to greet them, flanked by Rhyn and Cahal. She decided to not have extra guards as they would do little good should the *Laddel* attack. She halted her steed, and Rhyn rode up beside her on his gray warhorse. He looked relaxed, much to her chagrin.

As the riders came forward, Lachlei saw that they were not messengers, but nobility. Three warriors rode together with four guards. One warrior caught her attention. His wolf-gray mane, flecked with white, and brass eyes were unmistakable. His armor and surcoat bore the mark of the godling.

"Is that who I think it is?" Lachlei said, gazing at the warrior. "Is that Laddel, himself?" She glanced at Rhyn, who nodded.

"Wasn't your mother from the *Laddel* kindred?" Cahal asked.

"Ladara was Laddel's granddaughter, but I've only seen Laddel twice," Lachlei replied. She paused and considered the other two warriors. One she recognized as Ladsil, Laddel's son. But the other *Laddel,* she didn't recognize. She stared at him for a moment and back at Rhyn. There was a familiarity about the warrior.

"Something is wrong, Lachlei, to bring a godling here," Cahal said, interrupting her thoughts.

"The warrior on Laddel's right side," Lachlei said. "Who is he?"

Rhyn hesitated. "That would be Telek," he said. "First-blood."

Lachlei stared at the *Laddel.* There was a familial look between Rhyn and Telek that couldn't be disguised, despite Rhyn's *Lochvaur* features and Telek's obvious *Laddel* countenance, hair, and build.

Lachlei steeled herself and clapped her legs against her horse's sides. Cahal and Rhyn rode with her.

The *Laddel* guards parted and circled the three *Lochvaur.* Laddel rode forward, his brass eyes glowing in the oncoming night. "Lachlei," he said with a smile. "Daughter of my granddaughter. Please accept my condolences on the loss of Fialan. He was a great warrior-king."

Lachlei nodded. "Laddel," she said, smiling. "What brings the children of the wolf-god to Lochvaren?"

"The same thing that brings you to this place—Areyn Sehduk," he said.

Lachlei stared. "Areyn Sehduk?" she repeated in confusion. "The death god is here?"

Laddel considered her and then glanced at Cahal and Rhyn. His eyes rested on the warrior god. "Did you not tell her our true adversary, Rhyn-?"

"Rhyn," Rhyn'athel said firmly. "I suspected a demon…"

"But he did not know," interrupted Telek, his brass eyes holding Laddel's gaze for a few moments.

Lachlei recognized a private exchange in mindspeak between the two *Laddel* warriors, but could not eavesdrop. Instead, she met Laddel's gaze. "You say our quarry is none other than the death god?" she asked. "If that is so, he chooses his battles poorly. The *Silren* are twenty miles north of here—we have them on the run."

"Areyn knows there is the Truce to reckon with," Telek spoke up. His wolf eyes glittered in Mani's light. "He fears the warrior god's involvement and therefore remains covert in his actions. But once he destroys the *Lochvaur,* he will seek out the *Laddel.*"

"Telek is right," Laddel said. "Don't underestimate your foe, Lachlei, for he will destroy us."

"Then if Areyn Sehduk is here," she said. "Where is Rhyn'athel? The warrior god wouldn't leave us to fight alone."

"For the time being, he has," Laddel said. "The war is only between the *Silren* and *Lochvaur.* That may change if we do not fight now." He smiled. "But this is not the place for council. You and your warriors will be the *Laddel's* guests tonight while we plan our strategy."

Lachlei tilted her head in a short nod. "I accept your hospitality and the hospitality of the *Laddel.*"

CHAPTER FORTY-ONE

Fialan awoke to the cold dawn. He had refused to return to Lochvaur's fortress, and Eshe would not leave him. She had lain beside him during the night, and he had wrapped his cloak around them both. Fialan held her during the night, conserving what little heat their bodies had between them. She was pretty, he thought, and much stronger than he had given her credit for.

Yet his mind was still fixed firmly on Lachlei. Fialan had known that Lachlei might remarry if he were to die before she did. Such remarriages were not uncommon among *Eleion*, especially *Chi'lan*, whose lifespans were long, but who frequently died in battle. But Fialan had never considered how he might feel about it when he was dead—if indeed, he had any feelings about the matter. He had relegated death to the back of his mind. *If*, not *when*.

Fialan knew his jealousy was unfounded. He was, after all, dead, and the vows he and Lachlei had taken were dissolved. Yet, couldn't Rhyn'athel have saved him from Areyn? Lochvaur hadn't thought so, but Lochvaur was Rhyn'athel's son.

"There will be a day, Areyn, when I will exact my revenge."

"Really? Or will you let your brother do that?"

Fialan recalled the words between Lochvaur and Areyn. The barb Areyn shot at Lochvaur was exquisite. Painful and yet cut to the point. Would there even be another son of Rhyn'athel now that Areyn knew that Lachlei was the crux in this war? Fialan knew Lachlei would never consciously give herself to Areyn Sehduk—but he could deceive her or even rape her.

Fialan shivered in the cold, pulling Eshe closer for warmth. Eshe's eyes opened and she smiled. She sat up. "That's the first time I've slept alone with a man fully clothed," she said wryly.

Fialan sat up with her still in his arms and, feeling his face flush, began laughing. "I'm afraid this is my first time sleeping with a beautiful woman without taking advantage of the situation."

"Really?" Eshe said. She twisted around in his arms and kissed him.

Fialan pulled away. "Eshe, I can't..." he began.

A scream interrupted him. They scrambled to their feet. A large demon with the head of an eagle loomed over them. Like Flayer, the demon had the torso of a man with bat wings, but had the lower body of a bird of prey. Eshe flinched and buried her head in Fialan's chest. Fialan pushed her away gently and drew the ghost blade. "What do you want?"

The demon grinned, showing sharp teeth within the beak. "Areyn needs fighters," he said. "You and Eshe—by Lochvaur's own orders."

Suddenly, the world fell around them. Darkness closed around Fialan and dragged him down. He tried shouting for Eshe, but his voice made no sound.

Instead, all he could hear was roaring of the wind as it rushed by him. Then it stopped and he collapsed to solid ground.

Fialan felt sick. He had dropped the *Fyren* ghost blade and now lay in the mud. The light was blinding. Strong hands grasped him and pulled him to his feet. He could see little save dark figures. They weren't rough as they helped him regain his balance.

"Fialan!" Eshe called, her voice near panic.

"It's ok, Eshe," Fialan said. "I'm right here."

"I thought you'd be used to it by now, having gone through it once," Lochvaur's voice said wryly.

"Where are we?" Eshe said.

"We're in *Elren*," Fialan said. "Back in the world of the living."

◆◆◆◆

Do you think that was wise, Lachlei? Cahal asked in mindspeak as they followed the *Laddel* king back to their army.

Lachlei glanced at Rhyn, who seemed at ease with the arrangement. *Why?* she asked. *They are our allies.*

They could capture and ransom you, Cahal replied. *We could do naught.*

They could have destroyed us with their army and chose not to, Lachlei replied. *I sense no deception and nothing in my Sight indicates a danger.*

The Sight is not infallible, Cahal said.

Rhyn doesn't seem concerned, Lachlei replied.

Rhyn brought them.

You don't trust Rhyn? Lachlei asked. *I thought you were good friends...*

We are, Cahal said. *But he may not see the danger.*

Lachlei chuckled. "That doesn't sound like Rhyn," she said aloud.

Cahal shook his head. "No, it doesn't."

Rhyn had been riding in front of her, conversing with Telek. He glanced behind at the mention of his name. She caught his gaze and smiled and he grinned wryly. Telek noted the exchange with interest before returning to talk with the *Chi'lan*.

◆◆◆◆

"Cahal is wondering if this is a trap," Ni'yah remarked.

"Is it wise to speak with so many first-bloods about?" Rhyn'athel chided him. He disguised their conversation so it would not be understood, but he still believed that Lachlei might notice.

"Why not? They're on our side," Ni'yah said. "Laddel knows who I am already, and so what if Lachlei figures it out? She knows about Areyn now." Despite his disguise as Telek, Rhyn'athel noted that Ni'yah refused to take on a mortal body.

"That wasn't wise," he replied. "You shouldn't have told them about Areyn Sehduk."

"Why not?" Ni'yah's eyes glowed. "They're going to learn, regardless, brother. It's a matter of when, not if. It's better that the *Lochvaur* know now."

Rhyn'athel glared at him. "You're dragging me into this war."

"You're already in it, brother, or need I remind you who was so eager to become mortal for the sake of a woman? Areyn's demon steed didn't die of fright. The *Lochvaur* certainly wouldn't be pursuing the *Silren* if you weren't here."

Rhyn'athel said nothing. Instead, he stared ahead as they rode towards the *Laddel* encampment. "Areyn knows I'm here?"

"Most likely," Ni'yah said. "Your confrontation was impressive—Areyn will have to think you are behind this."

"Who knows about me?"

"Just Laddel. He will tell no one until I release him."

"Don't," Rhyn'athel said. "We may be able to discourage Areyn Sehduk enough to stop this war now."

Ni'yah met Rhyn'athel's gaze. "Do you really believe that? My brother, this is Areyn Sehduk we speak of, not some minor deity. You and he are opposites; he will never rest until he has destroyed everything you have created. If that means razing *Athelren* to its very foundations, he'd do it—if it weren't for you. You're the only thing he fears."

"Perhaps," Rhyn'athel said.

Ni'yah considered him. "Your mortality is affecting you," he said at last. "I didn't think it could happen, but I think it is."

"What?"

"You've never been this indecisive," Ni'yah said. "Careful, yes. But not like this. Your mortality is affecting your judgment."

"Don't be absurd."

"Am I?" Ni'yah said appraisingly.

"That doesn't sound like Rhyn."

Rhyn'athel turned at the sound of his name. He met Lachlei's gaze and grinned at her smile.

"Not affected?" Ni'yah snorted. "Smitten."

Rhyn chuckled. "This was your idea, brother."

"Unfortunately, not one of my better ones."

CHAPTER FORTY-TWO

The hospitality of the *Laddel* army assuaged Cahal's fears. Lachlei, Rhyn, and Cahal entered the *Laddel* main tent to find themselves treated as though they were *Laddel* royalty. Silver and agouti-haired warriors, many with silver or brass eyes bowed their heads in respect to her as she passed.

The *Laddel* were *Eleion* as were the *Lochvaur*, but their kindred showed the characteristics of the wolf-god, Ni'yah. They were shorter than the *Lochvaur*; indeed, next to them, Rhyn was a giant. He towered over most of them by nearly a foot. And yet, Lachlei sensed power within these warriors—a wildness she could not explain. Clad in mail, with long, wolf-colored manes and feral eyes, Lachlei knew their warrior abilities to be equal to her *Chi'lan* in many ways.

Two *Laddel* guards bowed as Lachlei entered the tent. All rose at her presence and she glanced at Cahal and Rhyn in puzzlement. Cahal looked perplexed, but Rhyn nodded.

Go in, he said. *You are Laddel nobility here.*

Lachlei stared at Rhyn. "What do you mean?" she whispered.

"You are the daughter of Ladara, the granddaughter of Laddel," Rhyn replied. "You are in line for the throne, albeit distantly."

Lachlei stared at the warriors. She had forgotten that the other kindreds weren't as egalitarian as the *Lochvaur* or the *Chi'lan*. The *Lochvaur* line of succession was earned, not inherited. Although the sons of the king were often challengers for the *Lochvaur* throne, there was no guarantee that they would rule, although it was tradition that a first-blood ascended the throne. Lachlei had forgotten the other kindreds chose their kings by blood-ties.

I know nothing of the Laddel, Lachlei objected to Rhyn. *Ladara became Lochvaur when she married my father...* She saw Rhyn grinning. *You're enjoying this, aren't you?*

Before he could respond, Laddel approached her and took her arms in the *Chi'lan* gesture of friendship. "I forgot that you might feel more comfortable being greeted as *Chi'lan* than a Queen, daughter of my granddaughter."

Lachlei returned the greeting. "Forgive me, great-grandfather, but as *Chi'lan* we treat all warriors as our equals."

"Indeed, *Chi'lan* Lachlei," Laddel grinned. "No doubt Rhyn'athel's influence."

Lachlei laughed. "You knew Rhyn'athel?"

Laddel glanced at Rhyn. "Indeed, and there are no other gods the *Laddel* would serve, save Ni'yah." He paused. "But, we are not here to discuss history, but to discuss the future. Areyn will destroy us if we do not unite against him."

He led her to a long table and bade her to sit. Servants brought plates of roast meat and bread, but the flagons stayed empty. "I would normally offer mead, but there are too many first-bloods at this table," Laddel said, glancing at Telek. "And we need our wits about us."

"Agreed," she said, drinking the water offered. "This is no time for celebration if Areyn is indeed here."

"He is," said Telek, meeting her gaze. "Make no mistake about it, *Chi'lan*, he has attacked the *Lochvaur* first because you are the greatest of the kindreds."

"We aren't the largest," Lachlei said. "The *Redel* are larger than us — they have more troops. So do the *Elesil*."

"But they are not *Chi'lan*," Laddel said. "During the war between the gods of light and darkness, it was Lochvaur and his *Chi'lan* who led us. They were the shock troops for the rest of us and they took the brunt of Areyn's assault. It isn't any wonder why Areyn has chosen to attack the *Lochvaur* again. It is a grudge that has lasted over two millennia."

"This is not a *Lochvaur* war — this is a *Chi'lan* battle only," Lachlei corrected him.

Laddel frowned. "The *Lochvaur* council hasn't given its approval?"

"Laewynd is blind to the threat."

"Blind or intentionally ignoring it?" Telek remarked. He gave Rhyn a knowing look.

"What do you mean?" Lachlei asked, noting the nonverbal exchange.

"Laewynd may be a traitor," Rhyn said.

Lachlei laughed but fell silent when the others did not join her mirth. "Laewynd may not be the most trustworthy of the council members, but he is no traitor," she said.

"Can you be sure of that?" Laddel asked. "He served Fialan for many years, but Fialan was a strong king."

"Are you implying that I am not?" Lachlei demanded, her eyes glittering in anger.

"No," Rhyn said. "No one here arguing your right or power. But it is unusual to have a queen on the *Lochvaur* throne."

"The *Haell* have a queen," Lachlei said.

"The *Haell* are a matriarchy. The only other is the *Falarel* and they are a secretive kindred," Laddel said. "They deal with no one, save perhaps the *Eltar*. I fear that your strength has surprised Laewynd, and he may try other means to control you."

Cahal nodded. "You did surprise Laewynd with your *Chi'lan* allegiance."

"I have always been *Chi'lan*," Lachlei stated.

"But not outwardly since you became Fialan's consort," Laddel remarked. He smiled at her surprise. "The *Laddel* know more than you think, Lachlei. We may keep to ourselves, but we are very aware of the happenings within the other kindreds." He paused. "Laewynd may have mistaken diffidence for weakness — something that I have learned long ago not to do. A sleeping dragon is still a dragon. And a twice first-blood is a very dangerous adversary."

Lachlei shook her head. "I still can't believe Laewynd would betray us. Laewynd is many things but he is not a traitor and he is not one to take power—he prefers to lurk in the shadow and deal. And Laewynd was a *Chi'lan*…"

"Perhaps, but not all those who take the oath to the warrior god serve him," Rhyn said. "We need those soldiers, even if we can't get the *Lochvaur* council's approval. There's too much at stake."

"If this is Areyn Sehduk," she said. "So far, I have the word of the *Laddel* and naught else."

Laddel glanced at Telek and Rhyn. "At one time, my word was good enough—what other proof do you need, Lachlei?"

"I don't know," she admitted. "I know there is a demon—I have seen him in the form of a *Silren*. But for you to say it is Areyn Sehduk…" She shook her head.

"Demons haven't been seen in this world for two millennia," Telek said. "The Truce has kept them in Areyn's worlds. Now, they appear again. Tell me that Areyn isn't behind this."

Lachlei met Telek's gaze. "I can't—but I need proof before I try to take control of the entire *Lochvaur* army. And if this were Areyn Sehduk, we'll need a lot more than just *Lochvaur* and *Laddel*."

"Then, the question remains—who will stand with us?" Laddel said. "The *Haell* will fight alongside the *Laddel*, but it will take time." "The *Redel* and *Lochel* may come to our aid," Lachlei admitted. "But Laewynd thought the *Redel* were massing to attack us. The *Elesil* are our allies, but they traditionally ally themselves with the *Silren*. If the *Elesil* enter the war with the *Silren*, we can't possibly hold our own without at least the *Redel*." She shook her head. "But the *Silren* have never traditionally served Areyn Sehduk—why the change?"

"Perhaps Areyn thinks he found a weakness against Rhyn'athel he could exploit," Laddel said, leaning back. "Look how indecisive we are already—we question the logic behind fighting this foe, when there should be no question."

The room fell silent and Lachlei gazed at each face. "What do you think, Cahal?" she asked.

Cahal shook his head. "I am not an advisor."

"Speak your mind, *Chi'lan*."

"Despite the lack of proof, something tells me to believe them. What we fought was supernatural, and only the warrior god saw us through this."

Rhyn saw us through this, Lachlei thought. *Not Rhyn'athel.* She turned and met Rhyn's gaze. "And your thoughts, Rhyn?"

"You know my thoughts, Lachlei," he replied.

"Tell me them anyway." Her gaze fell cold and hard on the North Marches *Chi'lan*.

"This is Areyn Sehduk," he said. "The Truce has ended, and the battle for our very survival has begun. If you ignore the problem, it will not go away but will continue to plague us. If not now, then later." He turned to Telek. "I was a fool for not seeing it sooner."

The wolf-god smiled, but said naught.

"I too have come to a decision," Lachlei said. "Instinct, as much as intellect and strength, must play a part in a commander's decision. I don't have much to go on, save what I have seen and your counsel. At this time, I must trust my instincts as a *Chi'lan* warrior." She paused. "Something evil killed Fialan—a demon or maybe even the demon god, himself. If this isn't the death god, then perhaps we will err on the side of caution. But if it is Areyn Sehduk, then it is my duty as Rhyn'athel's champion to fight him. I am with you."

At that moment, a scream ripped through the encampment. Warriors and gods were to their feet, swords drawn.

"Demon!" Telek said.

CHAPTER FORTY-THREE

Fialan's eyesight returned quickly. He was indeed in the world of the living once more, but time had changed dramatically in this world since he left it. Fialan had only been gone a few days in *Tarentor* time, but the season here was now approaching winter rapidly.

And yet, it was still *Elren*, the land of the living. The forest stretched for miles in all directions until it met the base of Lochvaren Mountains, the conifers frocked with glistening snow. The snow-capped peaks gleamed pure white in the contrasting sapphire-blue sky. Sowelu shone overhead, providing warmth where there had been none before. Fialan breathed deeply the cold, clean air and reveled in the feeling. It was as if he were alive again.

Eshe had wept on seeing the world of the living once more. The beauty of *Elren* had left her speechless, but the travel had drained her as it had many of the other *Braesan*—the Undead. While she rested, Fialan walked through the army, past the tents and warriors—and the demons that were constant reminders of the dead *Chi'lan's* slavery to Areyn.

One hundred thousand *Chi'lan* warriors had been brought back from the dead. They were *Braesan*, undead *Eleion*. Neither alive nor dead, their bodies were pale and their eyes held a reddish cast. The best and the greatest of the warriors to feed Areyn's war machine. Lochvaur had chosen exclusively *Chi'lan*, but whether this was by chance or intention, Fialan didn't know. Fialan found Lochvaur's tent and strode in, his eyes hardening as he met the godling's.

"So, you've betrayed us," Fialan said.

Lochvaur looked up. "You of all should not talk, Fialan. You left us."

"And so I'm dragged here?"

"The demons would've come for you, regardless. You're part of this war, Fialan—I can see your fate in the Wyrd."

"Spare me your platitudes," Fialan snarled. "I won't be party to any of this..."

"I see how you instill loyalty, Lochvaur," came Areyn's mocking voice from behind them. "Perhaps I could learn something..."

Fialan wheeled on the demon god. "You...you! If you touch Lachlei, I'll..."

Areyn smiled sardonically. "You'll what? Kill me? Rather unlikely, don't you think, Fialan? After all, if Rhyn'athel or his son can't kill me, certainly you can't."

"Be careful how you sling insults, Areyn," Lochvaur said. "Especially to the man who bested you in a swordfight."

The death god's eyes narrowed. "A small accomplishment—he is still dead."

"Small, perhaps, but notable," Lochvaur said. "Why are you here? You have what you want."

"My *Silren* and *Eltar* will be here soon," Areyn said. "You are to take orders from my captains."

Lochvaur said nothing, but anger smoldered in his steel eyes.

Fialan stared. "You're going to obey?"

"Of course," Areyn Sehduk said. "He's going to be the good soldier who follows orders, aren't you, Lochvaur?"

A muscle twitched in Lochvaur's jaw, but the godling merely gazed at Areyn.

With a yell, Fialan leapt at Areyn, swinging his sword. Flame surrounded the former *Lochvaur* king, and Fialan dropped to the floor, writhing. "Enough, Areyn!" Lochvaur snapped. "Leave him—your quarrel is with me."

"Indeed," Areyn said. The flames disappeared, and Areyn met the godling's gaze. "Remember, Lochvaur, who is your master," he said as he strode out.

Lochvaur glared after Areyn and then knelt beside Fialan's motionless body. He touched Fialan's forehead. "Fialan," he said. "Fialan, awake!"

Fialan started awake and stared at Lochvaur. Anger shone in his eyes, but Lochvaur shook his head. "Let us not quarrel, Fialan. For I am not your enemy, but your ally."

"My ally? You, who have doomed me to fight for Areyn?"

"Areyn would have you fight regardless." Lochvaur helped Fialan up. "Patience, Fialan. I know it is hard to trust me, but trust me, you must. No one—not even Rhyn'athel—holds my vengeance against the death god. Two thousand years or ten thousand years — I am a patient man, and I will have my revenge."

Fialan gazed into Lochvaur's eyes and shuddered. He could see the anger and hatred for the death god within Lochvaur's gaze. "You would've taken Areyn's anger though it was directed at me."

Lochvaur shrugged. "I have felt the death god's punishments before."

Fialan looked down. "There must be a way out of this—now that we are back in the world of the living."

"But our bodies are not part of this world," Lochvaur said. "We are tied to *Tarentor* as surely as if there were a chain around us."

"What if we tried to escape?" he asked.

"Don't," Lochvaur said. "If you did try, you are likely to feel terrible pain—worse than the jolt Areyn gave you."

"Then what do we do?"

"We obey orders and we wait—for the moment," Lochvaur said.

"That is not my nature," Fialan said. "I won't fight my own people."

"That remains to be seen, my young friend," the godling replied as Fialan left the tent.

◆◆◆◆

The demon was huge—a massive, dark creature that loomed over them. In the light of the third moon, it looked more imposing yet. It hovered above the encampment, dark and ominous. To Lachlei it looked like an amalgam of different creatures fused together haphazardly. Its head was that of a wolf; its body of a fireworm. Its bat-like wings beat furiously as it displayed its fierce, saber teeth.

Rhyn had been the first outside, his Sword of Power drawn. Lachlei stood beside him with *Fyren*, followed by Telek and Laddel. The *Laddel* warriors gathered around with spears and swords, torches lit. Some drew their longbows and nocked their arrows, awaiting Laddel's orders. Lachlei could see the hatred burn in their feral eyes as they looked upon one of the ancient enemies of the *Eleion*.

The demon screamed again, prickling Lachlei's skin and hair. Everything within her nature told her to hate it. She had never had such a visceral experience, except in the heat of the battle against Areyn. Perhaps it was the blood of the *Athel'cen* that coursed through her veins. She looked at Rhyn, whose expression was darker yet.

"Heath-stalker," Rhyn said. "Stay here." He glanced at Telek, who nodded and drew his sword. Lachlei stared. The *Laddel* warrior's sword glowed in the darkness; he carried a Sword of Power as well. They walked forward, Rhyn circling left and Telek circling right.

Lachlei started forward after them, only to feel Laddel's firm grip on her shoulder. "Don't—they've killed many demons before," he said.

Many? Lachlei turned back to Rhyn and Telek in wonder. *How could Rhyn have killed many? And what of Telek?*

The demon screeched, seeing both gods circling it. Rhyn's eyes burned with a bloodlust that Lachlei had only seen palely reflected in the *Chi'lan*. It was as though she had been transported back over two thousand years before. Was this how the battles between the *Eleion* and Areyn's creatures were before the Truce? Rhyn and Telek seemed to have stepped out of those times.

The demon struck at Rhyn. Rhyn parried and Telek charged, his brass eyes flashing in the cold moonlight. The demon twisted to meet the attack, only to have its talons severed as it sought to rake Telek. Rhyn swung his Sword, and the blade bit through the demon's armored scales. The Sword of Power cut through its neck, and the demon collapsed in a vile-smelling heap.

Rhyn'athel grinned as he met his brother's gaze. "It has been a long time," he said to Ni'yah. "I forgot how much I hate these things."

"Stupid heath-stalkers," Ni'yah remarked. "Areyn may not realize you're here yet. Or he may not admit it."

"Heath-stalkers?" Lachlei asked, looking at the body as it disintegrated into foul-smelling smoke. "There are types of demons?"

"Of course," Rhyn'athel said. "The heath-stalkers are fairly weak—a good adamantine sword can dispatch them."

"Then, Fialan wasn't killed by one of those."

"No," Rhyn'athel replied. He turned to Ni'yah. "Why would Areyn send a lesser demon?"

"A test, perhaps?" Ni'yah remarked. "They take little to create."

Lachlei stared at him. "What can we expect?"

"Arch-demons, certainly," Laddel said.

"And maybe worse," Rhyn'athel replied. "It depends on how far Areyn will go with this."

"One thing is certain…*Rhyn*," Ni'yah remarked, pausing and emphasizing Rhyn'athel's mortal name. "We'll be seeing more of these before the war is over.

CHAPTER FORTY-FOUR

Fialan returned to the tent where he had left Eshe sleeping. She was no longer there, and she had left her bedroll unmade. Fialan gazed at the bedroll in puzzlement and turned to Kiril as he entered the tent.

"Kiril," he said. "Have you seen Eshe?"

Kiril shook his head. In the bright sun, the big *Shara'kai* looked more formidable with his larger *Ansgar* frame and heavier bone. *Not as fast as an Eleion,* thought Fialan, *but he's probably stronger than any of us, save perhaps Lochvaur.* "I haven't seen Eshe at all—maybe she's getting something to eat."

"Eat?" Fialan repeated. "You mean we can eat? We need food?"

"You'll get hungry and thirsty soon enough," Kiril remarked. "It's almost like being alive. If I hadn't been in *Tarentor* for so long, I might actually think that I'm alive."

Fialan paused. *How close might these be to our real bodies?* he wondered. He closed his eyes and concentrated. Within his mind's eye, he felt the unmistakable touch of the Wyrd, and with it his power. His power wasn't entirely there, but his link with the Wyrd had returned. Just then he saw Eshe in his mind's eye with a small bundle in her hands, running as fast as she could away from the encampment.

"Eshe, no!" Fialan whispered.

"What?" Kiril said.

"Eshe is trying to escape," Fialan said.

Kiril's face turned pale. "Areyn will whip her." He paused. "Do you know where she is?"

Fialan nodded. "This way." Fialan led Kiril from the tent, past several more tents and westward into the forest. Here, Fialan paused and gazed at the tracks in the snow. There were a myriad of tracks even here, many of which continued into the forest. He tried to summon his Sight to determine which track Eshe had taken, but to no avail.

"Eshe went this way," Kiril said as he knelt down, examining one set of tracks in the snow. He pointed at one set that traveled northwestward.

Fialan gazed at the prints in the snow. "How can you be sure? There's too many to distinguish."

"I can," Kiril said. "I'm a tracker. Those other footprints were made some hours ago—these are fresh. They're about the same size of a woman's track, too." He sighed. "Damn it, Eshe," he grumbled. "You're going to get us all flayed for this."

Fialan turned to Kiril. "How do we know that we'll get caught if we try to escape?"

Kiril shrugged. "Our bodies are linked to *Tarentor*. If we go too far from Areyn or one of the demons, we'll lose them. Areyn doesn't need massive numbers of demons to look over us because we'll lose our corporeal selves." He paused. "At least, that's what Areyn has told us."

"Lochvaur believes that, too," Fialan mused. "We have to find Eshe."

"Follow me, then," Kiril said. He led Fialan through the snow in the forest. Fialan marveled at Kiril's strength as the snow began to run deep; the *Shara'kai Chi'lan* plowed through it tirelessly. "The deep snow has slowed her down," Kiril remarked. He stomped the snow around them so Fialan could see the tracks ahead. "You purebloods don't have the stamina of the *Shara'kai*."

Fialan studied the tracks. Although Eshe was tall for a woman, she was still not as tall as either Fialan or Kiril. By the tracks, it looked as if she was wading in the snow. He gazed at the long shadows and the tracks that seemed to go on endlessly. "That's true," he said. He glanced at Kiril. "She'd try to get where the snow might be less deep."

"That'd be higher ground," Kiril replied. He pointed to some rocks in the distance. "Eshe would go there and probably rest. Maybe for the night."

Fialan gazed at them. "It'll be dusk soon. Is there an easier way for us to parallel her tracks?"

Kiril nodded. "We're on the lee side of the hill where the snow collects. The higher we get along the ridge, the easier it will be to walk on." He pointed above them. "It'll be hard going 'til we get to the top of that rise."

Fialan nodded, trusting Kiril's ability. As they crested the rise, the snow level dropped to a few inches and they were able to walk along it towards the rocks ahead. As Sowelu started sinking lower in the horizon, they reached the rocky outcroppings. Cold and sweat-drenched in their armor, they climbed the rocks to overlook the land below them. Eshe sat next to a small pile of branches and deadwood she had collected and was busy striking her flint.

She looked up and saw them. Drawing her sword, she backed away. "No, Fialan!" she shouted. "I'm not going back!"

"Eshe! No!" Fialan said, scrambling down the rocks. He did not draw his sword. "Eshe, Lochvaur says there's another way."

"Kiril—tell him—I can't go back!" Eshe said. "Fialan, we eat and drink…"

"Eshe, you'll lose your form—we'll all lose our forms if we don't return," Kiril said. "Be reasonable. We can't leave the army…"

"That's what Areyn says," she said. "We don't know that! Maybe among the living we, too, can live…" She backed away from them.

"Eshe, no," Fialan said calmly. "Come back with me before the demons find us. There is another way."

"No!" Eshe turned and fled.

"Rhyn'athel's blood!" Fialan swore. He and Kiril ran forward, hoping to catch her.

Eshe shrieked and halted in mid run; her body caught in flame. Before Fialan could stop, both he and Kiril were caught in the fire as well. Excruciating pain, worse than anything Fialan had experienced ran through him. Unable to move, but writhing in agony, Fialan heard Areyn's mocking laughter.

I suspected you three would be the first to try to escape. You're predictable, Fialan.

Blinded now, Fialan could only suffer the torture and listen to Areyn's words.

What should I do with them, Lochvaur? They are yours.

Indeed, they are mine, Lochvaur said, his voice strong and clear in Fialan's mind. *Two of them were trying to keep the other from fleeing.*

It matters not, Areyn said. *They have violated my law. Will you take responsibility for them?*

Silence ensued.

Will you?

Damn you, Areyn. I'll remember this.

As you have so idly threatened me in the past. Will you take responsibility for their actions?

I will, Lochvaur said heavily.

Fialan fell unconscious and knew no more.

CHAPTER FORTY-FIVE

It was late when Lachlei and her warriors returned to their camp. Because the *Chi'lan* were in pursuit of the *Silren*, a full camp would take too much time to set up and break, so they bivouacked in the cold, huddled around their fires for warmth.

Rhyn'athel held Lachlei as she lay beside him, shivering in the cold. Despite her offhanded rejection of him before, she let Rhyn'athel wrap his arms around her and his cloak around both of them to keep her warm. Lachlei's proximity aroused him, but he knew his armor, even though it was flexible mail, would conceal it. He was glad she was facing away from him, or his expression would betray his emotions.

Lachlei's own emotions twisted inside her. Rhyn had awoken an old passion. She could feel his power as he held her. He reminded her of her beloved Fialan.

No. That wasn't it. Rhyn was Rhyn. Fialan, as dearly as she had loved her husband, was not the warrior Rhyn was. Fialan did not have Rhyn's intensity or his singular purpose. Lachlei had never met a man like Rhyn, save perhaps Telek. Laddel, too, seemed like Rhyn in a way, but even he deferred to Rhyn. Could Rhyn be a godling — or something else?

She had sworn to avenge Fialan, and yet Rhyn drew her to him even now. When he kissed her, she had wanted him. And yet, the hesitation was there.

She felt Rhyn shift. "Rhyn," she whispered. "Are you awake?"

"Yes," he said, his tone neutral.

"Are you worried about the battle tomorrow?" she asked.

Rhyn's response was a noncommittal shrug. "Perhaps."

Lachlei fell silent, content to feel his rhythmic breathing. "Why is Areyn here and not Rhyn'athel?"

"Who says Rhyn'athel isn't here?"

Lachlei turned her head, catching his smile. "Do you believe the warrior god is with us?"

"I do."

"Then this is a battle of the war between the gods," Lachlei whispered.

"Indeed," he agreed. "It is a part."

"Do you know about the war—the war between the gods?" Lachlei asked.

"A little—what has been passed down from Rhyn'el, Lochvaur's son."

She smiled; she had heard a hedge in his voice. She turned around in his arms, facing him. "What do you know, Rhyn?"

"What do you wish to know?"

"How did Rhyn'athel defeat Areyn?"

Rhyn'athel shrugged. "I suppose he just outfought Areyn," he said, not meeting her gaze.

Lachlei smiled as she saw his discomfort. "Rhyn'athel outfought the god of death?"

"Areyn is an *Athel'cen*, same as Rhyn'athel and Ni'yah," Rhyn replied. "He is a very powerful god, but Rhyn'athel is more powerful. Those three gods are Wyrd-born—their powers are beyond the other gods."

"So, why the Truce?"

"An *Athel'cen* can't be destroyed," Rhyn replied. "Their nature is woven through the Web of Wyrd. Rhyn'athel couldn't destroy Areyn Sehduk any more than Areyn could destroy him. The war had destroyed all the worlds and had even devastated a large portion of *Athelren*..."

"Why?"

Rhyn smiled sadly. "The *Fyr*."

Lachlei stared. "The *Fyr*? What is that?"

"The *Fyr* is the Eternal Fire of creation and destruction. The *Athel'cen* can use it, but no one else can—not even the other gods."

"What is it?"

"The power to create and destroy," Rhyn said, his eyes glowing in the ruddy light of the fire. "It exists within all things. Rhyn'athel and Ni'yah use it to create; Areyn to destroy." He propped his chin on one arm and met her gaze. "Why are you curious about the *Fyr*?"

"Could it be used against us again?"

"It could," he admitted. "But Areyn isn't that desperate. Not yet."

His confidence was reassuring, and Lachlei pulled herself closer to him. She could feel him respond as her body pressed against his. Her face was only a few inches from his. "Rhyn," she whispered. "I've reacted badly."

Puzzlement glinted in Rhyn's eyes. "What do you mean?"

"I never thought I could love another," she said. "And yet, I love you."

Rhyn stared at her as if not believing he had heard correctly. Lachlei pulled him towards her and kissed him. Rhyn took her in his arms and kissed her hungrily. She responded, sliding her hands over his mailshirt and unbuckling his swordbelt.

A scream shattered their passion. Rhyn was already on his feet, refastening the belt and drawing his sword. Another scream—this time louder—and Lachlei could see the anger in his eyes. "What is it?"

"Demon," Rhyn growled. His Sword of Power was glowing as he eyes followed the unseen menace above them.

Lachlei stood up, her silver eyes trying to see the demon. She had instinctively drawn her sword and could see something moving above the encampment, but nothing substantial. Rhyn's focus was so completely on it, that she found it easier to watch him than try to discern the demon in the dark sky.

Other warriors were to their feet as well. Rhyn's eyes glowed menacingly. "Reveal yourself, Heath-stalker!"

The demon screamed, and Lachlei caught her breath. The demon stood above them, its wings beating furiously. Its long serpent neck was furred, and it had the head of a wolf. Yellow eyes glowed as it growled at the warrior god.

Cahal was beside her, pulling her away from Rhyn. "No!" she snapped.

"Let Rhyn do his job!" Cahal hissed. "He's a demon slayer—let him kill it."

Suddenly, the demon screamed and dove, but not at Rhyn. Instead, the demon charged right at her. Lachlei swung *Fyren*, trying to focus on her power. The blade parried the demon's massive claws, throwing her backward. She heard Cahal's cry from somewhere behind her and saw the demon rise above her, its claws posed to grasp her.

A yell and a blinding flash. Black blood and drool poured from the slavering creature. Wings and claws whirled around her, and Lachlei thrust her sword upward as the demon bore down on her.

Lachlei could not breathe or see. The demon's weight crushed her. Then, for a moment, she saw a warrior glazed in light, his sword glowing in his hands. He looked like Rhyn, and yet wasn't. This warrior was powerful and terrifying. He thrust the sword deep into the demon and it thrashed.

Was it Rhyn'athel, himself? Her thoughts went back to Rhyn's words. He seemed confident that the warrior god was with them.

"Lachlei?" Rhyn's voice snapped her out of the vision. "Are you all right?" Gone was the warrior god, replace by darkness and demon-stench. Rhyn and several of the *Chi'lan* pushed the demon's body from her. As the body rolled off, Lachlei freed *Fyren* from the demon's chest. *Fyren* had cut through the demon's thick armor and into its heart.

"I think so," she said. Despite being covered in gore, Lachlei had not been injured. She found it odd that the demon tried to pick her up, not rake her. It had purposely avoided Rhyn, its obvious challenger.

Rhyn grinned as he saw the wound. "You killed it," he said. "I only managed to pierce its hide in the back."

Lachlei wiped the blood from her blade and considered Rhyn thoughtfully. "That's not what I saw," she said quietly, meeting his gaze.

Rhyn tilted his head. "What did you see?"

Rhyn'athel.

Rhyn started at the name. "Are you sure?" he breathed.

You are Rhyn'athel's champion, not me, Lachlei said. *That is why you were so certain Rhyn'athel is with us.*

Rhyn relaxed visibly. *Nonsense,* he said. *You bear the mark of Rhyn'athel.*

CHAPTER FORTY-SIX

Fialan awoke in a tent at the army's encampment. Every nerve burned within him, and he lay in agony for a while. Slowly, as the pain diminished, he was able to see again.

"Easy, Fialan, you've been through a lot."

As his eyes focused, Fialan looked up and saw his father's face. "Father?"

Lochalan nodded. He sat beside Fialan, looking much as Fialan remembered him. Fialan smiled as he realized how close he had come to resemble him. "Yes, my son, though I wish our meeting was under happier circumstances."

"Where are Eshe and Kiril?"

"They're both resting. You should rest as well."

"Lochvaur," Fialan said. "I heard Areyn and Lochvaur talking."

Lochalan shook his head, but said nothing. His eyes hardened. "What were you doing away from the army?"

"Eshe—she..." Fialan paused. "She was disoriented from leaving *Tarentor*. She wandered away and got lost," he lied. "Kiril and I went looking for her."

"A noble gesture, but one you shouldn't have made."

Fialan sat up. "Lochvaur. Where's Lochvaur?"

Lochalan hesitated.

"Father?"

"Lochvaur has taken the punishment intended for all of you."

"Punishment?" Fialan stared, remembering the conversation between Lochvaur and Areyn.

Will you take responsibility for their actions?

"A flaying," Lochalan said.

"No," breathed Fialan. "Why? If Areyn wanted to punish anyone, he should have punished me."

"Lochvaur is responsible for his men's actions," his father said. "Just as you would take responsibility for your own men."

"But a flaying?"

"The demons wouldn't have shown any mercy, my son. I don't think you would've been able to recover from those wounds on top of your new body."

"My new body?" Fialan stared at his hands. They looked the same.

"When you hit the perimeter, you burned off your body. That was the pain you felt. You're not up to full strength yet."

Fialan sat on the edge of the bed. His armor had been removed, and he was barefoot but he wore a tunic and breeches. "Where's Lochvaur?"

"Resting—as you should be."

Fialan tried to stand. Nausea assailed him as the room began to spin. He closed his eyes, fighting the heaves from his empty stomach before standing up.

"You're more stubborn than even I remember," Lochalan said. "You won't be up to strength for at least a day."

"I need to speak to Lochvaur," Fialan said. He glanced around and saw that Eshe and Kiril lay unconscious beside him. Both looked deathly pale, and their eyes were open and unseeing. Fialan stared at them in horror. "Eshe? Kiril?" He turned to his father. "Are they…?"

Lochalan barked a short laugh. "You were that way for nearly two days. They'll come out of it in time."

Fialan saw his armor and weapons on a chest nearby. He pulled the arming shirt and breeches on and slid the heavy hauberk over his head. "Father, I must speak to Lochvaur. I bring news that may help us."

Lochalan shook his head. "Very well, I will take you to him, but he may not see you."

"I'll take my chance."

◆◆◆◆

Lochalan brought Fialan before Lochvaur's tent. The tent flaps were closed and guards were posted outside the entrance.

"No one has been allowed inside—not since the flaying," Lochalan said. "It takes time even for a son of Rhyn'athel to heal from such terrible wounds. Luckily, we have that time—the *Silren* and *Eltar* are late."

"*Silren. Eltar.*" Fialan shook his head. "We are *Lochvaur* — not battle fodder."

"We are Undead—*Braesan*. We are expendable," Lochalan replied. He turned to the guards. "My son, Fialan, wishes admittance."

One guard shook his head. "No. We have orders from Lochvaur, himself. No one is to be admitted."

Fialan? Lochvaur's voice rang in his head.

Yes, it's me, Fialan replied.

Lochalan looked at his son in amazement. "You can mindspeak?"

Let him pass, came Lochvaur's voice.

"I'll explain later," Fialan said. He stepped into the tent.

Lochvaur sat in near darkness, cloaked and hooded, so Fialan could not see his face.

Fialan hesitated as he entered. "Lochvaur, I…"

"There is no need for apologies, Fialan," Lochvaur replied. His voice was raspy and barely audible. "Forgive my condition; I'm still not quite healed."

"By Rhyn'athel's sword!" Fialan swore. "Why? Why you?"

"Because Areyn can, Fialan. Areyn takes great pains to prove to me who has the upper hand. It's almost as if he doesn't believe it, himself."

"Does he have the upper hand?"

"What do you think?" Was there a tinge of ironic humor in his voice?

"I think Areyn does at the present, but he is like a man who has caged a terrible dragon," Fialan said. "He taunts the dragon, but isn't quite certain of the cage's strength."

"An apt description," remarked Lochvaur. "And now you know the game he and I play."

"A dangerous one."

"Is there any other kind to play?"

"What does Rhyn'athel think?"

"Rhyn'athel isn't involved in this. This is personal between Areyn and me," Lochvaur said. He paused. "Certainly, you didn't come to chide me over our little game?"

"No, though Eshe and Kiril still lie unconscious because of it," Fialan said.

"Eshe shouldn't have fled; Kiril and you shouldn't have gone after her."

"Perhaps not," Fialan said. "Would you like to know how we found her?"

Lochvaur stood up. "I was wondering who would be the first to no longer be Wyrd-blind…" Amusement colored his voice.

"You know?"

"I suspected—I've been feeling my own powers grow again, despite this poor facsimile Areyn calls a body…"

"But why?" Fialan mused. "Why can I mindspeak? Why am I starting to show my powers when I had none in *Tarentor*?"

"Because you're a creature of the worlds of the living, Fialan—just as I am," Lochvaur said. "Your powers are returning because you gain your strength from this world. We already have to eat and drink. The more of this world we take in, the less we are of *Tarentor*. We become of this world again, Fialan. The only other world that would allow us to gain our power back would be *Athelren*, itself."

"Because we came from *Athelren* originally," Fialan mused.

"You've been talking to Eshe—she remembers a time before when the *Eleion* came from *Athelren*."

"Then, it's true," Fialan marveled. "*Athelren* is our home."

"It always has been—and it will be so again," Lochvaur said. "And Areyn only suspects the depths of my power." With that, he shrugged off his cloak.

Fialan stared agape. Lochvaur was nearly healed. The lines were still there—ugly weals that crisscrossed his face, but they were healing rapidly. "Your face…"

"The scars will be gone within a few hours," Lochvaur said. "As I said, like you, I am growing stronger."

"But the pain…"

"Is inconsequential," Lochvaur grinned. "Areyn will have to double or triple his efforts to keep me contained. To keep you contained. To control the *Chi'lan*—the best *Lochvaur* warriors. All that takes power—power he can't use against Rhyn'athel."

"Or Lachlei," Fialan stared. "You chose the most powerful *Chi'lan*..."

"That is what Areyn wanted," the godling said slyly. "With each day, he will weaken..."

"And each day, we grow stronger," Fialan said.

"I hope you weren't fond of *Tarentor*, my friend," Lochvaur said as he drew his cloak and hood around himself once more. "We may yet find a way out of this."

Fialan turned to leave, but instead, paused. He gazed at the godling thoughtfully.

"You're curious about something?" Lochvaur asked.

Fialan hesitated. "I was wondering how you died," he admitted. "You are more than any *Chi'lan* warrior—indeed, more than any *Eleion*. It seems impossible to me that you could die."

"I *had* a mortal body."

"Yes, but you're part of *Athelren*, or the Wyrd..." Fialan felt at a loss for words. "Yes, Eshe came from *Athelren*, but you're more so..." He shook his head. "I can't explain it."

"It's that apparent even to my heirs?"

Fialan considered Lochvaur thoughtfully. "It's apparent to me. How apparent it is to the others, I don't know. How did you die?"

Lochvaur chuckled. "It seems your curiosity won't be satisfied easily, even with a straightforward answer. Areyn sent a small army of arch-demons and *Jotunn* to ambush me."

"But the Truce had already been agreed upon," Fialan objected. "The *Jotunn* and arch-demons were banished from *Elren* by then."

Lochvaur laughed. "So, they were—or so we thought." He raised a hand to silence Fialan. "Enough questions, my friend. I must rest, and Eshe is awakening."

Fialan nodded and left. As he greeted his father, he glanced back at the guarded entrance to Lochvaur's tent, wondering what exactly Lochvaur was and why Areyn Sehduk feared and hated him so.

CHAPTER FORTY-SEVEN

"What is Lochvaur, Kiril?" Fialan asked as he entered the tent where both Eshe and Kiril had lain comatose. Both were awake now. Eshe sat on her cot, drinking hot tea and eating what appeared to be hard tack. Kiril had drawn his sword and was idly swinging the blade back and forth, testing the new body. Beads of sweat ran down his bronze skin as he swung the broadsword over his head.

Kiril halted in mid-swing and gave Fialan a dark look. "Some way to greet your friends," he remarked.

"I'm glad you're ok," Fialan remarked brusquely. "But my father, Lochalan, already assured me that you'd come around."

"Well, that's sensitive," Eshe replied sarcastically. She bit into the hardtack and spit it out. "Awful. Simply awful."

Fialan took a slow breath inward. "Eshe, I'm glad you're ok."

She glanced at him and then looked away. "Kiril says you asked him to help search for me."

"I did."

"Why?"

"You shouldn't have fled."

"And why not?" Her silver eyes were unreadable.

"You would've been flayed."

"My skin seems remarkably intact," she replied, holding her hands outstretched for him to examine.

"Lochvaur's isn't."

A silence ensued. Kiril stopped swinging the sword and brought it point down into the dirt. "By Rhyn'athel's mane," he whispered.

Eshe blanched and looked away. "That was his choice."

"Yes, it was his choice," Fialan said evenly. "And Lochvaur took the punishment meant for us."

"I didn't ask him to do that," she snapped.

"No, you didn't. But you ought to be more grateful. Kiril and I took a dreadful chance trying to find you. I would've taken my punishment gladly if I had a say."

Eshe stood up and moved to draw her dagger. Fialan caught her arm. "Leave me alone."

"No," Fialan said. He eyed the weapon. "If you're going to draw it, *Chi'lan*, you'd better be prepared to use it."

"*Chi'lan*," Eshe spat. "We're *Braesan*. Undead. Unwanted and unloved by Rhyn'athel."

"I don't believe it—not for a moment," Fialan said. "I think your time in *Tarentor* has rotted your mind. You've listen too long to the demon's lies and now you believe them." He met her gaze coolly. "Listen, Eshe, there's still hope. There's always hope—even for the damned."

Eshe's hand wavered and she dropped the dagger. She collapsed on the cot weeping. "I don't know anymore, Fialan. I used to be so strong..."

Fialan held her and glanced at Kiril. Kiril nodded once and silently left the tent. He stroked her hair and kissed her. "Eshe, I'm so sorry."

Eshe dried her eyes on her tunic sleeve and smiled weakly. "It is I who should apologize," she said. "The demons would've flayed us had it not been for Lochvaur." She shook her head. "It is so like him to take our punishment."

"Why?" Fialan mused.

"Lochvaur feels responsible for us," she replied. "He's a good commander—he always has been. He never asked any of us to do something he wouldn't do himself. And, he always felt that the *Lochvaur* were his children—even if we all weren't descended directly from his bloodline."

"Do you know what he is, Eshe?" Fialan asked. "A godling, certainly, but I've known Laddel and Silvain, and neither is anything like Lochvaur."

"I don't know exactly what he is, except he is Rhyn'athel's son," Eshe admitted. "He was at least two thousand years old when I was living, but I don't think there were any *Eleion* alive who knew him that long ago. Perhaps he was one of the original *Eleion*." She kissed him, and Fialan held her as he stroked her hair. She was so unlike Lachlei, and yet, he sensed a strength within her that had been buried deep. "Why do you ask?"

"Curiosity, mostly. Why does Areyn fear him?"

"I don't know." She shook her head. "Those of us who saw Areyn's fear the first time took heart. But as the millennia passed, nothing seemed to come of it, and many of us gave up hope. We thought we had deluded ourselves into thinking we saw what we saw."

"I know what I saw. I saw fear in Areyn's eyes," Fialan replied. "Lochvaur spoke of a game he played with Areyn."

"A game?" Eshe mused. "Then it is a very old game. Areyn Sehduk has been Lochvaur's enemy as long as I can remember. This contention didn't start with Lochvaur entering *Tarentor*—it started well before that."

"Odd that a mortal would take on one of the most powerful gods. Unless he is something else." He looked into Eshe's eyes and smiled. "I can't be certain, Eshe, but I think Lochvaur has a plan to free us from Areyn's slavery."

Her eyes widened. "How?"

Fialan shook his head. "I don't know," he said. "But I know that with each breath of air, each drop of water, and each morsel of food I take from this world, I become stronger. You're becoming stronger too—perhaps that's why you fled—you felt this world permeating your body. If it continues, we may become part of the world of the living."

"Then, Areyn will have no control over us," Eshe said. She hesitated and then tentatively slid her arms around his neck and kissed him.

Desire exploded within Fialan and he took her in his arms, kissing her. Lochvaur was right—he was becoming more alive with each moment he spent in the world of the living. The part of him that was living was overwhelming his other senses. He wanted Eshe desperately now.

Suddenly, he pulled away as though invisible hands wrested him away from her. "No!" he shouted. "No! Not now!" He met Eshe's gaze as he staggered to his feet. "What's happening?"

"Areyn," Eshe replied as she stood up. "It'll hurt less if you don't fight it."

"He can control our actions even when he isn't here?"

"Areyn Sehduk can control everything we do if he so wishes. He'll force us to fight for him."

Fialan shook his head. Areyn gave them just enough freedom to believe that they were autonomous, only to rip it away and force them to acknowledge that they were subject to his will. Yet, Lochvaur had hope...

Kiril entered the tent. "The demons told me to get you both," he said, his jaw clenched as though fighting an invisible force. "The *Silren* army has arrived."

CHAPTER FORTY-EIGHT

"Where is Akwel?" demanded Silvain. The *Silren* king stood outside of Areyn Sehduk's tent, his ice-blue eyes hard as he surveyed the army. The army he had left Areyn with had been ten thousand strong. Now, counting the wounded, they were down to a mere thirty-five hundred and being pursued by the *Lochvaur* and the *Laddel.*

Silvain had come ready to confront the demon god on his apparent failure to secure victory beyond the North Marches. He rode with his guards from Caer Silren to take over the army. The godling had dismounted and strode to Areyn's tent, followed by his guards.

Areyn knew this even before he strode from the tent. "Silvain," Areyn said with a mocking smile. He crossed his arms and gazed at the tall *Silren* in amusement. It had taken very little for him to shield the *Braesan* from Silvain's senses. The *Silren* king was unprepared and walking right into Areyn's carefully laid trap.

"I demand that you explain yourself, Akwel," Silvain said. "My army is decimated and in retreat..."

"Unfortunate, but there are other players," Areyn remarked bored. "The *Lochvaur* bitch, Lachlei, seems to have some help."

"I'm taking the army back and returning to Caer Silren."

Areyn laughed. "Really, Silvain?"

Silvain stared at Areyn. "Why are you laughing?"

"Because I never thought you could be so blind," Areyn replied. "I would've thought a godling such as you could've seen through this guise."

Silvain looked taken aback. "What are you talking about, Akwel?"

"Let's drop the deception, shall we?" Areyn said. At that, the shell vanished and the death god stood before the *Silren* king. He stood before Silvain as a tall *Eltar* with a long, black mane and dark eyes.

Silvain retreated, only to find his guards gone; replaced by demons. "No," he gasped. "No..."

Areyn Sehduk smiled. "Your daughter had the right idea, Silvain, but you were too foolish to listen to her words. Cara serves Rhyn'athel. As you will serve me."

"No," Silvain said. "I am the son of Elisila, goddess of the heavens..."

"And I am Areyn Sehduk, the god of destruction. Elisila does not hear your prayers, foolish one, but I will. There is only one other god powerful enough to fight me and you eschewed him long ago."

The *Silren* king shuddered. Areyn knew he was considering his options, but also knew that Silvain had none. Even his first-blood powers could not hope to defeat the death god. "What do you want of me?" he asked at last.

Areyn smiled. "The same thing you want—the destruction of Rhyn'athel's kindred."

"Why? Why isn't Rhyn'athel here?"

"Rhyn'athel may already be here, but I doubt it," Areyn replied. "And why—I have my own reasons, Silvain. I am willing to bargain with you."

"Bargain? What would you bargain?"

"Your life and the lives of your kindred for your compliance."

"And if I refuse?"

"Then you serve me anyway as a *Braesan*—an Undead," Areyn replied. "Like my friend, Lochvaur."

"Lochvaur?" Silvain could not disguise the disbelief in his voice. "Lochvaur is here?"

"He serves me—along with his dead *Chi'lan*. You can serve me alive or dead, Silvain, it is your choice. But you will serve me."

Silvain looked around and saw the massive encampment where the *Braesan* now waited. He looked at his warriors who stood beside him, unable to help him. At last, he met the death god's gaze.

"What do you want me to do?"

◆◆◆◆

Deep within the *Athelren* Mountains, the great walled city of the gods sat beneath the blue skies. Overhead, the twin suns shone, making the white walls of the fortress-city glitter in their magnificence. Lofty towers and brilliant spires rose above those walls—their beauty conceived in one single thought of the *Athel'cen*. Within those walls were the castles of the gods, including the wolf-god's own hall.

Ni'yah smiled as he gazed at his handiwork. He was fond of the walled city, but found it too perfect. There was little challenge in *Athelren* and none within the city of the gods since Rhyn'athel had forced Areyn from the world of the *Athel'cen*. The displacement of the *Eleion* and *Ansgar* had much to do with his boredom—they provided a challenge that was now gone in this world.

Ni'yah strode through the open gates where the Watchers stood guard. They were creatures who took the form of silver dragons, but were not creatures of the *Fyr* as dragons were, but actual Wyrd-born creatures that Rhyn'athel brought forth from the Web to guard the city. They lowered their heads in respect as Ni'yah strode past them.

Once inside the gates, Ni'yah noted the stillness of the world. Nowhere was it more pronounced than here, in the great city of the gods. The glistening streets and towers were all deserted, save perhaps for the gods' own servants. The great halls, palatial residences, and garrisons were empty, just as the fields outside of the city lay fallow. It was spring, but there would be no crops. The gods didn't need sustenance, and there were few in this world who did.

He walked towards the palace of Elisila. It stood imposing before him, its tall columns stretched upward, holding a beautiful dome of starlight above.

"Ni'yah," came a voice. "I hardly expected to see you in *Athelren*."

Ni'yah turned and saw a beautiful woman with silver hair and pale blue eyes. She was tall and fair-skinned, wearing a dress that shimmered like the stars. Ni'yah grinned roguishly. "Elisila!" he said.

Elisila frowned. "I know that look," she said. "You're scheming…"

"Scheming? Me?" Ni'yah feigned an injured look. "Elisila, have I ever led you astray?"

"Many times," she said. "I should turn you out for that last little trick you pulled."

"It was a joke—no harm done," Ni'yah remarked. "Listen, I'm on an important mission. Rhyn'athel sent me."

Elisila's face grew darker. "Then, I don't want any part of it." She vanished.

Ni'yah smacked his head against a nearby column. "I forgot how touchy she is," he remarked to no one. With that, he vanished and rematerialized in Elisila's great hall.

It was as impressive inside as it was outside. The inlayed stone along the floor and wall sparkled like stars in a deep blue firmament. He gazed at her handiwork in appreciation. "Nicely done," he said.

Elisila sat on her throne at the end of the hall. "If Rhyn'athel sent you, I don't want to hear it," she snapped.

Ni'yah sighed. "OK, not Rhyn'athel. I'm here on my own behalf. Do you know Areyn is in *Elren*?"

"So is Rhyn'athel," Elisila shrugged. "The Truce is broken."

"Then you know Areyn Sehduk has control of the *Silren*," Ni'yah said. "He will enlist the aid of the *Elesil* as well."

Elisila paused. "Listen, Ni'yah, Rhyn'athel forced us all out of *Elren* long ago with that damn treaty. It's up to him to fix his mistake."

"Even at the cost of your own son's life?"

A muscle twitched in her face. "I've already lost one son to Areyn Sehduk."

"I'm not willing to lose mine," Ni'yah replied. "You still have Silvain—if you act now."

Indecision glowed in her eyes for a moment, and then she laughed. "Ni'yah, this is not my realm any longer. Go plead your case to sympathetic ears."

"There's no one else," Ni'yah said. "I need for you to speak to Conlan—tell him not to support the *Silren*."

Elisila smiled, but her smile was coldly patronizing. "You're *Athel'cen*, Ni'yah, not I," she said. "Certainly, you need not my insignificant power to obtain what you wish."

Ni'yah flashed his teeth, but it was not a smile. His brass eyes flashed with power, and Elisila would have withdrawn if she could. Instead, she met the wolf-god's gaze.

"I'm willing to play fairly for the sake of my brother, Elisila, but I will do what I must to ensure victory. As an *Athel'cen.*" With that, he vanished.

CHAPTER FORTY-NINE

Rhyn'athel insisted on keeping guard over Lachlei while she lay down to rest. Despite his exhaustion, he refused to lie down again. He sat on a stone beside her and admonished himself for being so lax. In his desire to make love to her, the warrior god had let his guard down—something he wouldn't have normally done.

What had disturbed the warrior god was not only the timing of the demon's attack, but also the purpose. The demon had gone after Lachlei—not him. Demons were notoriously stupid—and willing to follow orders precisely. The heath-stalker was ordered to capture Lachlei and bring her alive to Areyn.

It meant that Areyn knew Lachlei's future in the Nine Worlds' destiny. It meant that Areyn probably knew that the warrior, Rhyn, was none other than Rhyn'athel. It also meant that Areyn Sehduk was getting bolder. Or desperate. Or both.

Rhyn'athel gazed on Lachlei as he pondered the new patterns of the Wyrd. He admitted to himself that he had been directly responsible for the change to the Wyrd. But with all the *Athel'cen* in *Elren*, their presence complicated things considerably. The Wyrd didn't fully reveal the changes, but rather showed the ripples and how they could change the course of the future.

I never thought I could love another. And yet I love you, Lachlei had said. Rhyn'athel gazed on her face, wishing desperately that he had more time alone with her. She would have loved him.

The demon could have appeared at a worse time, Rhyn'athel admitted to himself wryly. If the heath-stalker had appeared a few minutes later, it would have forced Rhyn'athel to shed his body and reveal his true identity. Then, all would know, and the delicate game he played with Areyn Sehduk would end.

There would be another time, he silently promised himself.

He felt a touch on his shoulder and looked up. Cahal stood over him and grinned. "Gods, Rhyn, I don't know how you do it, but you need some rest."

Rhyn hesitated. He hadn't slept, and the fight with the heath-stalker had pushed this body to its very limit. He was exhausted, and yet Lachlei needed a guard. "Someone needs to watch Lachlei," he said.

"I will keep watch," Cahal replied. "Get some sleep—I'll alert you if the demons come around."

"But Lachlei..." he began.

"Will be safe if we're both near her," Cahal said. "Sleep beside her, Rhyn. I will keep watch." He grinned knowingly.

Rhyn chuckled and nodded. He settled down next to her and gently took her in his arms. Lachlei's eyes fluttered open for a brief moment, and she smiled as she felt his arms wrap around her. The warmth of her body relaxed him—as much as her feelings of love for him. He wanted her now, but Rhyn could not risk another chance encounter with the demons.

Lachlei was nearly asleep from exhaustion. She had stripped the gory mail, underlying arming shirt and padded leggings, and was down to a simple tunic and breeches. If she had to, she could don her armor quickly enough, but another demon attack would warrant Rhyn'athel protecting her at any cost.

As he felt her muscular frame against his, the warrior god relaxed. It was *when*, not *if*, and he accepted the fate with quiet confidence. He had waited this long, he could wait a little longer. He closed his eyes, hoping he would rest.

Yet, despite his fatigue, Rhyn'athel could not sleep. Instead, he pondered Lachlei's question—how the *Fyr* had destroyed the very thing it created and if Areyn would use it again. He had discounted it when he had spoken to her—another lie, if harmless—but in truth, Rhyn'athel had no answer. Rhyn'athel could not fully control two things, despite all his powers as an *Athel'cen*. One was the Wyrd; the other was the *Fyr*.

The Wyrd had created the *Athel'cen*, perhaps as guardians for it. Rhyn'athel likened it to a web or a tapestry. It wove itself into patterns that created and destroyed. At some point, it began to create. The *Athel'cen* and the *Guardians* were the result.

Rhyn'athel never understood the full reason behind his own existence, let alone the Wyrd's. It was mindless in many ways, and yet had a purpose. The *Athel'cen* were not the first of the Wyrd-born, but they were the most powerful. They could change portions of the Wyrd through their existence, but nothing could actually change the strands themselves or reweave them in another manner.

The *Fyr* was part of the Wyrd. Like the Wyrd, the *Athel'cen* could affect the *Fyr*, but it was dangerous and tricky to handle. Rhyn'athel drew on its power to create; Areyn called on it to destroy. Once it was unleashed, it was difficult to contain. The *Fyr* was the chaos to the Wyrd's order. Rhyn'athel had failed to control the *Fyr* when Areyn had unleashed it on the world. It had destroyed everything, save the walled city of *Athelren*.

Areyn would use it only in desperation, Rhyn'athel decided. Only if Rhyn'athel had the obvious upper hand.

But what could Rhyn'athel do if Areyn decided to unleash it?

"Rhyn?" Lachlei's voice drew him from his reverie. "Rhyn?" she murmured again, this time, her voice distant and dreamlike. The warrior god smiled as he slipped into her dreams.

I am here, beloved.

◆◆◆◆

"There's a large wolf following us."

Cara, the renegade daughter of Silvain, twisted in her saddle to look for movement. In the twilight, she could see nothing save shadows among the grasses that blew in the breeze. She turned to Haukel. "Are you sure?" She slowed her horse to a walk. The other *Silren* followed her actions.

"Quite—it's been following us for some time," Haukel said. "It's a big one, too—might be one of Areyn's Yeth Hounds."

Cara nodded slowly. Although the Yeth Hounds had not entered this world in two thousand years, she had seen shadows of demons fly overhead. "They normally run in packs, but this one might be a straggler. Let's be prepared. Everyone nock your arrows."

The *Silren* warriors pulled their light bows and nocked their arrows. They rode into a circle to cover their flanks. Suddenly, they heard a scream overhead. A shadow passed over them, and Cara released her arrow. The other *Silren* shot at the dark shadow in the sky. It circled once before heading southward.

"Hold your fire," came a strange voice.

Cara looked down to see an enormous gray wolf standing before them in the waning light. She lowered her weapon. "You can talk?" she asked. "What manner of wolf are you?"

The wolf grinned. "A wolf that would be your friend, Cara, daughter of Silvain, heir of the *Silren*," he said. "You'd just be wasting arrows on the demon if they aren't tipped with adamantine."

"Demon," she whispered as she watched the shadow head southward.

"You're in a precarious position, daughter of Silvain," the wolf remarked. "Outcast from your kindred, if you approach the *Lochvaur* and *Laddel*, you'll be shot before you could surrender—or even if they did accept you, you would not be allowed to fight."

"How do you know so much about me?"

"Rhyn'athel is not the only *Athel'cen* who hears your prayers."

Cara and Haukel glanced at each other. Whispers ran through the other *Silren* warriors. "Ni'yah?" she asked. "I had heard rumors that you still walked this world, but I scarcely believed it."

Ni'yah transmuted into his *Eleion* form and grinned. "There are other *Athel'cen* who walk this world now. You've already seen Areyn."

"Areyn Sehduk?" Haukel said, turning to Cara in wonder. "Could this be true?"

Cara's face darkened. "Akwel," she said. "I knew there was something wrong with him. But how do I know that you are Ni'yah? There are many treacherous spirits wandering this world now."

"I know all of you here serve my brother, Rhyn'athel," Ni'yah said. "And I know what Areyn said to you before you could talk to Silvain alone."

Cara stared. "What do you know of it?"

"Areyn threatened to expose those of you who are Rhyn'athel's followers."

"You didn't tell us that," Haukel said, turning to her. "How could he have known?"

Cara turned to Ni'yah. "That was a private conversation spoken in mindspeak."

"You know that only an *Athel'cen* has this much command of the Wyrd."

"You could be Areyn, trying to trick us," Haukel spoke.

"If I were Areyn, I wouldn't trifle with a small band of outcasts," Ni'yah replied. "But, as you know, Ni'yah would. The choice is yours." With that, he changed into his wolf form and turned to leave.

"Ni'yah, wait!" Cara said. The wolf paused and turned around. "Areyn has control of the *Silren*, doesn't he?"

"Yes, he does," Ni'yah replied. "Even now, he may be bringing more forces against the *Lochvaur*. If he succeeds in bringing the *Elesil* into this war, I fear the *Lochvaur* and *Laddel* may fall."

"Why have you come?"

"I need your help—to stop the *Elesil* from entering this war."

"You need *my* help? You're an *Athel'cen*."

"Well, yes, and I could appear to Conlan as Elisila and tell him to not join the *Silren*," Ni'yah said. "Or I could destroy the entire *Elesil* army with a single thought. But I'll have more than enough to do explaining why I went to Silvain's daughter for help."

Cara laughed. "You're doing this behind Elisila's back?"

"And Rhyn'athel's and Areyn's," Ni'yah said slyly. "Call it a favor to the wolf-god—and to Rhyn'athel, but my brother knows nothing of it yet."

A mischievous glint entered Cara's blue eyes. Haukel stared at her. "You're not thinking of going along with this creature?"

"I think we should," spoke Tora and a number of *Silren* murmured their agreement.

"I have to agree," Cara said. "We are sitting idly by now, when we should be in battle. If we can turn the war, let's do it. We're Rhyn'athel's warriors." She paused and gazed at Ni'yah knowingly. "Besides, it's not often one has an *Athel'cen* in her debt."

CHAPTER FIFTY

Conlan, the king of the *Elesil*, awoke in a sweat. The nightmares had begun again. They were Wyrd-dreams, he knew. As the last of the first-blood *Elesil*, Conlan was gifted with the Sight. He had heard the rumors of the *Silren* going to war against the *Lochvaur*. Now, the Wyrd-dreams painted a disturbing future.

Each dream became more vivid than the last. A warning or portent of sorts, but Conlan did not know how to respond to it. The Wyrd showed him demons swooping down to destroy the kindreds. His last vision was of the death god, Areyn Sehduk, himself; wielding the *Fyr* and decimating the entire world.

Conlan stood up, unable to shake the dream from his mind. He slid from the bed, careful to not wake Rani, his sleeping consort. He shrugged into a tunic and breeches, not certain what he would do, but he could not sleep. The dream was a portent from the gods, and he decided that he would not stand idly by while the kindreds were destroyed. He left the room.

As Conlan entered the passageway, he saw the moonlight enter through the stained glass windows that lined the corridor. He paused and stared out of one of the moonlit windows. He had spoken to no one about these dreams. No one, save perhaps another with the Sight could offer him counsel. He wished that Elisila would guide him, but the Goddess of the Heavens was silent.

Battles between kindreds were common. Border disputes were not unusual, but the bloodiness of North Marches was. Conlan had never known the *Silren* to put all to the sword as they had done. That brutality befitted the *Eltar* and *Falarel* more than children of Elisila.

Conlan had heard of Fialan's murder and grieved for the *Lochvaur* king. While being royalty precluded true friendship among rulers, Fialan had been the closest thing to a friend that Conlan had made among the Nine Kindreds. Rumors had it that a *Silren* had murdered Fialan—rumors that Conlan had not believed until he had heard about North Marches.

He stared out at the moon which shone over the land. It was Mani, the moon that heralded change. Staring at the moon, he heard a wolf howl, and the face of a woman flashed in his mind. Her white mane streaked with silver and pale blue eyes marked her as a *Silren*. She rode on a steed, leading a score of *Silren* towards Caer Elesilren.

As he made his way down the steps, one of his personal guards, Hakan, was climbing up. Like all *Elesil*, Hakan had a silver mane and silver eyes. He wore the dark blue colors of the House of *Elesil* with three eight-rayed stars. "My lord, I didn't expect to see you awake," he said.

"We have a visitor, Hakan?" Conlan asked.

"Yes," Hakan said. "The daughter of Silvain—she insists on speaking with you at once."

Conlan nodded. The woman in his Sight vision. "Bring her and her warriors to my meeting chambers and offer them food and drink. Tell them I will speak with them shortly."

◆◆◆◆

"I don't know if this was a good idea," Haukel said to Cara as they waited in the *Elesil* meeting chambers. Cara gazed at the opulence of the room that confirmed the *Elesil's* wealth. They had walked through corridors paneled in maple with marble floors. Everywhere, the banners of the *Elesil's* three stars hung as tapestries along the walls. Within the meeting chamber, the only light came from the fireplace and two sconces along the wall. They sat on oaken mead benches next to tables as they waited. Servants had brought breads, sliced cheeses, dried fruits, and spiced wine.

Cara glanced at Ni'yah, who had taken *Silren* form. He smiled and winked at her. She noted that he avoided the spice wine and thinking it wise, abstained as well. "I think we're doing the right thing," she said. "It isn't often that one has the favor of an *Athel'cen*."

"We could all be put to death as traitors, too," Haukel grumbled.

The massive bronze doors to the meeting room swung open. They all stood as a tall *Elesil* with a silver mane and eyes strode in, his countenance dark. He wore a small circlet and the robes of royalty, but his clothing was simple as if hastily thrown on. Guards flanked him as he entered the chamber. He scanned the *Silren* party until his eyes locked on Cara. "You—you're the one I've foreseen."

Cara glanced at Ni'yah, who shook his head. "I am Cara, daughter of Silvain," she said, sounding more confident than she felt. "I apologize for the hour I've come to you, King Conlan, but I fear Areyn Sehduk may have the upper hand if we delay this meeting."

Conlan's frown deepened. "Areyn Sehduk?" he repeated, his mind going back to the dream.

"Surely you already know that is why we are here," said Ni'yah. "We have had the dreams, same as you. We know that the death god walks this land. He has taken control of our kindred."

Conlan stared at Ni'yah. "What of Silvain?"

"My father does not know it is Areyn Sehduk, for Areyn has disguised himself as one of us," Cara said. "Areyn fooled me for a time, but what you see here before you are all of the *Silren* who escaped his powers."

Conlan gazed at the *Silren* present. "There's a little over a score here. This is all?"

"This is all," Cara said.

A silence ensued. Conlan seemed lost in thought for a while. Cara glanced at Ni'yah.

Don't worry, I have faith in Conlan, the god replied.

"What would you have the *Elesil* do?" Conlan asked at last.

"Don't enter the war," Cara said. "My father will ask that the *Elesil* fight alongside the *Silren* against the *Lochvaur*. He will ask in the name of blood ties. This you must not do lest all is lost."

Conlan turned away. "You come to me in the middle of the night with an odd request, daughter of Silvain," he said. "One would normally consider what you ask an act of treason."

"And one would normally consider a first-blood who ignored the warnings of his Wyrd-dreams to be a fool," Ni'yah spoke.

The *Silren* gasped. "What are you saying?" Cara hissed.

The wolf-god ignored her. "You've seen the battle that may come. You've seen Areyn's demons destroy your army on the battlefield. You've seen the decimation the *Fyr* will bring. Tell me, King Conlan of the *Elesil*, would it be wise to ignore such portents?"

Conlan's eyes widened. "Who are you?"

"Forgive him," Cara spoke. "He is a rash warrior…"

Conlan held up his hand. He gave Ni'yah an appraising look. "Who are you? I have told no one of these dreams."

Ni'yah smiled, but it looked more like a wolf snarling. "Just a meddler, Conlan, but one you can't afford to ignore."

Conlan considered the wolf-god for a moment and then laughed. "Apparently not," he remarked. He turned to Cara. "You keep strange company, Lady."

"Indeed, he made a persuasive argument to me as well."

Conlan gazed at her and then shook his head. "We will discuss this in the morning," he said. "In the meantime, you and your warriors are the *Elesil's* honored guests."

◆◆◆◆

Lachlei awoke before dawn, her body aching from her fight with the demon. She lay in Rhyn's grasp, her body entwined with his. She could not move without wakening him, and yet she could not lay there forever. She gazed on his handsome face, recalling the vivid dream.

In that dream she had made love to him. Wild, passionate love, but Rhyn had been the glowing warrior. Even now, she longed to love him. A slight smile on Rhyn's face suggested he had shared a similar dream. Maybe the same. But what was he?

Rhyn felt real. She could feel the rise and fall of each breath, the heat of his body, and the twitch of his muscles as he dreamt. If he were something else besides *Eleion*, wouldn't he be less real?

The legends of the time before the Truce spoke of spirit-creatures who served the gods—creatures of the elements. Could Rhyn be one of those? She scanned him with her powers as he lay with her. If he were a spirit creature, she could sense no seams, no chinks in his body. Everything was as though he was mortal. And yet…

Lachlei was certain she hadn't killed the demon. *Fyren*, for all its greatness, might have slowed the creature down, but it had been the warrior god's sword that slew the demon. What had Rhyn and Telek called it? *Heath-stalker?* They had spoken in the old tongue—the language of the *Athel'cen*—the language that *Eleion* came from.

As she lay beside him, she grew drowsy again. She closed her eyes for a moment.

Suddenly, she was woken by a rough shake. Lachlei gasped, and a hand quickly clapped over her mouth. She saw the glint of Rhyn's eyes in the dark. *Rhyn?*

Quiet, Lachlei, Rhyn's voice entered her head. *Do not even mindspeak.* It was a cold command that prickled fear in her. She glanced down to see he was sliding his hand to the pommel of his Sword of Power.

Lachlei strained to hear, but could hear nothing save the wind along the plains and the sounds of the encampment stirring. But Rhyn was as tense as she had ever seen him. She took a breath, and then another. *What did Rhyn sense she could not?*

A sudden scream. Before Lachlei could react, a winged beast was on top of them. Claws, fur, teeth, and wings were everywhere. With a yell, Rhyn drew *Teiwaz*, and it plunged into the demon as it bore down on them. For a split second, Lachlei saw Rhyn's blade pass *through* her as though it didn't exist. The demon lunged at her, grasping her with its claws. Rhyn's blade moved so quickly, Lachlei could not see it. The demon crumpled to the ground in a pile of smoldering ash.

The other warriors stared at Rhyn. The demon's claws had raked through his mail, and one poisonous spike embedded itself in his chest on the left side. Rhyn gripped the claw, and with some effort, pulled it from him.

He sheathed his sword and turned to her as the color began to drain from his face.

"Rhyn!" Lachlei gasped and caught him as he collapsed. Cahal and Tamar were beside her, helping her lay Rhyn down.

CHAPTER FIFTY-ONE

The clouds blanketed the sky. A storm was gathering, and the wind had picked up. The *Chi'lan* army was a half-day behind now that they pressed the *Silren* northwards into the forests between the Great Plain and the Lochvaren Mountains. Areyn had ordered the *Silren* to march northeastward to avoid getting bogged in the slower terrain, but now, they were entering the wooded hills of the *Elesil* domain. The *Elesil* king, Conlan, would allow passage, considering the *Silren* brethren.

Areyn had ordered Silvain to request the *Elesil* kindred's aid. In time, the *Elesil* would join the *Silren* in the battle—but it was time Areyn did not have. Short of forcing the *Elesil* to his will—something which would certainly take power from him—Areyn had to devise another solution.

Areyn had ridden northwest towards the foothills of the Lochvaren Mountains to be alone. He used this opportunity to slip away under the guise of scouting ahead, but in truth, he was weary of the mortals. He loathed their very existence, for they reminded him of his constant failure. Rhyn'athel's creations lived beyond their mortal bodies; Areyn's creations could not. That alone reminded Areyn of Rhyn'athel's power.

But it was more than that. Much more. The abomination called Lochvaur was much to blame for this. Lochvaur's very existence gnawed at the heart of Rhyn'athel's and his contention. Yes, Areyn owned Lochvaur, but in many ways, he did not. Lochvaur was something beyond Areyn's full comprehension. He was a godling, and much more.

Yet, there was a way to shift the balance of power for all eternity. The Wyrd had shown him Lachlei. Imdyr was jealous of her—a foolish notion since Areyn felt neither love nor passion. Lachlei was a tool, just as Imdyr was a tool, and the inconvenience of mortality was worth what he would gain: the final destruction of Rhyn'athel's power.

Areyn could sense Lachlei through the Wyrd. *Interesting*, he thought, as he let his mind play across the seemingly fragile strands of the Web of Wyrd. Fragile and yet stronger than the strongest adamantine, they wove across the Nine Worlds, gathering on the World Tree that held the very fabric of the universe together.

The Wyrd came before Areyn Sehduk and Rhyn'athel. Rhyn'athel had been the first of the three *Athel'cen*; Areyn, the second. Ni'yah had been the third and last of the Wyrd's gods. There had been others, much older and less powerful, such as Fala, Harbard, Sowelu, and Elisila. Nine gods and eight goddesses had been Wyrd-born. None of the other gods had been as powerful as the *Athel'cen*, and their hatred and jealousy over the newcomers had been pronounced. Rhyn'athel and Ni'yah had successfully established an uneasy truce, while Areyn Sehduk eschewed all compromise.

Yet the Wyrd now twisted interesting patterns. Lachlei's Wyrd-strand was like that of the *Athel'cen.* Areyn had spoken against Rhyn'athel's creation of such creatures—because Rhyn'athel had tied their lives so closely to the Wyrd that they might be able to affect the Wyrd as *Athel'cen.* Lochvaur had been such a creature—and now, it appeared that Lachlei might be, too.

If so, then her offspring could indeed change the balance of power. Areyn considered the possibilities. Imdyr, too, was tied with the Wyrd, but how, the death god could not be certain. If she bore Areyn's sons, they too would be powerful. Except…

The Wyrd Prophecy.

Areyn gazed at the strands with his immortal eyes. Normally, no one save *Athel'cen* and the dragons could see the slender Wyrd strands as they coursed through the Nine Worlds. Lesser gods and mortals of first-blood lineage could see the Wyrd within their mind's eye as flashes of insight. There were places where the Wyrd touched—where mortal and god alike could see part of the Wyrd and the World Tree, itself, but warden dragons heavily guarded those.

As he gazed at the Wyrd, it became evident that the patterns revolved around Lachlei. Imdyr was a little more than a second choice. The question was whether Rhyn'athel had entered the war. Had the warrior god sensed the change in the Wyrd? Rhyn'athel or Areyn might have even been the cause inadvertently. Ni'yah, as much as he was the lesser of the three, was still *Athel'cen* and might have changed the Wyrd with his presence.

Yet Areyn suspected the change came because of either himself or Rhyn'athel. Seldom did an *Athel'cen* affect the Wyrd in another section than where he had touched. Areyn considered the Wyrd and the thread where Rhyn'athel's fate wove through. As an *Athel'cen*, Areyn Sehduk knew he should be able to read the Web, but the path that Rhyn'athel's thread now ran through was murky and twisted. It was as though the warrior god intentionally twisted the strands so they were not readable.

"You won't find him there."

Areyn stiffened and turned. "I was wondering when you'd finally dare to show your face, Ni'yah. I was beginning to think you'd remain skulking in the shadows while the real warriors fight."

Ni'yah chuckled at the insult. "Is that the best you can do, Areyn? We both know you're the one hiding from Rhyn'athel."

Areyn's gaze narrowed. "Is Rhyn'athel here?"

"Can't you see that far—or is the all-powerful Areyn Sehduk blind?"

"I think Rhyn'athel isn't reckless enough to confront me. Peace makes a habit of platitudes and soon it becomes peace for the sake of peace."

"I think you'll find our brother to be far more aware of your actions, Areyn. He is, after all the more powerful of us three. It is your army that flees from the *Lochvaur* and *Laddel.*"

"That will change," Areyn replied. "Tell *our brother* that if he has entered the conflict that the Truce is over and that I will do what *is* necessary. Even if that means the utter destruction of the Nine Worlds."

Ni'yah laughed. "Be careful, Areyn, or you'll twist on the World Tree, skewered by *Teiwaz*. You don't want Rhyn'athel in this war. And Rhyn'athel already considers the Truce over."

With that, Ni'yah disappeared, leaving Areyn to ponder the wolf-god's words.

◆◆◆◆

The morning sun came streaming in, awakening Cara. For a moment, she thought she was back in her room in Caer Silrenel. As she awoke, she remembered her meeting with Conlan the night before. Cara closed her eyes and let the warmth of the down bed relax her. Even before her exile, she seldom slept in a real bed because of her duties as a commander. Now, it seemed a luxury. She had been so exhausted after so many days of hard riding that she had thrown aside her armor and arming shirt and crawled into bed, falling into a dreamless sleep.

Cara had slept so soundly that she had not noticed that the servants had entered and replaced her garments with clean ones or that a bath had been drawn for her. The *Elesil* had a tradition of woman warriors and had spared her the humiliation of wearing a dress. The tunic and breeches were soft cotton in the silver and royal blue colors of the *Silren*. They had also replaced the quilted arming jacket and the padded leggings.

Cara shook her head. She was vigilant and would have normally wakened when someone entered the room. Now, she strode over to the bath that looked so inviting. Touching the water, she found that it was still hot, and slid into it. The miles of hard riding and evading the armies had taken its toll, and she allowed the simple luxury to relax her.

As she lay in the hot water, her thoughts returned to Ni'yah. The wolf-god was well known for being a troublemaker, even when he had the best intentions. But he was also the brother of the warrior god and allied with Rhyn'athel. If Ni'yah felt that she could do something to change this war in the gods of light favor, then perhaps her efforts would not be in vain.

Reluctantly, she pulled herself from the bath and wrapped herself with a thick towel. Haukel and the other warriors would be waiting for her. Glancing at herself in the mirror, she noticed how hard her body had become in recent months. Her long, white mane, streaked with flecks of silver, needed cutting again so she plaited it to keep it out of her way. Her face was striking, but not beautiful, and she bore the scars of a warrior. Her nose was offset from being broken twice, and a thin scar cut across her forehead where she barely missed being poll axed. Most men found her intimidating, being both a commander and the daughter of the king.

A knock on the door brought her from her reverie. She threw down the towel and slipped into the tunic and breeches. "Come in," she said as she fastened her swordbelt around her waist.

Haukel entered and smiled. "You're looking relaxed, Commander. I trust you had a good night's sleep?"

Cara considered her captain. He, too, had cleaned up and was wearing fresh clothing, courtesy of the *Elesil*. "Indeed—I haven't had a rest like that in months. I take it that our warriors have been cared for?"

Haukel nodded. "There's food and drink in a small guest dining room just down the hall. They're all there."

"Good," Cara said. "Let's go." Haukel led her to the room. The door was open, and her *Silren* were sitting around two tables with platters of fruit, breads, and cheeses. All of them wore clean clothing—some in armor; most were clad simply in tunics and breeches. Her soldiers rose on seeing her.

"Commander!" Tora spoke.

"Please sit," Cara said as she and Haukel moved towards an empty place at the second table.

"Where's Ni'yah?" Cara asked, scanning the room.

"Gone," said Haukel. "His room is empty. It's as if he never existed." They sat down.

Cara chuckled and reached for some spiced dried fruit. "I'd be tempted to think that, except we're here in Caer Elesilren, under the hospitality of King Conlan."

"What do we do now?" Haukel asked.

"Well, my guess is that we're where Ni'yah wants us to be," Cara replied. "I'm assuming that he doesn't expect for me to sit idly by." She paused and smiled slyly.

"What are you thinking?"

"I am a commander without an army, and the *Elesil* might need a commander," she said.

"Are you suggesting we lead the *Elesil* into battle against our own people?"

"No, I'm suggesting we lead the *Elesil* into battle against the demons," she replied. "The *Lochvaur* could use our help."

Haukel shook his head. "I don't know if we can convince Conlan to lending us a few thousand of his troops to attack Areyn Sehduk."

"Perhaps not," said Cara with a gleam in her eye as she ate. "Perhaps it's a matter of how we ask him."

CHAPTER FIFTY-TWO

After breakfast, Cara led her *Silren* into the *Elesil* great hall and halted. As the doors opened, she stared at the great hall in wonder. The room glistened with white marble floors and rich, exotic wood. She strode across the three silver eight-rayed stars of the *Elesil* inlaid in the floor. Columns of stone rose upward to a vaulted ceiling where clerestories, filled with indigo glass, mimicked the night's sky above. The nobles' benches lined both sides of the hall as it led to the firepit and dais. The firepit lay before the thrones where Conlan and his queen, Rani, sat. Above the firepit, a hole opened to the sky.

Cara glanced from side to side. Although the *Elesil* were a brother kindred to the *Silren*, there were marked differences between the two. The *Silren* tended to be taller than the *Elesil* on average and had pure white manes or white manes streaked with silver. The *Elesil* had silver manes, similar to the *Laddel*, and had silver eyes; whereas, the *Silren* had ice-blue or silver eyes. There were other differences, much more subtle, that had more to do with their culture and philosophy. One was a warrior culture; the other, mainly agrarian.

The *Silren* were never as numerous as the *Elesil*, but were greater fighters. The *Elesil* were more content to stay in their lands and obtain what they needed through trade. Both methods had served them well. Until now.

Cara strode forward past the *Elesil* nobles and stood before Conlan and Rani. Rani was typical of most *Elesil* women, tall, beautiful, and fair skinned. She smiled graciously as she looked on Cara. Cara nodded, now realizing how different their worlds were.

"Conlan tells me that you've come seeking the *Elesil* aid," Rani said.

"I have," Cara said. "I am Cara, Daughter of Silvain."

"It appears that your father has sent a messenger as well," Rani said. "He has asked that the *Elesil* join the *Silren* in defeating the *Lochvaur* kindred."

A low murmur ran through Cara's warriors. Cara held up her hand for silence. "Messenger—what messenger?" she asked.

Conlan's gaze shifted to a *Silren* warrior who stood among the *Elesil* nobles that Cara had missed. Cara's eyes narrowed as her gaze fell on the warrior. It looked *Silren*, but was not. *Silren*-like, it had a long white mane and ice-blue eyes, but beneath the armor and the flesh, there was something else. Something sinister. The creature met her gaze coldly. "Your father wanted me to send his regards."

"Gods—what is that, Conlan?" she demanded, her hand on her hilt as she stepped forward.

"What do you mean?" Conlan said in confusion.

The *Silren* messenger strode forward. "What is wrong, Cara? Or do you go against Silvain's wishes?"

"I don't know you," she said. "I know every warrior in my father's personal guard, and you're not any of them." Cara could feel Haukel's gauntleted hand grip her arm. She shot him a look. *Be ready,* she mindspoke to her warriors. Haukel released her, and Cara strode forward towards the messenger.

The creature met her gaze. "I joined your father's guard after you left."

"Indeed, I would say he made a poor choice." Cara used her powers to try to sense what was behind the body. She felt a hard, cold shove, and the creature's eyes glittered menacingly.

"I don't know what you are, but you're no *Silren,*" she growled.

"Nonsense, I am everything *Silren,*" the creature said, drawing closer.

The creature made its move, but Cara was faster. She drew her adamantine blade and brought it down on the creature, cleaving through armor, bone, and sinew. Conlan yelled, but the *Silren* warriors already had their swords out to protect Cara as she fought the beast.

"Wait, your majesty," Haukel said.

The *Silren* messenger shed its body and grew in size. What stood before Cara was an arch-demon. Conlan and Rani withdrew in horror as Cara and the demon circled. The *Elesil* guards halted and stared.

"What should we do?" Conlan asked.

"Have your men ready with crossbows. Do you have adamantine-tipped quarrels?" Haukel asked.

"Yes." Conlan's eyes glazed over slightly as he relayed the message via mindspeak to his guards. "We should help her. My men are at the entrances so it can't escape."

Haukel shook his head. "I'll come in if she can't handle it, but she's as good as a *Chi'lan* warrior—maybe better."

The demon leapt at Cara. Cara slashed, dodging the sharp talons as they threatened to cut through her clothing. Now she cursed her decision to not wear mail. She had not expected a fight in the king's great hall.

The demon screamed as she sliced through its talons. Black blood splashed everywhere, and the demon charged, its blood-red eyes glowing. Cara retreated, but the demon pressed her. As the demon brought its claws around she dodged beneath its wounded arm and leapt onto its back. The demon screamed, swatting at her. Cara plunged her sword deep into the demon's back and rolled off as it thrashed.

"Now!" shouted Cara. The guards let loose a hail of quarrels. The demon staggered and fell. Cara wiped the blood from her face and walked over to the body. She pulled her sword out.

"Are you all right?" Conlan asked as he stood beside her. "What is it?"

Cara nodded. "I'm fine. It's one of those demons that have control of my kindred, Conlan. If you fight with my father's kindred, you, too, will be under its control."

Conlan looked at the demon and shuddered. Even now, the body was beginning to disintegrate. "What do you need, Cara of the *Silren*, to stop the demons?"

"We must stop the *Silren* from destroying the *Lochvaur* before it is too late," she said. "We fight the death god, himself."

Conlan looked grim. "We will destroy the demons together," he said. "Consider the *Elesil* army your allies."

CHAPTER FIFTY-THREE

You stupid fool, Ni'yah remarked. The wolf-god had appeared beside Rhyn'athel as he stood outside of his mortal body. *You took on an arch-demon. Areyn will now know you're here.*

Rhyn'athel glared at his brother and then turned to watch Lachlei kneeling beside his body. *I'm mortally wounded, aren't I?* Rhyn'athel asked.

Yes, your body is dying, he replied. *If you want to get the full effect of it, you can reenter it again.*

But Rhyn'athel wasn't listening. Instead, he stared at Lachlei. *What is she doing?* he asked in incredulity. He knew the answer. Lachlei's hands pressed against the wound, power flowing from her fingers: she was trying to heal him with her first-blood powers.

That wound is beyond most first-bloods, Ni'yah said, a grim smile on his face. *I've only seen Lochvaur and Laddel heal something that grievous.*

Rhyn'athel stared. *Could she do it?*

Doubtful, Ni'yah said.

She'd die in the attempt, the god said in wonder.

Lachlei's gaze was on Rhyn's graying face. *Rhyn'athel,* she thought. *Rhyn'athel, if ever there was a great Chi'lan champion, it is Rhyn. He took the blow intended for me.*

Very altruistic of you, Ni'yah remarked sarcastically. *Are you going to let her sacrifice herself?*

Rhyn'athel glared again at his brother. *Did I ask your help?* He knelt down beside her as she focused on his wounds. The claw had damaged his heart, torn into a lung, and then ripped through the blood vessels. No man, not even his son, Lochvaur, could withstand such a blow even with a first-blood healer present. And yet, could he make it look like she had healed him?

He felt her power pour into his body, healing what she could, but Lachlei was getting weaker. Areyn would already know Rhyn'athel was there—perhaps it didn't matter how. He focused on her, pouring his own power into her to channel back into his body. Lachlei grew stronger with the surge, and Rhyn'athel could feel the pull of the mortal body again. The color was beginning to return to his face, and he let himself be pulled back into the shell.

◆◆◆◆

Lachlei was near exhaustion when Rhyn's eyes opened. He gripped Lachlei's wrist and broke their contact. She would die if she continued. "Rhyn?" she whispered.

"By Rhyn'athel's sword," Cahal said, not believing what he had seen. "Lachlei—he was dead."

"Not quite," she whispered. "Not quite."

Rhyn took a breath and then another. His miraculous recovery would look suspicious, regardless of how slowly he appeared to heal. "Lachlei, you shouldn't have done that."

"No, Rhyn," she said. "Don't speak. You must heal."

"No, Lachlei," he said. "I'm not what you think I am…"

"I know what you are," Lachlei replied and met his gaze. Rhyn hesitated. *You're a Guardian, aren't you?* she asked. *The gods have sent you.*

Only one god, Rhyn thought. *Perhaps it was time to reveal who he really was…*

Cahal touched her shoulder. "Lachlei, the watchers tell us Areyn's army is on the move. We're likely to get more of those demons…"

"Prepare for the march," she said. "Let me know when we're ready."

"Don't wait," Rhyn said, his voice hoarse. He still had the metallic taste of blood in his mouth and felt weak, but the link between the mortal body and himself had not been quite severed. "Lachlei, you must go now…"

"Rhyn, you're in no condition to travel," she said.

And who would protect Lachlei? Ni'yah added in his mind.

Rhyn fought to sit up. Despite his mortal disguise, he had to heal himself quickly and give Lachlei enough power to protect herself. With each second, Rhyn'athel allowed himself to regenerate. Areyn would probably laugh if he saw the warrior god and his champion, injured and unable to continue.

"No, Rhyn," Lachlei said and tried to push him back down. Her strength was returning. "You've been mortally wounded."

"No, Lachlei," he replied. "You don't understand, do you? I can heal. Areyn's demons want you. If they capture you, Areyn will have you."

A cold wind blew between them, causing her to shudder.

"We must leave now," he said, his voice growing stronger.

Indecision flickered in her eyes.

"Have I ever led you astray?" he asked.

She met his steely gaze. Something within those silver eyes told her he was serious. She turned to Cahal. "We're going." She looked at Rhyn. "Can you stand?"

"I think so," Rhyn said, scrambling to get his knees under him. The last surge of power healed him, and he drew *Teiwaz*. The Sword of Power glimmered in response.

"Demons!" They heard the watch cry out. Warriors were already scrambling to arm themselves and turning to meet the threat. Lachlei was fastening the arming points of her quilted jack.

"Don't bother!" Rhyn snapped. "Get on my horse!"

Lachlei turned to see Rhyn's stallion standing nearby. She shrugged the mail hauberk over her shoulders and fastened her swordbelt. "What of my own horse?"

Screams echoed from the army's flank. A dark wave like smoke rolled over the *Chi'lan* and *Laddel* warriors as Areyn's army of dead warriors charged the flanks. Demons shrieked overhead and plummeted towards the warriors. A demon—a heath-stalker—flew at them, and Rhyn slashed at its claws. The demon shrieked and hovered just out of sword reach. The warrior god cursed Areyn and swung *Teiwaz*. The demon chattered and flapped its giant wings to stay away from the god's weapon.

"I can't protect you if you're away from me," Rhyn shouted.

Lachlei's expression darkened. "I am Rhyn'athel's champion," she said. "I should be leading my people." She leapt on her own warhorse and drew *Fyren*. "To me! To me!" she shouted.

CHAPTER FIFTY-FOUR

Fialan reined his horse and stared. Despite the overwhelming force that gripped him, he saw Lachlei and halted.

"By Rhyn'athel's sword!" he exclaimed. "That's Lachlei!"

Lochvaur reined his horse beside him. "So, it is," he said. His gaze fell on the warrior who stood beside her

Father...

Fialan glanced at the godling, overhearing Lochvaur's unguarded thoughts. *Rhyn'athel?* he wondered. Fialan followed Lochvaur's gaze to a warrior who fought a heath-stalker. He caught his breath and glanced at Lochvaur—he looked like Lochvaur—or Lochvaur looked like him.

Yet, even at this distance, Fialan could see a difference. The warrior who stood among the *Chi'lan* was powerful—more powerful than any creature Fialan had seen before. Light glowed like an aura around him, and he swung a Sword of Power that glowed bright with each cut.

This is the warrior god.

Fialan felt the pull of Areyn's magic. He would soon be unable to resist and have to fight. He turned to Lochvaur, whose face was grim. "That is your father," he whispered.

"I know," said Lochvaur heavily. "And these are my people. I will have to fight both." He drew his sword—a Sword of Power, Fialan noted—and closed his eyes. "May Rhyn'athel forgive us." He clapped his legs against the horse and charged forward, swinging the great blade.

Fialan resisted the pull. *How could he fight against his own army? His wife?* Pain shot through him, and even as he resisted, Fialan found himself, sword in hand, charging into the *Lochvaur* and *Laddel* ranks.

◆◆◆◆

A demon saw Lachlei as she rallied her troops. It dove towards her as she rode forward. Rhyn charged, but they were already too far away. Lachlei swung *Fyren*, slicing into the demon. The heath-stalker shrieked in agony as she cut into the demon's wing and sent it plummeting to the ground. Lachlei turned her warhorse and charged the demon, leaping off her horse and plunging *Fyren* into the demon up to her sword's hilt. She turned, her eyes glowing fiercely bright.

The warriors rallied. Swords drawn, they charged Areyn's troops. Then, suddenly, the fighting broke off and the *Chi'lan* stared in dismay at their adversaries. Lachlei ran forward, *Fyren* in hand.

"Charge! Charge!" she shouted and then stared. "*Chi'lan*? What manner of devilry is this?" She gazed at the warriors who attacked—they were *Chi'lan*;

not *Silren*, *Eltar*, or demons. Areyn's warriors forced Lachlei's *Chi'lan* into a retreat, fighting as they withdrew.

Rhyn leapt on his own horse and rode to her. "Lachlei!" he shouted grasping her arm and hauling her up to his saddle.

"What is happening, Rhyn?" she gasped as he carried her away.

"Areyn uses the dead against us," he said grimly. "He uses my own *Chi'lan* in this fight."

"Your own?" she began.

"Our own," Rhyn said hastily. Another heath-stalker swooped down on them, and Rhyn killed it with a single cut from *Teiwaz*. "Areyn has brought a hundred thousand *Braesan*—Undead."

"A hundred thousand?" Lachlei gasped. "Our army can't withstand that. Sound the retreat."

Retreat! Retreat! she heard Rhyn mindspeak across the battlefield. He glanced at her. "Rally point?"

"The knoll," she said and heard him relay the message in mindspeak to the troops.

Suddenly, the troops parted. Two warriors came riding towards Rhyn and Lachlei. Lachlei gasped as she saw a warrior that looked exactly like Rhyn riding towards them—and another, more familiar face.

"Fialan!" she gasped. *What is happening Rhyn? Why does that warrior look like you?*

The warrior god made no response. Instead, Rhyn'athel turned his horse around and met his son's gaze as both Fialan and Lochvaur reined their steeds. Their faces twisted in pain as they fought Areyn's power over them.

I can't control it, father, Lochvaur said. *Areyn is just too strong.*

Fialan drew his sword. *Lachlei, beloved,* he mindspoke. They started forward.

Rhyn'athel closed his eyes. *Forgive me, my son,* he whispered. *I will free you.* Flame shot between him and the *Braesan*. Their horses reared and turned away. Lochvaur and Fialan rode past Rhyn'athel and Lachlei.

The warrior god turned his horse and headed towards the knoll.

◆◆◆◆

Fialan glanced at Lochvaur as they rode on. "That was Lachlei!" he shouted to the godling.

"I know," said Lochvaur.

"Was that…?"

Lochvaur's glance silenced Fialan.

"What happened? We should have attacked," Fialan said.

Rhyn'athel has spared us the pain of fighting him, Lochvaur said in mindspeak.

Then, we are free?

Lochvaur shook his head. *Rhyn'athel has not chosen to free us yet.*

Fialan closed his eyes. "Lachlei," he whispered as he felt Areyn's power grip him again. He charged at the fleeing army, cutting through warriors as they retreated.

How could the warrior god betray him so? How could Rhyn'athel betray his own son?

◆◆◆◆

Chi'lan and *Laddel* archers defended the rally point. As Rhyn rode towards his army, demons and Areyn's warriors chased him. On arriving, the archers let loose their arrow storm, cutting down all. Rhyn sent a wave of fire through the *Braesan* ranks.

"Rhyn! We must retreat!" Cahal shouted as they rode up.

Rhyn turned to Cahal. "Get her a horse—I'll try to hold them off!"

Lachlei stared. "What are you saying?"

"Get off now!" Rhyn ordered. He grasped her around the middle, and with one arm slid her off his warhorse.

Cahal offered Lachlei a hand up. "Come on, Lachlei!"

Lachlei ignored Cahal and turned to Rhyn. "What are you doing?"

"Go!" Rhyn demanded. "Get the army out of here!" He spurred his horse forward.

"Come on, Lachlei—take my hand," Cahal said as she stood watching Rhyn leave.

Reluctantly, Lachlei grasped Cahal's hand and swung behind the *Chi'lan*. Cahal turned his horse and urged it away from the charging *Braesan*. "Retreat! Retreat!" Cahal shouted as they fled the Undead.

Rhyn'athel stared ahead at the oncoming warriors. He could obliterate Areyn's army, but with the energy Areyn would devour with that huge amount of death, the death god could regenerate them just as fast. Rhyn'athel turned and saw the demons coming in. They would lose the army to Areyn if he didn't do something now.

Cold anger welled inside him. Rhyn'athel was tired of the charade and tired of Areyn. He reined his horse and stood alone on the small hillock to face the approaching Undead. The warrior god drew *Teiwaz* and focused on his powers. With a single thought, a wall of flame rose from the ground and raced towards Areyn Sehduk's army. He closed his eyes as he heard the anguished screams of the *Braesan* and felt them pulled back to *Tarentor*. The wall of fire leapt up, consuming the demons as they flew towards him. When Rhyn'athel opened his eyes again, he saw Ni'yah standing beside him.

"You realize what you just did," the wolf-god said, his brass eyes meeting Rhyn'athel's gaze.

"I bought us enough time to return to Caer Lochvaren," Rhyn'athel replied brusquely. He turned away. "Where is Lachlei?"

"You destroyed the *Braesan* and the demons—Areyn will know now that you are here."

Rhyn'athel turned to meet the wolf-god's gaze. Despite the mortal body, he looked like an avenging god. "You wanted me in this war, brother. Now you have me. Be careful what you wish for."

CHAPTER FIFTY-FIVE

The flame raced towards the *Braesan*. The fires spread from one point and fanned out in a giant wall of blue flame. The demons fled from it, but the blaze consumed them. The Undead warriors scrambled to flee the inferno, but it quickly overtook them, too. Screams echoed across the battlefield and then were suddenly silent. The flame took all: *Braesan*, living, and dead. Even the blood-soaked grasses and bodies were consumed.

Fialan turned to Lochvaur and saw the godling grin before the flames hit them. Searing pain shot through Fialan, and he fell unconscious.

◆◆◆◆

Areyn Sehduk stared in shock at the inferno as it raced towards them. He spread his hands and drew on his dark powers, warding off the terrible magic. Imdyr, who still rode beside him, shrieked in terror, threw her hood over her head and pulled it down over her face. The flames lapped at his shield like the sea against the sand before dissipating.

The god of death stared at the devastation. The ground had been burned to the very soil, causing it to blacken. What little of his army survived were *Silren*—he had used the *Braesan* as his shock troops. No godling could have destroyed his power. No god could have done this—save one—not even Ni'yah, who was *Athel'cen*. His mind returned to the face of his old adversary, and again to the warrior who rode against him. The magic around the warrior had been impenetrable; his face had been familiar, and yet unrecognizable...

Rhyn'athel.

The name of the warrior god brought fear into Areyn's soul. Only Rhyn'athel had enough power to bring pain on the god of death. Only Rhyn'athel could have destroyed Areyn's Undead like this—and yet, Areyn had not been prepared for such a confrontation.

In truth, Areyn Sehduk had not expected Rhyn'athel to enter the war so early. The god of warriors was usually conservative, preferring to bide his time. Areyn had considered Lochvaur's claims of Rhyn'athel's return to *Elren* to be nothing more than boasts, but now he began to wonder how much the godling knew. Despite owning Lochvaur's soul and even forcing his submission, Areyn could not quite control the godling, nor could he read Lochvaur's mind.

Perhaps it was time to deal with the godling directly.

Areyn gazed at Imdyr, who cowered on her horse beside him. "Well, *Eltar* bitch?"

Imdyr shuddered and drew her hood back tentatively. "It was the god of warriors," she replied.

"I know that," he snapped. "How do I stop him?"

Imdyr shook her head. Fear filled her dark eyes. "I don't know," she whispered. "Rhyn'athel is powerful."

"But not invincible," Areyn replied. "It took a lot of power to shatter my defenses and destroy the *Braesan* like that. How much does he have?"

Imdyr eyes became unfocused for a few moments. "Rhyn'athel is more powerful than before," she said. "But then, so are you."

"Is he more powerful than I am?" Areyn Sehduk demanded.

Imdyr shook her head. "I don't know," she admitted. "You have grown in power over the years. It appears you are now equally matched."

"Equally matched," Areyn Sehduk licked his lips in anticipation. "Perhaps the godling knows more about this." At that, he summoned Lochvaur, who appeared before both of them.

Lochvaur stood in his new shadow body, arms crossed against his chest, his silver eyes defiant as they met Areyn's. He was a tall warrior — nearly as tall as Rhyn'athel — and imposing with broad shoulders, angular features, and piercing eyes. His Sword of Power hung at his side. He was something Areyn had never fully understood — not quite *Eleion*, but not quite god. He was the epitome of Rhyn'athel's arrogance. As long as Lochvaur existed, he would be a constant reminder that Rhyn'athel had been the more powerful god.

"What is this creature doing here?" Lochvaur said as he turned his baleful gaze on Imdyr.

Imdyr reined her horse backward in fear. Areyn raised his hand in a motion to stop her. "She serves at my whim."

"Then she is a fool," Lochvaur spat. He turned to her. "You'll regret your decision, dark one," he said. "Though you've already twisted the Wyrd to your purposes, haven't you? I know what you carry."

Imdyr grew pale. "This is a dangerous creature," she said to Areyn. "Why do you insist on using him?"

Areyn Sehduk had watched the interplay with interest. Lochvaur had seen something he had not. "Perhaps because the son of Rhyn'athel may still have some use to me," he replied.

"He will lead you down false paths."

"Really?" Areyn smiled. "I never said I trusted him." He turned to Lochvaur. "What is Rhyn'athel's plan?"

"Why don't you ask Rhyn'athel, yourself?"

Areyn resisted the urge to use his mace to smash the godling's sardonic smile off his face. "Because it's easier to ask you. You can't lie to me. Why is Rhyn'athel here in *Elren*?"

"Because you're here," Lochvaur replied. "You didn't think Fialan's death would go unnoticed?"

Areyn frowned. "It was the damn wolf-cur, wasn't it?"

Lochvaur grinned. "Ni'yah? He had something to do with it, yes."

Areyn's gaze narrowed. "You know nothing?" he demanded, circling the godling slowly with his horse.

Lochvaur stood rigid. "Why do you think Rhyn'athel would share his plans with me?"

"Because you are his son."

"Do you think my father would give the enemy easy access to such information?"

"I think you know more than you say." Areyn Sehduk considered Lochvaur thoughtfully. The godling showed no sign of fear. "I think you're holding something back."

"How can that be?" Lochvaur replied. "I can't lie—you've said so yourself. You own my very soul—I am the good little soldier who obeys your orders..."

Areyn's mace came crashing down. In a split second, Lochvaur had drawn his Sword of Power and parried. They stood for a moment, eyes locked, before Areyn broke the weapons' contact. "You task me."

"You wish the truth? You know I can't lie under your power."

"The truth? What truth?"

"You shouldn't have taken me," Lochvaur remarked, sheathing his sword. "I'm a danger to you, and yet you continue to keep me in chains while I wait and watch patiently for you to falter. Every day I plan for your destruction, but the Wyrd hasn't shown me the way yet. So, I bide my time and wait. You know I will destroy you, and yet you give me the means of doing so. It would be better if you freed me and sent me back to the Hall of the Gods to await the end of time when you and I will meet. Each day, I learn more and more what you are and hate you for it. Each day, I grow stronger with the knowledge I obtain. It won't be Rhyn'athel who will destroy you, Areyn. It will be me." He smiled coldly. "All it will take is one slip..."

Areyn's eyes narrowed. "I've heard enough of your prophecies..."

"You could stop that fate, if you so chose," Lochvaur said. "But you won't because of your arrogance and your hatred of me and what the *Eleion* and *Ansgar* stand for. We can no more be destroyed than *Athel'cen*, and for that we are punished. You torment me to soothe your own pride."

"I've heard enough of your prattle," Areyn Sehduk growled.

A slight smile played across the godling's lips. He turned to Imdyr. "The death god is a poor choice for lovers," he remarked. "He despises you and all that you stand for."

"Silence," Areyn snapped. "Prepare your warriors—we'll be attacking Caer Lochvaren within the week."

Lochvaur's smile was mocking. "As you wish, my lord," he said as he vanished.

“Caer Lochvaren?” Imdyr repeated after the godling vanished. “It will take months to siege their fortress. It’s winter, too—we won’t be able to launch an effective campaign.”

“No need,” Areyn said. “I have work for you to do.”

“Work?” she repeated.

“Work that will bring the destruction of Caer Lochvaren.”

CHAPTER FIFTY-SIX

Fialan awoke to the dim red sun of *Tarentor*. The ruddy sky stretched overhead as he lay on cold sand. The wind howled over the desert hills and Fialan knew it would soon be dusk. He groaned as he lifted his head. This time, his body ached all over. He felt a nudge as someone stood over him. *Tarentor* was so dark compared to *Elren* that it took time for his eyes to adjust. "Eshe?" he asked.

"I don't think Eshe would appreciate that." Kiril chuckled as he offered Fialan his hand. "She's much better looking than I am."

Fialan laughed and then groaned as the big man helped him up. "My head aches," Fialan said as he gazed at the bronze warrior. He looked around and saw that other warriors lay across the hills—thousands of them. Many were stirring as Fialan was, blinking in the dim light.

"Rhyn'athel doesn't hold back much when he decides to unleash his power," Kiril remarked.

"Rhyn'athel? That was Rhyn'athel?"

"Who else could destroy the entire *Braesan* with a thought?" the *Shara'kai* replied.

"Fialan?" Eshe's voice came from a few yards away.

Fialan blinked. "Here—Eshe!" he shouted. His eyes were still unaccustomed to the dark world, but he could see her shapely form as she came towards him.

She wrapped her arms around him and kissed him. "I missed you," she said. He responded to her kiss, but then Lachlei's image still burned in his mind.

Fialan pushed her away. "No, Eshe, this isn't right," he said. "Lachlei…"

Eshe shook her head. "Very well," she said. She smiled sadly and turned away.

"Eshe…" he began and gripped her arm.

"Fialan—I can't compete with the living," she said. "As long as we continue to fight in *Elren*, you may see your wife again. It is torture, Fialan, for as long as she lives, you can never have her." She freed herself and walked away.

"Do you want my advice?" Kiril asked as Fialan watched her help other warriors recover.

"No." He sighed. "Where's Lochvaur?"

"Areyn summoned him," Kiril replied. "No doubt to make him pay for Rhyn'athel's attack." He paused as he watched Fialan gaze on Eshe. "You'll get my advice anyway, first-blood. I think you're a fool."

Fialan met Kiril's gaze. "I didn't ask for your opinion."

The *Shara'kai* grinned. "No, but I'm good at giving it. She loves you."

Fialan shook his head. "Damn it, Kiril, I love Lachlei."

"And I loved Samara, but death got in the way." He shrugged. "Lochvaur tells me we may die dozens of times before the war ends. You're no longer of Lachlei's world anymore than she is of this one."

"Wise words, if there ever were," came Lochvaur's voice. They turned to see the godling standing beside them.

"Lochvaur—what happened?" Fialan asked.

"My father lost his temper," the godling grinned. "We should have a few days of rest before the demons come back for us."

"This is hardly rest," Fialan remarked, looking at the bleak landscape.

"It will have to do," Lochvaur said. "We'll be sent back to attack Caer Lochvaren by the end of the week."

"Is Areyn growing soft?" Kiril said scornfully.

Lochvaur chuckled. "No, the rest is not for us—it's for him. Areyn lost quite a bit of power with Rhyn'athel's attack."

"Won't that mean he'll use our energy to sustain him?" Eshe asked, shivering.

"Perhaps," Lochvaur said. "But I suspect he'd prefer the life force of the living over us. He did receive some energy when we all lost our lives, but it won't be enough. Areyn will need to feed again."

"Then he has been weakened," Fialan said. "Surely, this is the time for Rhyn'athel to strike."

"I wish it were," said Lochvaur. "But Rhyn'athel's display had its price. I suspect that flash of anger took much from Rhyn'athel, although he might not admit it. He had to overcome Areyn's magic—no mean feat."

"Should you be saying this?" Fialan asked.

Lochvaur shrugged. "I'm telling you something Areyn Sehduk already knows. An *Athel'cen's* powers are not boundless—there are things beyond their abilities, albeit few. What looked relatively effortless wasn't. Both Areyn Sehduk and Rhyn'athel suffered for it."

Fialan stared at the godling in amazement. He never thought that an *Athel'cen* might tire or require rest. Yet, Areyn required energy from the dead—did Rhyn'athel use the energy from the living? The thought intrigued him. If gods required nourishment, then perhaps they were not so different from their creations. The *Eleion* and *Ansgar* were perhaps closer to the *Athel'cen* than he thought. "How much did Rhyn'athel lose?"

Lochvaur shook his head. "I don't know, but it was probably not enough to worry about. However Areyn is growing in strength because of the dead. With each death, Areyn becomes powerful."

"But Areyn destroyed the Nine Worlds—wouldn't that have made him more powerful?" Fialan asked.

Lochvaur smiled. "It did—and he still couldn't defeat Rhyn'athel and Ni'yah when they combined forces. Even with all that death and destruction, Areyn Sehduk couldn't defeat them." He paused. "But enough of this. Let's return to my fortress, if the demons haven't smashed it to rubble. We'll need rest for the upcoming battles."

◆◆◆◆

Lachlei rode silently beside Cahal. She now had her own horse—one of her *Chi'lan* had found a steed whose rider had perished. While Cahal urged both horses forward, she had turned around when Rhyn sent the terrible wall of flames into the *Braesan*. Their horses had spooked, as had the others, forcing them to flee in the opposite direction. When they both finally controlled the warhorses, they had turned and seen a glowing warrior on a hill, sword drawn, with fire pouring from his steed's hooves. The flames had formed a wall of flame that rose hundreds of feet into the sky. She gasped as she saw tentacle-like flames wrap around the incoming demons and pull them into the fire. The roar was deafening as the fire rolled over the *Braesan*.

Part of Lachlei screamed as she watched the Undead *Chi'lan* disappear within the wall of flame. She knew Fialan was among them. Although logically Lachlei knew Rhyn had to destroy Areyn's oncoming army, she was aware she was watching Fialan's death.

What had she seen exactly? Lachlei wondered. *What mortal could call that kind of power to bear on an army?*

The *Chi'lan* and *Laddel* army had stopped in their retreat, stunned by the firestorm as it rolled over the valley. Many stood in awe as the final traces of blue flames burned themselves out along the grasslands. Hushed whispers ran through the warriors as Rhyn and Telek rode side-by-side from the knoll to rejoin the army.

Lachlei looked at Rhyn. The North Marches *Chi'lan* seemed unusually pale and subdued. No longer the glowing warrior, but one who looked strained and weary, he refused to meet her gaze. The *Laddel* warrior, Telek, rode on the opposite side. She could see that Telek and Rhyn were conversing, but could not hear their words. Telek looked up at her, and Lachlei was struck again at the similarity between them.

Concentrating, Lachlei found she could understand the conversation. The words were not quite *Eleion*, but were of the ancient tongue of the gods, which the *Eleion* language came from. She frowned. Very few knew that tongue—her mother, Ladara, had taught her some of the *Athel'cen* tongue, but she had never heard it spoken so fluidly before.

"...it should be possible for us to reach Caer Lochvaren before Areyn has recovered," Telek was saying. "How badly do you think you damaged him?"

"Enough," Rhyn said. "It should give us sufficient time."

"How are *you* doing?"

Rhyn paused. He looked up as if for the first time seeing Lachlei there. "I thought you cloaked our conversation..."

"I did..." Telek began and then turned and saw Lachlei. "You understand me?"

"I do," Lachlei replied.

Telek began to chuckle, but Rhyn held him with a look. "Twice first-blood," Telek said, speaking in *Eleion* again. "We'll discuss this later." He rode off.

Lachlei gazed at Rhyn. "What were you so eager to hide from me? That you wounded Areyn Sehduk? Is that even possible?"

Rhyn hesitated. "I don't know," he said.

"What did I see back there?" Lachlei asked.

Rhyn now met her gaze. "You saw what you saw, Lachlei. I make no excuse or apology for what I've done. I sent the *Braesan* back to *Tarentor*."

Lachlei stared at him for some time, even though he did not elaborate. Rhyn turned his horse southwest and pressed it into a walk. Cahal looked sideways at Lachlei, who nodded. Cahal turned and barked orders to the warriors to follow. They rode southwest for miles over the rolling hills until the sun climbed high above them. Only then did Rhyn turn to her as he reined his steed and gave the orders for the army to halt. "We should camp here," he said at last.

They were on the northern edge of Darkling Plain. As far as Lachlei could see, it would be a perfect trap to leave them exposed on the plains. "Wouldn't we be safer in the timber?"

"Normally, I would agree, but today, no," Rhyn replied. "We'll care for our wounded here—tomorrow we must make for Caer Lochvaren in haste."

"But Areyn's army…" Lachlei began.

Rhyn shook his head. "We'll be safe until we reach Caer Lochvaren. We need rest," he said. He met her gaze. "I need rest."

CHAPTER FIFTY-SEVEN

"You look awful," Ni'yah remarked. He looked down at Rhyn'athel, who sat alone beside a fire in the encampment.

Rhyn'athel looked up, his gaze weary. "Thank you. I'll remember that the next time you take on Areyn Sehduk." He drank a little hot water from a cup he had let heat in the fire. The air was cold and he shivered, unable to keep warm. The sky was now overcast and it was beginning to flurry. Rhyn'athel could not remember ever feeling this miserable or suffering this much pain.

"Maybe you should shed your mortal body," Ni'yah suggested, sitting beside him. "Go back to *Athelren* to recuperate..."

"I'm fine," he said. "Some food will help."

"It'll take more than food," Ni'yah remarked appraisingly. "How much protection did Areyn have around his troops?"

Rhyn'athel shook his head. "Enough."

Ni'yah noted that he did not meet his gaze. "How much, brother?"

"Areyn was expecting me, or at least had enough defenses so that only I could destroy them," the warrior god said. "You couldn't have done it; his shield was carefully constructed — he's grown in power. It wasn't as easy as it looked to destroy those defenses to annihilate the *Braesan*."

The wolf-god sat beside his brother and handed him some bread and cheese with strips of dried meat. "Eat—it'll at least help your body."

Rhyn'athel took the food and bit into the cheese and bread before trying the meat. It was hard to tear off. "You could've brought better food."

"I thought you wanted the mortal experience."

Rhyn'athel met his brother's gaze and chuckled. "That I did."

"If Areyn's defenses were that strong, then he knew you were here," Ni'yah said, returning to the subject.

"Perhaps—or perhaps he only suspected and that was a trigger point," Rhyn'athel replied, biting into the bread. "Whichever, he knows I'm here now. Areyn will take this war to the next level." He shook his head. "I can't leave—not now. Certainly not with his demons hunting Lachlei."

"I could protect her," Ni'yah said.

"Maybe, but I'm not willing to risk it."

Ni'yah paused. "Speaking of Lachlei, here she comes. We'll talk later." With that, he left.

"Rhyn?" Lachlei called. "I've been looking for you."

Rhyn smiled weakly. "Lachlei—I'm sorry. I needed some food and rest."

She considered him. His face was still pale and he looked tired. "Laddel's scouts inform me that we're not being pursued," she said. "How did you know?"

"I am not what I appear."

Lachlei smiled slightly. "I've noticed." She paused and waited, but Rhyn did not offer an explanation. "Telek and you seemed to be having an interesting conversation, in *Athel'cen*, no less. Are you a Guardian or something else?"

Rhyn hesitated. "It's difficult to explain."

"Just like your son?" she asked pointedly.

Rhyn'athel met her accusatory gaze in bewilderment. "My son?"

"You never told me you were married," Lachlei said.

Rhyn'athel frowned in puzzlement. "I wasn't."

She stared at him. "And you had a son? What of his mother?"

"It's very complex, Lachlei, and I really can't explain it to you right now..."

"Why not?" she asked. "Is she still alive?"

"You were married," he pointed out. "You have a son, Haellsil."

Lachlei met his gaze. "A son isn't something you hide from a lover..."

"Are we lovers?" Rhyn asked. "I would *like* to be yours..."

"I have never hidden my love for Fialan," she said. "And now..." Her voice cracked and she fell silent. She turned away, unable to speak. Her mind was filled with a vision of Fialan. It brought back all the sorrow and pain of losing him. Her soul still ached with the loss of the mind-link. She closed her eyes.

"It's Fialan, isn't it?" he said.

She turned to him. "He's alive, Rhyn—I don't know what I was thinking when we almost..."

"Lachlei," Rhyn said patiently. "Fialan is lost to you—just as my son is lost to me. Areyn has given them shells, but their souls are tied to him as surely as if they were in *Tarentor*. They fight for Areyn now, and there is nothing anyone can do to change that."

"I don't believe that," she snapped. "You're saying that Areyn Sehduk is more powerful than Rhyn'athel? That he can bring back the dead and Rhyn'athel can't?"

"It's more complex than that!" Rhyn said, his voice rising.

"Is it?" she replied. "Explain it to me! Tell me why the *Lochvaur* should serve Rhyn'athel instead of Areyn. Tell me why we're fighting this war when we all go to the demon god in the end. Tell me why your son serves Areyn Sehduk, demon-slayer."

Rhyn stared speechlessly at her. When he regained his voice, it was in a low, throaty growl. "You would defy the warrior god?"

"I would—if Rhyn'athel is truly so weak," she snapped. "Tell me why Rhyn'athel wasn't among us today. Why we must face our own people in battle. Why Fialan is dead..."

"Fialan is dead because Areyn Sehduk slew him," Rhyn said, his tone icy. "Rhyn'athel was with you today, whether you believe it or not. Areyn has ignored the Truce." He paused, rage glowing in his eyes. "And don't you dare defy the warrior god again."

Lachlei found that she could not move. For the first time, she was actually afraid of Rhyn. But, when she spoke, her voice was steady. "Why such loyalty,

Rhyn?" she asked softly. "You've been betrayed by Rhyn'athel, as I have. Look where we are. Look what we're fighting."

"Because Rhyn'athel created you as he created the Nine Worlds. His blood runs through our veins, Lachlei," Rhyn said.

"Then he needs to take responsibility for what has happened," she said. She stood up and left.

Rhyn watched her leave. As Lachlei left, she thought she heard him say: "He has, Lachlei. He has."

◆◆◆◆

Imdyr rode across the windswept plains south towards Caer Lochvaren. Cloaked in invisibility, she rode past the *Chi'lan* and *Laddel* armies as they bivouacked in the cold fields under the graying sky. Imdyr paused and reined her horse. She guessed by the size of the army that they had maybe thirteen thousand. Most of the dead in battle had been *Laddel*, but the *Chi'lan* had taken a substantial loss.

She gazed on the encampment, trying to sense the warrior god. Areyn Sehduk had a right to fear this *Athel'cen*, if Rhyn'athel could sweep aside the death god's powers like wind through dry leaves. Despite the tremendous power Areyn wielded and her loyalty to the gods of darkness, Imdyr felt drawn towards Rhyn'athel's power. The strength and resolve was beyond anything she had experienced.

Imdyr hesitated. Entering the camp of her enemy seemed unthinkable, and yet, she hungered for Rhyn'athel's power.

You'll regret your decision, dark one.

Even now, the godling's words taunted her. She had given herself completely to the demon god. Now, there was regret. Areyn was right when he said she was just a tool for him to use. Like any tool, once used and broken, she too would be cast aside. In her lust for power and control, Imdyr found she had none. Areyn had control. She would have nothing. She hated Areyn now. There were no rewards for servitude—only death. Even the *Silren* who now served him from fear were slowly being destroyed to sustain Areyn Sehduk's power. And what use would she be when he was through with her?

Yet, Imdyr had seen hope in Lochvaur's defiance. Lochvaur had no fear of Areyn, only hatred. Imdyr still might be able to turn from Areyn's power. Yet, even as she thought this, Imdyr knew she could not. Not now. If she entered the *Lochvaur* camp, Rhyn'athel would learn her secret and destroy her. How could he not? There would be no forgiveness now.

I know what you carry, Lochvaur had said.

How could the godling see where Areyn could not? If Lochvaur could see, then Rhyn'athel surely could. Imdyr shuddered. She was twice cursed. She dug her heels into the steed and rode past the army towards Caer Lochvaren.

It took Imdyr a few days to reach the city-fortress of the *Lochvaur*. She gazed at the stone walls, keep, and the palisade fence wall that encircled the lower area of the city. The buildings within were wooden, not stone. She doubted that even the great hall or the council chambers were made of anything better than wood.

She paused now and focused on her face and hair. As she concentrated, she held the vision of Lachlei in her mind's eye. Her hair became red-gold and her eyes became silver. The trappings of her horse shifted to gold and red. Her own armor changed to silver in color and her surcoat was red and gold.

When the transformation was complete, Imdyr knew she looked exactly like the *Lochvaur* queen. Only the most powerful *Eleion* or a god would be able to see through her guise.

She spurred the horse forward and entered through the gates. The guards saluted her as she rode in, but Imdyr ignored them. Riding through the lower gate and upward towards the main gate of the city, she barely glanced at the wooden shops and homes, nor at the people who were preparing for a siege. *Lochvaur* soldiers were everywhere, but again, she paid them no heed nor bothered to salute as she passed. At last, she reached the hall where the *Lochvaur* council sat. She dismounted, thrusting the reins into a guard's hand and strode in.

The hall was dark, save for the light from the clerestories. It was late afternoon and the sun was already beginning its descent behind the Lochvaren Mountains. As Imdyr walked in, she saw a shadow move among the shadows.

"Lurking in the shadows as always, Laewynd?" she said, her voice dripping with scorn.

"I'm surprised you got through the guard, Imdyr," Laewynd said as he stepped from the darkness. His silver eyes glowed menacingly. "Even a second-rate *Chi'lan* could see through that disguise."

The rebuke stung, but Imdyr simply narrowed her gaze. She transformed into her *Eltar* shape. "It won't be me who will be called a traitor, Laewynd," she said. "Can you give me Caer Lochvaren?"

"Can you give me the throne?" Laewynd said.

Imdyr smiled. "You could've had it months ago if you had challenged Lachlei."

"If I challenged Lachlei." He chuckled. "Lachlei is too popular among the people; I am not. I had hoped she would let me handle the affairs of state—and for a time, she did..."

"You thought to make her a puppet since you couldn't bend Fialan to your will. Only she has proven as headstrong as her former husband." Imdyr smiled. "So, now you wish to depose her and take the *Lochvaur* throne? You have the *Lochvaur* army."

"They're not loyal to me—they are loyal to her. They would never turn on Lachlei."

Imdyr smiled coldly and changed back into Lachlei's form. "Then, let's give them someone to be loyal to. They want Lachlei—we will give them Lachlei."

CHAPTER FIFTY-EIGHT

"She has a point," Ni'yah said, as he watched Lachlei leave.

"Whose side are you on?" Rhyn'athel demanded. All around them, the warriors prepared for what little rest they could, oblivious to the fact that two gods spoke in their midst.

"Yours, but sometimes I don't know why," the wolf-god said. "Honestly, brother, she's right you know. You haven't been interested in this world for two millennia."

"The Truce…" he began and then fell silent. Even Rhyn'athel was tired of his own excuses. *Why had he abandoned his Eleion all these years?*

Ni'yah smiled. "See? It's different down in the trenches. That's why I've stayed here instead of *Athelren*."

Rhyn'athel gazed at the wounded and battle-weary *Eleion*. How different it was in *Athelren* with its shining walls, lofty towers, thick forests, and towering mountains. The peace of *Athelren* had dulled him while all this time, Areyn Sehduk had been plotting his revenge. "I have been gone too long."

"Indeed—I saw Lochvaur in battle," Ni'yah said.

The warrior god scowled. "I did, too," he admitted. "We had agreed that he should stay in Areyn's realm…"

"But not to rot," Ni'yah said.

"It was your idea."

The wolf-god said nothing.

"Do you deny it?" Rhyn'athel pressed. "I was against it, if I recall."

Ni'yah frowned. "Yes, it was my idea, and Lochvaur agreed. But it has been too long. Areyn will bring him back to fight against us along with the greatest of the *Chi'lan*. Regardless of the warriors you gather, we can't defeat one hundred thousand of the very best of your blood."

"Why didn't I see this?" Rhyn'athel mused. "The Wyrd showed nothing of this."

"Areyn is *Athel'cen*—same as you or I," Ni'yah shrugged. "The Wyrd doesn't reveal everything we set into motion."

"No, but I should've seen this—how many warriors have we lost?"

"Two thousand or so," Ni'yah said. "You'd have lost more if you didn't retreat."

"I should never have agreed to allow Lochvaur to go to *Tarentor*."

"Lochvaur agreed to go to *Tarentor* to keep the Truce—and to remind you that every day your people are in Areyn's hands."

"Don't you think I've thought about Lochvaur every day since his death?" the warrior god said heavily. "He's my son, Ni'yah."

"And the *Eleion* and *Ansgar* are your people. I would've thought you'd at least consider claiming the *Lochvaur*—your blood runs through their veins."

"Peace—the argument is pointless. The Truce is broken now. Now I must find a way to keep Areyn from escalating this war to the rest of the Nine Worlds." Rhyn'athel paused and shook his head. "Two thousand lost and now Lachlei despises me."

"She just saw her dead husband—she is confused. Give her time."

"Time isn't something I have," Rhyn'athel replied. "Nor does she."

◆◆◆◆

Lachlei left Rhyn, her mind in confusion. *Gods! Did he have to be so damn loyal to the warrior god?* She knew the answer. Rhyn was a Guardian, and that alone would make him beholden to Rhyn'athel. Guardians were lesser spirits—not gods, not *Eleion*. Something in between. Yet he had been eager to make love to her—something Guardians seldom did.

And she nearly loved him. Now her emotions were mixed. Fialan was here in this world. Even if Fialan were dead as Rhyn said, Lachlei couldn't break the vows she made to him. He had been her husband for three years. She barely knew Rhyn. She had not even known he had a son. What other secrets might this Guardian possess?

And yet—she could not deny her feelings for Rhyn. He had saved her life now countless times, and she had saved his once. He had been her counselor and her friend. He had been at her side since Fialan's death. But now Fialan was alive. That changed things.

"Lachlei," Cahal's voice interrupted her thoughts. "We need a first-blood to tend to the wounded."

"Where's Rhyn?" she asked, and then fell silent. She met his steady gaze. "Show them to me—I'll do what I can."

Cahal led her to the wounded. The numbers were staggering. Men and women alike lay with terrible battle wounds. The anguished cries rang out over the field as healers did what they could to staunch the bleeding and bandage the injuries. Laddel was speaking with Telek when Lachlei arrived. Telek looked up, and Lachlei found herself staring into brass eyes that spoke of terrible power.

What are you? she wondered. *A Guardian?*

"I am *Telek*," the warrior said. *But I am known by many names.* He turned his wolf gaze back to the man they were working on.

Laddel glanced up. "My son, Ladsil, is working with Rhyn. We could use your help as a healer, Lachlei."

"This way," Cahal said, leading her to the wounded at the far end.

Lachlei glanced at *Telek* and then at Cahal. "What is Telek?"

Cahal shook his head. "I don't know."

"He's powerful, whatever he is."

Cahal nodded. They stepped over and walked around many with superficial wounds until they stood before wounded that had been laid haphazardly.

Lachlei halted in horror. Many were not her own, but *Braesan* from Areyn's own army. Their skin was deathly pale, and their silver eyes held a reddish cast to them. The stench of death was unmistakable. Rhyn had been kneeling beside one, while Laddel's son, Ladsil, worked on one of Lachlei's own warriors.

"The *Braesan* have become mixed with our own," Lachlei said. "Damn Areyn for using our own dead!"

Rhyn looked up, his face grim. "I can't do anything for them," he said.

"Why not?" Lachlei asked softly.

"It's part of Areyn's dark magic," he said. "Look." He touched the man's arm.

The *Braesan* screamed in agony and writhed under Rhyn's touch. Rhyn pulled his hand away. Ugly red welts appeared where Rhyn touched him.

"By Rhyn'athel's sword," Lachlei breathed. "Would it do that for me?"

Rhyn shook his head. "No, but you'd damage him further if you tried to heal him," he said. "His body is Areyn's creation, not Rhyn'athel's. We can't save them." He drew his sword.

"What are you doing?" Lachlei gasped as Rhyn knelt down beside the man again.

Rhyn looked up. "The only thing I can to ease his suffering." He looked at the man, regret in his face. "Forgive me, Lochsil," he murmured. "Loyal warrior." With one quick thrust, he plunged the blade in the man's chest. The man shuddered once and lay still. His body became ash and blew away in the breeze.

"You just killed him," Lachlei said, when she found her voice. "You killed a wounded man."

Rhyn looked grim. "I destroyed the body of a *Braesan*—an Undead. He was already dead, Lachlei. He will return to fight against us."

She shuddered. "You would kill Fialan?"

Rhyn's face hardened. "Like I would kill my own son," he said. "Lachlei—I do what I must…"

But she had already turned from him and focused on her own wounded.

CHAPTER FIFTY-NINE

"We can't stay here," Rhyn said. A few hours after caring for the wounded, he had joined the other commanders in an impromptu meeting in a small grove of trees where the army had bivouacked. Each one of the commanders was a familiar face: Lachlei, Cahal, Tamar, Kellachan, Laddel, Ladsil, and Telek. Each one looked as exhausted as he felt.

The strain of destroying Areyn's Undead, combined with the battle, maintaining an impervious shield, and keeping the mortal guise had left Rhyn'athel with few reserves. He could not access all his powers as a mortal as easily as he could as a god. *So, this is what it is like to be mortal*, he thought. The seemingly endless supply of power was not there.

"Why can't we stay?" Lachlei asked, but there was no challenge to her voice—only weariness. She closed her eyes in exhaustion. Healing what wounded she could had sapped most of her energy. Looking around at the other first-bloods, Rhyn could see that the wounded alone had taken a heavy toll on them. "You said we'd be safe until Caer Lochvaren."

Rhyn frowned. He had spoken too soon and was now paying for his optimism. "I assumed that I destroyed most of Areyn's minions. He managed to shield some of them—primarily the *Silren*. He's gone to the *Eltar* and will bring warriors from their kindred."

"The *Eltar*?" Cahal spoke. "Damn those demon spawn! As if we didn't have enough trouble with the *Silren* and probably the *Elesil*."

"The *Elesil* are not our concern," Telek spoke. He met Rhyn's gaze. *I believe I've taken care of that.*

"How can they not be?" Lachlei asked.

"If Telek says they're not our concern—we can assume they're not our concern," Laddel spoke sharply.

Lachlei glared. "I can't simply take his word on it!" she snapped. "I have a whole kindred at stake..."

"Lachlei," Rhyn said. "Telek has taken care of the *Elesil*."

"How, Rhyn?" she turned on him. "How could one man suddenly change an alliance? He couldn't possibly travel to Caer Elesilren and back from here in the time necessary—it's almost a hundred miles."

Rhyn glanced at Telek, whose face was unreadable. He looked around at the faces. Cahal and Tamar exchanged glances; Rhyn knew that they already had suspicions as to who he and Telek really were. Laddel already knew Rhyn'athel was there, and there were whispers among the *Laddel* kindred that the wolf-god was among them.

"Lachlei," Rhyn said. "Perhaps it is time for me to explain something..."

"The first-blood *Laddel* are shapeshifters," Laddel said suddenly. Rhyn and Telek glanced at each other, but said naught.

"Shapeshifters?" Lachlei stared.

"We've inherited the ability to change shape just as my sire, Ni'yah," Laddel said. "It's been a long-kept *Laddel* secret. Telek transformed into a wolf to cover the great distances between us. He has spoken to Conlan already."

She turned to Rhyn. "Did you know?"

"I knew Telek was seeking to keep the *Elesil* out of the war, but I didn't know the particulars," Rhyn'athel replied, eyeing his brother. "What did you do?"

Telek seemed distracted as he and Laddel were engaged in a private mindspoken conversation. He glanced at the others. "I found a small band of *Silren* renegades, loyal to Rhyn'athel. They've spoken to Conlan already—I suspect Conlan will stay out of this war or if he does enter it, will enter it on our side."

"Do you think they would let us cross their lands?"

Telek nodded. "I think it likely."

Lachlei gazed at Rhyn. "Why didn't you tell me this about the *Laddel*?"

"He was sworn to secrecy," Laddel replied before Rhyn could speak. "We guard our secret closely—and now that you know, I would ask that you too keep our secret. It has given the *Laddel* an advantage over the many years against our enemies."

"Shapeshifters." Lachlei shook her head. "My mother never spoke of it."

"Your mother, Ladara, had the ability," Laddel said.

"My mother was a shapeshifter?"

"Indeed—quite a good one," he replied.

"While this is very interesting, it doesn't change the matter that we should be heading back towards Caer Lochvaren," Telek said impatiently. "That will be the first place Areyn will bring his troops once he summons the *Braesan* again. He'll wait for the *Eltar* and *Silren* reinforcements, but that still doesn't give us much time. "

"How far will he push us?" Cahal asked.

"As far as he thinks he can," Rhyn replied. "Areyn doesn't want to bring Rhyn'athel into this war."

Lachlei shook her head. "We could use his help about now. Our scouts tell us the passage through the Lochvaren Mountains is almost snowed-in. It'll be slow going if we take the King's Highway in our retreat."

"Then we'll have to chance the *Elesil* lands," Laddel said. "We'll only be running through a short cut before we enter *Haell* and *Laddel* lands."

"Risky—we might enter a trap if the *Elesil* decide it is in their best interest to fight alongside the *Silren*," Lachlei replied.

"We could send *Laddel* scouts ahead," Rhyn suggested. "They should give us advanced warning."

Lachlei turned to Rhyn. "If we do get caught, can you destroy the *Braesan* again?"

The commanders fell silent as all eyes turned to Rhyn.

"You're asking me to challenge Areyn Sehduk again," he said softly.

Lachlei's eyes were cold. "Yes."

"I was successful because I surprised him," Rhyn replied at last. "Even so, it took more power than I anticipated. What's more, he'll be expecting my challenge now."

Lachlei met his gaze. "Can you do it again, Rhyn?"

Rhyn'athel nodded grimly. "I can."

CHAPTER SIXTY

Imdyr walked from the *Lochvaur* council's hall. Laewynd was a fool — greedy and power-hungry — one who was easily twisted to Areyn Sehduk's purposes. She knew not all the *Lochvaur* were like him, but as long as there was one or two willing to betray the rest, the *Lochvaur* were defenseless. She smiled at the irony. A great kindred would be brought to ruin over one man…

"Lachlei!"

Imdyr turned to see Kieran approach. She looked at the warrior, trying to recall the names Laewynd had briefed her on. "Kieran?" she said. "What are you doing here?"

"I heard you had returned," he said. He stared at her quizzically with his one good eye, as though trying to determine what was different.

Imdyr smiled wanly. Perhaps this was not going to be as easy as she thought. "We need our army," she said. "We took massive casualties against the *Silren* and there are rumors that the *Elesil* may enter the battle."

"What about Laewynd and the rest of the council?"

"I was in the chambers talking with him," she said. "I convinced him that we needed the troops. He'll talk to the others on the Council."

Kieran stared. "We've never been able to get the Council to agree — especially Laewynd."

"Well, Laewynd was the stumbling block, and now it's all clear," she said smoothly.

"That's good," Kieran said. He paused. "How bad is the damage? Who's commanding the army now?"

"Cahal's in command for the moment," she said. "We're retreating toward the plains."

"What happened to Rhyn?" Kieran asked.

Imdyr hesitated. She did not recall Laewynd mentioning someone named Rhyn. "Rhyn? He's dead."

Kieran stared at her. "Are you all right?"

Imdyr began walking. The conversation was not going the way she intended it to. "I've been very tired," she said. "Perhaps I'll get some rest."

"No doubt you'll be seeing Wynne and Haellsil."

She nodded wordlessly and left.

◆◆◆◆

The *Laddel* scouts had returned telling Lachlei that the *Silren* were on the move again. More *Silren* reinforcements were only a few hours behind them. Exhausted, Lachlei, Rhyn, Telek, Laddel, and the other commanders roused the warriors for a forced march southward towards the Great Plains of *Elesilren*. As they rode forward, the trees soon became sparse and the mountains diminished into rolling hills. A cold wind blew from the north, making the slow trudge southward more unpleasant.

"We should find more defensible ground," Rhyn'athel said as he rode beside Ni'yah. "We can't afford a fight here."

Ni'yah nodded, glancing over at Lachlei. "She seems aloof," he said.

"I destroyed the entire *Braesan* army — including Fialan. Lachlei does not forgive me for that," Rhyn'athel said, using his power to make certain that none could overhear their conversation.

"Most unfortunate," Ni'yah remarked.

"In her eyes, I am no better than Areyn." Rhyn'athel fell silent.

Ni'yah shook his head. "I can't advise you on this, brother. This is something Lachlei will have to come to terms with herself. Logically, she knows you did what you had to. Emotionally, the rip in the mind-link is too new. Every time she sees Fialan, it becomes a reminder of what she lost."

Rhyn'athel nodded, pondering the wolf-god's words. "The others are beginning to suspect who I am."

"Well, you don't destroy an enemy's army in flames without drawing some attention to yourself. Frankly, I'm not surprised."

"Except Lachlei," Rhyn'athel remarked. "She of all my warriors should recognize a god's power, and yet she's convinced herself that I'm a Guardian or a very talented first-blood."

Ni'yah chuckled. "Indeed, those whom we are closest to we are often blind to as well. Perhaps deep inside she realizes who you really are, but she is denying it. After all, how can a mortal fall in love with a god?"

Rhyn'athel smiled ruefully. "And how can a god fall in love with a mortal?" He fell silent. "Despite your trickery to coerce me into this world, I must admit I've been away from *Elren* for far too long. I can feel their loyalty, Ni'yah. What's more, I'm not just their god anymore — I'm one of the *Chi'lan*. Their loyalty is not to some detached deity, but to me. I've experienced what they've experienced, and now I've earned their respect. By becoming mortal, I've become worthy of them."

"Ironic, isn't it?" Ni'yah grinned. "Despite the shortcomings, mortality does have its advantages."

Rhyn'athel chuckled. "But what to do about Areyn?" he said, becoming somber. "The *Braesan* are a concern."

"Areyn now has the upper hand," Ni'yah agreed. "We could create more warriors…"

Rhyn'athel shook his head. "Each warrior I bring forth will take power I need to fight Areyn directly. And each of those warrior's deaths will feed Areyn. I can destroy the *Braesan*, but what victory does that give me? Areyn has grown too powerful for me to directly wrest the *Braesan* from his control. And yet, I must find a way to deprive him of the dead."

Ni'yah grinned.

Rhyn'athel glanced at the wolf-god. "What are you thinking?"

"That occasionally, my brother, you show flashes of genius, despite yourself."

Rhyn'athel considered Ni'yah thoughtfully. "What did I say?"

"You must deprive Areyn of his dead."

Rhyn'athel gave Ni'yah a long, measuring look. "If I remove Areyn's source of power, I will weaken him."

"Indeed, and Areyn's penchant for destroying his own warriors could be his downfall," Ni'yah replied. "Returning a hundred thousand warriors from the dead takes power—power that Areyn must replenish."

"And he insists on controlling them, especially Lochvaur."

"Especially Lochvaur," the wolf-god agreed. "Your son is draining Areyn's power. But Areyn dares not free Lochvaur for a moment or risk losing control of a dangerous enemy."

Rhyn'athel leaned back in his saddle. "Holding back Lochvaur would take vast amounts of energy. That much energy would drain even me. Could Areyn be relying on something else to bring the *Braesan* to *Elren*?"

"A Runestone?"

Rhyn'athel thought for a moment and then shook his head. "Areyn wouldn't use it—it resonates too much with my own power. It might actually burn him to use one."

"The Gateway, then," Ni'yah said. "The Gateways are neutral ground."

Rhyn'athel nodded slowly. "If I were wishing to conserve my power—I would use the Gateways."

"Rather archaic, don't you think?" Ni'yah remarked. "And not very defensible."

"But very much like Areyn," Rhyn'athel replied. "Areyn uses what he can against me, such as it is."

"The Gateway would stop travel both ways—if Areyn is indeed using it."

Rhyn'athel smiled thoughtfully. Perhaps there was a way to defeat Areyn.

CHAPTER SIXTY-ONE

Kieran watched as the woman who called herself Lachlei walked down the path that led from the Council Hall to the Great Hall. Already, the city was steeped in shadows as the sun had dipped behind the mountains. It felt as though it was an ominous portent. Something was wrong.

This was not Lachlei. This was not the woman whom he had fought against in one-on-one combat for the crown. This was not the woman who spared his life. The woman he spoke with now was arrogant and aloof, something he had never seen in Lachlei. Nor had the war changed her — Lachlei had fought for Lochalan in battle before. Even when Lachlei had lost Fialan, she had not acted like this.

Now, the one who claimed she was Lachlei had brushed aside Rhyn's death as if it had been a non-event. In the past, Lachlei had not spoken of Rhyn in Council, and although Kieran knew little of the North Marches *Chi'lan*, Kieran knew that Lachlei had been close to Rhyn. He had seen Rhyn by her side at the coronation and in the Great Hall. She had even appointed Rhyn one of her commanders.

Kieran tried to summon the Sight, but to little avail. Like most *Eleion* gifted with the Sight, the visions came unbidden and in flashes. Now he saw nothing, but he trusted his instincts as a warrior. Those instincts told him that whoever this was, it was not Lachlei.

But who could he trust? Certainly not Laewynd, even if he had originally been against giving Lachlei the army. Kellachan was with the *Chi'lan* army — assuming he was even alive. The other Council members were dubious at best. Perhaps Moira could be trusted, but she was as political as the others.

"Is something wrong, Kieran?" Laewynd's voice came from behind.

Kieran turned around. "I just spoke to Lachlei," he said. "She's behaving oddly."

Laewynd seemed to scrutinize Kieran's features. "Perhaps she is weary from the battle."

"Perhaps," Kieran agreed, but even to his ears, he sounded unconvinced.

Laewynd smiled slightly. "Is there a problem?"

"I don't know."

"Perhaps you should accompany Lachlei with her troops." He paused. "For the Council."

Kieran nodded. "For the Council," he said.

"You will leave tomorrow before sunrise," Laewynd said. "I suggest you get some rest."

◆◆◆◆

It was late when Wynne awoke from a dream. The older *Laddel* woman, who had been Lachlei's nanny, threw her robe on and slid from bed. Seldom did she have Wyrd-dreams, but when she did, she heeded them. This one had been especially vivid.

The vision was disturbing. Troops were coming—*Silren* and *Eltar* troops from the north along with Undead and demons. They had taken Caer Lochvaren and put all to the sword. Wynne shuddered as she recalled the dream. It was clearly a warning—but how much time did she have?

She had heard Lachlei had returned to Caer Lochvaren, but Wynne had not seen her. It was odd that Lachlei would not see her own son. Perhaps Lachlei was preoccupied. Or perhaps the battle was going poorly. Her mind drifted to Rhyn. She sensed that the enigmatic *Chi'lan* would do all within his power to stop that from happening. But maybe that would not be enough. The demons and the Undead suggested the old enemy of the *Lochvaur* and *Laddel* had entered this world again: Areyn Sehduk.

Haellsil began crying in the other room. Wynne changed the baby, picked him up, and gently rocked him to sleep in her arms. His blue infant eyes had changed to silver now and he gazed at her with an intensity that she had also seen in Fialan. Haellsil had lost his father and would most likely lose his mother. And now, with the Wyrd-dream, Wynne suspected they were all in peril.

She put the baby back in his cradle and quietly left. Opening up the door to the main hall, she nodded to one of the few *Chi'lan* left to guard them both. They were sitting around the table playing a game of dice. On seeing her, they rose.

"Lady Wynne," spoke Kerri. Kerri was a younger *Chi'lan* with very little experience.

Wynne smiled. "*Chi'lan*, I will be out for a few hours. Can you summon someone to watch over the young prince while I'm gone?"

"Certainly, Wynne," Kerri said and paused, seeing the *Laddel* woman's concern in her eyes. "Is something wrong?"

Wynne shook her head. "I don't know, but I'm about to find out. I will return in a few hours."

Wynne left the *Chi'lan* and hurried out of the main hall. The skies were overcast and threatened snow. As she approached the main gate, she hesitated. It had been a long time since she had invoked the *Laddel* blood-magic, but she knew if she did not, lives might be lost. She slid unnoticed out of the main gate and continued past the shops and the second gate. The lower town was teeming with *Lochvaur* soldiers preparing for the march that lay ahead.

With so much chaos, no one noticed as the lone *Laddel* woman slipped out the lower gate and into the night. The air was cold and her breath rose as frosty steam. She glanced back once and then focused on her power. Wynne felt the characteristic twist in her stomach, and when she opened her eyes she knew she had changed.

No one noticed the small gray wolf as she padded into the night.

CHAPTER SIXTY-TWO

Fialan stared across the plains and his heart sank. In the distance, he could see the walls and keep of Caer Lochvaren glisten in the last of Sowelu's rays. He turned to Lochvaur, who sat on his mount, grim-faced. "They won't have a chance against us, will they?"

Lochvaur said nothing. There was really nothing to be said. The line of *Braesan* warriors stretched across the Darkling Plain like an impenetrable wall. The *Lochvaur* warriors would die at the hands of their ancestors.

"Maybe you can tell Rhyn'athel?" Fialan said.

Lochvaur shook his head. "Areyn Sehduk knows Rhyn'athel has entered the war. Areyn has focused his entire power on blocking me and shielding the *Braesan* from Rhyn'athel. His shield is impenetrable."

"Is that possible?" Fialan asked. "I thought Rhyn'athel was more powerful."

Lochvaur turned his baleful gaze at Fialan. "He is, Fialan, but Areyn is close to his match. The Nine Worlds are a universe of opposites, my friend. For every Rhyn'athel, there is an Areyn Sehduk. Such is the way of the Web of Wyrd. If Areyn were gone, another would take his place. The Wyrd strives for balance."

"But Areyn has grown in power."

"He has, but so has my father." Lochvaur sighed. "If there was one mistake my father made, it was giving Areyn the dead. Areyn uses us to fuel his fight against Rhyn'athel."

"But he doesn't use you?"

Lochvaur smiled grimly. "He can't. I'm too powerful, and I'd destroy him."

"What do we do?" Fialan asked. "Imdyr will bring my army and we will destroy them. Damn Laewynd! I never trusted him. I wish I had told Lachlei my fears."

"What's done can't be undone," Lochvaur said. "But there may be other players in this the Wyrd has yet to reveal."

Fialan glanced at Lochvaur, but the godling's face remained expressionless. "Other players? Have you seen something in the Wyrd?"

Lochvaur smiled slightly. "Perhaps I have."

◆◆◆◆

It was still dark when Kieran and Imdyr/Lachlei led the *Lochvaur* army out of Caer Lochvaren. Thirty thousand strong, they marched eastward toward the Darkling Plain into the glow of the rising sun. Once or twice, Kieran spied a small wolf or coyote following their army. It flitted through the grasses, barely noticed by anyone. Other than the wolf, there was no living creature for miles around.

"Where are we going?" Kieran asked, turning to Imdyr/Lachlei.

Odd, he thought. Even the magpies and camp-robber birds that normally followed a large army were absent. The sky was overcast, and a cold wind came from the north.

Imdyr/Lachlei smiled as she reined her horse. "We'll be meeting up with our own warriors," she said.

Kieran shivered slightly as he gazed on Imdyr/Lachlei. His suspicions were slowly being confirmed—whoever this was, she was not Lachlei. Her carriage was wrong for the *Lochvaur* queen, and he noted that she held the reins in her right hand. While Lachlei was typically ambidextrous, Lachlei held the reins with her left hand to have her right hand free for her sword. "Who are you?" Kieran demanded.

Imdyr/Lachlei hesitated. "What do you mean, Kieran?"

"I'm tired of this charade!" he snapped, drawing his sword. "I don't know who you are, but you're not Lachlei!"

"What are you saying, Kieran?" a *Lochvaur* commander named Rivalan spoke. He glanced at Imdyr/Lachlei. "Have you lost your mind? Of course, she's Lachlei!"

Kieran pointed his blade at her throat. "Are you?" he demanded. "Your game's up, sorceress! I know the queen of the *Lochvaur*, and you're not her!"

Imdyr laughed. "Very good, Kieran," she said, resuming her form as an *Eltar*. The *Lochvaur* soldiers gasped. "But it's too late for you."

Kieran raised his sword to strike her, but she vanished in the wind. Rivalan stared. "What does this mean?" he asked.

Kieran frowned. "It means we've been led out of Caer Lochvaren and have left the city defenseless…"

Rivalan turned to speak, but his mouth hung open in shock. Arrows rained down onto the *Lochvaur* troops. Before he could shout his orders for retreat, an arrow penetrated his gorget and he fell. His last vision was of a hundred thousand *Braesan* charging towards them.

◆◆◆◆

Cara reined her horse and looked down at the *Braesan* as they charged towards the *Lochvaur* army. She rode beside Conlan at the head of the *Elesil* army. The king of the *Elesil* looked grim as they watched the charge. Cara glanced at the *Elesil* troops. Forty thousand strong, but they could not possibly withstand the *Braesan's* full might. She compared the two armies.

"Gods," Haukel exclaimed, "Cara, there must be…"

Cara raised her hand for silence. Haukel glanced at her, but did not continue. He did not have to. Cara knew what he was thinking. The same thoughts were on Conlan's face as well. A hundred thousand *Braesan* were more than the *Elesil* expected. Even with the *Lochvaur* army, they were still outnumbered.

"What do we do, Commander?" Haukel asked at length.

Cara stared at the army as it advanced. "We're outnumbered, but with the *Lochvaur*, we might be able to trap Areyn's army between the two."

"If the *Lochvaur* don't turn on us," Conlan said.

"Do you have any better ideas?" Cara asked.

Conlan shook his head. "The Wyrd shows me nothing."

Cara smiled grimly. "I don't see anything either. I wish Ni'yah were here."

"The wolf-god?" Conlan asked. "That old trickster? Why wish him here?"

Cara made no reply. Instead, she gazed at the army. "Trickster," she murmured. "That's it, Conlan."

Conlan considered her. "What?"

"We trick them. Make the *Braesan* think we're bigger than we are," Cara said. "You know any illusions?"

"Battle illusions? Some, but they're not very good."

"Mine aren't either, but maybe together..."

Conlan smiled, comprehending her plan. "Do you think we could do it?"

Cara shrugged. "It's better than nothing."

CHAPTER SIXTY-THREE

"To me! To me!" Kieran shouted. The old *Chi'lan* warrior brandished his sword to rally the troops in the confusion that followed. Although most were not *Chi'lan*, they were still trained soldiers and quickly sought order in the battle's confusion.

The enemy looked like *Lochvaur*, but Kieran had never seen soldiers such as these. They were deathly pale and their silver eyes glowed with a red cast. Nor did they wear the red and gold colors of Rhyn'athel, but the black and red of Areyn Sehduk. Yet they fought like *Chi'lan*, and when killed their bodies disintegrated on the wind.

It's like they're not alive, Kieran thought. He cleaved through several before his horse was taken from under him. Forced to fight on foot, Kieran led the retreat.

A battle-horn rang out. Kieran saw several of the *Braesan* make a charge. Two of the Undead warriors stood out. One was a great warrior who rode through the *Lochvaur* army, swinging a great Sword of Power. The other was Fialan.

Kieran stared. "Fialan?" he gasped. He parried a blow from a *Braesan* and turned to see the dead *Lochvaur* king ride towards him. "My king?"

Fialan reined his horse; pain twisting his features. "Kieran!" he spoke through locked teeth. "Get the *Lochvaur* out of here!"

"How? How can this be you?"

A powerful force snapped Fialan's head around and his eyes glowed red as he looked on Kieran. "I am dead. We are all dead—all *Braesan*. Areyn controls us now."

"Areyn—Areyn Sehduk?" Kieran stared. Another *Braesan* attacked, and Kieran was forced to retreat. If this were true, he wondered, how could they escape? They were not far from the *Elesil* lands—perhaps they could head deeper into the Darkling Plain and lose the Undead in its rolling hills. He grasped the reins of a riderless horse as it ran past him and swung into the saddle. At that moment, another battle-horn rang across the fields.

Kieran looked towards the east and a large army appeared. But even as he hoped it might be the *Chi'lan*, he fell into despair. The warriors who charged wore the blue and silver of the *Silren* and *Elesil*. The army was huge—a hundred thousand warriors or more—standing amid an ethereal mist that swirled around them. The battle-horns rang in earnest now and the *Braesan* paused.

Kieran stared and his heart sank. "Rhyn'athel," he muttered. "May I die well."

◆◆◆◆

Areyn gazed hungrily at the open gates of Caer Lochvaren. A few thousand soldiers were all that was left. He would feed tonight; relish in the final deaths of the *Lochvaur*. When they had destroyed Caer Lochvaren and razed it to the ground, he would turn on the *Chi'lan* and *Laddel* army and feed from them. And there would be nothing *Rhyn'athel* could do to stop him.

His *Braesan* would finish the *Lochvaur* army. Imdyr was gathering his *Eltar* army. He would then turn on the other *Eleion* and eventually the *Ansgar*, finally destroying Rhyn'athel's hold on *Elren*.

What do you want us to do, my lord? Flayer asked. *They are unprotected.*

Areyn considered the arch-demon in amusement. "Raze the city. Put everyone to the sword." He paused. "But bring me Laewynd. Alive."

◆◆◆◆

Wynne fled as quickly as her wolf legs could carry her. She did not stay to see the *Lochvaur's* army obliteration nor did she pause until she entered Caer Lochvaren. Heedless of the guards who tried to stop her from entering in wolf form, she fled through the lower town and halted only when she entered an alleyway near the merchant shops. Wynne waited as the soldiers ran past and transmuted into her *Laddel* form. She continued past the main gates and into the great hall. The few *Chi'lan* who had stayed behind to guard Lachlei's son were drinking and playing games.

"Wynne!" Kerri said, spying the *Laddel* woman. "Where have you been?"

"We have no time," Wynne said. "The army is being destroyed as we speak. Caer Lochvaren is defenseless—we must leave now!"

Another *Chi'lan* named Tragar laughed. "Wynne, what do you mean?"

"We must leave now!" Wynne said, pushing by them and entering Lachlei's quarters to pick up Haellsil and some items.

Kerri followed her inside. "Why? I heard Lachlei was with our troops."

Wynne whirled around. "That was not Lachlei. It was a shapeshifter—an *Eltar* sorceress who serves Areyn Sehduk."

Kerri stared at Wynne. "Are you insane? Of course that was Lachlei."

Suddenly an explosion threw them to the ground. Wynne clutched Haellsil desperately to prevent him from falling. The infant began crying.

"What in the gods' names?" Kerri exclaimed.

Tragar threw open the door. "We're under attack!"

"Attack?" Kerri gasped and glanced at Wynne who nodded.

"We won't be able to win this. There's a secret passage that leads out of the city," Wynne said. "Without the army, Caer Lochvaren is indefensible."

Kerri nodded. "Do you know the way?"

"I do," Wynne said. "Gather the *Chi'lan* and anyone else you can find and follow me."

◆◆◆◆

"What is going on?" Laewynd demanded as the demons dragged him before Areyn.

Areyn smiled condescendingly. He wondered how blind Laewynd actually was to the true nature of what held him. The demons had assumed *Silren* bodies—the guise was incomplete, and even a *Lochvaur* without a drop of god's blood in his veins would have seen it.

But Laewynd was blinded by greed. Areyn had seen this before in many men and used their desires to twist them to his own end. At last, the death god would taste the High Council's blood.

"You promised!" he whined. "You promised I'd be king over Caer Lochvaren."

"And so you are," Areyn said. "You are king over all you survey." He laughed.

Laewynd shuddered. "That *Eltar* bitch…"

"Has done my bidding," Areyn said. "As you will serve me one last time."

The roar of demon flame drowned out Laewynd's screams.

◆◆◆◆

Flames engulfed Caer Lochvaren as the demons descended on the *Lochvaur* city. The *Silren* rode through the gates, slaughtering anyone who dared oppose them. Demons attacked from above.

"There's a portal that leads into the mountains!" Wynne shouted above the roar. People were following her and the few *Chi'lan* guard, hoping to escape the slaughter as the fire swept across the buildings.

Wynne held Haellsil close to her. They had made their way through the back alleys to where the keep stood. "Tragar, there is a passage which leads from the keep to a cave within the mountains."

"To me! To me!" Kerri shouted as another volley of fire rained down and she saw people flee in panic. "Gods! We've got to get people out of here!"

Wynne shook her head. "*Chi'lan*, the city is already lost."

"I don't believe that," said Tragar. "Kerri, Garhan, you take Wynne and Lachlei's son to the passage. Zars, Niels, and I will round up whoever we can." He led the other two *Chi'lan* warriors away.

Kerri's grim expression told Wynne that she did not believe they would see Tragar or the others again.

"I'm sorry, Kerri," Wynne said. "I only wish I had found out in time."

Kerri paused as they entered the keep. People pressed around them as Kerri threw open the doors to the keep. "It's all right. If he can find a way to get out, he will. Tragar is *Chi'lan*."

Tragar was Chi'lan, but even a Chi'lan would not survive, Wynne thought darkly as the crowd jostled her towards the escape tunnel. She said nothing of her thoughts, instead winding her way down the stairs that were carved from the native stone. It was slick with moss, and Wynne held Haellsil close as she stepped downward. One fall and she was likely to never stand up again with the throng pushing around her.

Darkness swallowed them. Wynne could feel the panic rise within her until her eyes adjusted. She felt a firm hand and looked to see Kerri pulling her along. "Come on, Wynne, we'll be out of here soon."

The sound of the battle became muffled and then—nothing. The silence was eerie. All Wynne could hear were the ragged breaths of those around them. *How far?* she wondered.

"There's a door!" came a voice. Wynne could barely discern oaken doors ahead. She watched as several warriors pulled the bar away from the doors. They pushed, and a crack of light streamed in. The crowd surged and shoved the doors open. Wynne nearly stumbled as the throng forced her out and into the blinding light of morning. She nearly wept to see the red rays of Sowelu as it crested the mountains and feel the cold mountain air. They stood amid the pines as more *Lochvaur* left the tunnel.

"You're all right," said Kerri. Wynne touched her face and realized she was weeping. Haellsil began crying.

Wynne picked up a skin of milk she had brought. "I'm all right," she said. Though where they would go, she had no idea.

◆◆◆◆

Lachlei reined her horse and gazed into the valley where, just beyond, lay the shining walls of Caer Lochvaren. She turned to Rhyn and smiled. "Gods, Rhyn, it'll be good to be behind Caer Lochvaren's walls again."

Rhyn returned the smile, but he was not as certain. Something was nagging him, even though his connection to the Wyrd seemingly showed everything to be all right. Something was wrong, but he could not place what it was.

Telek met his gaze. *What do you suspect?* His wolf eyes mirrored his concern.

I don't know, Rhyn said. Areyn's power was growing, but how he was not sure. They continued riding into the valley, apparently unchallenged.

The valley was actually a series of hills that led to the plain which Caer Lochvaren overlooked. The approach was concealed—if one did not know that the city was there, it could be easily missed.

Even as they rode, tension began to mount. Rhyn said nothing, but continued to reach out with his senses, trying to discern something wrong. He felt Areyn's shields and found them impenetrable. *Was that even possible?* he wondered.

It was when they climbed the hill that overlooked the valley into Caer Lochvaren that both Lachlei and Rhyn reined their horses in disbelief. Smoke rose over what had been Caer Lochvaren. The gates were ripped asunder and the walls laid low.

"By Rhyn'athel's sword!" gasped Lachlei. "Areyn has been here!"

CHAPTER SIXTY-FOUR

The *Elesil* and *Silren* army rode down the hill into the battle. Kieran turned to fight the next *Braesan*, but a curious thing happened. The *Braesan* began to retreat. The *Lochvaur* soldiers stared in puzzlement as the Undead withdrew.

"What is this? A trap?" Kieran said aloud. The other *Lochvaur* look no less puzzled. Some began pursuing the fleeing *Braesan*; others stood as Kieran did, confused by the Undead's actions. The *Braesan* had the advantage—what were they doing?

"Rhyn'athel! Rhyn'athel!" A *Silren* woman led a charge right into the *Braesan* lines, swinging her broadsword.

"They're with us!" Kieran exclaimed. "To me! To me! Warriors of Rhyn'athel!"

The *Lochvaur* soldiers took up the cry. "Rhyn'athel! Rhyn'athel!" They charged the *Braesan*. Caught between two armies, the *Braesan* fell back. Then, as suddenly as the *Braesan* appeared, they disappeared.

"Gods! What manner of devilry is this?" Mirin spoke. She was one of the *Lochvaur* soldiers standing beside Kieran.

"Perhaps none," Kieran said as he watched the mist disappear and the *Elesil* ranks shrink in number. "This is first-blood doing, or I'm not a *Chi'lan*. I have heard of such illusions, but I have never seen them." He stared at the woman who rode towards him. She was a warrior among warriors, even though her white hair and blue eyes distinguished her as *Silren*. A warrior bearing an *Elesil* surcoat rode beside her. His bearing suggested first-blood or at least nobility.

"Who is she?" Mirin whispered.

Kieran shook his head. "She's *Chi'lan*."

"She can't be, she's *Silren*," the soldier replied.

Kieran shook his head. "*Silren* or not, she's *Chi'lan*," he said. "I'd bet my life on that—she bears the look of one who serves Rhyn'athel."

"Who's in charge?" the woman called as she rode forward. The *Elesil* rode beside her.

"I am," Kieran said. She turned her ice-blue eyes on him, and he repressed a shudder. She was indeed *Chi'lan*. Only Lachlei held more power in her gaze.

"The *Lochvaur* owe you a debit of gratitude," he said. "I am Kieran, *Chi'lan* warrior and member of the *Lochvaur* High Council."

"I am Cara, daughter of Silvain." Cara turned to the Elesil warrior. "This is Conlan, king of the *Elesil*. We were told you needed help."

"That we did. If you hadn't arrived, we would've been destroyed."

Cara gazed over the soldiers. "Where's your queen? Where are the *Chi'lan*?"

"I don't know. We were led this way by a shapeshifter posing as Lachlei," Kieran said. "She led us into this trap."

Cara glanced at Conlan. Alarm glowed in the *Elesil* king's eyes. "What about Caer Lochvaren?"

Kieran's eyes widened as he realized the implications. "By Rhyn'athel's sword!"

"Gather what warriors you can—we have a hard ride ahead," Cara said. "Hopefully, we're not too late."

◆◆◆◆

Rhyn reined his horse and stared at the *Braesan* materializing before the army. The *Laddel* and *Chi'lan* army were caught between the Areyn's army of living and his army of *Braesan*. The *Chi'lan* and *Laddel* were thrown into confusion. "How?" he roared. "Damn him! Damn Areyn and his demon spawn!"

"It's a trap!" Lachlei shouted.

"Rhyn'athel! Rhyn'athel!" Cahal shouted. "Charge!" The *Chi'lan* commander broke from the other commanders with sword brandished, leading a charge directly at the *Braesan*. The *Braesan* attacked and forced them into a retreat.

Ni'yah reined his horse beside his brother, his brass eyes wide in shock. "How could we have not seen this?"

Rhyn'athel made no reply. For the first time, he felt completely helpless against Areyn. He focused his powers on the *Braesan* army, but this time he was met with a strong rebuff. He turned his powers on the *Silren* and *Eltar*, and still nothing.

"Brother!" shouted Ni'yah.

Rhyn'athel shook his head.

Lachlei rode up, *Fyren* drawn and already bloody. "Do something!"

"I'm trying!" Rhyn'athel turned to Ni'yah. "We must break his link to *Tarentor*, it's the only way."

Lachlei glanced at them. "While you argue, my army is getting slaughtered." She brandished *Fyren*. "To me! To me!" she shouted, clapping her legs against the warhorse's sides.

"What are you doing?" Rhyn demanded.

"I'm leading us out of here!" she shouted and took off.

"No! Lachlei! Wait!" Rhyn shouted, but she was already out of earshot. The *Braesan* were driving her army towards the gates of Caer Lochvaren where the *Silren* and *Eltar* waited. Rhyn knew that she would try to turn the army eastward to evade the trap. It was risky and required greater speed.

Ni'yah grasped Rhyn'athel's arm. "Leave her! If we have a chance to stop them, it's now. Both our powers combined."

Rhyn'athel nodded and drew *Teiwaz*. Ni'yah drew his own sword, *Dagaz* and crossed it against the warrior god's own blade. Flames leapt from the two *Athel'cen* swords and raced towards the *Braesan*.

◆◆◆◆

"Lachlei!" Cahal shouted as Lachlei rode to the front lines. Cahal was still on his warhorse, but she could see both he and his horse were injured.

"Cahal!" Lachlei said. "Retreat! East!"

"East?" Cahal repeated. He paused. "Lachlei, look! By the gods of light—what is that?" She followed his line of sight to the hill she had left.

Lachlei stared as well. Two glowing warriors sat on their steeds with swords crossed, flames racing towards the *Braesan* as they advanced. But the flames halted before the Undead troops. They did not touch the enemy lines, but the enemy could not advance.

A scream came from above. Lachlei looked up to see demons appear overhead. One flew right for her. Sheer chaos followed. Her warhorse reared and threw her to the ground. She rolled and within moments, the demon was on top of her. Lachlei thrust *Fyren* upward as the arch-demon slashed down on her. A poisonous talon slashed through her armor and grazed her skin. She slid from the demon's grasp and turned to face it.

"Behind you!" shouted Cahal, but it was too late.

A blow from behind hit her helm and she fell to her knees stunned. The poison began to burn in her veins. She fell unconscious and knew no more.

◆◆◆◆

"Lachlei!" Rhyn'athel saw the demons swoop towards her. He broke contact with Ni'yah's sword and spurred his horse forward.

"Rhyn'athel! What are you doing?" Ni'yah shouted.

Rhyn'athel turned back. For a moment, he looked as if he would answer. Instead, he rode through the enemy to reach Lachlei. He arrived to see the demon grasp her and disappear.

"NO!"

The rage the warrior god felt was indescribable. He unleashed his power, slamming it against Areyn's shields, but to little avail. Rhyn'athel was weakening—he could feel it with each death—his power was slipping from him and slowly feeding Areyn Sehduk.

"What are you doing?" Ni'yah said, riding now beside him. "She's gone."

"No, she's not!" Rhyn'athel said, his eyes glowing.

"Even if she isn't, we're being destroyed."

"Lead the army away," Rhyn'athel said. "I must find her."

"Don't be a fool! I can't stand up to Areyn!" Ni'yah snapped.

"You'll have to until I return." Suddenly, he was gone, and the entire *Eleion* army stood twenty miles away on Darkling Plain. The *Braesan*, the demons, the *Eltar*, and the *Silren* were gone. Instead, the *Chi'lan* and the *Laddel* were now looking at the *Elesil* and *Lochvaur* army.

"By Rhyn'athel's mane!" Cahal said, pulling his helm off and staring the two armies. He turned to Telek. "Rhyn did this, didn't he?"

Telek smiled grimly. "Yes, he did. He's gone after Lachlei. Gather what's left of our army. Rhyn has given us some time, but not much."

CHAPTER SIXTY-FIVE

Lachlei awoke in chains. A sharp pain knifed through her shoulder as she moved, bringing her back to consciousness. She groaned. Her stomach was queasy, and she had a throbbing headache. Her last memory was fighting one of the demons when she was clubbed from behind. Now she lay in the mud, covered with blood and dirt. She was in an encampment with tents around her. *Eleion* warriors with dark manes and dark eyes strode past her, a few glancing down and smirking as they saw her pull against the chain.

Without a distinguishing landmark, she had no idea where she was, except in a forest. She could be near the Great Plains of *Elesilren* or further away. She knew that she was in the enemy's camp, but saw neither *Braesan* nor *Silren*. These *Eltar*, she suspected, were reinforcements.

She moved and became violently ill, vomiting. The pain in her shoulder stabbed through her. *Poison,* she thought. *The demon used poison. But why did it keep her alive?*

"So, this is the great Lachlei," spoke a sardonic voice.

Lachlei tried to focus on the wound in her shoulder, but found she could not heal it. She was either too weak or the demon poison counteracted her magic. Instead, she looked up, wiping her eyes clear of the mud with her good hand. The manacle pulled against her and she frowned. Whatever the reason, her captors were keeping her movements limited.

An *Eltar* woman strode into view, flanked by two guards. She was tall with dark, plaited hair, and wore black mail. Her arms were crossed, and she scowled at Lachlei as the *Chi'lan* queen lay there. Lachlei stared back at her.

"What are you staring at?" the *Eltar* demanded.

"I didn't know the death god used children," Lachlei said. "How old are you? Sixteen? Seventeen?"

The woman's face twisted in anger. She kicked Lachlei in the stomach. "Get up, bitch! My lord will be coming for you."

The kick sent Lachlei into another round of retching. The *Eltar* smiled, enjoying Lachlei's predicament. When Lachlei stopped heaving, she looked up at the woman. "Who are you? Who is your lord?"

"I am Imdyr, high priestess and consort of Areyn Sehduk," she said. "Areyn is my lord; he will soon be your lord."

Lachlei said nothing. The girl was mad; that much she was sure of. Imdyr strode up to Lachlei and grasped her by the hair. "I don't see what's so special about you," Imdyr sneered. "A great *Chi'lan* warrior laid low by demon poison."

Lachlei brought her hand up in a palm-heel strike, hitting Imdyr hard under the chin and sending her sprawling backwards. Her guards caught her, and one moved towards Lachlei, sword drawn. Lachlei backed against the tree, but she had nowhere to go.

"Wait, Tarel!" Imdyr barked out. Tarel halted and glanced at Imdyr. "Areyn wants her alive."

"Pity," Tarel remarked. His eyes raked over Lachlei and he grinned. "Perhaps we can amuse ourselves in other ways."

"Just try," Lachlei growled, her silver eyes locked on the *Eltar*. "You'll find yourself missing vital parts."

The *Eltar* laughed. "I like a challenge," he said, gripping her chin and pressing the blade against her neck.

Lachlei could feel his hot breath against her face. She wondered how much damage they would inflict on her if she broke his neck now.

"Enough, Tarel!" Imdyr snapped. "I don't think Areyn would appreciate having his prize spoiled."

"Pity," Tarel remarked. "I could show you what a real man is like."

"How would you know? Or have you experienced one?"

Tarel brought his arm back to strike. Lachlei's knee impacted his groin and sent him sprawling. The other guard leapt forward, but Imdyr gripped his arm. "Don't," she said, her dark eyes glittering menacingly. "Areyn will have his fun with her soon enough." She turned to Lachlei. "In the meantime, bitch, you'd better behave yourself. I can't hold my men off you if you continue to taunt them." She turned to the guard again. "Pick him up!" she snarled as she glanced at Tarel. As the other guard helped Tarel up, the *Eltar* gave her a murderous glance before stumbling away.

◆◆◆◆

Rhyn'athel rode through the night. At first, he had thought he could track the demon without following the trail, but he soon realized that Areyn was blocking his powers. The Wyrd was now a confusing tangle of threads, many branching out along the World Tree. He gazed on the threads as he rode, but with so many *Athel'cen* in one place, there was no clear path. Without a clear trail, Rhyn'athel was forced to follow the thread the demon laid across the Wyrd.

Lachlei. His thoughts were on her and nothing else. The loss of the army, the *Braesan*, and even *Elren*, itself, were inconsequential. Areyn knew the new Wyrd prophecy, and he would do everything within his power to keep Lachlei from the warrior god. Even if it meant killing her. Areyn would destroy her rather than to have the balance decided.

Rhyn'athel admonished himself for failing to stay beside Lachlei. He had stayed away in deference to her feelings, but had left her unguarded. Even if he could not have her, Rhyn'athel could not bear seeing her at the mercy of the death god. The anger now burned hot inside him, and he used all his powers to search for her.

Nothing. He slowed his warhorse as he gazed into the night's sky. Something was blocking his ability to sense where she was. Areyn should not have been able to do it. Something else. Something of a very old line. Could Areyn have found a Wyrd-blood to serve him?

Wyrd-blood. That would explain Rhyn'athel's apparent lack of power. If Areyn had a Wyrd-blood serving him, he would be able to hide much. Rhyn'athel hoped he'd be able to find Lachlei in time before Areyn…

Rhyn'athel forced the thought from his mind. He had never been jealous, but the thought of Areyn alone with Lachlei angered him. The anger drove him forward, and he urged his horse faster.

If he could only rescue her in time…

CHAPTER SIXTY-SIX

Lachlei sat back down in the mud and considered her options. Despite her powers, Lachlei found she could neither open the adamantine manacles nor break the chains that bound her to the tree. There was some spell that prevented her from opening the fetters. She looked around, but saw nothing she could use to her advantage, so she sat and tried to think of possible ways of escape.

The *Eltar* guards leered at her and she frowned. She doubted their fear of Areyn's reprisal would hold them back for very long. They seemed more fearful of Imdyr than Areyn, which suggested that perhaps they had not dealt directly with the death god yet. Imdyr was another matter. Lachlei could sense her power, despite her young age. Could she really be Areyn's high priestess and consort? Consort? The implication disgusted her and she shook her head, trying the clear the image of the demon lord taking advantage of the girl.

Imdyr was not much more than a child, really. Despite her bravado, Imdyr was still very young and probably emotionally immature. Lachlei knew nothing of the *Eltar* worship of Fala and Areyn, but she suspected that Imdyr had never had a true home once she was made a high priestess. Maybe she was apprenticed by the old priestess whose job she eventually took over. Lachlei tried to think back when she was so young — she had always been levelheaded, but many that age were impressionable and malleable. It would take little for a god like Areyn to twist Imdyr to his will, especially because the *Eltar* already encouraged it.

Lachlei had heard of children being given up to serve a god, but the concept was foreign to her, since Rhyn'athel had no priests or priestesses; simply *Chi'lan*. The *Chi'lan* were traditionally *Lochvaur*, but there had been *Eleion* from other kindreds and even *Shara'kai* who chose to be Rhyn'athel's warriors.

Perhaps she could talk to Imdyr—gain her confidence? She looked back at the guards who still leered at her. If she had more time—but time was something Lachlei did not have. Not if she was to be brought before the demon lord in chains or if the guards decided to move on her. She could handle one guard while chained, but not if they both moved against her.

Laddel had mentioned that her mother had been a shapeshifter, having inherited the power from Ni'yah, the wolf-god. Lachlei wondered if perhaps she had inherited the wolf-god's powers as well.

Twice first-blood, Telek had said when she overheard a bit of Rhyn and his conversation. Perhaps that combination made her more powerful than she originally thought. But what should she focus on becoming? Something small, perhaps. A rodent? She closed her eyes to concentrate, focusing her powers on becoming a mouse.

Suddenly, she was thrown to the ground. Lachlei threw up her hands only to have them jerked above her. She tried to kick, but Tarel already had her pinned to the ground. He clapped a hand over her mouth as he pressed a knife against her throat.

"Scream and you die," Tarel growled. He removed his hand from her mouth and slid his hand under the arming shirt and hauberk to loosen the padded breeches. He grinned at his companion. "We'll take turns."

Not fear, but anger exploded inside Lachlei mind. Her guts twisted, and suddenly she found herself free of the chains. She tried to yell, but her voice was the scream of an animal. Looking down at her feet, she saw large paws instead of hands. She looked up at the guard, who was just as surprised as she was seeing a red wolf standing in place of a woman.

Ni'yah, Lachlei thought. *The Laddel are descended from him.* It made sense that the easiest form to take would be that of a wolf. She wondered how she managed the transformation. Perhaps it was her anger or desperation.

"What is that, a witch?" Tarel's companion gasped, pulling her out of her reverie.

"I'll show it how we deal with Rhyn'athel's witches," Tarel said. He brandished the knife and leapt at her.

Lachlei leapt on the *Eltar*. Tarel screamed as she lunged at his throat, her teeth closing around the soft skin and pulling back. A sharp pain ripped through her side as the man flailed.

Then, Lachlei was suddenly *Eleion* again. She pulled Tarel's dagger from her side and stared at the man as he lay dying, his throat ripped out. The other *Eltar* guard screamed and fled in horror.

Lachlei bent over and retched. The smell of blood was overwhelming and it sickened her what she had to do.

Lachlei turned and saw that Tarel carried *Fyren*. She took the swordbelt from around the dead man's waist and buckled it around her own. She hesitated. Would it even change with her? She paused, trying to decide what to do.

"Where is she?" Lachlei heard Imdyr's voice from the camp. Lachlei turned and fled into the thick forest, but she knew they would track her. Each gasp of breath was white-hot as she ran; her side ached with the knife wound. When, at last, she didn't think she had the strength to continue, she stopped at a tree to catch her breath.

She drew *Fyren* and stared at it a long while. Would it change with her if she tried again? Her clothes had changed when she turned into a wolf. Maybe her sword would too.

She sheathed *Fyren* and closed her eyes. She now concentrated on becoming a wolf. At first, nothing happened. But then, she felt her guts twist and when she looked down, she had changed back into a wolf. *Fyren* had changed with her. She sighed in relief and padded deeper into the forest.

◆◆◆◆

Lachlei moved quickly through the forest, hoping to evade her captors. In wolf form, she was faster than she could move as an *Eleion*. In retrospect, she should have realized the easiest form to take would be a wolf—legend had it that Ni'yah, after all, was a wolf when he assumed a different form. And yet, she was not a true lycanthrope. Her clothing had remained intact when she changed back and took *Fyren* from the *Eltar* guard. *Fyren* had changed with her when she transmuted.

It had been an hour since she escaped the chains. Her wolf guise proved handy when the *Eltar* search parties combed the forest. The other guard may or may not have reported that she had changed into a wolf—and if he did, would Imdyr believe him?

Lachlei stopped now. The smell of blood was overpowering, and she was feeling weak. She turned and looked at the long gash along her ribcage. She was bleeding again, and she tentatively licked the wound. The point of the dagger had entered just below the last rib. With so much adrenaline pumping through her body and her fear of the *Eltar* recapturing her, she had not had time to assess the damage.

She had lost a lot of blood. Furthermore, the dagger had penetrated her liver and part of her spleen. Lachlei realized she should have been dead, but for her first-blood constitution. She would die if she could not transform back into an *Eleion* and use her healing powers.

She lay down and tried to concentrate, but she was too weak. She heard a demon scream overhead and closed her eyes. By the time the demon found her, she would be dead. Areyn would have a victory. Perhaps he would make her a *Braesan* like he had Fialan and force her to fight against her own people. But, she would be with Fialan at last…

Another demon screamed. This time, much closer.

The thought of joining Fialan did not comfort her. Instead, she opened her eyes and saw a demon land nearby. It clacked its jaws together and approached her. She closed her eyes again, not wanting to see the end.

Rhyn'athel, help me, she thought.

Suddenly, there were sounds of steel clashing against claws. The demon screamed, and Lachlei opened her eyes to see the glowing warrior attack the creature. The Sword of Power plunged deep into the beast and it shrieked loudly. The warrior turned to her.

Lachlei? a familiar voice came into her mind.

Rhyn? she thought, but she had no strength left to mindspeak.

"Shhhh, beloved," Rhyn said absently. "You're badly hurt."

She felt his hands move along her ribcage and she whined softly. *How did he know it was her in this wolf body?* She felt his warm hands heal the organs and close the wound. As she began to gain strength, she opened her eyes and

lifted her head. To her amazement, she was in *Eleion* form again. "You came for me," she whispered.

Rhyn smiled. "Of course I did," he said. "Save your energy and let yourself heal. We have some hard riding ahead of us, and Areyn's demons are looking for you."

Lachlei stared at the smoldering body of the demon nearby. "Imdyr," she said. "There was a girl named Imdyr who claims to be Areyn's consort. She had me captured."

Rhyn looked puzzled. "Imdyr?" he said. "I don't recognize the name. A girl, you say?"

"Yes—just sixteen or seventeen," Lachlei said. She slowly sat up. "Do you have any water? Those beasts didn't give me any."

Rhyn handed her his canteen and she drank greedily. "Odd, I don't know of any Imdyr." He seemed lost in thought.

Lachlei gave him a long appraising look. "Why should you? She's *Eltar*."

Rhyn smiled. "You're right, of course," he said. "I shouldn't."

"How did you find me? We need to get out of here..."

"Easy," he said, pushing her back down. "Rest a bit. The demons won't attack while I'm with you. I found you through the Wyrd, but it wasn't easy. Areyn tried to keep you from me."

Lachlei stared at him for a moment. *What are you?* she wondered, but instead, she asked, "What about our army?"

"Cahal, Telek, and Laddel are leading them away from Caer Lochvaren. They'll be joining what's left of the *Lochvaur* army."

"And the civilians?" Lachlei felt her mouth go dry. *What about Haellsil and Wynne?*

"Your son is all right," Rhyn said. "Wynne had enough foresight to escape before Caer Lochvaren was razed."

"How many civilians escaped?"

Rhyn frowned. "Maybe ten thousand."

"Ten thousand?" Lachlei closed her eyes. "Out of forty thousand civilians? What of the army?"

"Maybe twenty thousand if we include the stragglers, but the *Elesil* have joined us."

"By *Teiwaz*, Rhyn," she whispered. "The *Lochvaur* have nearly been exterminated."

"Many have sought refuge in the Lochvaren Mountains," he said.

"And you left the army to find me?" Lachlei asked, her temper beginning to rise. "You shouldn't have come."

"What was I to do? Leave you to Areyn?"

"If need be. I can take care of myself."

"Not against Areyn Sehduk," Rhyn replied, his voice rising.

"And you believe that you could do something against the god of death?"

"Yes, I do."

"You would have to be *Athel'cen*."

Rhyn said nothing but met her gaze. When he finally spoke, his tone was measured carefully. "I make no apology, Lachlei. Now, if you are well enough to ride, I suggest we do so. We have a long journey ahead of us."

CHAPTER SIXTY-SEVEN

Lachlei rode silently beside Rhyn. She now regretted their argument. She had shown Rhyn no gratefulness for saving her life, something she now wanted to do, and yet when she turned to speak to him, he silenced her with a glance.

She suspected that they were in the forests northeast of Caer Lochvaren, not far from the King's Highway, but just east of the mountains. The forest was broken with large meadows and the land was rolling, not flat. Lachlei heard the screams of the demons overhead, but Rhyn appeared unconcerned. Instead, he seemed to look into another world; his eyes slightly out of focus. They continued to ride southward through the forest for hours until dusk.

Rhyn reined his horse and dismounted.

"Why are we stopping?" Lachlei asked.

"We should rest," Rhyn replied. "We have another full day and night's travel before we reach the army." He looked into the sky, scanning it for something.

"What about the demons?" Lachlei asked, dismounting from her horse. She stretched slowly and looked up where he was gazing, but saw nothing. "What are you looking for?"

He glanced down at her and smiled. "Patterns in the Wyrd," he said. "With the *Athel'cen* in this world, the Wyrd is changing at an alarming rate."

"The *Athel'cen* are here?" Lachlei asked.

"Of course," he said, distractedly as he stared at something she could not see. "You wouldn't expect Areyn's presence here to go unanswered, do you?"

Lachlei gazed at Rhyn for a while, but he did not elaborate. "What about the demons?" she ventured.

He glanced at her again. "They're following us, but they know I'm here so they don't dare make their move." He paused. "Did you see Areyn?"

"No," Lachlei said. "Just his *Eltar* and the woman named Imdyr."

Rhyn looked puzzled and let his eyes glaze over again. "Imdyr," he murmured and then shook his head as his eyes came back into focus. "Odd, I can't see her."

"Rhyn," Lachlei began. "I'm sorry I…"

The North Marches *Chi'lan* shook his head and grinned. "Lachlei, I understand." He gripped her shoulder affectionately. "Stay close to me. I'm the only reason the demons aren't coming for you."

"Why are they after me? Because I'm Rhyn'athel's champion?" Lachlei asked.

"It has something to do with that, yes," he said. He turned and began gathering dead wood for a fire.

"Won't the fire attract the demons?" Lachlei asked.

"They already know we're here," he said. "It doesn't matter. They won't attack tonight."

Lachlei followed him silently. Rhyn seemed more enigmatic than ever now. She wanted to ask about the *Athel'cen* and how he knew that they were in *Elren*. She wanted to ask him how he could see the Wyrd when no mortal could. She had a million questions and no answers. She wanted to trust him, but he seemed unwilling to say much more.

She helped gather the firewood and made a small fire in a clearing where the wind had blown the snow from the ground. As the shadows deepened, they sat and ate in silence. Lachlei gazed at Rhyn, feeling very much alone in her thoughts. The North Marches *Chi'lan* was aloof, apparently concentrating on something far away. Lachlei bit into the hardtack and grimaced. She stood up and searched her horse's pack for more edible food, but found little.

"Just hardtack, Rhyn?" she asked.

Rhyn shrugged. "I was in a hurry."

Lachlei laughed and sat beside him. "I would imagine so. Why did you come after me?"

Rhyn smiled grimly. "Isn't it obvious?" he asked.

Lachlei felt a twist in her stomach. It was not the answer she was prepared to hear. Instead, she spread a bedroll beside the fire, hoping that the layers would at least keep her dry, and lay on them. She looked into the skies and saw that wisps of clouds were beginning to form. A shadow passed swiftly overhead and she shivered as she felt the presence of a demon.

"You're safe," Rhyn assured her, looking up. "They won't come near."

"There's no way I can sleep," she muttered. "Not with those things flying above us."

"You should sleep. We have a long ride ahead."

Lachlei closed her eyes, but her senses were on alert. She could see the demons with her Sight, passing overhead and circling like hungry wolves. Each scream caused her to jolt fully awake. At last, she turned over and looked at him. "I can't sleep."

"Nor, I," he admitted. "The demons require too much of my attention."

"Can you tell me a story?" she asked, propping her head with her hands.

He grinned. "I think I can. What do you want to hear?"

"About Rhyn'athel," she said.

"Rhyn'athel?"

"You seem to know more about *Eleion* history than anyone I've ever known. Certainly, you know more about the warrior god than I do. And I am his champion."

Rhyn smiled. "I suppose I do. What would you like me to tell you? How he defeated Areyn the first time?"

She shook her head. "No. Tell me a story I haven't heard."

"How about the story of where he falls in love with a mortal woman?"

Lachlei smiled as she closed her eyes. "He did?"

"Oh yes," Rhyn said. "Rhyn'athel's brother, Ni'yah, played a trick on the warrior god and convinced him to come to *Elren* to see his champion. Ni'yah led Rhyn'athel to her and he fell hopelessly in love…"

Lachlei opened her silver eyes. "Was she pretty?"

"More lovely than the goddesses of *Athelren*," Rhyn replied. "But that wouldn't have mattered; for he saw her heart and knew she was the embodiment of the *Chi'lan*."

"How romantic," Lachlei murmured as she closed her eyes again. "Did she love him?"

"She didn't know he was a god, for he had taken an *Eleion* form. She turned from him because she loved another she could not have…"

"Then, she was foolish."

"Perhaps," said Rhyn, amusement coloring his voice. "Or perhaps she was blinded by her love for another. She didn't know he was Rhyn'athel."

"I would think she would know if there was a god in her midst," Lachlei said sleepily. "I would."

"Perhaps you would," Rhyn said. He fell silent.

Lachlei found herself drifting off to sleep in spite of her edginess. "Rhyn?" she murmured. "Did Rhyn'athel finally win her love?"

Rhyn said nothing for some time. Lachlei found she could not stay awake and eventually drifted off. Her rhythmic breathing told him she was asleep. Even so, Lachlei thought she heard him speak softly. *I don't know, beloved. That part of the tale is still unfinished.*

◆◆◆◆

Rhyn'athel stared at the Wyrd threads as they coursed through the world. The patterns were changing rapidly, leaving gaps where there had been none before. Three *Athel'cen* within the same world was too much of a focal point for the Wyrd not to be changed. Areyn knew it, too, and sent the demons to find a hole in Rhyn'athel's defenses. But there were none. Rhyn'athel had been careful to construct an impenetrable shield. The demons could not find a breach within his powers. Not now. Rhyn'athel would shed his mortal body before allowing them to take Lachlei again.

But he could feel a tremor along the Wyrd. The Eternal Fire that fed the Wyrd was crackling against the slim fetters that held it in check. He could sense the *Fyr*-dragons move though the flames of creation and destruction. They were normally dormant, but now they awoke. He could feel their presence throughout the Wyrd strands.

Rhyn'athel closed his eyes. It would not be long before one escaped that fiery realm.

◆◆◆◆

Lachlei awoke to sunlight breaking through the trees. She shivered in the blankets by the dying embers. She looked to see Rhyn already packing his equipment.

"You've been up a while," Lachlei remarked, sitting up. "Couldn't you sleep?"

"No," Rhyn said. "I'll sleep when we return to the army."

"It's the Wyrd, isn't it?"

Rhyn looked at her appraisingly. "What do you know about it?"

"What you've told me," she said. "But I can feel something happening. I can't describe it."

Rhyn smiled grimly. "Nor can I. Because it's never happened before."

Lachlei closed her eyes, and a vision of whirling fire filled her mind's-eye. "It's almost like a maelstrom of fire and light."

Rhyn had been cinching the girth tighter on his horse. His head snapped around. "You've seen it?"

"Just now." She stared at him. "I'm the focal point, aren't I?"

Rhyn nodded. "You are."

"Why?"

Rhyn made no reply. "Come on, let's ride. The sooner I get you back to the army, the sooner you'll be safe."

Lachlei stared at him, but again, Rhyn offered no explanation. She gathered her bedroll and tied it to her saddle. Without a word, they mounted and headed southward, trailed by demons.

Chapter Sixty-Eight

Rhyn and Lachlei had ridden most of the morning southward towards the Darkling Plain. They had spoken little, but Lachlei pondered Rhyn's words. She had seen something of the Wyrd—a maelstrom where she was the focal point. She was certain Rhyn knew why, but the North Marches *Chi'lan* refused to discuss the matter.

As they rode forward, they entered a small meadow. Something dark lay in the center. At first, Lachlei thought it was a demon, but as they approached, she saw the pity in Rhyn's face.

The creature was long and reptilian with glossy black scales and four legs. Its wings, battered and torn, lay at awkward angles; Lachlei was certain they were broken. Deep gashes ran down its body as though raked by huge claws. Its massive head lolled to one side, and its jaws were open, exposing sharp teeth. It was longer and much more substantial than the elusive fireworms she had seen occasionally in the Lochvaren Mountains.

"Is that a dragon?" Lachlei asked in wonder.

She stared at the creature. She had never seen a dragon, given that they dwelled in the Eternal Fire and in the Wyrd, itself, but it fit the description of one. Its hot body had melted the snow where it lay and scorched the dried meadow grasses beneath it. The snow that had not melted was bright red with blood.

Rhyn had already dismounted and walked over to the beast. The dragon's skin was becoming gray. Lachlei dismounted and followed him. She walked over to Rhyn, who knelt beside the creature's head. Rhyn was saying something in a series of clicks and hisses that she could not understand. The creature answered him in the same language.

"He's one of the *Fyr*-dragons," Rhyn said, glancing up at her. "There must have been a break in the *Fyr* and he slipped through into *Elren*, but the journey nearly killed him."

"A *Fyr*-dragon?" Lachlei repeated. "You mean he lives in the *Fyr*?"

Rhyn nodded. "The *Fyr* is a great power of creation and destruction. Only the *Fyr*-dragons can live within it," he said, running his hands along the creature's scales.

"How do you know its language?" she asked.

Rhyn acted as though he had not heard her question. He continued to touch the creature's scales as it spoke in its strange language.

"Is it—dying?" Lachlei asked. She felt an overwhelming sadness for the creature—as terrible as it was, it was also beautiful to behold. It opened its cat-like eyes and groaned in pain.

Rhyn frowned and shook his head. "Yes," he said sadly. "These are creatures that can't live outside of *Fyr* for very long. His name is Haegl."

Lachlei knelt down beside the dragon. She laid her hands on the creature's skin. It was warm to touch, but she could tell it was rapidly cooling. *Haegl,* she thought.

The dragon looked into her eyes. *Help me, Eleion.*

Lachlei started and stared at Rhyn. "Can we heal him?" Dragons and *Eleion* held no animosity towards each other; in the past, both seemed willing to leave each other be.

"Yes, but it won't stop him from dying," Rhyn said. "He can't live outside the *Fyr* for long."

Athel'cen, help me, the dragon said plaintively.

Athel'cen? Was that a plea to the gods? Or did the dragon mistake them for gods? Lachlei turned to Rhyn. "He must be delirious—we must try something." She placed her hands on the dragon and began to concentrate on its wounds. Rhyn knelt beside her, running his fingers along the dragon's wounds. They healed under his touch. The dragon's skin began to darken and grow hotter. Soon, Lachlei could not touch the creature for fear of burning her hands. She watched as Rhyn continued to run his hands along the hot scales.

As she watched, she saw a change come over Rhyn's face. She saw power flash in his eyes, and the dragon's body glowed where he touched him.

I only sought to free myself from the Fyr, the dragon said. *We belong to the Wyrd as well. Is this so evil?*

Rhyn shook his head. *No.*

Then free us and we will be forever indebted.

"What's happening? Rhyn?" Lachlei asked, but he did not answer. Instead, a slight smile touched his lips. His eyes glimmered with pity.

Very well, Haegl, you are free.

The dragon lifted his head and met Rhyn's gaze. *You have my deepest gratitude. Dragons do not forget.* The dragon slowly stood up and turned to Lachlei. *And you, Eleion, I will not forget your kindness. Dragons will remember their life-debt. We will serve Rhyn'athel's heirs. Call on us in your hour of greatest need.*

Lachlei stared. "But you owe me nothing. It was a gift."

Haegl met her gaze. *And so is my promise.*

Rhyn and Lachlei backed up, and the black dragon drew itself to its feet. With a roar, the dragon leapt into the air, his wings beating gracefully as he flew northwards.

Lachlei looked at Rhyn in puzzlement. "What was he talking about? Did he think you freed him from the *Fyr*?"

"Perhaps he did." Rhyn did not meet her gaze. Instead, he watched the dragon as it flew out of sight.

"That's impossible," Lachlei said. "That would take the power of a god."

"Indeed, it would take an *Athel'cen*," Rhyn agreed.

"What did he mean that he would serve Rhyn'athel's heirs?" Lachlei asked.

Rhyn shrugged. "What do you think it means?" He returned to his warhorse and mounted it.

"Perhaps he meant the *Lochvaur*—we are all Rhyn'athel's heirs," she said.

Rhyn said nothing. Instead, he rode forward. "Let's get going—we have many miles to cross."

She stared at him as if looking at him for the first time. "What is wrong with you?" She mounted her horse and spurred it after him. "You've been aloof ever since you've rescued me. What is wrong?"

"Are you so blinded by anger that you can't see what I truly am?" Rhyn replied.

"What?" Lachlei said. "You're a *Chi'lan*, certainly, and a powerful first-blood."

"Is that all?"

"I thought perhaps you might be a Guardian."

"A Guardian," growled Rhyn. "Weak spirits incapable of anything save perhaps the most rudimentary magic." He reined his horse and looked at her. "What I did was free the *Fyr*-dragons from the *Fyr*."

Lachlei stared at him. "That's impossible."

"Not for me," Rhyn said. "Damn it, Lachlei! The *Chi'lan* warriors have figured out who I am, but my own champion is blind!"

"What are you saying? That you're a god?"

"Who else could kill arch-demons as easily as heath-stalkers? Who else could thwart Areyn's attempts at trying to capture you or destroy our army? Who else would directly challenge Areyn Sehduk?"

Lachlei laughed. "Really, Rhyn? If you were a god, don't you think we'd be winning this war?"

Anger flashed in his face. "Areyn is a powerful god—almost as powerful as I am. Lachlei, I became mortal because I love you. I've wanted you since you spoke to me the night when Fialan's pyre lit the sky over Caer Lochvaren…"

"How do you know about that?" Lachlei demanded, staring at him. "You were there?"

"Of course I was there," Rhyn said. "Areyn murdered Fialan—I couldn't let that grievance slide—and then I saw you." He paused. "There isn't a day that goes by that I haven't wanted you…"

She gaped at his admission. "Leave!" She drew *Fyren*.

Rhyn looked down at the blade and smiled grimly. "Do you think that blade would stop me if I decided to take you? With as many opportunities as I've had…"

Fear gripped Lachlei. Rhyn—or whatever it was—*had* opportunities, as recent as the night before. The nights when they had lain together under the stars flashed in her memory. She recalled, ruefully, that she had been attracted to him, despite herself. Perhaps he was a demon—maybe a life-leech or another evil creature. Whatever he was, Rhyn was no god—that she was certain. "Leave me alone, whatever you are. I never want to see you again."

Rhyn'athel shook his head. "Lachlei, I love you. I loved you since I first saw you, when you swore vengeance against Fialan's killer. That is what brought me to your side, and now you would take on your most dangerous enemy without me. Lachlei—think this through—this is no ordinary demon you're fighting. You will be fighting Areyn Sehduk."

"I know, but I can't love you."

"That's not true," Rhyn snapped. "I know what you feel inside, but you keep it so buried that you've fooled yourself into believing you can never love another."

"I love Fialan."

"Fialan is dead! Worse than dead—he's *Braesan,* which makes him part of Areyn's troops. Lachlei, don't look for comfort from the dead—they do not give it."

Lachlei's eyes flashed in anger. "Leave now!"

"You haven't heard a word I've said, have you?" Rhyn said evenly. "I can't protect you if you send me away now. There are demons trailing us, and only my power keeps them at bay. We'll argue about this later when we return to the army, but I won't leave you now."

"I don't need your protection, Rhyn," she replied. "I don't need you. Leave me alone!"

Rhyn bowed his head. "Lachlei, you don't know what you're asking."

"I do, and you must leave now."

He met her gaze. "By my own blood, Lachlei, you have your wish. I won't return. But do not call on me in your darkest hour, for I will not hear your cries."

Rhyn'athel drew his sword, took it between his hands and raised it above his head. *Ille vauri swaerya. Ille athelren!*

The sword glowed and in a flash of light, Rhyn'athel vanished.

CHAPTER SIXTY-NINE

Lachlei stared in shock at the place where Rhyn and his charger had been. No ordinary *Eleion* could have disappeared like that. Not even a godling had the power to leave as Rhyn had done. Lachlei could only think of one creature who could have done it.

Do not call on me in your darkest hour, for I will not hear your cries.

Rhyn's warning chilled her. She stared at the place where he had been, her mind numb and her heart heavy. He had spoken in the god's tongue, swearing by his own blood he wouldn't return. His second command had been to *Athelren.*

Athelren—the home of the gods.

The Chi'lan warriors have figured out who I am, but my own champion is blind...

My own champion... She took a breath and then another. Could he have been...? She couldn't finish the thought. She began to weep. What had she done to her kindred? What had she done to herself?

Why hadn't Rhyn told her who he really was?

A demon cry brought her around. She stared into the sky to see a dark winged creature in the distance. Lachlei spurred her horse to a canter and glanced at the creature. Did it see her? Could it sense her presence?

Without Rhyn, Lachlei didn't know. She scanned the road ahead. The meadow changed to thick pines, but she knew as long as she remained on the road, she would be a target. Going cross-country might save her.

Lachlei turned her warhorse and urged it over the berme, hoping the snow wasn't deep. The horse stepped and sunk in just above the pastern, so she clapped her legs against its side to step up the pace. The warhorse stepped through the snow carefully, trying not to slip or injure itself.

A scream echoed through the forest, louder now, and Lachlei hoped the demon had no supernatural senses to search for her. She doubted she would be so lucky and closed her eyes to concentrate on shielding herself.

Do not call on me in your darkest hour, for I will not hear your cries.

Lachlei chewed her lower lip. She would normally ask Rhyn for his guidance, and now she had none. *I won't call on you,* she silently promised him. The dragon Haegl said he would come to her aid in her time of need, but how could she call him? She tried using mindspeak, but saw and felt nothing. Perhaps the dragon meant that it would aid Rhyn only or perhaps only Rhyn knew how to call it.

Lachlei considered turning into a wolf, but then, she would not have her warhorse or her provisions. She could hunt as a wolf, but she wondered how successful she would be at it. Attacking an *Eltar* in close quarters was one thing; hunting for scarce food was another. She decided she was better off as an *Eleion* unless she had to give up her horse.

She was still a first-blood and had powers—perhaps now was the time she used her magic. The strength of the *Chi'lan* had always been in battle. Without something like a Sword of Power, she could not focus her magic as effectively as she had seen Rhyn do, but she was still powerful—perhaps powerful enough. She took a few more breaths to try to calm the pounding in her ears, but her mouth was dry. She could barely speak the words in the god's tongue: *Illa ara sceadu, galdor lochvarel...*

Suddenly, she saw movement on her left. Lachlei drew her sword and turned to see a *Chi'lan* woman astride a horse with sword drawn. Lachlei sighed in relief and lowered her blade. The illusion did likewise. The magic had worked. She was looking at a replica of herself.

"*Vala!*" *Go!* — she ordered the apparition, sending it away from her. The doppelganger was an illusion that would leave no tracks, but she knew demons were not necessarily observant. The illusion turned her horse and rode through the forest at a speed Lachlei was envious of. The screams of the demon were close now, and she spied a copse of thick firs not far from her.

She urged her horse towards them, hoping the boughs would provide some concealment from above. As her warhorse approached the trees, the snow became deep, and the horse balked. She leapt from the saddle and plowed into thigh-high snow. She grasped the reins and pulled her horse forward into the thicket.

Her first-blood senses alert, she could feel rather than see the demon as it passed. She could do nothing to hide her tracks, but perhaps it would not see them from that far above. She concentrated on an impregnable shield to conceal herself. As she did, she felt the cold grip of the demon.

It was not a heath-stalker as she had hoped, but an arch-demon. She felt it as it casually inspected her shield. The demon considered it as though it was not completely certain if she was there or not. Then, she heard a triumphant cry and a flurry of wings as the demon raced away after the doppelganger.

Lachlei shivered violently. She was drenched with sweat, which her padded arming shirt had soaked up. The cold wind blew through her, and her fingers were growing numb. "By Rhyn'athel's sword..." she muttered and then stopped herself. She doubted Rhyn'athel would show much mercy to her now.

She leaned against the warhorse and it whickered softly. She pulled off her leather gauntlets and ran her hands over the horse's hide. It was good to feel the animal's warmth and the painful tingling in her fingers told her she was restoring circulation. She slid her gauntlets back on and considered her options.

It was a fine time for her to order Rhyn to leave, she admitted. But the anger had been smoldering for some time. Perhaps it had been seeing Fialan again or watching Rhyn dispatch *Braesan* with such callousness. Perhaps it had been his advances towards her, when he knew she still loved Fialan. Perhaps it had been her reaction to him. She had wanted him, despite herself. He had voiced the tension both of them had felt.

Was Rhyn truly a god? She had laughed in his face at the claim, yet now she was not so certain. There were only three *Athel'cen*. Could he have been Rhyn'athel? She recalled the battles they fought; each time, Rhyn used power beyond anything she had ever seen. Lachlei had explained it away that he was a talented first-blood, nothing more. Yet, looking back on his powers, she had known all along that he had done more than any mortal.

Her first clue should have been the Sword of Power, she decided. No Sword of Power existed, save Laddel's. It had passed through her at one point, leaving her unscathed. She had chosen to ignore it at the time—why? The Sword of Power should have cut her in half and yet, it had not touched her. He had destroyed Areyn Sehduk's defenses and brought utter destruction on the *Braesan*. Furthermore, Rhyn's Sword had the warrior rune carved in its blade: *Teiwaz. God-Warrior.* Rhyn'athel.

Lachlei closed her eyes and shivered again. Why had she been so blind? Was what Rhyn said true, that all the other *Chi'lan* had long ago recognized him? If so, they must have thought her foolish. Perhaps she had let her anger cloud her judgment. She had been angry at Areyn for killing her husband and Rhyn had been the only one to lash out at. Her feelings towards Rhyn had further complicated matters and made her angrier yet. In her anger and resentment, she had driven him away, demanding that he leave her.

Do not call on me in your darkest hour, for I will not hear your cries.

Was she no longer Rhyn'athel's champion? Had he truly forsaken her? She resisted the urge to pull off her gauntlet and pull back the sleeve of her mailshirt and arming jacket to see if the mark was gone. She did not need to know this right now. She shivered again, but this time grasped her horse's reins and began the slow, agonizing trudge through the deep drifts. Forsaken or not, she would die of exposure if she did not continue.

Rhyn had told her they were a day and night away from the army, but that had been at his pace, on a road, and without dodging demons. She guessed that she was forty or fifty miles from her army—maybe farther. At this rate, it was unlikely she would make ten miles in a day. She didn't dare take the road—that would be the first place the demons would look for her.

Lachlei had enough food and water for three days or maybe longer if she stretched the rations as far as she dared. She did not have a bow, so hunting was unlikely. After that, she could survive a week or better if the snow held out or if she could find water. Assuming she could find the army in that time and Areyn had not destroyed them.

The snow became less deep, and Lachlei stomped her feet to try to restore circulation in her toes. Her leather boots and breeches were soaked. Still, riding was better than walking, and she slid a numb foot into a stirrup and swung herself into the saddle.

Another scream from above told her that the demon had discovered her ruse. Lachlei cursed. She had not expected the demon to return so soon. She urged the horse onward, unwilling to search for another hiding place just yet. She concentrated and sent another doppelganger out, hoping to confuse the demon.

The screams grew louder, and without Lachlei's urging, the warhorse broke into a gallop. Lachlei turned and saw the demon overtaking her. She drew *Fyren* and twisted in the saddle in time to slash at the demon as it bore down on her.

At that moment, two things happened. *Fyren* bit deep into the demon and the warhorse passed under a snag. The boughs smacked Lachlei hard, throwing her off her steed and into a snow bank. She tumbled and lay stunned.

The demon, angry and wounded, landed nearby. It considered Lachlei as she lay motionless in the snow. Lachlei groaned and fought to keep conscious. She could see the slavering creature as it clicked its beak together in pleasure at seeing her so incapacitated. Lachlei moved her leg and cried out, nearly blacking out from the pain. It did not take her first-blood senses to know it had twisted and broken in several places. She could not flee, and *Fyren* lay many yards away.

Lachlei pulled her dagger from its sheath. It was woefully inadequate, and given it was what she had, she decided to try another tactic. *Demon,* she mindspoke to it. *Why do you come for me?*

The arch-demon hesitated and laughed. The horrible grating sound hurt her head, and Lachlei winced. Perhaps this had not been her best idea, she thought ruefully. She slid her hand against her broken leg and concentrated.

Why do you come for me? she persisted.

Lord Areyn wants you brought to him. The demon replied.

Lachlei felt the bones begin to knit in her leg. *Why does Areyn want me?*

The demon laughed again. The tenor was decidedly more unpleasant. *You will find out, mortal woman.*

Really? To kill me as he killed Fialan? I would've thought he'd send a second-rate lackey like you to dispatch me.

Not to kill… the demon said and gazed on her hungrily.

Lachlei suppressed a shudder. Instead, she met the demon's yellow eyes. *How far was she away from Fyren? Could she get to the sword before it could stop her?*

You don't frighten me, she mindspoke to it. She shifted her legs slowly to try to get her feet under her. *Areyn doesn't frighten me. Go tell your master I serve Rhyn'athel.*

The demon laughed again. *A strange way to serve the warrior god by sending him away,* the demon said. *You can explain that to Areyn when you satisfy him.*

A knot twisted in her stomach at the mention of Rhyn'athel. *What makes you think you'll be able to capture me? A second-rate, soul-less lackey that has less worth than the filth on my boots…*

The demon snarled and leapt at her.

Lachlei was on her feet, slashing at the demon, focusing all her power into the adamantine blade. The creature screamed as the dagger buried into it up to the hilt. Its massive tail thrashed and slammed her to the ground. Holding her with one talon, it pinned her to the earth, claws digging into her.

I grow tired of this little game, mortal, it sneered and yanked the dagger from its chest.

Lachlei screamed as she felt the burning poison enter her. The poison was like fire in her veins, and she writhed uncontrollably. As she opened her eyes, Lachlei saw *Fyren* several yards beyond. She reached out in desperation. "*Fyren*!" she screamed.

Suddenly, the sword was in her hand. She could not see it any more, blinded by the poison, but felt its familiar hilt. The demon shrieked as she thrust the blade upward, holding onto it with all her strength. Black demon blood poured around her. Her last cognizant image was of the demon falling on top of her. Lachlei fell unconscious.

CHAPTER SEVENTY

Lachlei awoke cold and sick. How long she lay beneath the demon, she had no idea. She was soaked with blood and melted snow. She tried to move slowly, but every nerve screamed in agony. It was the poison—fortunately, this demon had used it with the intention to sedate her, not kill her. She thought back to Rhyn when he had taken a full shot of demon's poison. She had healed him then, but now she suspected that Rhyn had helped her quite a bit—no one recovered from those terrible injuries that fast. Not even a first-blood.

Lachlei groaned and pushed the demon off her. Despite the gore, the demon had inadvertently saved her life by falling on top of her when it died. The heat from its massive body had kept her from freezing to death. She sat up and began retching uncontrollably; her stomach emptied its contents. After a few minutes, she stopped when there was nothing left but bile. She knew it was the poison that made her so ill.

Lachlei looked around. It was late afternoon by the long shadows of the trees. There would be other demons looking for her now that she had slain an arch-demon. She stared at the creature's bulk, still smoldering hot against the grass. It had melted the snow around them. As she looked at the creature, it began disintegrating. She stood up and staggered. For a minute, her body threatened more retching fits, but it subsided. She focused on shapeshifting into a wolf, but it took too much power and left her feeling sick and exhausted. She had to find shelter—a place to make a fire and dry her clothing before she froze to death. Without food, she doubted she would have enough energy to do much anyway.

Is this how Rhyn intended her to die? Sick from demon poison; cold and alone? Lachlei inadvertently recalled the nights she had spent in his arms, so close to loving him, and yet, so distant. Despite herself, she missed him terribly.

"Rhyn," she whispered. "Forgive me. I spoke rashly."

Do not call on me in your darkest hour, for I will not hear your cries.

Lachlei nodded. She did not expect forgiveness. She searched for her dagger and found it lying on the ground, not far from her. She pulled *Fyren* from the arch-demon's fading corpse and smiled grimly, looking at its blade. Rhyn had said its adamantine came from *Athelren*—of course, it would slay demons. Areyn had felt its bite as well, she thought. The evil she had sensed along the darkened blade could only be Areyn Sehduk.

Her enemy.

She looked at *Fyren* and thought of *Athelren*, something nagging at her poison-addled brain.

Ni'yah.

There were three *Athel'cen*. Rhyn had said that all three *Athel'cen* were in *Elren*. If the *Laddel* had been involved, certainly Ni'yah had been with them.

Her mind brought forth the image of Telek. So like Rhyn, and yet, different. She had seen the sibling likeness and thought that Telek and Rhyn were related somewhere by blood. Each time she had seen Telek, she had seen Rhyn conversing with him. Of course, they had been brothers.

Odd that only once had she actually heard a portion of their conversation and they had broken it off. Rhyn had been exhausted then from destroying the *Braesan* and Telek had been distracted. Even so, they would slip in their familiarity with each other in front of her. Their conversations about the demons seemed odd then, but made sense now that Lachlei knew who they were.

Ni'yah was the god of her mother's kindred, the *Laddel.* Ni'yah had been her mother's god. Lachlei, having been raised with the *Lochvaur*, had been a follower of Rhyn'athel, not the wolf-god. But she was half *Laddel* and a first-blood of Ni'yah. She closed her eyes and concentrated on Telek.

"Ni'yah!" she whispered. "Wolf-god, I've never prayed to you, but I do so now. Rhyn'athel has abandoned me through my own fault and will not hear me. If you have any pity for Rhyn'athel's fallen champion and your kinsman, aid me."

The cold wind whispered its reply.

Lachlei stumbled to the edge of the melted ground, scooped up a handful of slushy snow and shoved it into her parched mouth. Survival was the first step. She could cut a lean-to with her dagger, but she doubted it would give her much protection against demons should they come around again. She scanned the area, but she could see little of the terrain in the dense pines. Still, she suspected higher, rocky crags might be more defensible and would provide adequate shelter against the wind.

She turned and walked parallel to the road. Her horse was gone and she doubted she'd be able to find it again in so much timber, assuming the demons hadn't killed it. She could see rocky crags not far from where she stood. She followed the ridgeline, trudging through calf-deep snow, her feet becoming numb. In the waning light, she could now discern that the rocks ahead were not a natural formation, but ruins from an earlier time.

A lone howl rose up from somewhere in the fading light. It was close. Lachlei felt a supernatural chill run through her. She hesitated and drew *Fyren* once more. Using her powers, she tried to sense the presence out there, but sensed nothing—not even a wolf. She stared at dark forms of the trees and shuddered. Her cold mind must be playing tricks on her, she decided.

She made her way up the small hill to the ruins and halted. The stones were flat gray and stood like sentinels of an age long past. This had been a small shrine to the gods of light. It was very ancient and covered with dead vines and snow. She walked over to the shrine and dug away some of the vines with her cold fingers. The runes marked this clearly as an *Athel'cen* shrine—a shrine to Rhyn'athel and Ni'yah. As she traced the runes with her fingers, she could still feel the power within their cuts. It offered sanctuary.

Lachlei breathed a sigh of relief. The runes were of another age—a time before the Truce that somehow survived the *Fyr.* The power was of that age, ancient and terrible. Back then, *Eleion* fought *Jotunn* and demons; the ward glyphs held a magic lost to all, save the gods and the *Braesan*. Legends said those runes were wards against demons. Perhaps Ni'yah had heard her prayers.

Lachlei turned and walked to the nearest thicket of spruce trees. The bows on most were springy, but she found one with dead branches, snapped them off and carried them back into the ruins. She walked in and dropped her small bundle of wood. The shrine had been small, maybe ten feet by six at the most. The roof was long gone—probably thatch or some other material—as was the altar where offerings were left to the gods. Snow filled the little chamber, and Lachlei was forced to kick and scrape the snow back to the stone floor beneath. She was surprised to see the floor intact and the runes still marked as though carved recently.

She ran her fingers along the runes, feeling their power. These too were ward glyphs. Before the Truce, Guardians had roamed the world, many settling in the shrines of the gods they served. Lachlei recalled ruefully how she believed Rhyn had been a Guardian. The Guardian of this shrine could have imbued the runes with its own magic to prevent demons or other evil creatures from entering or destroying this shrine.

Another howl, this time farther away. Lachlei paused and listened. Wolf cries had never been a cause for concern, yet now, something within her memory told her that these were. Lachlei shivered, her fingers stiff as she laid the wood on the floor. She touched the branches. "*Solu*!" The wood caught fire, and she stripped her gauntlets from her hands.

"By Rhyn'athel's mane," she exclaimed. The flesh of her fingertips was white, signaling frostbite. She pulled her boots off and looked at her feet, finding them mottled white as well.

The howl came again, this time joined by another and another. Lachlei shivered and gazed into the darkness beyond the shrine's threshold.

Something was wrong. Lachlei's senses told her that this was no ordinary wolf pack. If Rhyn had been here, he would have known exactly what she was hearing. But, she reminded herself, Rhyn was gone and she was alone. Instead, she touched the ward glyphs that guarded the threshold, hoping to activate their magic. She tried to recall the old stories of howling—of demon wolves that searched for their prey.

Demon wolves—that sounded familiar, but why? Lachlei closed her eyes, trying to concentrate, despite her cold. The arming shirt was becoming stiff and heavy with ice, but she did not dare remove her armor. She pulled her cloak off, laid it by the fire, and sat on it. She was hungry and hypothermic, but had nothing to maintain her energy.

The howling brought her around. Demon wolves—what were they? Wolves of Areyn. Dire Wolves. She threw another branch on the fire and tried to think. She was so cold.

Rhyn, I'm sorry.

With her cold, came exhaustion. Despite herself, she felt her eyes slowly close. She did not see the glowing eyes in the forest beyond.

CHAPTER SEVENTY-ONE

"Now, what do we do?" Cara asked. She sat in a tent with Conlan and the *Lochvaur* and *Laddel* lords. After the *Chi'lan* and *Laddel* troops materialized on Darkling Plain before the *Elesil*, all agreed to parley and plan their next strategy. "The Undead will surely come back and Areyn Sehduk has control of my kindred."

"We don't know if the *Braesan* will return," Conlan said. "With the show of force that we've seen, I would think it would cause the death god to pause and rethink his strategy."

"Rhyn isn't here," Telek said. "He's gone after Lachlei."

Kieran frowned. "Can he rescue her?"

"If anyone can, it'd be Rhyn," Cahal stated. "The problem is, how long could it take and why does Areyn want Lachlei?"

Telek smiled ruefully. "Rhyn is up against Areyn's strongest magic—he'll have difficulty finding her."

"Assuming she's alive," Conlan said. "Your Rhyn could be riding into a trap."

"Lachlei is alive," Telek said before the *Lochvaur* could object. "Areyn will only kill her if presented with no other options. Lachlei is the focal point in this war."

Laddel stared at his sire. "You never told me that."

"You didn't ask, and I wasn't in the mood to tell you," Ni'yah remarked.

"It doesn't matter," Cahal spoke up. "What matters is that we're forced to fight the *Braesan*. They wait; they bide their time. They will attack us again with greater numbers."

"I saw Fialan," Kieran remarked. "He told me that he was dead."

Laddel nodded grimly. "They use our own dead against us."

Cara stared at them. "How can we win when we fight our own warriors?"

All eyes turned to Telek. The god took in a deep breath. "I am not as powerful as Rhyn. Areyn planned that assault carefully and managed to hold back Rhyn's powers." He paused and met Laddel's gaze. "It wasn't our intent to show our powers this soon."

"And why not?" Cahal said. "Let's end this charade. We all know who is here."

Ni'yah smiled wryly. "Is that so, my young *Lochvaur*?" He looked around and saw confirmation on the *Eleion's* faces. "I would be careful voicing your thoughts so openly. You don't want the war Rhyn and I would give you. It would mean a total unmasking of all power. The *Eleion* have not seen such horror in nearly two thousand years."

Silence ensued.

"Then, what do we do?" Laddel asked. "Fight until each of us are slaughtered and turned to *Braesan*? I, for one, have no desire for that fate."

Ni'yah stood up and gripped his son's shoulder. "No, I wouldn't ask you to do that. We need to hold on for a little longer. Rhyn and I have a plan."

"How much longer?" Cara asked. "They're twenty miles away. Our scouts already have seen Areyn's demon wolves and other more foul creatures..." She stared as Ni'yah suddenly stood up.

"What is it?" Laddel asked as he saw the wolf-god's lip lift in a snarl. "Demons?"

"May the *Fyr* take him!" Ni'yah snarled. "Damn *Athel'cen* and that stubborn creature whom I call brother!"

"What's wrong?" Cahal asked.

Ni'yah ignored Cahal. "I must leave now," he said to Laddel. "It's too complex to explain, but if I don't Lachlei will die."

"What of our armies?" Laddel asked.

"Do what you can—my shield should protect you." With that, Ni'yah leapt through the tent flap. He turned into a wolf in mid-air and loped across the Darkling Plain.

◆◆◆◆◆

Lachlei awoke to growling. The fire had died and she lay on the blanket freezing and shaking. The terrible cold had made her delirious and exhausted. She wondered why she was even awake—those who suffered from hypothermia fell into a sleep, never to awaken again.

The growling continued and Lachlei reached for *Fyren's* hilt. As far as she could tell, she was still in the little shrine, curled up and shivering. She lifted her head and groaned. Everything took energy from her body—energy she did not have. And yet, the growling continued.

She forced herself to sit up and use her Sight. Something was wrong. Terribly wrong. She looked out of the threshold and saw dozens of glowing eyes and stumbled to her feet. Her numb feet were bare from when she had taken off her boots. Pain shot through her, and she nearly doubled over. Lachlei looked down and saw her feet were mottled white and her toes were turning black as if terribly bruised. She cursed herself. She should have put her boots and stockings back on once they had dried. Now she could not run—she could not even walk—and she doubted she could fight. Lachlei glanced at her hands—she had left them bare too, but had tucked them against her body. She at least had their use.

So, Rhyn, this is how I die, she thought bitterly. *Half frozen and eaten by Areyn's demon wolves.*

But, they were not just demon wolves, Lachlei knew. They were Areyn's Yeth Hounds—supernatural dire wolves that would follow their prey relentlessly.

Lachlei decided she would take some of them out if they dared enter the shrine. She had not much wood left, so she threw the last on the embers and rekindled the fire. She did not dare to try to put on her boots with the wolves outside.

Lachlei waited, but the Yeth made no movement. It soon became apparent that they were not going to attack. She looked at the threshold in wonder—the ward glyphs gleamed with their own light. Whatever she had done must have activated the very old magic.

"This is a shrine to the *Athel'cen*," she reminded herself aloud. The magic was good against the demon wolves, but what of the heath-stalkers and arch-demons? And even though it protected her from her enemies, it would not keep her from freezing to death or dying of thirst or starvation.

The sanctuary was a cell. She had walked into a trap.

The demons knew she would have to come out soon or die. Either way, Areyn would have her. Lachlei almost despaired now and searched her mind for anything that might help her. She sat down again and ran her fingers along her frozen feet, trying to heal them the best she could with what little energy she had left before sliding her stockings and boots back on. Unless she reached Laddel or Ni'yah soon, she was likely to lose some toes.

Lachlei pushed those thoughts aside. "I will not die a coward," she said aloud. If necessary, she would die in battle. But then she would become a *Braesan* and serve Areyn against her people. Lachlei shook her head. Even a valiant death—one that she did not fear—would feed her enemy, the death god. Her mind returned to Rhyn. She had been angry with him and spoken rashly, but had she truly driven him away? She could not believe he would abandon her to death or worse to his ancient enemy—if he were Rhyn'athel.

But Lachlei knew little of the warrior god save what she learned from legends and old writings. Most of what she knew focused on his powers and his actions—not his personality. Rhyn had admitted he had taken mortal form for her—could mortality have affected him?

She did not have the answer and Rhyn would probably deny it, she admitted to herself wryly. "Rhyn," she whispered. "Rhyn—I was wrong, I'm sorry," she said. "You've proven your point—I can't do this without you."

Silence followed.

Lachlei drew *Fyren*. The adamantine blade shimmered blue in the darkness. "Rhyn, I go to die—I don't expect forgiveness, though I ask for it. If I can't live through this, at least let me die well."

She took a deep breath of the cold air and charged out of the shine, swinging her sword.

CHAPTER SEVENTY-TWO

Lachlei charged from the shrine, swinging *Fyren*. She could see the demon Yeth wolves now—ghost white with red eyes and ears. They had long, saber-like fangs that shone in the darkness. The moment she stepped past the glyph wards, they charged her. *Fyren* bit deep into the first wolf and she slashed again, cutting deep into the one next to it.

Lachlei summoned what power she could and focused it against the Yeth. A wave of blue fire issued from *Fyren's* blade and rolled over the wolves, throwing them backwards. Lachlei pushed forward, using the blade to clear a path of those Yeth Hounds which had been unaffected by her initial blast.

But there were too many. Lachlei continued to fight her way through, even when she heard the screams of demons above her. One wolf lunged past her defenses and threw her to the ground. She struggled against it, but its teeth clamped around her throat, slowly suffocating her. She slammed *Fyren's* blade into it repeatedly, but it would not let go. Sharp teeth sliced into her sword arm, forcing her to drop *Fyren*. She tried to cry out in pain, but she could not even do that. She was completely at their mercy and she could do nothing. She fought to stay conscious.

Suddenly, Lachlei heard a massive fight somewhere ahead. Yeth were snarling and yipping in terror. The wolf that held her fast released her and she gasped for breath. She sat up and grasped *Fyren*. She stared in shock as she saw she was face-to-face with the largest wolf she had ever seen.

"Lachlei," the wolf said sternly, staring at her with its brass eyes. "Get up!"

"Who are you?" she stammered as she clambered to her feet.

"A foolish romantic," the wolf replied. "Climb on my back and we'll get out of here."

Lachlei sheathed her sword and grasped handfuls of his fur with her cold hands. As she touched his fur, she felt warmth run through her. She was dry, and her pain was gone. She stared at her right wrist and saw there was no mark on it.

"Rhyn?" she stammered as she climbed onto his back.

"No, Ni'yah," the wolf replied. He leapt forward, bowling the snarling demons over.

"You heard me?"

"Surprisingly, yes," he replied. "But I'll admit, I have a soft spot for you."

Lachlei buried her face in the warm fur and almost wept as she hung on. "What of Rhyn?"

"Probably sulking in *Athelren*—he'll get over it after a couple hundred years," Ni'yah remarked.

"Then, he is..."

The wolf-god glanced back with an incredulous grin. "Mortals have never failed to amaze me. How you can be so powerful, and yet so blind to the truth?"

"You're insulting me?"

"Well, it's not every day a god gets a captive audience," Ni'yah chuckled as he padded through the forest. "Unless you'd like me to hand you over to the Yeth again."

Lachlei stared for a moment at the wolf-god and then began to chuckle. "The stories don't do you justice, Ni'yah," she said. "I had no idea you had such a sense of humor…"

"It balances Rhyn'athel's lack of humor," he replied. "Anyway, you know that I've been called a meddler and a trickster. Certainly, humor would be a part of it."

Lachlei smiled and held on as the wolf continued to lope through the forest. Despite the cold, she felt comfortable on the wolf-god's back—no doubt due to the god's magic that had also healed her. She looked up and saw that the sky was lightening between the treetops. It would soon be dawn.

Mile after mile, the wolf-god loped effortlessly. The sun soon shone over the horizon, peering through the trees, and still they continued. At last, Ni'yah slowed down as they approached a meadow.

"Why are we stopping?" Lachlei looked back apprehensively.

"We're safe—Areyn's demons won't attack you while I'm here," he said. "We're almost to Darkling Plain, and you and I need to talk."

Lachlei hesitated. *What would the god say to her?*

"Are you hungry?" the wolf looked up at her.

"Famished."

"Then I suggest you check your horse's packs—if I recall, you had a few days worth of provisions."

Lachlei looked up and saw her warhorse standing in the meadow, pawing the snow to graze on the grass beneath it. She slid off Ni'yah's back and stared at it. "Where did you find him?" she asked and turned to Ni'yah. To her surprise, he was no longer a wolf, but in *Eleion* form. "Telek—there was such a familial resemblance," she said shaking her head.

"Being Wyrd-born does that to you," Ni'yah remarked. "But, I'm surprised you noticed the resemblance between Rhyn'athel and me. Most are thrown off by my gold eyes and silver hair."

"I knew you and Rhyn were related the moment I saw you. I just couldn't see how," she admitted. She walked over to her horse, pulled out one of the rations, and stared at it quizzically.

"I took the liberty of improving the food," Ni'yah said. "Rhyn'athel is great at creating and swordsmanship, but he's a lousy cook. Toss me a ration—there should be one for me as well."

Lachlei laughed and then shook her head as she handed Ni'yah the packet. She pulled out the bread, leaned against her horse and began to eat.

"What's so funny?" Ni'yah asked, seeing her expression.

"A few hours ago I was nearly dead, frostbitten, covered in demon blood, and ready to die in battle. Now I'm having breakfast with one of the most powerful gods in the Nine Worlds."

"The Wyrd spins strange patterns."

"You heard my prayer. How?"

"I didn't have much of a choice," he said wryly. "You're really quite a powerful first-blood when you focus your magic. I was surprised you decided to stay in Fialan's shadow as long as you did."

Lachlei winced, but held her temper. "I loved Fialan."

"Nobody, least of all Rhyn, would dispute that claim. But you ask something that is beyond even his power to grant."

"I know," she muttered, "and I behaved like a fool. It's just that I wasn't prepared to fall in love so soon." She pulled her flask from the saddle and took a swig. Honey-sweet spiced wine filled her mouth. She swallowed it. "Metheglyn?" she remarked. "Are you trying to get me drunk?"

"No, that's for me," Ni'yah said. "Rhyn'athel would have my hide if I touched you. He really does love you."

"I know," she said wistfully. She fell silent and ate the meat in the ration.

"Do you love him?" He paused. "As Rhyn, I mean. Not as a god."

Lachlei thought back. Rhyn had been closer to her than anyone, save perhaps Fialan. He had seen her at her worst and best times and still loved her. And yet, she had tried to distance herself from him as their relationship had taken a new tenor. Why?

She knew the answer even before she asked the question. Fear. The damage the torn mind-link had done seemed irreparable. Seeing Fialan again had simply opened the wound. And yet… Lachlei closed her eyes. Even now, she missed Rhyn terribly. She had never thought she could feel this way about another man, but Rhyn's leaving left an emptiness within her. Lachlei wished she had not banished him. Rhyn had loved her deeply—perhaps more deeply than even Fialan had loved her—and now, Lachlei admitted she loved him.

She turned to see Ni'yah chewing on his bread with a wry smile.

"You already knew," she accused him. "You know I love him."

"Yes, but you didn't know, did you?" Ni'yah remarked. "Not until I asked." He paused. "Hand me that flask of metheglyn."

Lachlei held the flask in her hand for a moment and then eyed the wolf-god. "You're going to talk with him, aren't you?" She asked as she handed it to him.

Ni'yah uncorked the flask and took a swig. "You've made a bit of a mess of things for me," he admitted. "Rhyn'athel is rather displeased at me anyway."

"Why?"

"Because I'm a meddler," Ni'yah grinned. "How do you think he found out about you?"

"You?"

"If anyone is to blame for this, it's me," he said, taking another swig. "You were the bait to get Rhyn'athel interested in *Elren* again."

"You used me?" Lachlei stared.

"I saw Fialan die," Ni'yah said. "I knew it was Areyn, but I couldn't convince Rhyn'athel. So, I suggested that he see the damage done firsthand..."

"The night of Fialan's pyre," Lachlei said. "I can't believe this—you brought him when I asked Rhyn'athel for vengeance?"

"He told you, did he?"

"You knew he'd fall in love with me."

"Oh yes, I did." Ni'yah grinned and caught her fist in mid punch. "That's no way to treat the god who rescued you from Areyn's demons." He chuckled and shook his head as she lowered her arm. "*Lochvaur*. You all have Rhyn'athel's temperament, you know."

"You deserve a good beating," she remarked, crossing her arms.

"Why do you think I'm not in *Athelren*?" he said slyly.

Lachlei laughed, despite herself. She then met his gaze. "You'll talk to him, won't you?"

Ni'yah considered her carefully. "I might."

"What do you want?" she asked.

A wolfish gleam entered Ni'yah's eyes and he smiled. "I'll have what I want," he replied. "Don't worry; Rhyn'athel will be responsible for this debt, not you."

"Why doesn't that put me at ease?"

"Because I'm a troublemaker," Ni'yah said. "Now go. Your army needs you, and I must talk to Rhyn'athel. Don't worry; you'll be under my protection until you reach them."

Lachlei nodded and finished her ration. She hesitated and met Ni'yah's gaze. "I think I owe you something anyway," she said. She walked over and kissed him. "Thank you."

Ni'yah grinned. "You tempt me sorely," he said, shaking his head. "But Rhyn'athel would truly skin me alive." He disappeared, leaving Lachlei to mount her horse.

CHAPTER SEVENTY-THREE

Lachlei rode southward along the road through the forest. After an hour, the trees thinned and rolling hills of grassland replaced coniferous forest. She hesitated and scanned the area, using the Sight. She could feel the demons pursuing her, and yet, she could feel another power holding them at bay.

"Ni'yah," she whispered. "Thank you."

If the god heard her, he made no reply. Lachlei could sense her army five miles ahead even though she could not see them. The rolling hills of the Darkling Plain made it impossible for her to see beyond a mile, but she knew Cahal and Laddel were leading them in a retreat. A small demon contingent was harassing them; pushing them southward towards a larger army of *Braesan*. Lachlei knew they would not last.

"What have we here?" came a voice.

Lachlei turned and saw two *Redel* warriors, their arrows aimed directly at her.

"Put your hands up, pretty one," said the *Redel* who had spoken. He was a tall *Eleion* with a gold mane and gold eyes. Like all *Redel* warriors she had seen, he was well over six feet in height with a thin, muscular build. The bow he used was light—not like the heavier longbows that the *Lochvaur*, *Laddel*, and *Haell* used. Still, at this range, it could probably pierce her armor. His partner was a slightly older *Redel* with silver streaks through his gold hair. He had an unpleasant glimmer in his eyes as he considered Lachlei.

"By Rhyn'athel's mane, I don't have time for this!" Lachlei snarled. She raised her hands to give her a few moments to think about what she should do. She had been so focused on returning to the *Lochvaur* that she had not bothered to scan the area for other *Eleion*. "This is *Lochvaur* land."

"*Redel* land," the first replied. "You and your army have entered *Redel* claims. We intend to take our land back."

Lachlei stared at him. "Redkellan brought his army?" she asked.

"Ten thousand strong. We intend to defend our right to the plain."

Lachlei could not believe her fortune. Ten thousand. Fialan had been friends with Redkellan. She used the Sight and found that the *Redel* were only a mile away. If she could speak with the *Redel* king... "Lead me to Redkellan," she said.

"After we have a little bit of fun," said the second *Redel* with a smirk. "Get off your horse."

"Now!" the first one ordered, aiming his arrow at her chest.

Lachlei considered them. Even if they had not left their thoughts unguarded, Lachlei knew what they were planning. The *Redel* soldiers were exclusively men and had none of the *Chi'lan* discipline. They often used war as a reason for raping and looting. They thought she was an interesting prize and they would have some fun before perhaps turning her over to Redkellan.

Perhaps if she had been a noncombatant, Lachlei would have been horrified. But, she had seen far worse and was annoyed. She began to dismount, sliding her hand to *Fyren's* pommel as she turned her back to them.

"Careful!" demanded the first.

Lachlei leapt off, drawing *Fyren* in mid-leap and swinging the blade. It sliced through the first *Redel's* bow, and whirling around Lachlei slammed the blade into the second. The second *Redel* shot, but the arrow went wide. It slammed into her armor and buried itself into her shoulder.

Lachlei yelled in pain and rage, cutting into the *Redel*. The soldier staggered back as *Fyren* bit deep into his chest. She felt the death rattle and pulled the blade from the man as he collapsed. She turned on the first *Redel*, who stared at her in fear.

"By Sowelu," the man gasped. "What are you?"

Lachlei slammed *Fyren* point first into the ground. Focusing on the arrow, she grasped the shaft and pulled it out, healing herself as she did. She snapped the arrow and threw it before the astonished *Redel* soldier. "I am *Chi'lan* and you will take me to Redkellan. Now!"

She pulled *Fyren* from the ground, wiped the blade, and sheathed it. The soldier watched, but made no move. She turned to him. "What is your name?"

"Redsil," the *Redel* replied. He glanced at his dead companion. "We can't leave him."

"Then, pick him up," Lachlei replied impatiently as she mounted her horse. "You do have a horse around here, don't you?"

"Yes," he said and hesitated.

"Get your horse and sling the body over it. If you're worried about the blood price, I'll pay it," she snapped. She glanced into the sky. She could not be sure how long Ni'yah's shield would last. "We have to go now!"

Redsil slung his comrade over his shoulder and trudged towards a thicket. She rode beside him to be certain he did not try to flee or trick her. Two horses were tied to an oak tree. Redsil slung his dead companion over one of the horses and took the reins and tied it to the saddle horn of the other horse. He mounted his horse and glared at her. "I should kill you…"

"Don't flatter yourself. I've been killing arch-demons and Yeth Hounds; your sword is no threat. You try to kill me and I'll see to it your head is on a pike," Lachlei replied. "Lead me to Redkellan now."

Redsil rode forward. Lachlei followed, scanning the skies for the demons. Ten thousand *Redel* were not enough to destroy the demon army, but they would buy her own *Lochvaur* and *Laddel* time.

A lone howl echoed across the prairie. Lachlei's horse became antsy and tossed its head in fear. Redsil reined his horse and looked back at Lachlei. "I've never heard wolves in daylight."

"Those aren't wolves," she said. "Unless you count the demon kind among them. They're Yeth Hounds. Areyn must have broken Ni'yah's power—if we don't get to your army, you friend won't be the only one feeding Areyn." She pressed her steed into a gallop, not waiting for the *Redel's* response.

Lachlei glanced back to see Redsil press his horse to a gallop. A dozen white wolves materialized behind them. *Release the second horse!* She mindspoke to him. He needed no further urging and cut the reins to the second horse. His horse shot forward in blind panic, freed from its burden. The other horse turned, and the Yeth leapt at it, tearing it to pieces. Still, other Yeth filled in the gaps. Lachlei spurred her horse forward, hoping to avoid the demons. She heard Redsil's scream, but did not look back. She knew the Yeth had caught the *Redel* soldier.

Up ahead, she could see the *Redel* army. Archers were already scrambling to ready themselves along the lines as she rode towards them. She hoped none of them would take aim at her. She glanced back and saw that the Yeth were rapidly closing on her. Lachlei urged her horse onward, but she knew that her warhorse was stretched to its limits.

Fire! Damn it! Fire! She shouted in mindspeak as she came into range. A volley of arrow flew overhead, and she saw some of the Yeth go down. Adamantine-tipped arrows, Lachlei realized. While their archers did not have the range of the *Lochvaur* longbow men, Lachlei knew that the *Redel* archers could be as deadly in short range.

Lachlei rode through the lines and reined her horse. The Yeth halted in dismay and turned back as a hail of arrows greeted them.

"Lachlei?" spoke a familiar voice. Lachlei turned to see a handsome *Redel* with gold hair and eyes approach her. His surcoat showed a golden sun on a blue background. "By Sowelu's rays, is that you?" he asked incredulously.

"Redkellan?" Lachlei said. "Thank the gods you are here. Those were Yeth Hounds..."

Redkellan nodded. "I know. We heard that the *Lochvaur* were in our territory, but I didn't expect an army, and I didn't expect you. Where's Fialan?"

Lachlei stared at the *Redel* prince. "Didn't you hear?"

Redkellan frowned. "Hear what? There's been rivalry among the *Redel* princes for the throne—I've been busy."

Lachlei gazed at him for a moment before answering. How would the *Redel* act towards a *Lochvaur* queen? "Fialan is dead..."

"Dead?" Redkellan stared. "Who's king now?"

She smiled. "I am."

Redkellan's eyes widened for a moment and then he laughed. "Come with me," he said. "We must discuss this."

"But the demons..."

"My warriors will take care of them," he said. His gaze narrowed. "I believe we have some matters to discuss."

◆◆◆◆◆

Redkellan led Lachlei into his tent and they sat down in two chairs next to a table. A portable woodstove burned next to a cot, and Redkellan motioned a servant to fill two flagons with mead.

Lachlei raised her hand. "As much as I would like to drink with you, I fear I must pass," she said.

Redkellan nodded. "You're first-blood—I forget," he said with a smile. "It amazes me how those with gods' blood in them have no resistance to alcohol."

"The first-bloods' curse," she remarked, and he chuckled.

Lachlei at one time might have considered Redkellan with interest. He was young—no more than fifty years old—and like his father, had achieved his position through combat, not blood. He was handsome in a rough way, with braided gold hair and golden eyes. His nose was broken and a large scar ran from cheekbone to throat. Although his father had been king, neither Redkellan nor his father had any godling blood, which made his achievement remarkable. But Lachlei did not doubt that there were first-blood challengers among the *Redel* princes who were causing friction.

He removed his gauntlets and Lachlei smiled as she saw the mark of Sowelu on his forearm: a many-rayed sun. "I see the sun god has chosen you as his champion," she said.

Redkellan glanced at the mark and nodded. "The combat wasn't easy. Some are still contesting my right."

"Indeed," Lachlei said. "But that doesn't explain what you are doing on *Lochvaur* lands."

Redkellan leaned back and took a draught of the honey-wine. "Darkling Plain has always been under contention between our two kindreds. My father, Redhael, gave up that right for the sake of peace with the *Lochvaur*, but with the current contention for the throne, it would seem that the old treaties are invalid."

"But you're Sowelu's champion," she said.

"Not all recognize me as such."

"They didn't argue when Redhael took the throne."

"Redhael had a larger army and more lands than I do," Redkellan replied. "He was older when he ascended the throne. I don't have the support he had."

Lachlei met his gaze. "So, those who can build the largest army and take the most lands are most likely to take the throne," she said.

"Indeed," Redkellan remarked. "But what is the *Lochvaur* army doing on Darkling Plain?"

"You have spies," she said. "You know we're being pursued."

Redkellan leaned forward, his gold eyes glittering. "Yes, by *Silren, Eltar,* and demons. Very interesting."

Lachlei frowned. "Then, if you know…"

The *Redel* prince shrugged. "This is not the *Redel's* fight," he said. "We have our own problems."

"Areyn Sehduk killed Fialan," Lachlei interrupted him.

Redkellan fell silent and considered her. "If that is so, then we should be seeing the *Athel'cen.*" He shook his head. "This is not a *Redel* fight."

"It should be," Lachlei said. "Join me against them."

Redkellan chuckled and shook his head again. "This is not our fight, Lachlei."

Lachlei considered the prince carefully. "I can give you what you want."

Silence ensued. Redkellan acted disinterested, but Lachlei could sense interest behind his shield. "And what might that be?"

"The throne to the *Redel* kindred," Lachlei said, sounding more confident than she felt.

Another silence followed. Lachlei watched as Redkellan weighed her offer. "You've piqued my interest," he admitted. "How would you put me on the *Redel* throne?"

"I have my ways," she said.

He shook his head. "No mystery. If I am going to risk the lives of my army I must know how you plan to put me on the *Redel* throne." Redkellan smiled sardonically. "It seems odd that a *Lochvaur* queen who is pursued by two kindreds and demons could offer the crown to another kindred."

Lachlei hesitated. The support of the *Lochvaur* would not be enough to give the *Redel* crown to Redkellan. Her mind strayed back to the wolf-god—how much would Ni'yah willing to do? She could not say. "An *Athel'cen* fights with us," she said.

Redkellan's eyes widened. "Is that so?"

Lachlei nodded. "He would look on those who help the *Lochvaur* with favor," she said.

"Favor is not enough," Redkellan said dismissively. "I need more than favor. I need a victory."

"Help me and I promise at least one *Athel'cen* on your side," Lachlei said, wondering how she might accomplish it.

The *Redel* prince grinned as he quaffed the last bit of mead. "I don't believe you," he said at last. "I don't think you or anyone has that power…"

"Very well, then you take an awful chance, don't you?" Lachlei said, standing up.

"Where are you going?" Redkellan asked.

"Back to my army," Lachlei replied.

"But the demons…"

Lachlei smiled grimly. "I have slain arch-demons, Redkellan," she said. "I am not afraid." She walked out of the tent.

"Lachlei," Redkellan began.

She turned and met the *Redel* prince's gaze. "Yes?"

His eyes narrowed and he shook his head. "They said you were a *Lochvaur* sorceress, but I didn't believe them. Now I do."

Lachlei laughed. "Really? I didn't know I had such a reputation."

"My own *Redel* will join you—though only the gods know why."

CHAPTER SEVENTY-FOUR

"Demons!" the watch shouted.

It was still dark when Cahal awoke to yells and the strident call of the battle-horns. He leapt from his bedroll, still in armor. He nudged Kieran, who lay not far away in the commanders' tent, with his foot. "Demons, Kieran! Demons, Laddel!"

"Gods!" groaned Kieran. He pulled himself from bed. "This is the third time tonight."

"They're keeping us awake," said Cara. "They're wearing us down."

"She's right," said Laddel. "The demons don't need sleep."

"What about the *Braesan*?" Cahal asked.

Laddel shook his head. "I don't know. But I suspect that if they need rest, it is for their bodies in this world." He clapped a few warriors on the back. "Let's go."

They ran outside and stared into the sky. The clouds blanketed the sky, blotting out the light from the stars and the moons. As Cahal heard the last notes of the battle-horns die, he gazed into the sky.

"There!" Cahal said, pointing to the forms that moved against the clouds. There were several.

"By the wolf's mane," said Laddel, his brass eyes gazing at the creatures. He drew his Sword of Power.

The demons shrieked and flew towards them, claws outstretched. The *Laddel* and *Chi'lan* archers were ready. A hailstorm of adamantine-tipped arrows flew towards the demons. Some avoided the barrage, but many were hit and fell. The warriors on the ground charged the wounded demons and attacked.

Screams of men and demons filled the night. Another battle-horn rang out and Cahal turned to see fighting along the flank. Even from this distance, he could see the pale warriors attack the *Elesil* troops. "Damn! Damn!" he shouted, grasping a horse and climbing into the saddle. "Conlan! The *Braesan* are attacking your men!"

Conlan was already on his horse, riding towards his troops. A demon swooped down, talons bared. Conlan drew his sword, but the demon was already on top of him, ripping the *Elesil* king and his mount to shreds.

Cahal charged, blinded by fury. He swung his adamantine blade, slicing deep into the creature. It shrieked, trying to rake its claws against Cahal. Cahal jumped back. The demon turned back onto its prey.

"Rhyn'athel!" shouted Cara and leapt at the demon. Together, Cahal and the *Silren* princess attacked the demon. Cahal's final stroke decapitated it. The demon collapsed, and they pushed the corpse off what was left of Conlan.

"Oh Conlan!" Cara cried, cradling the *Elesil* king's head. The silver eyes were already glazing over. She tried frantically to heal him, but the demon had ripped one of his arms off and huge gouges ran down his body.

Cahal looked at Laddel, who stood by. The godling shook his head. *I think this is even beyond my sire's ability.*

Cahal gripped Cara's shoulder. She looked up with angry blue eyes. "Come on, *Chi'lan*," he said gently. "We can do naught for him now."

"Cahal, he was my friend."

"I know, *Chi'lan*," he said. "We've lost many friends because of Areyn Sehduk. We'll build a pyre when this is over."

"*Chi'lan*," she said grimly. "I have wanted to be called that all my life. Now, I look on the king of my brother kindred and I am not so certain. Is this what the warrior god demands of you?"

Cahal shook his head. "The *Chi'lan's* way has never been easy. It isn't what the warrior god demands; it is what we give freely. It is something we do, not because it is easy or painless, but because it is right."

"Conlan knew this," Cara said.

"Then I count him as *Chi'lan*," Cahal said. "Just as I count you as one." He paused. "Come on, *Chi'lan*. We have a battle ahead."

◆◆◆◆◆

Cara led the *Elesil* to the front lines. Although they had no weapons like the *Chi'lan* and *Laddel* longbows, they had archers and stood ready along the front lines. *Laddel* and *Chi'lan* mixed between them, fortifying the archers' lines with long-range defense. Pikemen made a line before the archers, hoping to provide some protection in case of a charge.

Cara rode behind the archers, in front of the warhorses and infantry. Cahal, Laddel, and the other commanders rode with her. "Damn," she said. "I wish the wolf-god was among us."

Laddel smiled grimly. "Indeed. But I, for one, wouldn't argue if Rhyn'athel fought beside us."

She looked at him. "You look much like your sire. I didn't have much time to thank him when we entered this war."

A howl echoed through the line. Laddel stiffened; his brass eyes narrowed as the howling continued. Cara felt an involuntary shiver run through her.

"What is it?" Cahal asked.

"Areyn's Yeth Hounds."

"Yeth Hounds?" Cahal repeated.

"The demon hounds of Areyn. Dire wolves."

"We've seen them," Cara said. "They're very tough to kill." She looked into the night. Slowly, thousands of red glowing eyes appeared, one after another. "By the warrior god's sword, how many are there?"

Laddel shook his head. "Could be as many in number as our army. Maybe more."

Without warning, the demon wolves attacked. The *Eleion* sent a barrage of arrows into the creature's lines, and the wolves screamed as the adamantine tips of the clothyard shafts penetrated and pinned them down. Some ran through, only to be waylaid on the pikes. The pikes were not adamantine tipped and did no damage, but it kept the demons at bay. Those that came through the pikes, the foot soldiers and cavalry made short work of.

As the bodies of the dying demons began to pile up, Cara grew fearful. They would soon run out arrows. How many demons were there? She glanced at Laddel and Cahal, who looked grim.

"Yeth!" shouted the archers.

A white wolf leapt through the lines, its eyes glowing red as it headed right towards Cara. Her horse reared as the demon leapt for her. She slashed at the beast as it threw itself on her, but it knocked her from the saddle. For a moment, everything was teeth, fur, and claws as the demon tried to rip her throat out. She felt the crushing jaws around her gorget. and she slashed and stabbed.

Then, everything was still. Cara could hear her name called out and felt strong hands pull her to her feet. She was covered in blood—demon blood.

"Are you all right?" Cahal asked. He and Laddel were standing beside her. She nodded, staring stupidly at the demon's body as it turned to dust before her eyes. "Are you wounded?"

"No," she said. "Watch out!"

More demon wolves broke through their ranks. The archers were out of arrows. Demon wolves were everywhere, suddenly materializing inside the ranks. The *Eleion* fought back, but they were weary and the demons were fresh. Cara wondered now if perhaps this might be their last stand. She looked in the sky; dawn was breaking. Even so, she doubted she would see midday.

Then, I die as Chi'lan, she thought.

◆◆◆◆◆

A battle-horn rang out, and there was a pause in the fighting. Cara turned and saw another *Eleion* army charge forward. She and Cahal glanced at each other. "What in the gods' names?" she exclaimed.

Cahal stared. "They're *Redel*," he said, noting their armor and surcoats emblazoned with a sun.

"*Redel*? What are they doing in this battle?"

Cara's gaze fell on a lone rider at the thrust of the attack. Her red-gold surcoat emblazoned with a dragon of Rhyn'athel shone even at this distance. "There's a *Chi'lan* among them."

Cahal began laughing. "Lachlei! Lachlei!" Soon all the soldiers picked up his cry.

CHAPTER SEVENTY-FIVE

"Admit it; you're still in love with her."

Rhyn'athel sat on his throne in the Hall of the Gods. The great mead hall was empty, save for the two. The firepit sat cold, and a breeze blew through the vast room. If either had been in their mortal bodies, they would have felt the wind's bite much more. It echoed Rhyn'athel's dismal mood.

Admit it; you're still in love with her.

Ni'yah's words stung, but like most of his barbs, the words held truth. That was why most gods detested Ni'yah—indeed, that's why Areyn despised the wolf god. Rhyn'athel suffered his brother's tongue, because despite the harshness, Ni'yah had a clarity that sometimes Rhyn'athel lacked. And, although Rhyn'athel wouldn't admit it, he had brotherly affection for the wolf-god.

Rhyn'athel glanced at Ni'yah, but refused to meet the wolf-god's gaze. "Love is a foolish mortal emotion…"

Ni'yah grinned. "Brother, you're not the only god to have fallen for a mortal woman."

Rhyn'athel stood, towering over his brother. "You—you dragged me into this! I should skin your miserable wolf-hide and hang it on my door as a warning for those who dare to meddle."

Ni'yah chuckled. "I'd probably deserve it, too. But this doesn't alter the circumstances, my brother. The *Lochvaur* are at Areyn's mercy without you. And Lachlei will become his…"

A muscle twitched in Rhyn'athel's chiseled jaw. He turned his silver eyes away. "Lachlei doesn't love me."

"She loves you—but she also loves a memory."

"I can't give her what she asks. It is not in anyone's power, save Areyn's."

"Then, Lachlei is lost to you." Ni'yah shook his head. "And with her, so shifts the balance."

"Lachlei would be Areyn's when she died," Rhyn'athel replied. "I can do naught."

Ni'yah leaned back on the armrest of his own throne. "Are you so quick to relinquish the battle?" He shook his head. "And I thought you were always the more powerful. I guess I was wrong."

Rhyn'athel turned to him. "What are you saying?"

"For a victor, you're a coward!" Ni'yah said, his voice dripping with scorn. "I'm surprised that the great warrior god cowers in the face of a lesser deity. Perhaps I've overestimated you…"

Anger flashed in Rhyn'athel's eyes, and before Ni'yah could respond, he held the wolf-god off the floor by the neck and shoved him against a wall. The tip of *Teiwaz* pressed into Ni'yah's throat. "I should cut your tongue out," Rhyn'athel said.

Ni'yah's brass eyes glanced at the Sword of Power. "For speaking the truth?" he said, his voice strained.

"For your annoying prattle."

"For the *truth*," Ni'yah croaked. "Areyn has you cowed. He will take the Nine Worlds from you bit by bit, until there is nothing left and you can no longer stop him."

"But the Nine Worlds…"

"The Nine Worlds were ravaged before and we managed to rebuild. Is our power so weak, we cower at creating again? Are you willing to let Areyn gain the upper hand in this war?" He paused and a gleam entered his eyes. "Do you want him to make love to Lachlei?"

Rhyn'athel's fist closed tighter around Ni'yah's throat, but he did not move the Sword. He met Ni'yah gaze with fierce determination. "Areyn wouldn't dare."

"Areyn would defile her. He'd rape her and force her to bear his demon offspring—the sons that should be yours…"

Rhyn'athel released Ni'yah. The wolf-god landed unsteadily on his feet and ran his fingers over his sore neck.

"Has your time as a mortal made you Wyrd-blind?" Ni'yah said, still rubbing his neck. "Her godling sons will change the balance."

Rhyn'athel shook his head. "There's a fork in the Wyrd strands."

"Your sons may bring Areyn's ultimate destruction or Areyn's sons may bring yours."

"But Lachlei is the junction," he said at last. "She doesn't love me, Ni'yah. She loves Fialan, and I can't even bring him back."

"Perhaps not now," said Ni'yah. "I think when this war is over there should be some changes, my brother."

Rhyn'athel nodded, sheathing his sword. "I won't take her as Areyn would, but I won't have her be the pawn of the gods or the pawn of the Wyrd. It must be her choice."

"We are all pawns of the Wyrd in one way or another," Ni'yah said. "But you are right, my brother. Lachlei must decide. And so a mortal woman holds the fate of the Nine Worlds and the destiny of the gods." He grinned wryly. "I couldn't have thought up more mischief if I had tried."

Rhyn'athel chuckled. "Indeed."

"Go to her, brother. I think she'll surprise you."

◆◆◆◆◆

The sun rose above the Darkling Plain, casting all in its red glow. Lachlei rode forward with Redkellan at her side. She swung *Fyren*, her full anger unleashed on the demon hounds. Several tried to attack her, but she gathered her power and flung them away in a blast of supernatural fire. All around her, she could hear her name as a battle cry. The *Lochvaur*, *Laddel*, and *Elesil* took up the cry and began slaying demons, renewed by her presence. The demon hounds and *Braesan* fled and disappeared as the warriors converged.

Lachlei raised her hand, amid the shouts of victory. She was covered in blood and looked weary. Cahal rode towards her, a grin on his face. Following him were the other commanders. "I thought you might need some help," she said.

"Yes, we could use a little help," Cahal said.

"It looked like you might," said Redkellan.

Lachlei nodded. "This is Redkellan. He's agreed to aid us."

Cara looked at the *Redel* prince in mistrust. "I didn't know that the *Redel* were so eager to aid the *Lochvaur*."

Redkellan gazed coolly on Cara. "A *Silren*? I thought you served Areyn."

Cara drew her blade and lunged. Cahal pulled her back. "Easy, they just saved our hides."

"I don't care," she snapped. "*Redel* dogs!"

"Enough, *Silren*!" Lachlei snapped. "If anyone should be angry, it should be me for your kindred's role in nearly destroying mine. I take it you're one of the dissenters?"

Cara nodded. "I am Cara, daughter of Silvain."

"Good, we can use you," Lachlei said. "I see *Elesil* here—where's Conlan?"

A silence followed.

"Conlan's dead," Cara said. "A demon killed him tonight."

Cahal looked at Lachlei. "Where's Rhyn? He was supposed to rescue you."

A shadow crossed Lachlei's face. "I don't know," she said. "He left."

Laddel stared at her. "Will he return?"

Lachlei met his gaze. "I sent Telek to find him. It depends on how persuasive he is."

Then, you know he is Ni'yah, Laddel mindspoke.

Yes, she replied heavily. *And I know who Rhyn is.*

You don't know if he will return?

No.

Laddel's face became grim. *Then, we are lost.*

CHAPTER SEVENTY-SIX

Lachlei dismounted her steed and stood, wounded and bloody, on a hill overlooking Darkling Plain. She was weary and had not even the reserves to heal herself. Her arm ached from a cut she received from a Yeth hound, and it hurt to even breathe. She stretched slowly, rubbing her cramped thigh muscles with her good hand. She could still carry a sword—that was all that mattered now.

The shadows were growing long again. The hours since the morning victory had slipped by all too fast. Her warriors recovered what few clothyard shafts and adamantine-tipped arrows there were. They had pulled the wounded deep inside their lines, hoping to heal them. Lachlei had done what she could, not even bothering to heal herself now. Her own safety seemed meaningless with so many wounded. Even now, she could see the torches of Areyn's army marching ever closer to her own weary troops. They needed to flee—to escape Areyn unrelenting pursuit—but they also needed rest.

"Lachlei!" Cahal spoke. She turned and looked at her second-in-command.

"Cahal," she said.

"You know we found Wynne and Haellsil."

She caught her breath.

"They're alive and with the noncombatants," he said quickly. "*Chi'lan* Kerri got them out of the city before Areyn razed it."

Lachlei lowered her head and wept. "Thank the gods," she whispered. "What of our noncombatants?"

"Ten thousand at most," he said.

"And our warriors?"

Cahal shook his head. "It's grim, Lachlei. We have about a thousand *Chi'lan* left. Our *Lochvaur* are maybe twenty thousand. The *Laddel*, maybe five thousand. The *Elesil* are twenty thousand and the *Redel* at about ten thousand. Maybe sixty thousand total."

"Sixty thousand," she sighed. "I would normally dream for such an army, and yet it seems like nothing compared to Areyn's might. He could bring a hundred thousand — five hundred thousand, a million—against us because he has the dead. How can we fight against that?"

"He also has the *Eltar* now as well as the *Silren*," Cahal said. "Who knows what other kindreds will fall to him? But our army isn't unified either. Already, we've had to break up fights between the *Elesil* and *Redel*—they're enemies, you know."

"I know," Lachlei said heavily. "Damn it, Cahal, why do we have to fight each other?"

He shook his head. "I don't know. All it does is serve the death god." He paused. "It's not safe out here, Lachlei. Come back to the tent, get something to eat and have Laddel take a look at that arm."

"All right, I will in a little while," she said, trying to smile. "Go ahead without me—I'll be with you soon."

Lachlei watched as Cahal mounted his horse and rode back. She could see it in his eyes that he did not expect to live through this final battle. None of them did. Without Ni'yah or Rhyn'athel, they were doomed.

In despair, her thoughts turned to Rhyn. How Lachlei longed to see him again. Part of her knew what he was, and yet she still could not believe it entirely despite the fact that she had spoken to Ni'yah who admitted Rhyn was the warrior god. If Rhyn were Rhyn'athel, he would certainly have a plan to get them out of this.

But that was not why she missed Rhyn so, Lachlei now admitted to herself. She missed *him*. Ni'yah had showed her she had fallen in love, despite herself. Lachlei wished she had not banished him. Rhyn had loved her deeply—perhaps more deeply than even Fialan had loved her.

Snarling pulled her from her reverie. Lachlei's horse screamed as a Yeth Hound leapt on her. She rolled with the massive demon on top of her, and her injured arm flailed upward to protect her throat. The Yeth sank its dagger teeth into her arm and shook, breaking bone and sinew. Lachlei screamed in pain and fought to grasp her sword or dagger hilt—anything to fight the demon hound. She brought her legs up and kicked, but the Yeth was relentless.

Suddenly, it was gone. Lachlei lay for a moment, her breath ragged and painful with every shallow gulp of air. Her arm was in shreds, and the familiar coppery taste of blood filled her mouth. Her vision blurred, and she saw a glowing warrior astride a stallion, wielding a Sword of Power. The Yeth Hounds slunk away from the warrior, and he rode towards her. She closed her eyes, too weak and overcome with pain to speak. When she opened them again, she looked into a familiar face.

"Rhyn?" she whispered, but her voice came out as a croak.

"Shhhh," Rhyn whispered to her. "You're badly wounded." He touched her, and she saw the glow around him once more.

"Am I dreaming?" she murmured. She began to feel warm, and the pain disappeared.

"Shhhh," he repeated. He touched her ribs where they had broken and punctured a lung. His fingers touched her shredded arm, and it became whole again. The damage was extensive—had he not arrived, Lachlei would have died.

Lachlei opened her eyes. "You've come back to me," she said confused. "Or am I dead, and you too? Will we have to join Areyn's legions?"

Rhyn smiled. "No, we're not dead," he said. "And I doubt Areyn could have me in his legions."

Lachlei slid her arms around his neck, pausing for a moment to see that her arm was whole. “Rhyn,” she whispered. “How…?”

“Shhhh, you’re still healing.”

“No, listen to me,” she said. Rhyn fell silent and met her gaze. “Gods, I don’t know what I was thinking, but I was wrong. I was wrong, Rhyn.” She pulled his face towards hers. “I love you.” She pulled him to her and kissed him.

It was as though all the penned-up emotions inside her were released. Energy crackled between them, white hot, as she felt his eager response. He took her in his arms and held her, his silver eyes filled with desire and longing for her.

“Areyn’s army,” she said.

Rhyn shook his head. “Don’t worry, beloved, there will be time enough for battle. Areyn won’t reach us yet.”

Lachlei stared into his eyes. “The greatest warrior,” she whispered. “And I was too blind to see.”

Rhyn’s lips caressed her throat. “You were preoccupied, beloved.” He slid her helm off and slid the mail coif to her shoulders. He began to untie her tresses and ran his fingers through her red-gold hair.

Lachlei returned his embrace as she slid from her armor. “You should have told me, Rhyn’athel. You should have told me.”

CHAPTER SEVENTY-SEVEN

Ni'yah loped into the *Lochvaur* camp in wolf form. The sentries backed away as the huge silver wolf, glazed in light, came bounding in. He transmuted into his *Eleion* form, a *Laddel* warrior with radiant armor and a Sword of Power that glowed white-hot. Many of the sentries had nocked arrows, but lowered their bows.

"I am Ni'yah," the wolf-god said. "If you want to live, you'd best bring me to Laddel and Cahal."

Laddel strode forward through the crowd that was gathering, followed by Cahal, Tamar, and Cara. The *Laddel* King stared at his father for a moment. "What are you doing here?" he demanded. "Do you know what this means?"

"Fine way to greet your sire," Ni'yah snapped. "How many wounded do you have?"

"Do you know this creature?" *Chi'lan* Kian asked, turning to Laddel.

Laddel glanced behind at the *Lochvaur* apprehensively.

"Tell them who I am," Ni'yah said.

"Then, the war's begun," Laddel whispered.

"It never ended—tell them!"

Laddel turned to the *Lochvaur*. "This is Ni'yah, brother of Rhyn'athel."

"Telek is the wolf-god?" Cahal asked. "Then, I was…"

"Your guess, young *Lochvaur*, was right," Ni'yah said.

"What does this mean?" Cahal looked around. "Where's Lachlei—she should know."

"Lachlei already knows—she's with Rhyn'athel," Ni'yah said. "I need your wounded now, and I need you to stop your orders to advance. We wait on Rhyn'athel's orders."

A murmur ran through the *Lochvaur*. "Rhyn'athel? Rhyn'athel *is* here?" exclaimed Cara. She stared at Ni'yah. "The warrior god is here?"

"Indeed. The *Chi'lan* know him as 'Rhyn,'" the wolf-god replied.

Another murmur ran through the *Lochvaur*. Cahal grinned broadly. "Rhyn? Rhyn has returned?" He stared at the wolf-god. "And he is truly Rhyn'athel as we thought?"

"Rhyn'athel!" laughed Tamar, clapping Cahal on the back. "By the gods! I knew there was more to Rhyn than meets the eye. And here I thought a mere mortal had bested me!" The *Chi'lan* warriors surrounding them chuckled in appreciation.

"I guess your reputation is still intact," Cara remarked.

"But what of the death god's army?" Laddel asked.

"I've taken care of that—we have several hours ahead of us to rest and prepare," Ni'yah replied. "If you're up to fighting for the warrior god," he added wryly.

Cahal laughed. He turned to his men. "Rhyn'athel! Rhyn'athel!" he led the cheer.

◆◆◆◆

Lachlei awoke beside the warrior god, still wrapped in his embrace. She slowly turned in his arms and gazed up at the stars. It was still dark, and the stars were still in the same position as they had been when they made love. They lay under his cloak, warm against the chilly air. Lachlei relaxed against him, enjoying the heat and feel of the warrior god's body, pressed against hers.

"What is wrong, beloved?" Rhyn'athel asked.

"The stars…" she began.

"Time has stopped," he said simply.

"How?" she began and then laughed. "Of course. What about our army?"

"They are resting," Rhyn'athel said. "They will need it for the battle." He kissed her. "Beloved, something troubles you."

"Why didn't you tell me who you really were?"

Rhyn'athel sighed. "I would have, if I thought I could. I had hoped to keep my identity secret long enough to keep the Truce intact. It was foolish notion. It's complex, beloved, but even I can't see the entire future. Every time a god interferes, it causes the Wyrd to change. I knew Areyn was here and hoped to stop him before it came to this…" He shook his head. "I'm sorry for the deception, beloved, but it was necessary to keep Areyn from knowing that I was involved."

Lachlei gazed at his face. "Some first-blood I am — I didn't even recognize a god within my own *Chi'lan*."

Rhyn'athel smiled wryly. "It was difficult to keep my identity concealed from you, anyway. But I didn't lie to you when I told you I was a demon slayer."

She kissed him. "No, you didn't."

"And you would've felt differently about me if you had known I was a god."

Lachlei met his gaze. "Do you believe that?"

"Deities inspire awe and fear, but seldom love," he said. "Perhaps you might not have, but I couldn't risk it. Being a god can be lonely, Lachlei. When I saw you for the first time, I knew I had to have you. But to appear to you as a god…"

"You became mortal for me," she said, shaking her head. "I still can't believe it."

Rhyn'athel nodded sheepishly. "Not one of my well-thought out plans," he admitted.

"Rhyn, I would love you regardless of what you are," she said, laying her head against his chest. "I am glad you returned. When you left, a part of me died."

Rhyn'athel smiled at her use of his familiar name. "If there is anyone to blame for my return, it's Ni'yah."

"Ni'yah?" she grinned. "I knew that trickster wouldn't fail me."

Rhyn'athel stared at her. "You sent him?" he asked incredulously.

"I guess I did. He saved my life, Rhyn. I asked him to convince you to come back." She kissed him. "I'm glad he did."

"His meddling brought me here in the first place," the god remarked.

"I know. He told me."

Rhyn'athel frowned. "What else did he tell you?"

She slid her arms around his neck. "That you love me very much." She kissed him again. Rhyn'athel responded, kissing her slowly. She pulled away and gazed into his eyes. "Rhyn," she whispered. "Not all the kindreds are involved in this—are any of the other gods involved?"

"No, this time it is between Areyn Sehduk and me," the god said. "The other gods won't take sides—not this time. Only Ni'yah has joined my side." He smiled wryly. "Even now, he's preparing our troops." He slowly sat up, keeping her pressed against him. "We shouldn't tarry long, beloved, even if I have stopped time. Areyn will eventually become wise to it."

Lachlei sighed. "I suppose you're right." She met his gaze. "Rhyn, there is something else that bothers me—Fialan ..."

"I know," Rhyn'athel said grimly. "I would've prevented Fialan's death if I could've, Lachlei. But Areyn killed Fialan."

The words made Lachlei shiver, and she pressed her head against the god and wept. He held her gently. "Fialan hates it, I know—I could see it when he fought against us. But he was powerless to do anything." She looked up again to see the god's eyes strangely bright.

"I know," he said. "All the dead serve Areyn, even the *Chi'lan*. Even my son, Lochvaur…"

Lachlei closed her eyes and shook her head. "Your son—Lochvaur. That was Lochvaur?"

Rhyn'athel nodded. "I told you it was hard to explain, but yes, the man who rode next to Fialan was none other than Lochvaur."

Lachlei felt sheepish. She opened her eyes to see Rhyn'athel grinning at her. "What's so funny?"

"You are," he said. "You drove me away and yet were jealous over a nonexistent lover." Lachlei tried to look angry, but Rhyn'athel pulled her closer and kissed her. "I couldn't quite explain to you Lochvaur's existence—it was far too complicated."

"I see," Lachlei said and fell silent. "Did you love her?"

Rhyn'athel glanced at Lachlei in puzzlement. "Love whom?"

"Lochvaur's mother."

Rhyn'athel chuckled. "Lochvaur had no mother. Lochvaur was a product of my power, Lachlei, just as the *Eleion* and *Ansgar* are, only more so." He shook his head. "Lochvaur is difficult to explain, but he is my son."

"But he serves Areyn."

"Not willfully. He is *Eleion*, which makes him mortal, thus, when Areyn took the dead, he also took Lochvaur. I didn't want it that way, but Lochvaur and Ni'yah talked me into it."

"I don't understand."

Rhyn'athel kissed her. "Now is not the time for the full explanation. Just accept that because he is mortal, he fell under Areyn's domain."

"As do all mortals." Lachlei shivered again. "I don't want to serve Areyn," she whispered, tracing the lines of Rhyn'athel's face. "I couldn't bear to part from you again."

"You won't," Rhyn'athel said. "I swear on my sword, *Teiwaz*, I will never let that happen."

Lachlei kissed him, relishing in his response to her touch. His lips slid from her lips to her neck and down to her breasts. "Shouldn't we return to the army?" she asked. She pulled away to see disappointment in his eyes.

Rhyn'athel smiled. "Another hour will give them more rest," he said, pulling her close again. "I've waited a long time for this, Lachlei. A very long time…"

Chapter Seventy-Eight

Rhyn'athel rode back to the army with Lachlei riding beside him. Gone were the mortal trappings now as he rode his white steed into camp. His fiery eyes were glazed with light, and his adamantine armor shone brilliantly in the darkness. The long, red-gold mane flowed behind him like a banner. The *Lochvaur* and *Laddel* warriors paused and stared as the god rode past. Tamar grinned as he saw the god ride past with Lachlei. "Rhyn'athel! Rhyn'athel!" he called out.

Others took up the cry, and soon the entire camp was chanting the warrior god's name. Lachlei glanced at Rhyn'athel. "I believe you're enjoying this," she remarked dryly.

Rhyn'athel grinned back. "I should've never agreed to the Truce, beloved," he said. "These are my people, and this is my world. Ni'yah was right—I've been gone far too long from the *Eleion*."

Ni'yah turned and saw his brother ride forward amid the cheering warriors. He had been speaking with his son, Laddel, when the warrior god rode up. "You took your time," he grumbled.

Rhyn'athel grinned and dismounted. "It *was* your idea, brother," he said, glancing at Lachlei as she dismounted and stood beside him.

Ni'yah laughed. "Indeed it was," he said knowingly.

"How many warriors do we have ready to fight?" Lachlei asked, distracting them.

Ni'yah glanced at Laddel. "Sixty thousand warriors, total—completely healed and rested," the *Laddel* king replied. "Ten thousand noncombatants, of which we're able to arm two thousand."

"But they are not skilled," Cahal said, striding up. He paused as he met Rhyn'athel's gaze. "My lord, I am your humble servant," he said, bowing his head.

"Cahal—no," Rhyn'athel said, gripping the commander's arm. "You are my friend, not my servant. Those who fight for me, who serve me as *Chi'lan*, are my warriors and my friends, not my slaves. I am proud to count you as a friend." He turned and met Cara's gaze. The daughter of Silvain stood among the warriors silently. "And you, Cara of the *Silren*, you wish to ask something of me?"

Cara hesitated, her ice-blue eyes betraying her fear. "My lord, I..." She felt Cahal's grip on her shoulder and steeled herself. "Conlan is dead."

Rhyn'athel nodded. "I know; he served me well. There will be changes err the battle is over, *Chi'lan*."

"*Chi'lan*?" she whispered in puzzlement, and then smiled as she caught his knowing look. "I am *Chi'lan*..."

"As are you all."

"Very well, *Chi'lan* Rhyn'athel, what shall we do?" Cahal asked. "Areyn Sehduk has us hopelessly outnumbered with creatures that can't die. We can't kill what is already dead—and many are our own fallen comrades."

"Areyn may bring the *Jotunn* here as well," Ni'yah remarked. "If he brings those into this world, we can assume that the war will spread to other worlds."

"It's a risk I'll have to take," said Rhyn'athel. He raised his arms and drew a glowing diagram of a battlefield in the air. "Areyn, for all his bluster, is a poor tactician. He holds such contempt for life that he's willing to sacrifice troops for the most casualties. He uses his warriors foolishly, depending on sheer numbers rather than their skill. We can use that to our advantage..."

"But if his warriors can't die, he has a good reason to rely on overwhelming numbers," Laddel said.

"Indeed, but he expects the gate to his world will stay open," said Rhyn'athel, grinning at Ni'yah. "He will have a nasty surprise when he finds the gate shut and guarded."

"Many of the warriors were our own *Chi'lan*," Lachlei said.

Rhyn'athel nodded. "And the *Silren* and the *Eltar* fight for Areyn out of fear. Trust me on this, beloved. We will defeat him here and now on Darkling Plain."

Lachlei smiled. "Very well, continue."

"We keep our lines mobile and high on these ridges," Rhyn'athel continued, pointing to the blue drawings. "Longbow men, here, will be our primary weapon to take out the charge. If any get through, we'll have to handle them hand-to-hand."

"What of the noncombatants?" Cahal asked.

"We'll have to have someone lead them away from the fighting. The two thousand armed noncombatants will have to be their protection." He paused. "With such small numbers, I can't afford to lose any more *Chi'lan*."

"What if Areyn tries to outflank us?" Lachlei asked.

Ni'yah grinned. "They'll have a nasty surprise." With that, he vanished.

◆◆◆◆◆

Ni'yah stood on a pass within the Neversummer Mountains. Not far from the ice dragon caves lay the great glaciers that moved slowly towards the sea. The jumbled seracs stood like giant towers, but Ni'yah knew they were constantly shifting. The seracs slowly tumbled down the frozen mountains towards the ocean, moving just a few feet per day. They stood iridescent blue and green, like oddly colored sentinels, guardians to a world beyond.

For indeed, they were. Before Ni'yah stood a great gate; two upright posts and a bar that lay across the top. It was covered with frost and ice from thousands of years of cold and blowing snow, so much so that it appeared to be hewn from the ice, itself. But Ni'yah knew what lay beneath was adamantine, riddled with Runes. A gateway into Areyn's worlds.

The wolf-god stood at the gateway and focused on it. The power within the gateway flashed, and a wall of ice-blue flame filled its portal. From one of the seracs, a creature rose from the ice. A fifty-foot long crystal dragon with translucent blue and green scales now stood at the gateway. Ni'yah grinned at his handiwork. "They'll be no returning from the dead from this gateway, Areyn," he said.

Chapter Seventy-Nine

The stars had begun to move again in their journey across the sky. It would be only a few hours before Areyn's troops attacked. Lachlei rode her stallion where the noncombatants were making final preparations for a retreat. Carts and wagons, pulled by oxen, old horses, mules, and burros lumbered slowly westward through the pass in the ridge.

"Wynne! Wynne!" Lachlei called as she rode beside each wagon. Each driver shook his heads as she passed, calling. A tightness filled her throat as she searched for the wagon or cart that carried her son, Haellsil. Wagon upon wagon clattered by, each with no sign of her son or Wynne. Could they have gotten lost in the fighting? Could Areyn have killed her son? The fear turned to panic, and she rode frantically beside each wagon calling Wynne's name.

"My lady!" came a voice.

Lachlei reined her warhorse abruptly. She turned to see a golden haired *Eleion* with gold eyes astride a white charger. His cloak flowed behind him, glowing brilliantly, and his armor was fiery gold. Even from this distance, Lachlei could feel heat radiate from him. She stared at the man speechlessly.

"My lady," he said again as he rode towards her. "Your son, Haellsil, and his caretaker are safe. They're in one of the first wagons making their way over the pass. I can get them if you'd like."

Lachlei found that she had caught her breath while gazing at the god — for god, he had to be. "No, that's all right," she said when she found her voice. "I didn't know Rhyn would take care of this."

The god smiled; the warmth seemed to wash over her. "I'm afraid this is Ni'yah's doing. He has called in some favors at the last minute, it appears." He shrugged.

"Thank you," she whispered and turned her horse around to ride back down. A massive wolf appeared beside her. and her warhorse shied as she reined the beast.

"Can you give me prior warning before you do that?" she snapped.

The wolf-god shrugged. "Rhyn'athel sent me to find you," he said. "Areyn's army is nearly at the bluffs."

"Rhyn didn't tell me he would have a god watching over the noncombatants," she said.

"You didn't ask," Ni'yah remarked. "But you have nothing to worry about —Sowelu will care for them."

Lachlei glanced behind at the brilliant rider. "Sowelu? The sun god?" she asked.

"He doesn't have much to do at night." The wolf wagged his head in laughter. It looked almost comical, if he had not been a god. "Sowelu can't stand up to Areyn Sehduk directly, but he's powerful enough to protect them until either I or Rhyn'athel arrive."

Lachlei stared at the wolf-god. "What does a god do to make another god indebted to him?"

Ni'yah grinned evilly, and a mischievous gleam crept into the god's yellow eyes. "Sowelu told you about that, did he?"

Lachlei chuckled at the wolf-god's expression. "I don't want to know what you'll hold Rhyn'athel to for this," she said. "Or what the *Lochvaur* will owe you."

Ni'yah teeth gleamed. "You're my great-granddaughter and half *Laddel*, even if you carry the *Lochvaur* traits. Both you and the *Lochvaur* have already given me what I want," he said.

"And that is?"

Ni'yah grinned and vanished as they approached Rhyn'athel, astride his charger giving last minute orders to Cahal. Lachlei stared at the place where Ni'yah vanished before riding beside the warrior god.

Rhyn'athel turned to her. "The archers are ready with fifty arrows a piece," he said. "Five thousand longbow men. They may not hit their mark every time, but they should decimate Areyn's ranks enough…" He paused. "What's wrong?"

"Ni'yah…" she began.

Rhyn'athel laughed. "So, he's been talking about debts, has he?"

"He says the *Lochvaur* and I have already paid his debt—how?"

"That rogue," he chuckled. "I guess in a way, you have."

"How?"

"Gods gain power in many ways, Lachlei," Rhyn'athel said. "Ni'yah has ensured the *Laddel's* survival and their placement within the kindreds."

"Through me?"

"Through you—and through your sons."

She hesitated. "My *sons*?"

"My sons," he said, smiling.

"How would you…" she began and then fell silent. Of course, he would know—he was a god, she reminded herself. Her mind was thrown into a whirl of confusion and mixed emotions. Was she pregnant? She would not know for a month, but she did not doubt his word. Did he only intend to be with her through the battle or long enough to ensure her carrying his sons to term? What did this mean?

It means that I love you very much, he said in response to her unspoken questions. He held her gaze. *I will never leave you, beloved.*

◆◆◆◆◆

Areyn Sehduk reined his demon steed and gazed at the bluffs. No longer did the guise matter—the *Silren* and *Eltar* were his to command now. Their lives, their souls, their very life force was his, and he relished them. They shrank from him in terror as he rode among them, but they were unable to resist his power. Even Silvain, the son of the goddess Elisila, could do nothing to resist him.

Imdyr rode beside him, astride her own demon mount. Her dark eyes were languid as her powers touched the Wyrd and beyond. Areyn considered her thoughtfully. She was looking less gaunt and more *Eleion* now. She had been eating, perhaps to keep her strength up because the magic she used required so much energy. And yet, perhaps there was something more…

Fialan rode beside him as well. The *Lochvaur's* baleful gaze was constantly on Areyn now. He did nothing to disguise his hatred and contempt for the death god. Forced to serve Areyn, the *Lochvaur* king despised him. If the former *Lochvaur* champion could, he would try to destroy the death god. Areyn smiled at the man's foolishness.

"Rhyn'athel is here," Imdyr said aloud, snapping Areyn from his thoughts. The *Eltar* sorceress's eyes were still unfocused. "He has brought the wolf-god with him."

"Rhyn'athel," Areyn Sehduk repeated, and felt the chill of fear creep into him. His old adversary was powerful. And yet, Rhyn'athel had not fought him until now—now that Areyn was powerful and filled with the blood and life force of so many who had died. He turned to see Lochvaur grinning. Areyn slammed his mace into the *Lochvaur*, sending him sprawling from his horse. "It is little matter, worm," he growled. "Rhyn'athel can't save you—you are mine."

"Perhaps," said Lochvaur, wiping the blood from his face. The baleful stare was back. "But it will be a pleasure to see you spitted on his sword, writhing in agony."

"Go from my sight, worm!"

The smirk returned. "As you wish, my master," Lochvaur said scornfully. He mounted his stallion and rode forward.

Imdyr gazed at the dead *Chi'lan* warrior as he rode off, and then she turned to Areyn. "That one will betray you."

Areyn Sehduk laughed. "He can do naught," he said. "But Rhyn'athel can. What other gods are with Rhyn'athel?"

Imdyr shook her head. "None save the wolf."

"None?" Areyn smiled as he gazed at the bluffs ahead. "How many troops?"

"Sixty thousand," she replied.

Areyn grinned. It would be a slaughter.

Chapter Eighty

Rhyn'athel's gaze suddenly became unfocused. There it was again—something elusive and yet steady. He could sense it probing his army, looking for tactical advantage anywhere it could find it. It was indefinable, shifting and changing with each shield he reinforced. His frustration built as the magic discovered apparent chinks in his impenetrable defenses.

Lachlei glanced at him. "What's wrong?" she whispered.

Rhyn'athel turned to her, anger on his face. "There's something out there that can sense through my defenses," he said. "It's almost as if…" He paused and shook his head. "It's almost as if I'm fighting a Wyrd-blood." He gazed on Lachlei thoughtfully.

"A Wyrd-blood? You mean a god?"

Rhyn'athel smiled as realization crept into his eyes. "Of course," he murmured. "The Wyrd-blood will hide from me, but not from you." He paused. "Lachlei, I must use you to find the Wyrd-blood who is working for Areyn Sehduk."

"What must I do?" Lachlei asked.

"Let me into your mind," he said.

Lachlei nodded and at once felt Rhyn'athel's presence inside her thoughts. She nearly became overwhelmed with his presence. He had not needed permission to enter her mind, as he swept aside her barriers as casually as she might bat away an insect. Lachlei found herself blending into the god's mind—it was terrifying, and yet exhilarating. It was as though he had mind-linked with her, but, it was more than a simple mind-link.

Lachlei/Rhyn'athel began to search for the elusive Wyrd-blood. Lachlei could sense it probing her mind around the edges. She fought to shield herself, but felt Rhyn'athel's power gently hold her firm.

Let it sense you, the warrior god spoke.

What did Rhyn intend to do?

Suddenly, Lachlei felt a flash of power—like a wave surge crash around them. She shivered as she saw Rhyn'athel bare his teeth and his eyes snap into focus.

I have you now…

◆◆◆◆◆

Imdyr screamed and grasped her temples. She fell from the demon steed and thrashed in terrible pain. "No! No! No!" she cried. "Stop him! Stop him!"

Areyn watched implacably as she writhed before him. Several *Eltar* leapt to her aid, trying to hold her as she shook uncontrollably. Then, Imdyr became still. "Bring her to me," Areyn said.

The *Eltar* dragged Imdyr before him. She was sobbing hysterically. "He found me!" She gurgled as she met Areyn's gaze with her own wild eyes.

"Who found you?" Areyn asked.

Suddenly, Imdyr became rigid. A light that was not there before shone in her eyes. She opened her mouth, but her voice was not her own. "So, Areyn, you've given up your disguises," she said.

Areyn quavered and then steeled his gaze. "Rhyn'athel."

Imdyr smiled sardonically. "I didn't think any of the Wyrd-blood survived our last encounter. Using a child to find me—I thought you were more powerful than that."

Areyn's gaze narrowed. "I don't need the bitch to defeat you, Rhyn'athel. I have enough power and warriors enough to destroy your tiny army."

"Foolish words spoken by a coward," Imdyr said. "We'll see how brave you are when you're writhing on *Teiwaz's* blade."

Areyn backhanded Imdyr, throwing her to the ground. "Get her out of my sight!" he snarled.

Imdyr rose and shuddered. She fled on foot, terrified of the death god. Areyn turned to the shrinking *Eltar*. "Prepare for battle."

◆◆◆◆◆

"That was cruel," Lachlei said, gazing at Rhyn'athel. The link she had felt between them severed abruptly, leaving her empty and confused. "That poor girl..."

His eyes were emotionless. "I am not here for kindness," he said. "The *Eltar* girl was Areyn's tool to get to me—to see where he could not. I had to make her useless to him." He smiled grimly. "You, most of all, should feel no pity for Imdyr. She would've given you up to Areyn had you not escaped." He shook his head. "I should've realized she was a Wyrd-blood when you mentioned her name because I couldn't see her. Only Wyrd-bloods have the power to evade a god's powers."

"What is Wyrd-blood?" she asked.

"Several millennia ago, the goddess Fala took Areyn as a lover."

"Fala took that demon as a lover?" Lachlei asked incredulously.

"Areyn was not always evil, beloved," Rhyn'athel replied. "And he is a powerful god in his own right."

Lachlei shuddered at the thought.

"Fala gave birth to twins—Eltar and Mai—the founders of those kindreds."

"But shouldn't they have been gods?" Lachlei asked.

"They should have, but Fala was one of the ancient ones, the *Laeca,*—the ones that came before the *Athel'cen.* Fala's offspring were mortal — called Wyrd-blood. Not quite gods, but their powers could circumvent some of our own. Areyn and Fala used them during the wars. The girl is the last of that line."

"Not quite gods? Demons, then?"

Rhyn'athel shrugged. "You could call them demons, but I've considered them akin to my *Eleion*."

"What happened to them? Did you destroy them?" Lachlei gazed at Rhyn'athel, whose emotions were now unreadable.

He shook his head. "No, though Ni'yah wanted me to do so. Perhaps I should've listened to him because the Wyrd twists itself into new patterns with each choice I made. Eltar, Fala, and their kindreds joined me against their sire."

"They fought on our side?"

"Ironic, isn't it?" Rhyn'athel smiled sadly. "They paid with their lives. In the Battle of the Nine Worlds, Areyn slew all Wyrd-blood, save Lochvaur and Laddel—or so we had thought. One must have survived."

"Lochvaur? Lochvaur is Wyrd-blood?" Lachlei asked. "I thought he was first-blood."

"He is that, too, and much more," Rhyn'athel replied.

Ni'yah rode up beside them before Lachlei could respond. "Areyn's troops are advancing." He grinned. "Whatever you've done, you've angered him."

Rhyn'athel gazed at the oncoming lines. "Good. His temper is his downfall." He turned to Lachlei. "I realize it is your place to make the speech before a battle, beloved," he began.

Lachlei laughed. "That is because we have had not had you lead us."

"Indeed," he said with a wry smile. He rode out in front of the troops and drew *Teiwaz*, the Sword of Power. At once, Rhyn'athel became the fiery god she had seen before. How easily it was for him to shift between the two, she thought. The *Chi'lan* and their horses stood steady, but there was an awed murmur throughout the lines.

"My *Lochvaur* and *Laddel*!" he shouted, and his voice thundered over the land. "Areyn rides towards us, leading his vast army. He scorns your very existence and seeks to destroy you. And yet, Areyn knows naught of what truly you are created from. For the *Lochvaur* are my own, just as the *Laddel* are Ni'yah's. Each one of you is a part of me. Each time Areyn takes you he robs from me…" He paused and his gaze settled on Lachlei. "No longer."

Ni'yah broke into a grin. "At last!" he said in a low voice that only Lachlei could hear.

Lachlei glanced at Ni'yah. *What could this mean?* she wondered, not daring to hope…

"We fight today, not just for our lives, but for our futures," he said. "Mortal you are, and mortal you will be, but it will be my choice now, not his. You will fight today, but you do so for your freedom. Freedom from Areyn!"

The warriors banged their swords against their shields. "Rhyn'athel! Rhyn'athel!" they chanted.

"Fight with me, die for me, and you'll be rewarded," Rhyn'athel said. "Live and you will see a greater world!"

"Rhyn'athel! Rhyn'athel!"

Rhyn'athel rode back into the lines. "They're at the bluffs," he said, turning to Lachlei. "Give the command to fire."

CHAPTER EIGHTY-ONE

Areyn's army had halted its advance. The rolling fields of Darkling Plain had given way to a bluff that rose from several hills and joined the foothills of the Lochvaren Mountains. The bluff wasn't steep, but its rocky slopes and winding cart path made for a difficult charge.

Areyn Sehduk rode forward on his demon steed. The *Eltar* and *Silren* parted in sheer terror, but the dead *Chi'lan* warriors held their ground. Their silver eyes gazed at the death god in contempt—there was no fear in the *Braesan*. Fialan sat on his steed beside Eshe and watched as the death god approached Lochvaur, who stood beside his charger. The son of Rhyn'athel met the death god's gaze fearlessly.

"Why have you halted?" Areyn demanded, dismounting the demon steed. "The *Lochvaur* are up there."

"I will not lead them," Lochvaur replied. His silver eyes held contempt for the god.

"You *will* not?" Areyn demanded. "You have no will save mine. You do as I command."

Lochvaur laughed. "Rhyn'athel has suffered your insolence enough, as have I. Soon you will have no control over us."

Eshe turned to Fialan. "What is he doing? Baiting Areyn?"

Fialan shook his head in wonder. "I don't know," he whispered.

Areyn raised his mace to strike Lochvaur, but the godling caught his wrist. "I wouldn't be too eager to inflict punishment, Areyn," Lochvaur said menacingly. "My father will take each blow out of your own hide."

"You will do as I say," Areyn growled, but lowered the weapon.

"For the time being," Lochvaur said. "But we are walking into a trap."

"A trap?" Areyn laughed. "Your sire has only sixty-thousand troops. I hardly call it a trap. Attack now!"

Lochvaur smiled coldly. "As you wish, my lord," he said sardonically. "It will be a pleasure to die for you one last time."

◆◆◆◆◆

Lachlei brandished her sword and rode out, her gaze on the approaching army below. "Archers—Ready!"

The longbow men nocked their arrows and pulled back. "Mark your targets!" she heard Cahal order them.

There were Lochvaur among Areyn's troops, she reminded herself. *Lochvaur such as Fialan…*

"Steady!" she shouted as she saw the *Braesan* charge the hill.

Forgive me, my old friends, she thought.

Trust me, came Rhyn'athel's voice in her head.

Her face became grim. "Fire!" she shouted.

A maelstrom of arrows flew overhead. They roared as they flew towards their targets. Wave after wave of arrows arced across the sky and slaughtered the charging warriors. Lachlei watched in amazement, half expecting fire to come raining down on her troops as it had at Caer Lochvaren.

Yet when the flames came, they came not from Areyn, but from Rhyn'athel. Blue ethereal flame shot across the sky and arced into Areyn's army. Areyn's warriors fell as they charged. *Braesan*, *Silren*, and *Eltar* bodies lay in piles as they fell and still, they came.

Lachlei stared at the bodies and the fire in wonder. She turned and saw Rhyn'athel smiling as he watched the decimation of Areyn's army. "Where is Areyn's counter?" she asked.

"Where indeed?" Rhyn'athel chuckled. He glanced at Ni'yah knowingly as though they shared a private joke.

"Take away his source of power," said Ni'yah calmly, "and he has naught to strike with. Ironically, he is doing it to himself."

◆◆◆◆◆

Arrows hailed around Areyn Sehduk's army, cutting down the living and dead alike. Adamantine tipped, the arrows killed demon as well as *Eleion*; dead as well as living. The arrows felled the *Braesan;* their bodies disintegrated in the air.

Fialan and Eshe rode forward, despite the hail of arrows. Fialan knew he could not disobey the death god's commands, and yet, he stopped and watched as the battle commenced. Something was wrong. With each dead soldier, there should have been two to take their place—and yet, the bodies were piling fast. The demons were coming through the ranks, and the arrows cut them down, too.

"Fialan!" cried Eshe as she fell from her horse, an arrow piercing her chest.

"Eshe!" Fialan cried. Knowing the pain he would suffer, Fialan dismounted and ran to her. He held her in his arms. She was coughing blood.

"Fialan," she said hoarsely. "Something is wrong."

"You're wounded," Fialan said, looking at arrow protruding from her chest. "If I only I could heal you…"

"No, something is wrong with Areyn—don't you feel it?" she said.

Fialan looked up. The numbers of advancing troops were thinning. "There are no replacements." He grinned. "We should be regenerating…"

"But, we're not," Eshe said triumphantly. "Rhyn'athel has broken Areyn's power."

Fialan paused. "But, then you will die…"

"We are already dead, Fialan." With that, the life force within the shell vanished, and she crumbled into dust.

Fialan bowed his head and wept. He never saw the flames as they engulfed him.

◆◆◆◆◆

Areyn snarled in rage as the ethereal flames raced down the bluff towards the *Braesan* and the other warriors, powerless to stop it. Areyn drew on the energy of the dead, shielding part of the army against the torrential flames. Yet, with their deaths, there was nothing. Their life forces no longer fed him. Frantically, Areyn tried to draw his soldiers from his world, only to find the gateway shut. The shield collapsed, and the ethereal fire consumed all in its path.

The living *Eleion* broke ranks and fled in terror. Only the demons remained. Areyn drew on their dark power, such as it was, and established a shield. He turned to a demon captain. "Flank them!" he shouted. "Take five thousand and crush his army while I attack with the rest."

Areyn watched as the demon captain left. Rhyn'athel and Ni'yah had somehow effectively broken his link between his own world and this one. And his own dead were given him nothing in power—nor had the living, for that matter. It was as though his power source had simply vanished. Without the dead to feed from, Areyn was weakening. He would have to return to his realm, accepting defeat once again.

Unless...

There was still the *Fyr*—the Eternal Fire.

Chapter Eighty-Two

Lachlei gazed at the slaughter below them. She turned to Rhyn'athel who grinned at her. "How?" she asked. "Rhyn, how did you stop Areyn?"

"Areyn relies on the dead for his power, beloved," Rhyn'athel said. "He assumes he can bring as many dead as he needs."

"You had Ni'yah close the Gateway in the north," Lachlei said, the answer dawning on her. "Areyn used the Gateway to bring the dead through."

"Normally, he would use his own powers to bring them forth, but his time in this world has weakened him," Rhyn'athel remarked. "He's had to feed to keep the *Silren* guise and has had to feed to keep both the living and dead under his control. And, he has had to maintain a shield to keep me from finding him…"

"But you have had to maintain your body and keep yourself hidden from Areyn," Lachlei said.

"But I do not control you or these forces," Rhyn'athel said. "Nor does my power come from destruction. My power is in creation, Lachlei. Areyn and I are opposites."

"But you can destroy…"

"Just as Areyn can create," he remarked. "But Ni'yah and I chose long ago where we would draw our power."

"Then, the battle is won…"

"Not quite," Rhyn'athel said, gazing below. "I must still confront him, and I must take from him that which is rightfully mine."

Lachlei met his gaze. "Will Areyn accept it?"

Rhyn'athel grinned. "Probably not, but it is not his choice any longer. The *Chi'lan* belong to me, beloved, be they alive or dead. Areyn can take those who follow him, but Ni'yah and I will deny the source of his power."

"How?"

A battle-horn rang across the fields. Lachlei felt a chill run through her. She turned her horse and saw an army along the hills of Darkling Plain. She turned to Rhyn'athel. "Who are they?"

"*Chi'lan*," Rhyn'athel replied.

She stared as the army stood ready. "*Chi'lan*? There aren't any more *Chi'lan*, Rhyn," she said.

"Lochvaur and Fialan will be leading the warriors against the demons."

◆◆◆◆◆

Lochvaur reined his horse, and grinned at Fialan, Kiril, and Eshe who sat on their own warhorses beside him. They had appeared on Darkling Plain, sandwiching the enemy between themselves and the *Lochvaur* and *Laddel* lines.

"Hold your position!" Lochvaur shouted as he rode down the front lines. "We won't be fighting our own any longer! We fight for Rhyn'athel now!" A cheer rang over the plain as the godling's message was passed through the *Chi'lan* ranks.

Fialan stared at the godling. One moment, he had been kneeling beside Eshe, weeping for her; the next moment, he was here, astride a warhorse.

Fialan looked down at his body. Armored in mail, his surcoat bore the colors of Rhyn'athel, not Areyn. He took a deep breath, allowing the acrid air to fill his new lungs and turned to Lochvaur in wonder. The godling rode up to him and grinned. No longer did the godling have the pale skin and red cast around his eyes; he looked *Eleion*, not *Braesan*. None of the former *Braesan* did. They looked like a powerful *Chi'lan* army.

"Feels better to have a real body, doesn't it?" Lochvaur remarked.

"It's real?" Fialan asked. "You mean that we're not tied to Areyn any longer?"

"No," Lochvaur replied. "Though technically, this body doesn't belong here either. We're tied to *Athelren* now—not *Tarentor*."

"*Athelren*?" Fialan repeated. "Then, then—we're Rhyn'athel's warriors again?"

"As we always have been," Lochvaur said with a wry smile.

"What if we choose not to fight?" Kiril asked. Fialan turned to look at the *Shara'kai* in wonder. In his new body, Kiril looked impressive—a more fearsome warrior, Fialan could not imagine, save Lochvaur, himself.

Lochvaur became somber. "That is your choice, *Shara'kai*. My father will not control us the way Areyn controlled us. It is not in Rhyn'athel's nature to do so."

Kiril grinned. "Then, it's true—the warrior god has freed us." He laughed. "I will fight for a god such as Rhyn'athel."

"What of you, Fialan?" Lochvaur asked. "You have grievances against the warrior god."

Fialan turned and looked at Eshe. She was more beautiful now, and she smiled at him. Fialan felt a twist in his gut as he realized how much he loved Eshe. He had chosen to stay with her—to die with her rather than save himself. What of his loyalty to Lachlei?

Even as he wondered, he already knew the answer. His death had severed the bond between him and Lachlei. Death *did* change things. He smiled wryly at Eshe, before turning back to Lochvaur. "Damn you!" he growled in mock anger. "You planned this…"

"Did I?" Lochvaur said. "I don't see how—I hadn't any powers while I was under Areyn's control."

"I don't believe that," Fialan said. "By Rhyn'athel's blood, Lochvaur, you know I'd follow you back to *Tarentor* if you asked. Don't you think I owe that much allegiance to the warrior god?"

"This is why I chose you as second-in-command." He grinned. "How would you like to be known as a demon-slayer? Flayer is bringing five thousand against us."

"Demons," Fialan laughed. He drew his blade—no longer *Fyren's* doppelganger, but a broadsword made from *Athelren's* adamantine. "It would be a pleasure to see one writhe on my sword."

◆◆◆◆◆

Areyn shuddered as he felt Rhyn'athel's power bear down on him. Rhyn'athel's power surrounded him, threatening to crush him from this world. The *Braesan* were gone—wrenched from his grasp as though he never had control over them. Their deaths could no longer feed him, and his link with *Tarentor* was slipping fast.

Lochvaur's mocking words haunted him now. The godling must have known Rhyn'athel's plan. Yet, how Lochvaur kept the knowledge from Areyn, the death god did not know. Areyn mistrusted Lochvaur even though the godling had been under his control the entire time in *Tarentor*. Lochvaur was not like his sire in one crucial way—Lochvaur's desire for vengeance was beyond anything seen in the Nine Worlds. It rivaled Areyn's hatred for Rhyn'athel. That alone had made Lochvaur dangerous.

But Areyn knew Lochvaur would get his chance at vengeance now that Rhyn'athel and Ni'yah had torn away his power. He could go to the Gateway, but his Sight within the Wyrd showed a Gate Guardian. He could defeat it, but he would be forced to flee back to *Tarentor*. No, the *Fyr* was the only way.

Areyn shed his mortal body, gathering what little power remained to him. The demons would be destroyed. The *Eltar* and *Silren* would fall back—no longer under his control. But, he would have the strength to release the deadly eternal fire from his realms. With a shudder, he felt the slender flames slip through his grasp as he released the fire.

Thunder rolled across the plains, and violet lightning streaked across the sky in a pattern that unmistakably caught the filaments of the Wyrd threads. Areyn grinned, feeling his link establish to *Tarentor* and his other worlds again. The dead's energy strengthened him once more, and he looked up at Rhyn'athel's troops in satisfaction.

Let's see how you handle the Fyr, Rhyn'athel.

CHAPTER EIGHTY-THREE

Demon warriors charged Lochvaur and his *Chi'lan*. No longer *Braesan,* the *Chi'lan* attacked the demons in fury. Their bodies, now from *Athelren*, made them immortal, and they could not be killed. The demons fell to their swords and spears.

Thunder rolled across the plain, stained black with demon blood. Fialan looked up to see instead of stars, dark clouds with violet lightning shimmering across them.

Lochvaur finished impaling Flayer on his sword and looked up. Dread crossed the godling's face as his silver eyes darted from one end of the horizon to the other.

"What is it?" Fialan asked.

"I've seen skies like this once before," Lochvaur said. "Can you see the Wyrd filaments or the branches of the World Tree being shaken?"

Fialan stared into the sky. The violet flames licked the stars and coursed along in a spinning fashion. Ethereal and beautiful, yet altogether sinister, the fire seemed to arc across the sky. "I see something, but I can't describe it. Like a dance of fire, only woven…" He shook his head.

"Damn demon!" Lochvaur said. "Areyn is releasing the *Fyr*—I thought we had weakened him enough."

"What does this mean?" Fialan asked. When he heard no reply, he turned to Eshe. "Eshe—what is it?"

"It's our destruction," Eshe said, her face pale. "Unless Rhyn'athel can stop it."

◆◆◆◆◆

"You knew it was a possibility," Ni'yah said as the flames raced across the sky. His voice was as hard as his brass eyes. He met his brother's gaze. "I can't stop it—you know that."

Rhyn'athel gazed at the fire. "I know," he said. "It is something I must do."

"What is it—the *Fyr*?" Lachlei asked, her terror creeping into her voice. What had Rhyn said about the *Fyr*? She tried to remember, but none of what she could recall would help her battle this power.

Rhyn'athel turned to her. "Stay with Ni'yah—no matter what happens to me."

"What are you doing?"

"What I must do, Lachlei." Rhyn'athel reached over and caressed her cheek. He met her gaze. "I love you." He drew *Teiwaz*, clapped his legs against his warhorse, and rode forward.

Rhyn, no! Lachlei shouted in mindspeak, but she heard no acknowledgment. His form glowed as he rode forward and faded on the wind.

She turned to Ni'yah. "Will he live through it?"

Ni'yah turned to her, his brass eyes filled with worry. "I don't know."

◆◆◆◆

Rhyn'athel rode forward, his eyes focused on the flames of the *Fyr*. They swirled ahead of him, dancing like the Northern Lights. Yet, unlike the Auroras, Rhyn'athel could see a pattern and a purpose to them. They ran along the World Tree's trunk and through its branches; across the filaments that wove the great Web of Wyrd—the Web of Fate. He stared at the flames, both beautiful and deadly.

Rhyn'athel had used the *Fyr* when it was contained. Like the Wyrd, the *Fyr* was the power of creation and destruction. Like the Wyrd, an *Athel'cen* could only affect it, not fully control it. He and Ni'yah had used it to create life. Areyn had used it to destroy. It would destroy again if he did not stop it.

As *Athel'cen*, the higher gods believed nothing could destroy them, but Rhyn'athel had long wondered about the Wyrd and the *Fyr*. Even the higher gods were beholden to both: the Wyrd controlled the *Athel'cen* destinies and the *Fyr* gave them life. But could they destroy the *Athel'cen*? Rhyn'athel and Ni'yah had argued the philosophical points, but to no avail. They simply did not know, and neither wanted to find out, even though Ni'yah wryly suggested they try its powers on Areyn Sehduk.

Rhyn'athel stared at the flames as they spread across the fiber of the Web. Areyn did not care if he destroyed all in his quest for power. He would rather destroy all than give into Rhyn'athel. The warrior god concentrated, but the power of the *Fyr* was too great for him to simply control. There was only one way, and that was to transmute into pure energy and join it. Only then, Rhyn'athel knew he might be able to control it.

But at what cost?

The god stared at the *Fyr*. He might lose himself to the Eternal Fire. He would not be dead, but he would be trapped for eternity. Without him, the *Eleion* would not survive, even under Ni'yah's protection. Areyn Sehduk was too powerful for Ni'yah to defeat alone, and the death god would gain the upper hand in this battle for power. His sons would not survive, and Areyn would finally have control over all the worlds, save perhaps *Athelren*. But, in time, even *Athelren* would fall, regardless of the other gods and goddesses. Areyn was too powerful to be held at bay for long.

But the Fyr would destroy all.

Rhyn'athel closed his eyes. He knew what he had to do. He shed the corporeal shell he had so carefully constructed. Areyn must not win now.

Without a body, he was free to sense the Wyrd and its patterns. It gave him no hope—no answer to his questions. It merely stopped at his decision point. The future was completely unknown. His destruction would shake the World Tree at its very foundations.

Perhaps there would be another *Athel'cen*; another warrior god created from his own energy.

Perhaps; perhaps not.

His thoughts were of the *Eleion*, the *Lochvaur*, his son, his unborn sons, and Lachlei before he leapt into the *Fyr* and was consumed…

◆◆◆◆◆

The foundations of the Nine Worlds trembled. Tremors ran across the Darkling Plain causing the battle to halt. Demons and *Eleion* stared into the sky as the Wyrd strands streaked across it. Dark lightning coursed across the filaments.

Fialan turned to Lochvaur, who watched the patterns of the Wyrd race through the sky. "What does it mean?" he asked.

Lochvaur gazed at the sky stoically and shook his head. "I don't know, Fialan. I hope my father knows what he is doing."

Farther up the battlefield, Areyn Sehduk smiled.

Rhyn'athel was no more.

◆◆◆◆◆

Lachlei hung her head and began to weep. Rhyn'athel was gone—she could feel it as the Wyrd shifted. *Why, Rhyn? Why?* she silently asked. She felt a hand on her shoulder and looked up. Ni'yah's brass eyes glittered in concern.

"He's gone, isn't he?"

The wolf-god shook his head. "I don't know, Lachlei. I can't see into the Wyrd with this. The path isn't there…"

Lachlei wiped her tears and met his gaze. "Is there a chance he might survive?"

Ni'yah sighed. He shook his head. "I don't know—it's the *Fyr*, Lachlei. Only the dragons survive it, themselves being creations of it."

"Then, there is a chance," Lachlei said fiercely. "We do have hope."

"A foolish hope, perhaps," Ni'yah said. "Come, we must meet with Lochvaur and the others."

"Lochvaur? Rhyn's son?" Lachlei asked.

The wolf-god nodded. "Lochvaur might have a better idea for fighting Areyn than I do. He was under Areyn's dominion for nearly two millennia."

"Lochvaur is still not as strong as he would like to think he is," a voice came from behind them.

Lachlei turned her horse. Before her stood Areyn Sehduk. Beside him stood two demons holding Lochvaur, who struggled against the chains that bound him.

CHAPTER EIGHTY-FOUR

Lachlei and Ni'yah's warhorses spooked. Lachlei leapt from her own before it threw her. Ni'yah dismounted and stood beside her. "Let them go," he said quietly. "You won't be able to hold them now that Areyn is here."

Lachlei released her horse and it scampered away, terrified of both Areyn and the demons. She drew her sword, *Fyren*. The long sword felt woefully inadequate against the god.

Four demons flanked Areyn at either side. They were not the heath-stalkers, but arch-demons. They had raptor heads and gazed at her hungrily; their yellow eyes glowing as they considered her. Yet, it was Areyn who drew her attention.

Areyn Sehduk was a handsome god, Lachlei had to admit, despite his *Eltar* features. Dark, piercing eyes and a long black mane, Areyn was as tall as Rhyn'athel and as muscular. He wore black mail and no surcoat. A dark Sword of Power hung at his side.

Despite herself, Lachlei felt strangely drawn to the death god as much as she had been drawn to Rhyn'athel. She could see a resemblance between Areyn and Rhyn'athel. The warrior-hardened features, the angled jaw-line, the fierce expression—he reminded her of Rhyn'athel.

Could they be brothers? she wondered. She glanced at Ni'yah, whose gaze was riveted on the death god. There was a resemblance between Areyn and Ni'yah, too — she had not seen it between them because of Ni'yah's wolf-like hair and eyes. But now, having seen all three *Athel'cen*, Lachlei could discern their similarities. Ni'yah and Rhyn'athel considered themselves brothers, being *Athel'cen*. Areyn was *Athel'cen*—did that make him Rhyn's brother?

Lochvaur struggled against the fetters on his wrists, ankles, and neck. Stripped and bloody, he met Areyn's gaze with a feral look that spoke of hatred.

Areyn laughed. "So, you will destroy me, Lochvaur? Where is your power now that your sire is destroyed? Where is the great Rhyn'athel now?"

Lochvaur was facing Areyn, but he held Lachlei's gaze. "He isn't destroyed. You of all should know this."

Ni'yah glanced meaningfully at Lachlei. *If what he says is true, he knows more than I do but, it could be the ramblings of a madman.*

"Rhyn'athel is gone," Areyn replied with such finality that Lachlei closed her eyes. "Nothing survives the *Fyr* save that which belongs in it." He turned and slammed his mace into Lochvaur. The *Chi'lan* warrior went limp in the chains. "I'll deal with you later," he growled.

Ni'yah had already transmuted into his wolf form and leapt at Areyn. The wolf's massive jaws closed around the death god's gorget, but Areyn threw him off with ease. Suddenly, Ni'yah stood chained beside Lochvaur's limp form, unable to move as the fetters wound around his body.

"Leave him alone," Lachlei growled, raising her sword. It was a bold, defiant gesture, but one she knew was hopeless.

Areyn turned to Lachlei, his dark eyes considered the *Chi'lan* woman thoughtfully. "I think not," he said with a sneer. "I think they'll make fine pets. Don't you think?"

"I think if you were as powerful as you say, you'd free them," Lachlei said. "They can't hurt you."

Areyn laughed. "A brave goad, Lachlei, but I think not. Even I know my own limitations when handling fellow *Athel'cen* and their spawn. Ni'yah, for all his meddling can indeed be dangerous. And Lochvaur..." He paused and his countenance darkened. "Lochvaur is dangerous indeed."

"Why are you toying with me—certainly not to taunt me," Lachlei said.

"Rhyn'athel is gone, Lachlei—the *Fyr* consumed him as it will consume all. You're alone now, and you alone must make a choice."

"Choice?" Lachlei snarled. "What choice could you offer me?"

"Lachlei, don't listen!" Ni'yah said.

"Silence, cur!" Areyn snapped, and a muzzle twisted around the wolf-god's jaws. "Your brother is gone, and as usual, you haven't the power to deal with me." He turned back to Lachlei. "He meddles in the affairs of mortals without understanding what damage he causes. Lachlei..." His tone was almost a throaty purr. "Lachlei, they've kept so much from you."

Lachlei took a slow breath. "What have they kept from me?"

Delight flickered in Areyn's dark eyes. "You don't know, do you?" Areyn said. "Neither Ni'yah or Rhyn'athel bothered to tell you your destiny? Funny how *that* slipped their minds."

"What destiny?"

"Lachlei, Rhyn'athel was never in love with you. Gods such as the *Athel'cen* are incapable of love. Oh, we have needs and desires, but they are much different than anything a mortal experiences...."

"That's not true," Lachlei said.

"Really? Did Rhyn'athel mind-link with you?" Areyn smiled as he saw the doubt form in her eyes. "Gods can't mind-link with mortals, Lachlei, because we are very different from you. While you may satisfy us for a short time, there is no love, not as you know of it."

Lachlei forced herself to stare ahead at the demon god, but her mind was reeling with his words. Could Areyn be telling the truth? Rhyn'athel had not offered to mind-link with her as first-bloods did. Perhaps Rhyn'athel did not because he was a god—in that case, Areyn was right, Rhyn'athel could not mind-link with her. She forced herself to recall Rhyn'athel's last words. "Rhyn loves me."

"Rhyn is it?" Areyn chuckled. "My, my, how he duped you! Poor girl!"

"Silence!" Lachlei snapped. She raised her sword defensively. "Would you like to feel *Fyren's* bite again?"

Areyn smiled, but his smile was patronizing. "Lachlei, don't you think as a god, I could have anything I desire? Even you? Your pathetic attempts at defending yourself are hardly worth noticing. Still…" He grinned. "Wouldn't you like to know why 'Rhyn' was so eager to bed you?"

Lachlei's face flushed slightly, but she kept her gaze steady and her guard up.

"The sons you'll bear will change the balance of power," Areyn remarked. "The Wyrd has shown us all this. Rhyn'athel naturally decided to seduce you to be certain it was his offspring, not mine."

"That can't be true…"

"Can't it?" Areyn asked. He glanced at Ni'yah. "Why don't you ask the meddler? He'll tell you the truth." With that, the muzzle slipped from the wolf's jaws.

Ni'yah moved his jaw back and forth in an effort to restore feeling to it. "Don't believe him, Lachlei. Rhyn'athel loves you…"

"Is it true about my sons?" Lachlei asked. "Is that why Rhyn…"

"Lachlei, he's twisting the truth around," Ni'yah said. "That was a consequence of Rhyn'athel's appearance in this world on the Wyrd…"

The muzzle snapped around his jaws once more, and the wolf-god tried fervently to paw it off. Areyn laughed. "You see, Lachlei? Ni'yah can't deny that Rhyn'athel used you. I would've done the same, except Rhyn'athel kept such close guard over you; I couldn't get my demons through."

"The demons you sent after me…"

"Were to capture, not kill you," Areyn Sehduk remarked. "I'm more honest about my intentions, even if they aren't particularly honorable."

"Why do you tell me this?" she said. "Why now—now that Rhyn'athel is…" She couldn't finish her statement. The thought of Rhyn being gone for good was unbearable. Still, if the warrior god had tricked her as Areyn had said…

"Because there is a slight problem," Areyn said. "Even though I have won, I don't have full victory yet, Lachlei. Only you can give that to me."

"How?" Lachlei asked.

"You carry Rhyn'athel's sons already," Areyn said darkly. "They should be my sons, not his."

"I see," Lachlei said, frowning. "If you're so powerful, why don't you simply change it?"

"It's not that easy," Areyn Sehduk admitted. "You're a twice first-blood with blood from both that cur and from Rhyn'athel. I can kill you or even take you by force, but I can't control you fully. Your power blocks my abilities."

"My power?" Lachlei mused. *What power?* she wondered. As far as she knew, she had no great power—certainly none that she could use against Areyn. *Unless…*

Unless Rhyn'athel had left her some type of protection.

Her gaze strayed to Lochvaur, and saw he was conscious once more. His face was bloody and swollen, but Lochvaur held her with his own steady gaze, so reminiscent of Rhyn'athel. She glanced away, hoping that Areyn did not notice.

"Your power," Areyn continued. "Lachlei, Rhyn'athel is gone now. I can restore this world to what it was and return the *Lochvaur* to you, if you wish. You can be the greatest *Eleion* queen in history."

"Really?" she asked.

"I could bring back Fialan," Areyn said slyly. "You know I could do it. Rhyn'athel granted me the souls of the dead when we first divided the Nine Worlds. I could return your beloved husband to you. And all I ask in return is for you to be my consort. To let me destroy Rhyn'athel's sons and make you my queen."

Lachlei's gaze had shifted to the wolf-god's steady gaze. He could not speak or even communicate to her in mindspeak, but his brass eyes spoke plainly. *We are all lost if you give in to him.*

Lachlei recalled Rhyn'athel's earlier embrace. Had she fooled herself into thinking that the warrior god could actually love her? Areyn had said the *Athel'cen* could not love the way mortals did and Ni'yah could not deny Rhyn had used her. Yet, the wolf-god thought there was more, much more, than Areyn had said.

If Rhyn'athel had only wanted to make her pregnant, he could have done so any time without her permission or love. Instead, Rhyn'athel had taken a mortal body—for her?

Not entirely for her. He had hoped to change the balance of power between himself and Areyn—to take back something that belonged to him. And now, Rhyn was dead.

But was he? Rhyn had told her the greater gods such as Ni'yah, Areyn, and he could not be destroyed. None of the *Athel'cen* could be destroyed because they were part of the Wyrd. And part of the *Fyr.*

Free me, Lochvaur's voice rasped in her head. *Free me, and I can return Rhyn'athel...*

Lachlei hesitated. *Lochvaur could mindspeak when even Ni'yah could not.* She remembered what Rhyn'athel had said about Lochvaur—how he had been a special type of Wyrd-blood. *What are you?* she asked Lochvaur.

I am Athel'cen.

Lachlei almost looked at Lochvaur, but forced herself to stare into Areyn's eyes. *Could it be true? Could Lochvaur have been the only Athel'cen who had not been Wyrd-born?* Her mind whirled with the knowledge. Rhyn'athel had said Lochvaur had no mother, but she had not understood it until now. Lochvaur was more than a godling—but could he be enough?

"Lachlei?" Areyn asked. He moved closer to her, and she slid instinctively towards Lochvaur and Ni'yah.

"Areyn, I…" Lachlei said, hesitation creeping into her voice. She had one place left to look—the Wyrd, itself. She used her Sight, hoping it would give her a glimpse of the future.

"Lachlei, I can be anything you desire," he said. He met her gaze. "You know that."

A vision from the Wyrd flashed before her eyes. She forced herself to look where only Lochvaur had seen. She smiled. *Of course.*

Lachlei's gaze narrowed on Areyn. "You're a clever liar, Areyn," she said grimly. "I won't whelp any of your spawn. I am a *Chi'lan* warrior. I serve Rhyn'athel."

Areyn's face twisted in rage. "Then, you will die."

"So be it."

With a yell, Lachlei charged. Areyn brought his sword up to parry, but Lachlei spun around and slammed *Fyren's* blade into Ni'yah's shackles and sliced through Lochvaur's chains in two cuts.

"No!" Areyn bellowed.

Blinding pain ripped through her as she felt the full force of the god's wrath. She could feel the organs within her burst and the burning coppery taste of blood filled her mouth. She collapsed to the ground, writhing. It would not be long before she entered *Tarentor* with the other *Lochvaur* dead.

Was this what Fialan felt when he died? she wondered. And yet she clung to life. She was certain she could not see, but Lachlei watched the battle unfold before her.

Lochvaur leapt up, eyes blazing. Gone were his wounds, and he now wore glowing armor. He drew a Sword of Power and plunged it into Areyn. At the same time, the wolf-god transformed into his *Eleion* shape. He swung his sword and it cut into Areyn, sharp and quick.

The death god bellowed in pain and rage. Lochvaur pulled back his sword and thrust into the ground, point first. The earth shook, and a gateway opened. A single glowing warrior astride a black dragon flew through the gateway and bore down on Areyn Sehduk. Lachlei's gaze met Rhyn'athel's, and for a moment he smiled at her before turning on Areyn.

Areyn recoiled, and his blade parried *Teiwaz.* Thunder shook the ground as *Teiwaz* cleaved through the death god's blade and into his chest. Areyn writhed in terrible pain, and the screams from the god echoed across the plain. Then, they were gone in a flash of light.

Lachlei let the darkness take her and knew no more.

CHAPTER EIGHTY-FIVE

Areyn fled across the Wyrd as Rhyn'athel pursued him. The god of warriors brandished his sword as the black dragon flew into the Wyrd through the *Fyr*. They were now *between* the worlds where the *Fyr* and the Wyrd met. The violet flames of the *Fyr* licked all around them, but Rhyn'athel felt nothing, protected by Haegl's magic. The flames' roar was nearly deafening, and it swirled about him in a maelstrom of color and light.

This has to be hurting Areyn, Rhyn'athel shouted over the din.

Haegl grinned, showing all of his very sharp teeth. *He fears you more that the pain of the Fyr. Too bad no dragons will bear him. He might have had allies if he had not tried to control us so readily.*

Rhyn'athel could barely see Areyn's form ahead of him. He would try to flee to *Tarentor*, but even there, there would be no hiding.

Areyn halted in dismay. He stood at the base of the World Tree and turned around. The World Tree was a huge, silver-barked ash. Its branches spread across the roof of the universe, itself. From it, the Web of Wyrd and the flames of the *Fyr* swirled about its branches and spread across the Nine Worlds.

The pain from the *Fyr* was intense. Areyn, however, would gladly suffer the pain if only to avoid Rhyn'athel's rage. The agony that the *Fyr* wrought was inconsequential in comparison. Areyn knew what his brother could do. He fled towards *Issa*, not *Tarentor*, hoping perhaps to trick the warrior god.

You may fool Rhyn'athel, but not for long, came a hated voice. Areyn Sehduk halted and stared into the flames. A *Chi'lan* warrior emerged with his Sword of Power drawn.

Lochvaur? But how? Areyn began, but saw another *Athel'cen* emerge from the flames.

Areyn turned and fled as Lochvaur charged, swinging his Sword. Ni'yah, now in wolf form, leapt after the death god. Areyn turned and drew on his power. Dark flames from the *Fyr* wrapped around both. With a cry, the fire consumed Lochvaur. Areyn laughed. *So, the godling sought to destroy him?* Areyn Sehduk now turned his full fury on Ni'yah.

You, too, will die… Areyn thrust his dark Sword of Power into the wolf-god, pinning Ni'yah against the trunk of the World Tree. The wolf-god snapped and writhed as the sword twisted in his chest. Ni'yah changed into *Eleion* form and tried to pull the blade from his chest, but Areyn was too powerful.

A blast threw Areyn backwards and Lochvaur was there. Areyn blinked. The godling was more powerful than Areyn realized. He pulled the blade from Ni'yah's chest, letting the wolf-god fall to his knees at the base of the World Tree.

Now, Areyn, Lochvaur said coldly. *It is time we truly fought.*

Fear held the death god as he saw that there was none in the godling's eyes. *Could Lochvaur destroy him?*

A shriek and a rush of wings came overhead. Areyn looked up in time to see Rhyn'athel and the dragon bear down on him. Rhyn'athel swung *Teiwaz,* and it bit deep into Areyn. Areyn screamed and sent wave upon wave of fire at the warrior god. He hit the dragon square on, but the dragon did not halt his charge. Haegl's teeth closed around Areyn's form before disappearing into the flames.

Rhyn'athel bellowed and again thrust *Teiwaz* deep into Areyn's chest, spearing the god against the World Tree. Blinding pain shook Areyn. He was trapped; he could not escape.

Yield!

No!

The pain became excruciating. Rhyn'athel twisted the blade. Areyn met the warrior god's gaze as they stood inches apart. Rhyn'athel smiled coldly. *Yield, Areyn, or you will find yourself in chains.*

No!

You've broken the Truce, brother.

Ni'yah broke the Truce.

The Truce was between you and me, Rhyn'athel said. *Can you deny it?*

Areyn remained silent, the pain slowly pummeling him into submission. *No, I swear by the Wyrd Strands, I will keep the Truce.*

Not good enough, Rhyn'athel said. *My warriors—the Chi'lan belong to me.*

And the Laddel, Ni'yah added. *Those who serve Rhyn'athel and me belong to us.*

Areyn's eyes focused on Lochvaur, who stood beside his father with arms crossed. *Take them! Take those vile creatures!*

He heard Lochvaur's mocking laughter.

And Elren? Ni'yah demanded.

Areyn bared his teeth. *The Truce. No more.*

Not good enough, the wolf-god said, standing next to Rhyn'athel, opposite of Lochvaur.

Areyn Sehduk met Rhyn'athel's gaze. *And if I were to agree?*

The warrior god smiled grimly. Areyn knew what Rhyn'athel was thinking. *If you were to agree, then I would have you.*

As you do now. It changes naught. If you wish an empty promise, I will give one now. But Elren is still mine if I choose it.

Rhyn'athel pulled *Teiwaz* from Areyn's chest. *Go,* he said. *The next time you return to Elren, it will be your last. My sons will see to that.*

Areyn fell to his knees. He looked up to see the black dragon looming over him.

Go back to your worlds, Rhyn'athel said in disgust. Areyn, weakened and in pain, fled. The black dragon pursued him to the border of *Tarentor.*

◆◆◆◆◆

Ni'yah looked at his brother. *You should've gotten his word.*

Rhyn'athel shook his head. *It matters little. He will still fight over Elren until the end of time. His word means naught.* He turned to see Lochvaur gazing at him. *We have work to do.*

Lochvaur nodded and vanished.

Ni'yah eyed his brother. *Elren is too tempting for Areyn Sehduk.*

Indeed, said Rhyn'athel. *But he now knows I am not afraid to enter the fray. This alone may keep him away from the Fifth World.*

Until he thinks he has an advantage.

Until then.

Chapter Eighty-Six

Lachlei awoke in terrible pain. She lay in a pool of her own blood. *Fyren* lay beneath her, broken in two, but her hand was still on its hilt. It must have broken when she cut the adamantine chains that held the gods. Now she lay dying, caked with mud. Not quite dead, but nearly so, she could feel her body tense and then relax in a slow and weird convulsive spasm. She was rapidly fading from consciousness, but instinctively fought as death threatened to close her eyes.

Once or twice, Lachlei opened her silver eyes to stare into the dead face of a *Silren* warrior. His ice-blue eyes stared vacantly ahead, glazed over in death. His white mane was stained crimson now since his helm was cleaved in two. As far as she knew, he could have been one of many *Silren* she had killed. Lachlei gazed in pity at her dead adversary.

So, we embrace each other in death, Lachlei thought grimly. *For we could not do so in life.*

Lachlei's thoughts turned to Rhyn'athel, Ni'yah, and Lochvaur. They were gone. Perhaps it was just as well, she thought. She had given everything for Rhyn'athel—even at the sacrifice of her own life and the lives of her sons. She hoped that the warrior god had vanquished Areyn Sehduk—perhaps she had given Rhyn enough time.

Where were the healers looking for the wounded? she wondered. Lachlei knew she had led a successful attack, but maybe the *Lochvaur* kindred had lost. If that were so, then there would be no healers—only carrion and scavengers. It was said that the *Silren* and *Eltar* did not bother with their own wounded, let alone the enemy's.

The *Silren* warrior could have easily been a *Redel, Elesil,* or even *Lochel,* she reflected. *If we're not defending ourselves against the Silren, we're fighting the Redel, Eltar, Elesil, or any other of the Nine Kindreds. We can't keep killing each other; there must be a peace.*

Lachlei closed her eyes. How ironic that in death, she could see something she had never seen while alive. Her thoughts drifted to her son, Haellsil, and she wondered who would care for him now. Haellsil, who would never know his father, now would lose Lachlei.

Something made her open her eyes again. A dark shape fluttered into view. It took her dying mind a few moments to recognize the shape: a raven. It would be followed by other scavengers: magpies, foxes, crows, wolves, and other opportunists. The raven hopped towards her boldly, cocking its head to one side as if studying her to determine how much of a challenge she would be.

Lachlei grasped the hilt of her broken sword and tried to pick it up. The weight was too great, and it clattered along the ground. She tried again, and this time brought it forward. With all her might, she flung her hand outward, but her fingers loosened, and the sword skittered away out of reach. Lachlei groaned in pain and closed her eyes.

That is hardly any way to greet your lover.

"Rhyn?" she rasped. Lachlei forced her eyes open. "You're alive..." She tried to focus on the figure that stood before her, but her vision was blurred. She felt his gentle hands slide along her body. The pain was suddenly gone, and her vision cleared.

"You can't kill an *Athel'cen*," Rhyn'athel chided her lightly. "You know that." The warrior god knelt beside her. "How do you feel?"

Lachlei smiled wryly. "Do you want to know?"

Rhyn'athel's silver eyes glittered mischievously. "I suppose not," he admitted. "Taking the brunt of Areyn's wrath is bad enough for a god—I can't imagine what it might do to a mortal." He offered her his hand.

Lachlei took it and found herself pulled into his arms. Rhyn'athel kissed her passionately. "I thought you were lost," she whispered. "Even Ni'yah couldn't be sure. Only Lochvaur..."

"Lochvaur is much more than he appears," Rhyn'athel agreed.

"He said he was *Athel'cen*," Lachlei said. "But you said he was Wyrd-blood."

Rhyn'athel grinned. "Yes, he is both and neither. It's very complex..." He continued to kiss her.

"Evidently." She pulled away and looked at him quizzically.

"What is it, beloved?" Rhyn asked. "Something is troubling you?"

"Areyn said that as *Athel'cen* you couldn't love," she said.

"Did he now?" the god of warriors said, kissing her again.

"Rhyn?" Lachlei said as his lips moved to her throat. She pushed him away. "He said you chose me because of the sons I would bear..."

"He told you about the Wyrd prophecy, did he?"

"Then, it's true..." Lachlei said, feeling her anger rise. "That's why Ni'yah couldn't deny it."

"Areyn is a master at twisting the truth to his own purpose," Rhyn'athel replied. He traced the lines of her face with his fingers. "Lachlei, I fell in love with you the moment I saw you. The Wyrd prophecy came later—because of my love for you..."

"Then, you loved me before you knew of the prophecy?"

"Oh yes," he smiled.

"But, you can love? Areyn said..."

"Areyn can't love, beloved," he said. "But I can. Areyn speaks of his own experience as *Athel'cen*—he can't speak for either me or Ni'yah."

Lachlei smiled wryly. "I guess I was foolish to listen to him."

"Not foolish, just unprepared," Rhyn'athel said. "Many have fallen for Areyn's lies, I assure you. And some of those have been gods."

"What happened with the *Fyr* and what happened when you challenged Areyn?" Lachlei asked.

"Later, beloved," Rhyn'athel said. "It is time we rejoined our army." He held *Fyren* out to her, whole as though it had never been broken. "You'll need this."

"Our army?" she said, staring in wonder at the blade.

"Have you forgotten about your army?" came a wry voice.

Lachlei turned and saw Ni'yah sitting on a horse, leading two others. "Ni'yah?" she spoke.

The god grinned. "It seems, lady, I am in your debt. But your army awaits you."

"The *Chi'lan*? We were decimated," Lachlei whispered.

Ni'yah glanced knowingly at Rhyn'athel.

Rhyn'athel shook his head. "No, beloved," he said. "Your warriors await."

They mounted their horses and rode forward. Through the smoke, Lachlei could see row after row of *Chi'lan* warriors. She stared at them and then glanced at Rhyn'athel in wonder. There were faces she recognized, but many she did not. The warriors began to cheer as they rode by.

"Rhyn'athel! Rhyn'athel!"

To her surprise, Lachlei began to hear her own name mixed into the chants. "Lachlei! Lachlei!"

She glanced at Rhyn'athel in wonder. "Why are they cheering me?"

"When you freed Lochvaur and me, you tipped the balance back in our favor," Ni'yah replied. "Rhyn'athel used much of his power to contain the *Fyr*, he couldn't return to fight Areyn without our help."

Lachlei stared. "Is that true?"

Rhyn smiled slightly. "My brother tends to exaggerate things, but yes, you brought me back."

Lachlei laughed. "So I did get my revenge after all," she said.

"Indeed," said Rhyn'athel, but his gaze was distracted. He reined his horse before a warrior. Lachlei stared at the man who stood before them. It was Lochvaur, but the last time she had seen him, he had either been in chains or as a glowing warrior. Looking on him now, Lachlei stared at the godling in awe. He was nearly as impressive as his father, looking like Rhyn'athel in mortal form. He was a tall *Chi'lan* warrior with a hardened gaze. Rhyn'athel dismounted his steed. They embraced in the typical *Chi'lan* greeting, gripping both arms.

Lochvaur laughed and hugged Rhyn'athel. "Father!" he said.

"I told you I wouldn't abandon you to Areyn," Rhyn'athel said.

"I never lost faith." He paused. "Even if you did need my help." He turned and nodded at Lachlei. "Lachlei."

"Lochvaur," Lachlei said. "I am glad to meet you under less dire circumstances."

"Indeed," Lochvaur said, considering her carefully. "So, you are the mortal woman who defied Areyn Sehduk." He met his father's gaze, and Lachlei could sense something unspoken passed between the two. "There is someone you should meet," he said. He turned and nodded to a *Chi'lan* warrior who stood back among the other warriors.

"Hello, Lachlei," Fialan said.

CHAPTER EIGHTY-SEVEN

Cara stared as an army of warriors, larger than anything she had seen yet, filled Darkling Plain. "By Rhyn'athel's mane—who are they?" She turned to Haukel, who shook his head.

"They're not the *Braesan*," Haukel said. "They look alive."

Cara's eyes scanned the warriors. Red and gold manes and surcoats shone in the sun. "They're *Chi'lan*," she whispered. "But I've never seen so many."

"Not all *Chi'lan*," came a familiar voice. "Though I suspect Rhyn'athel considers me one of his warriors."

Cara turned and saw the *Elesil* king standing beside her. "Conlan!" she gasped and hugged him. "By the gods! You were dead!"

"*Were*," Conlan said. "But not of this world, either. Rhyn'athel forced Areyn to give up his warriors."

"Areyn has lost the dead?"

Conlan shook his head. "Not entirely. Those who were loyal to Rhyn'athel will return to the Hall of the Gods. And I suppose, those who have aided Rhyn'athel's cause..."

"Then, you won't be staying?"

He shook his head. "Not long. I've already spoken to Rani, she is now queen of the *Elesil*." He eyed her as she lowered her head. "What's wrong?"

"I don't know," Cara admitted. "I've felt so..." She shook her head. "Damn it, Conlan! I've felt responsible for your death."

"The price of being *Chi'lan*..."

"*Chi'lan*," she muttered. "I don't know what it means to be *Chi'lan*."

Conlan gazed at her, his silver eyes filled with sympathy. "You do, Cara, but right now, you feel lost. Your kindred is nearly destroyed because of what Areyn did."

"Why didn't Rhyn'athel stop this?"

"Why does the Wyrd weave the web it does?" Conlan shrugged. "Who can say? And if the god would answer to you, would he give you an answer that would satisfy you?"

Cara smiled grimly. "I suppose not."

Conlan gripped her shoulder. "You have much work to do, *Chi'lan*, to rebuild your kindred. Your father is still among the living."

"Silvain is still alive?" she said. "He won't speak to me."

"Perhaps not now, but he'll need you." Conlan looked at the other renegade *Silren*. "He'll need all of you to rebuild what is left." He hugged her. "Go—find Silvain, *Chi'lan*."

Cara nodded. She mounted a horse and led the *Silren* towards the enemy's wounded.

◆◆◆◆

"Fialan?" Lachlei whispered. Before her stood her former husband as she had remembered him. Fialan stood next to Lochvaur and a *Chi'lan* woman.

Lachlei ran to him and they embraced. Rhyn'athel watched stoically as Fialan held her and kissed her.

◆◆◆◆

Brother? Ni'yah's voice spoke in Rhyn'athel's mind.

Not now, Ni'yah, Rhyn'athel said heavily. *I don't want to discuss this. I knew it could happen…*

◆◆◆◆

Lachlei pulled away and glanced back at Rhyn'athel. "It is good to see you, Fialan."

Fialan smiled at her. "Indeed, Lachlei," he said, glancing at Eshe. "It looks as though things have changed." He paused. "Walk with me."

How could she explain her love for the warrior god? Dread filled her heart. "Fialan, I…"

"Listen to me, Lachlei," Fialan said. "I know already about Rhyn'athel…"

"You do? How?"

"Lochvaur—he told me."

"How does he know?"

"Lochvaur is, well, he's more than a godling, even though he won't admit it," Fialan said. "Lochvaur told me that death had a way of changing things. He was right."

"Fialan," she raised her hand, causing him to fall silent. "I believed you were dead. I was your wife, and I will respect that vow if you hold me to it, but many things have changed since we parted. I could not love you as before. I am Rhyn'athel's now."

"I know," Fialan said. "I understand now that I was never intended for you—you were intended for Rhyn'athel. I didn't believe it until I saw you at Caer Lochvaren. I love you and I always will, but I know that you and I were not meant to be." He paused. "Do you love him?"

"Deeply, Fialan. I have never loved anyone more."

"I know this. I could never be here with you, and you would have to come with me to *Athelren*. But, it is not your time." Fialan shook his head. "What of Haellsil? And what of your unborn sons?"

"You know of them already?" Lachlei asked, frowning. "Does the entire army know?"

Fialan chuckled. "They may. Lachlei, our son, Haellsil, will be a great warrior in his own right, but the sons you will carry will be greater still. They'll be sons of Rhyn'athel, same as Lochvaur."

Lachlei glanced at Eshe, noticing her for the first time. She could see the fear in Eshe's eyes. *Fialan? Could Fialan have fallen in love with her?* "You love her, don't you?"

"Eshe?" Fialan smiled. "Yes, I do. One doesn't go through *Tarentor* and battles without feeling something for those who fight beside you. Somewhere in this war, I fell in love with her."

"Then, you release me?" Lachlei held her breath. *Could Fialan have found his soul-mate as she had?*

"There is nothing to release, Lachlei, my death broke our bond. We have no mind-link, and even Rhyn'athel would recognize that," Fialan said. "I owe Rhyn'athel this, if naught else."

Lachlei held him, tears streaming down her face. She laughed. "Fialan, I will always love you."

"And I, you." Fialan paused. "Go to him, Lachlei." He kissed her on her forehead and smiled.

Lachlei turned and strode back to Rhyn'athel. Rhyn'athel straightened, wonder on his face. "Lachlei?"

Lachlei smiled and took Rhyn'athel in her arms. "Rhyn, I couldn't leave you," she whispered as they embraced.

Chapter Eighty-Eight

Lochvaur turned to Fialan. "It's time for you to go," he said. "And it is time for me to say good-bye."

Fialan stared. "You're not coming to *Athelren*?"

Lochvaur shook his head. "Areyn Sehduk still exists, my friend. *Athelren*, for all its grandeur and beauty, bores me greatly. I'm a warrior first, Fialan. Why do you think I accepted my fate in *Tarentor*?"

"You could've left at any time," Fialan said in wonder. "Areyn wasn't keeping you there—you allowed yourself to be his slave. Why?"

"The way to defeat one's enemy is to know him," Lochvaur said with a wry grin. "Neither Rhyn'athel nor Ni'yah could enter Areyn's realms or learn Areyn's secrets—but I could."

"You were a spy." Fialan shook his head. "Areyn Sehduk misjudged you."

"Indeed, he did."

"But, where will you go?" Fialan asked. "You will have no body in this world."

Lochvaur glanced at Lachlei. *Ah, but I will,* he replied in mindspeak.

Fialan stared at him. *You can be reborn?*

I like the name 'Lachlan.' It means 'champion'— did you know that? Lochvaur said casually, an evil glint in his eyes. *With each incarnation, I do change. I become stronger, but I do forget much. Farewell, Fialan. Perhaps in another life, we will meet again.*

With that, Lochvaur disappeared. Fialan felt swept up and the world spun around him. Then, Fialan and the other *Chi'lan* found themselves staring at a great walled fortress, gleaming white, at the base of mountains so tall they touched the sky. Twin golden suns shone in the sapphire sky.

Eshe laughed. "We're here, Fialan! We're in *Athelren*!" She hugged Fialan.

"Lachlan," Fialan said, thoughtfully. "It has a ring to it."

◆◆◆◆◆

Cara and Haukel rode among the *Silren* wounded. The battlefield was burnt and bloody, filled with the dead, the dying, and scavengers. Thousands of *Eltar* and *Silren* bodies lay in the sun. She looked from side to side at the carnage. Those *Silren* still alive looked on her with hatred—she wore the red and gold colors of the warrior god, not the colors of the *Silren*. Both she and Haukel dismounted.

"What are you doing here?" demanded a lower-ranked *Silren* noble named Essil. "Isn't it enough that you've served the enemy?"

Haukel gripped Cara's shoulder, but the daughter of Silvain was not dissuaded. She smiled grimly. "I was not the one who fought for the death god," she said. She looked around. "Where's my father?"

Essil shook his head. "He won't see you."

"I think he should be the one to decide that," she said. She looked over and saw her father's standard. As she walked towards the standard, she saw the carnage of what had been the top *Silren* nobles. Nearby lay her father, Silvain. Not dead, but wounded. He looked up at her with pale eyes.

"You," he whispered. "My daughter…" He stared into the sky. "You've come to gloat—to watch an old man die."

"No," Cara said softly. "I've come to take you home."

"You're *Chi'lan*," he spat.

"I am Rhyn'athel's warrior," she said. "I am also your daughter."

"You can't be both."

"I am," she said. She glanced up at Haukel, who knelt on Silvain's other side. She laid her hands against his wounds, using her first-blood powers to heal him. "Help him up." Together, Cara and Haukel brought Silvain to his feet.

"What are you doing?" Silvain asked.

There was pity in Cara's smile. "We're going home."

CHAPTER EIGHTY-NINE

EPILOGUE

"The gales are early this year."

Modolf stared out of the window at the dark clouds and the angry gray-green swells of the North Sea. A *Shara'kai* of *Eltar* and *Ansgar* mix, Modolf inherited his stature from his *Ansgar* side. He stared at the sea, his own dark eyes in turmoil as he heard the baby cry again.

"She's dead," Saeunn said. Saeunn was his wife of three years. The shock of silver that ran through her hair was the only indication she was *Shara'kai*. "She lost too much blood in the birth. The child's alive—a boy. He looks *Eltar*, same as his mother."

"What is a pureblood doing here?" Modolf mused, staring out at the sea. He had heard rumors of a war among the *Eleion*—news traveled even to this far place. He frowned. "Maybe she was an exile."

"Maybe. And maybe she got lost."

"Did she tell you her name?"

"Imdyr."

Modolf spat. "*Eleion* name. I bet she was a witch."

"She was practically a child," Saeunn said. "She wanted her baby called *Allarun*."

Modolf frowned, staring at the sky. The gales were early. "We should leave the child to the gods," he said at last.

Saeunn stared. "You can't be serious—it'll die."

"Then, that's what the gods want."

"It's not what *I* want."

Modolf frowned again. Saeunn had lost their own son in a stillbirth only a week ago. "We can try again."

"No." Saeunn shook her head. "He'll be my son."

Modolf looked into the sky again. A storm was coming.

◆◆◆◆◆

Lachlei held her infant son, Lachlan, rocking him gently. His twin brother, Elsonre, had already fallen asleep in their crib. They looked alike in many ways, but Rhyn'athel had assured her that they were fraternal, not identical, twins. Perhaps they looked so much alike because they looked like their father. They had his steel-colored eyes, and their hair was deep red and streaked with gold. Even at a few months old, their faces were angular and held their father's strong jaw line.

The infant yawned and closed his eyes. It was nearly dusk and well past his bedtime. Lachlei had relieved her servants, hoping to perhaps spend a quiet night in her chambers.

It had been a year since Rhyn'athel's victory over Areyn. The *Lochvaur* had reclaimed and rebuilt Caer Lochvaren and now Lachlei had private quarters built from stone rather than wood. Stone would eventually replace wood throughout Caer Lochvaren, making the city impregnable except to the longest sieges. Rhyn'athel had helped design the city after his own fortress-city in *Athelren*.

Rhyn'athel had stayed with the *Lochvaur*, helping them repair the terrible damage done. Rhyn was constantly beside them, whether training *Chi'lan* or guiding the building and repair of the fortifications.

Rhyn'athel had stayed with Lachlei. He had adopted Fialan's son as his own and had already taught Haellsil to speak at two years old.

Lachlei heard a noise and turned. She saw Rhyn'athel standing beside her.

"He's very much like his father," she remarked smiling.

"Lachlan?" Rhyn'athel grinned. "I'm not surprised."

"He has a fiery temper and the most piecing silver eyes," she said. "A born troublemaker and a warrior, if there is such a thing."

The warrior god chuckled. "That, I don't doubt." He kissed her. "What of Elsonre?"

"He's a thinker—I think a tactician," Lachlei replied. "Analytical. They almost complement each other. I might think you'd have planned them this way."

"Planned?" Rhyn'athel said, with an expression of feigned innocence. "Beloved, would I have planned such an occurrence?"

"Ni'yah is a bad influence, and you are a bad liar," she replied. She gazed at Lachlan. "He's finally asleep—do you want to hold him?"

Rhyn'athel took his young son in his hands and cradled him gently. "They are so like me," he admitted. His eyes held a glimmer of sadness. He walked over to the crib and gently laid the baby next to his brother.

Lachlei leaned against him. "What is wrong, Rhyn?" she asked. She met his gaze. "You're leaving, aren't you?"

Rhyn'athel shook his head. "I cannot lie to you," he confessed. "I can't stay in this world for much longer—I must return to *Athelren*."

"It's that damn Truce, isn't it?"

"Yes," he admitted. "I can't stay here."

"What happened in the *Fyr*, Rhyn?" she asked. "You never told me the entire story."

Rhyn'athel shrugged. "There isn't much to tell, beloved. In order to control the *Fyr*, I had to become part of it. A definite risk, yet one I was willing to take. Within the fire, I met the dragon, Haegl, once again."

"Haegl—the black dragon you rescued?" she said in wonder. "What happened?"

"The dragons are creatures of the *Fyr*, but their lives are tied to it. I agreed to give him what he most desired for what I desired."

"Control over the *Fyr*—for what?" she mused.

"Their freedom from the *Fyr*." He smiled. "It seemed a fair trade. But even with the dragons' help controlling the *Fyr*, I hadn't enough power to break through to *Elren*. Your freeing Ni'yah and Lochvaur allowed me a way back."

"It was Lochvaur. Despite all the torture, he still defied Areyn Sehduk. Why does Areyn despise Lochvaur so? Areyn's hatred for him seems to even surpass his hatred for you."

"Areyn hates me as much, but can't do much to me. But there is a Wyrd prophecy that Areyn fears that may someday come true…"

"That is?"

"That one of my sons may destroy him."

"But you said *Athel'cen* can't be destroyed," Lachlei reminded him.

Rhyn'athel shrugged. "Not any way that I know of." He paused. "When I returned, I pinned Areyn against the World Tree. He agreed to abide by the Truce for the time being."

"That's all?"

"I won my dead," Rhyn'athel said. "Those who serve Ni'yah and me are no longer Areyn's."

Lachlei shook her head. "In all that fighting—in all those battles—what did you win?" she asked.

Rhyn'athel pulled her close. "You." He glanced at his sons. "And them. And, of course, Ni'yah's and my warriors."

"But you could not gain *Elren*?"

"Areyn would give me *Tarentor* before giving me *Elren*, beloved," Rhyn'athel replied. "Even if I forced him to swear by the blood that flowed in his veins, his word means naught. He would still continue to undermine me." He sighed. "Lachlei, *Elren* is but one of my worlds. I have three others that must be looked after—and Ni'yah can't shoulder all my work."

Lachlei's throat tightened. "Rhyn, will you return?"

Rhyn'athel closed his eyes and held her. "No," he whispered. "I can't…" He held her as she wept.

"I wanted you to see Lachlan and Elsonre grow up. I wanted you to stay with me forever…"

"Do you think I would abandon you?" Rhyn'athel chided, gently lifting her chin to meet his gaze. "Don't you think I will see my sons grow? Lachlei, I will always be with you, you know that, even if I can't be here in *Elren* with you."

"I know," she said, drying her eyes.

Rhyn'athel smiled and ran his fingers through her hair. "Ah, Lachlei, it won't be long when we are together in *Athelren*."

"By a god's reckoning or a mortal's?"

"By my own reckoning," Rhyn'athel replied. "I cannot bear to be parted from you long." He sighed. "I have already spoken to Cahal—he will be Lachlan and Elsonre's foster father. And then, of course, there is Ni'yah…"

Lachlei laughed, despite her tears. "Are you trying to corrupt your sons?"

Rhyn'athel chuckled. "Ni'yah isn't my first choice as a role model, but he is my brother and an *Athel'cen*. He can teach my sons what they need to know." He took her hands and kissed them, placing a ring on her finger. It was a simple band of intertwining patterns. *Beloved,* he said in mindspeak. *You will not be far from me.*

Lachlei stared at him as he opened his mind to her. *You wish to mind-link?* she said in awe. *Is that even possible with a mortal?*

I will make it possible, beloved. Will you accept it?

Yes. Lachlei closed her eyes as she felt the mind-link form between them. Rhyn'athel's presence within her mind was almost overwhelming. *Like staring into the sun after being in the dark,* she thought. His fierceness, power, and love flowed through her. Slowly, the force of his presence dimmed. When she opened her eyes, she knew he was gone.

Gone, and yet, not. Lachlei could still feel the warrior god's presence and emotions as he left her. *Loneliness. Regret for leaving her. Love.*

Lachlei twisted the band on her finger, and it glowed softly in the waning light. Rhyn was with her even now. The mind-link was his gift to her; his promise that he would never leave her. This time, nothing would break the mind-link. Not even death.

She walked to the window and stared into the twilight sky. The stars were slowly winking into the velvet night. The link between them caressed her gently.

Rhyn was right. It would not be long.

PEOPLE, PLACES, AND THINGS IN LACHLEI

Lochvaur

- Cahal—chief guard and *Chi'lan* warrior.
- Elrys—Council Member.
  Fialan—King of the *Lochvaur*, killed by Areyn Sehduk.
- Haellsil—Infant son of Lachlei and Fialan.
- Kellachan—cousin to Lachlei and Fialan.
- Kerri—Younger *Chi'lan.*
- Kian—*Chi'lan* warrior who brings the bodies of Fialan and his men back.
- Kieran—*Chi'lan* warrior who sits on the Council.
- Lachlei—queen of the *Lochvaur, Chi'lan.*
- Laewynd—Leader of the high council member.
- Lochynvaur—Father of Lachlei.
- Moira—Council Member.
- Talar—Council Member.
- Tamar—*Chi'lan* warrior.
- Tarchon—Council Member.
- Tragar—*Chi'lan* in charge of guarding Haellsil.

Silren

- Akwel—Areyn Sehduk's guise.
- Cara—daughter of Silvain.
- Galen—a noble who served Akwel.
- Haukel—a rebel Silren, loyal to Rhyn'athel.
- Silvain—king of the Silren, son of Elisila.
- Tora—a rebel Silren, loyal to Rhyn'athel.

Elesil

- Conlan—King of the *Elesil.*
- Hakan—guard of Conlan.

Laddel

- Ladara — granddaughter of Laddel, mother of Lachlei.
- Laddel—King of the Laddel, son of Ni'yah.
- Ladsil—son of Laddel.
- Telek—Ni'yah's *Laddel* name.
- Wynne—Lachlei's personal lady-in-waiting.

Eltar

- Imdyr—mother of Allarun—Wyrd Blood—Last of Areyn's and Fala's line.
- Tarel—*Eltar* guard.

***Braesan*—The Undead**

- Eshe—*Chi'lan* Soldier.
- Kiril—*Chi'lan* Soldier, *Shara'kai,* bronze-skinned.
- Lochalan—Father of Fialan.
- Lochvaur—Son of Rhyn'athel, founder of the *Lochvaur* kindred.

Redel

- Redhael—Father of Redkellan
- Redkellan—King of the Redel
- Redsil—Redel soldier

Demons

- Flayer—an arch-demon
- Slayer—an arch-demon that took a warhorse's form

Place names and terms

- Adamantine—An ore when tempered is stronger than the hardest substance. Has magical properties as well. Scarce in *Elren,* it exists primarily in *Athelren* although there are ore deposits in *Tarentor.*
- *Ansgar*—a younger race, less warlike but shorter lived than *Eleion*
- *Athel'cen*—Three gods who were born from the Wyrd. Considered the most power of the gods.
- *Athelren*—World of the gods
- Caer Lochvaren—Main city of the *Lochvaur*
- *Chi'lan*—Lochvaur warriors dedicated to fighting for Rhyn'athel
- Darkling Plain—The boundary plain between the *Lochvaur* lands and other lands to the east.
- Demons—Are more or less twisted creations of Areyn Sehduk designed to carry out his orders. Unlike *Eleion* and *Ansgar,* they have no life-force beyond their bodies, but have no concept or fear of death. They can't be reasoned with nor do they have a free will. They do their master's bidding and their emotions mirror the dark emotions of Areyn Sehduk. There are many types of demons, but the ones that the *Eleion* recognize are the Heath-stalkers (lesser demons), Yeth Hounds, life-leeches, and Arch-demons.
- *Eleion*—a race of people with long lives, but still mortal, who are the descendants of the gods.
- *Elren*—Land of the Living

- *Fyr*-Dragons—creatures who exist within the *Fyr*
- *Fyren*—Fialan's and later, Lachlei's sword. Lochvaur's first sword, forged from adamantine from *Athelren*.
- Heath-stalkers—The Heath-stalkers are the lesser and most plentiful demons. Called Heath-stalkers because before the Truce, they would travel the wilderness in search of victims. They feed off the blood and souls of the living.
- Iamar—Second moon
- Lochvaren—Land of the *Lochvaur.*
- Mani—moon of ominous portents.
- Nine Kindreds—The *Eleion* split into nine clans or kindreds, named after the founder. They are *Lochvaur*, *Lochel*, *Redel*, *Elesil*, *Silren*, *Laddel*, *Haell*, *Eltar*, and *Falarel*.
- Nine Worlds—In this universe, there are nine separate worlds, each connected to each other through the World Tree, which is the source of the Web of Wyrd. The Wyrd runs throughout the Nine Worlds. Originally, there had been just the Web of Wyrd, which created the gods. Rhyn'athel is credited with created the Nine Worlds and fixing them to both the World Tree and the Wyrd, although there had been previous worlds created by lesser gods and goddesses such as Harbard and Fala. Most of those worlds are only half-worlds, coexisting with the Nine. The main worlds in question are: *Tarentor*, *Isa*, *Jotunnren* or *Jotnar*, *Elren*, and *Athelren*. The other three worlds of Rhyn'athel aren't mentioned, but they're considered lesser aspects of *Athelren* as *Isa* and *Jotnar* are considered lesser aspects of *Tarentor*. Of all the worlds, *Jotnar* is perhaps the most *Elren*-like place.
- North Marches—a town and later an area that bordered the northern part of Lochvaren. Under dispute between the *Silren*, *Eltar*, and *Lochvaur*.
- *Shara'kai*—half blood, usually a mix between *Ansgar* and *Eleion*
- *Tarentor*—Land of the Dead—Areyn's Realm
- The *Fyr*—The fire of creation and destruction
- The World Tree—The structure or universe which holds the Wyrd, the *Fyr*, and the Nine Worlds together.
- Tomah—First moon.
- Yeth Hounds—Demon hounds of Areyn Sehduk.

Gods, Goddesses, and Dragons

- Areyn Sehduk—god of death, *Athel'cen.*
- Elisila—goddess of the heavens.
- Fala—goddess of the earth and darkness, associated with night.
- Haegi—black Fyr-dragon.

- Harbard—god and guardian of the Wyrd. Guardian of the Gateways.
- Issa—goddess of winter/ seasons.
- Jera—goddess of the spring/ harvests.
- Ni'yah—the wolf-god, trickster, *Athel'cen.*
- Nim'he—goddess of the sea.
- Rhyn'athel—god of warriors, *Athel'cen.*
- Sowelu—god of the sun

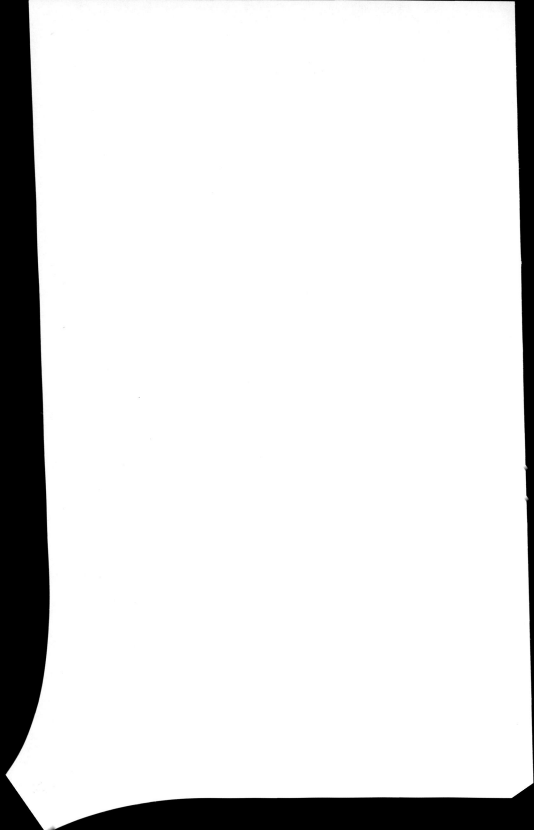

ABOUT THE AUTHOR

M. H. Bonham, (sometimes known as Margaret H. or even Maggie Bonham to throw off her publishers) is a six-time awarding winning professional author. She started her career as a rocket scientist (yes, it is rocket science) and quickly switched to a software engineer and systems administrator, where she insisted that Y2K was just a figure concocted for how much a computer geek can make in one day after convincing the newspapers the world's computer systems are going to crash.

Taking her money and running, Maggie learned through racing sled dogs that dogs are a lot like computers (they don't do anything you want unless you speak their language and can be just as stubborn). She holds the prestigious three-time Red Lantern Award at the American Dog Derby (the oldest sled dog race in North America) and was featured in the Ashton Daily News as the only musher whose ten-dog team chased a Pomeranian into the backyard of the local gossip columnist. Despite such harrowing experiences, she has braved whiteouts in Wyoming and swamps in Minnesota (as well as the fearsome Idaho Pomeranian) and learned much about dog and wolf behavior. She's a world-renown expert in canine behavior and training having been published by Penguin Putnam, John Wiley and Sons, Barrons Educational Series, TFH, Sterling, Dragon Moon Press and Yard Dog Press. She's lost count how many articles she has published in various consumer and trade magazines and websites, but figures it's over a hundred by now. Otherwise, she has no life because she has 27 books in print.

She is the author of *Prophecy of Swords* and *Runestone of Teiwas*, both heroic fantasy books in the Swords of Destiny Series published by Yard Dog Press, which share the world with Lachlei. Her next book with Dragon Moon Press will be *Howling Dead*, a cyberpunk werewolf mystery/romance. Her work has also appeared in the *Four Bubbas of the Apocalypse, Small Bites, Houston, We've Got Bubbas, A Time To...* and *Flush Fiction* anthologies and *Lorelei Signal, Kidvisions* and *Tales of the Talisman* magazine, and *Amazon Shorts*. She writes science fiction, fantasy, and mystery, having taken courses appropriate to a software engineering background such as Anglo Saxon, Latin, and Beowulf. When she's not racing her geriatric sled dogs, she's climbing mountains, hiking, and practicing Shotokan Karate (she's a brown belt) and Ninjitsu. She is currently working on her master's degree in Liberal Studies. She shares her home at 4000 ft – where most people swear there isn't any oxygen and you can't find that altitude on the high altitude directions for cake– with four Malamutes, six Alaskan Huskies, a tortoiseshell cat, the deer, elk, foxes, coyotes, mountain lions, bobcats, and bears, and her husband, Larry, who indulges her lunacy. Visit her website at www.shadowhelm.net and www.lachlei.com, and visit her blog at shadowhelm.livejournal.com.

Our titles are available at major book stores and local independent resellers who support Science Fiction and Fantasy readers like you.

Alien Deception by Tony Ruggiero -(tp) - ISBN-13: 978-1-896944-34-0
Alien Revelation by Tony Ruggiero (tp) - ISBN-13: 978-1-896944-34-8
Alphanauts by J. Brian Clarke (tp) - ISBN-13: 978-1-894063-14-2
Apparition Trail, The by Lisa Smedman (tp) - ISBN-13: 978-1-894063-22-7
As Fate Decrees by Denysé Bridger (tp) - ISBN-13: 978-1-894063-41-8

Billibub Baddings and The Case of the Singing Sword by Tee Morris (tp)
- ISBN-13: 978-1-896944-18-0
Black Chalice, The by Marie Jakober (hb) - ISBN-13: 978-1-894063-00-5
Blue Apes by Phyllis Gotlieb (pb) - ISBN-13: 978-1-895836-13-4
Blue Apes by Phyllis Gotlieb (hb) - ISBN-13: 978-1-895836-14-1

Chalice of Life, The by Anne Webb (tp) - ISBN-13: 978-1-896944-33-3
Chasing The Bard by Philippa Ballantine (tp) - ISBN-13: 978-1-896944-08-1
Children of Atwar, The by Heather Spears (pb) - ISBN-13: 978-0-88878-335-6
Clan of the Dung-Sniffers by Lee Danielle Hubbard (pb) - ISBN-13: 978-1-895836-05-0
Claus Effect, The by David Nickle & Karl Schroeder (pb) - ISBN-13: 978-1-895836-34-9
Claus Effect, The by David Nickle & Karl Schroeder (hb) - ISBN-13: 978-1-895836-35-6
Complete Guide to Writing Fantasy, The - Volume 1: Alchemy with Words
- edited by Darin Park and Tom Dullemond (tp)
- ISBN-13: 978-1-896944-09-8
Complete Guide to Writing Fantasy, The - Volume 2: Opus Magus
- edited by Tee Morris and Valerie Griswold-Ford (tp)
- ISBN-13: 978-1-896944-15-9
Complete Guide to Writing Fantasy, The - Volume 3: The Author's Grimoire
- edited by Valerie Griswold-Ford & Lai Zhao (tp)
- ISBN-13: 978-1-896944-38-8
Complete Guide to Writing Science Fiction, The - Volume 1: First Contact
- edited by Dave A. Law & Darin Park (tp)
- ISBN-13: 978-1-896944-39-5
Courtesan Prince, The by Lynda Williams (tp) - ISBN-13: 978-1-894063-28-9

Dark Earth Dreams by Candas Dorsey & Roger Deegan (comes with a CD)
- ISBN-13: 978-1-895836-05-9
Darkling Band, The by Jason Henderson (tp) - ISBN-13: 978-1-896944-36-4
Darkness of the God by Amber Hayward (tp) - ISBN-13: 978-1-894063-44-9
Darwin's Paradox by Nina Munteanu (tp) - ISBN-13: 978-1-896944-68-5
Daughter of Dragons by Kathleen Nelson - (tp) - ISBN-13: 978-1-896944-00-5
Distant Signals by Andrew Weiner (tp) - ISBN-13: 978-0-88878-284-7
Dominion by J. Y. T. Kennedy (tp) - ISBN-13: 978-1-896944-28-9
Dragon Reborn, The by Kathleen H. Nelson - (tp) - ISBN-13: 978-1-896944-05-0
Dragon's Fire, Wizard's Flame by Michael R. Mennenga (tp)
- ISBN-13: 978-1-896944-13-5
Dreams of an Unseen Planet by Teresa Plowright (tp) - ISBN-13: 978-0-88878-282-3
Dreams of the Sea by Élisabeth Vonarburg (tp) - ISBN-13: 978-1-895836-96-7
Dreams of the Sea by Élisabeth Vonarburg (hb) - ISBN-13: 978-1-895836-98-1

Eclipse by K. A. Bedford (tp) - ISBN-13: 978-1-894063-30-2
Even The Stones by Marie Jakober (tp) - ISBN-13: 978-1-894063-18-0

Fires of the Kindred by Robin Skelton (tp) - ISBN-13: 978-0-88878-271-7
Firestorm of Dragons edited by Michele Acker & Kirk Dougal (tp) - ISBN-13: 978-1-896944-80-7
Forbidden Cargo by Rebecca Rowe (tp) - ISBN-13: 978-1-894063-16-6

Game of Perfection, A by Élisabeth Vonarburg (tp) - ISBN-13: 978-1-894063-32-6
Green Music by Ursula Pflug (tp) - ISBN-13: 978-1-895836-75-2
Green Music by Ursula Pflug (hb) - ISBN-13: 978-1-895836-77-6
Gryphon Highlord, The by Connie Ward (tp) - ISBN-13: 978-1-896944-38-8

Healer, The by Amber Hayward (tp) - ISBN-13: 978-1-895836-89-9
Healer, The by Amber Hayward (hb) - ISBN-13: 978-1-895836-91-2
Hounds of Ash and other Tales of Fool Wolf, The by Greg Keyes (pb) - ISBN-13: 978-1-895836-09-8
Human Thing, The by Kathleen H. Nelson - (hb) - ISBN-13: 978-1-896944-03-6
Hydrogen Steel by K. A. Bedford (tp) - ISBN-13: 978-1-894063-20-3

i-ROBOT Poetry by Jason Christie (tp) - ISBN-13: 978-1-894063-24-1

Jackal Bird by Michael Barley (pb) - ISBN-13: 978-1-895836-07-3
Jackal Bird by Michael Barley (hb) - ISBN-13: 978-1-895836-11-0
JEMMA7729 by Phoebe Wray (tp) - ISBN-13: 978-1-894063-40-1

Keaen by Till Noever (tp) - ISBN-13: 978-1-894063-08-1
Keeper's Child by Leslie Davis (tp) - ISBN-13: 978-1-894063-01-2

Lachli by M. H. Bonham (tp) - ISBN-13: 978-1-896944-69-2
Land/Space edited by Candas Jane Dorsey and Judy McCrosky (tp) - ISBN-13: 978-1-895836-90-5
Land/Space edited by Candas Jane Dorsey and Judy McCrosky (hb) - ISBN-13: 978-1-895836-92-9
Legacy of Morevi by Tee Morris (tp) - ISBN-13: 978-1-896944-29-6
Legends of the Serai by J.C. Hall - (tp) - ISBN-13: 978-1-896944-04-3
Longevity Thesis by Jennifer Tahn (tp) - ISBN-13: 978-1-896944-37-1
Lyskarion: The Song of the Wind by J.A. Cullum (tp) - ISBN-13: 978-1-894063-02-9

Machine Sex and other stories by Candas Jane Dorsey (tp) - ISBN-13: 978-0-88878-278-6
Maërlande Chronicles, The by Élisabeth Vonarburg (pb) - ISBN-13: 978-0-88878-294-6
Magister's Mask, The by Deby Fredericks (tp) - ISBN-13: 978-1-896944-16-6
Moonfall by Heather Spears (pb) - ISBN-13: 978-0-88878-306-6
Morevi: The Chronicles of Rafe and Askana by Lisa Lee & Tee Morris - (tp) - ISBN-13: 978-1-896944-07-4

Not Your Father's Horseman by Valorie Griswold-Ford (tp) - ISBN-13: 978-1-896944-27-2

On Spec: The First Five Years edited by On Spec (pb)
- ISBN-13: 978-1-895836-08-0
On Spec: The First Five Years edited by On Spec (hb)
- ISBN-13: 978-1-895836-12-7
Operation: Immortal Servitude by Tony Ruggerio (tp)
- ISBN-13: 978-1-896944-56-2
Operation: Save the Innocent by Tony Ruggerio (tp)
- ISBN-13: 978-1-896944-60-9
Orbital Burn by K. A. Bedford (tp) - ISBN-13: 978-1-894063-10-4
Orbital Burn by K. A. Bedford (hb) - ISBN-13: 978-1-894063-12-8

Pallahaxi Tide by Michael Coney (pb) - ISBN-13: 978-0-88878-293-9
Passion Play by Sean Stewart (pb) - ISBN-13: 978-0-88878-314-1
Plague Saint by Rita Donovan, The (tp) - ISBN-13: 978-1-895836-28-8
Plague Saint by Rita Donovan, The (hb) - ISBN-13: 978-1-895836-29-5

Reluctant Voyagers by Élisabeth Vonarburg (pb) - ISBN-13: 978-1-895836-09-7
Reluctant Voyagers by Élisabeth Vonarburg (hb) - ISBN-13: 978-1-895836-15-8
Resisting Adonis by Timothy J. Anderson (tp) - ISBN-13: 978-1-895836-84-4
Resisting Adonis by Timothy J. Anderson (hb) - ISBN-13: 978-1-895836-83-7
Righteous Anger by Lynda Williams (tp) - ISBN-13: 897-1-894063-38-8

Shadebinder's Oath by Jeanette Cottrell - (tp) - ISBN-13: 978-1-896944-31-9
Silent City, The by Élisabeth Vonarburg (tp) - ISBN-13: 978-1-894063-07-4
Slow Engines of Time, The by Élisabeth Vonarburg (tp) - ISBN-13: 978-1-895836-30-1
Slow Engines of Time, The by Élisabeth Vonarburg (hb) - ISBN-13: 978-1-895836-31-8
Small Magics by Erik Buchanan (tp) - ISBN-13: 978-1-896944-38-8
Sojourn by Jana Oliver - (pb) - ISBN-13: 978-1-896944-30-2
Stealing Magic by Tanya Huff (tp) - ISBN-13: 978-1-894063-34-0
Strange Attractors by Tom Henighan (pb) - ISBN-13: 978-0-88878-312-7
Sword Masters by Selina Rosen (tp) - ISBN-13: 978-1-896944-65-4

Taming, The by Heather Spears (pb) - ISBN-13: 978-1-895836-23-3
Taming, The by Heather Spears (hb) - ISBN-13: 978-1-895836-24-0
Teacher's Guide to Dragon's Fire, Wizard's Flame by Unwin & Mennenga - (pb)
- ISBN-13: 978-1-896944-19-7
Ten Monkeys, Ten Minutes by Peter Watts (tp) - ISBN-13: 978-1-895836-74-5
Ten Monkeys, Ten Minutes by Peter Watts (hb) - ISBN-13: 978-1-895836-76-9
Tesseracts 1 edited by Judith Merril (pb) - ISBN-13: 978-0-88878-279-3
Tesseracts 2 edited by Phyllis Gotlieb & Douglas Barbour (pb)
- ISBN-13: 978-0-88878-270-0
Tesseracts 3 edited by Candas Jane Dorsey & Gerry Truscott (pb)
- ISBN-13: 978-0-88878-290-8
Tesseracts 4 edited by Lorna Toolis & Michael Skeet (pb)
- ISBN-13: 978-0-88878-322-6
Tesseracts 5 edited by Robert Runté & Yves Maynard (pb)
- ISBN-13: 978-1-895836-25-7
Tesseracts 5 edited by Robert Runté & Yves Maynard (hb)
- ISBN-13: 978-1-895836-26-4
Tesseracts 6 edited by Robert J. Sawyer & Carolyn Clink (pb)
- ISBN-13: 978-1-895836-32-5
Tesseracts 6 edited by Robert J. Sawyer & Carolyn Clink (hb)
- ISBN-13: 978-1-895836-33-2

Tesseracts 7 edited by Paula Johanson & Jean-Louis Trudel (tp)
- ISBN-13: 978-1-895836-58-5
Tesseracts 7 edited by Paula Johanson & Jean-Louis Trudel (hb)
- ISBN-13: 978-1-895836-59-2
Tesseracts 8 edited by John Clute & Candas Jane Dorsey (tp)
- ISBN-13: 978-1-895836-61-5
Tesseracts 8 edited by John Clute & Candas Jane Dorsey (hb)
- ISBN-13: 978-1-895836-62-2
Tesseracts Nine edited by Nalo Hopkinson and Geoff Ryman (tp)
- ISBN-13: 978-1-894063-26-5
Tesseracts Ten edited by Robert Charles Wilson and Edo van Belkom (tp)
- ISBN-13: 978-1-894063-36-4
Tesseracts Eleven edited by Cory Doctorow and Holly Phillips (tp)
- ISBN-13: 978-1-894063-03-6
Tesseracts Q edited by Élisabeth Vonarburg & Jane Brierley (pb)
- ISBN-13: 978-1-895836-21-9
Tesseracts Q edited by Élisabeth Vonarburg & Jane Brierley (hb)
- ISBN-13: 978-1-895836-22-6
Throne Price by Lynda Williams and Alison Sinclair (tp)
- ISBN-13: 978-1-894063-06-7
Too Many Princes by Deby Fredricks (tp) - ISBN-13: 978-1-896944-36-4
Twilight of the Fifth Sun by David Sakmyster - (tp)
- ISBN-13: 978-1-896944-01-02

Virtual Evil by Jana Oliver (tp) - ISBN-13: 978-1-896944-76-0